TITLES

by Kyell Gold

TITLES

Production copyright FurPlanet Productions 2019

Artwork © Rukis and Amon Omega 2019
https://www.furaffinity.net/user/rukis/
https://www.furaffinity.net/user/amonomega/

Published by FurPlanet Productions
Dallas, Texas
www.FurPlanet.com

Hardcover ISBN 978-1-61450-503-7
Softcover ISBN 978-1-61450-504-4

First Edition 2019

For my wolf and cat
Who remind me what's important

Contents

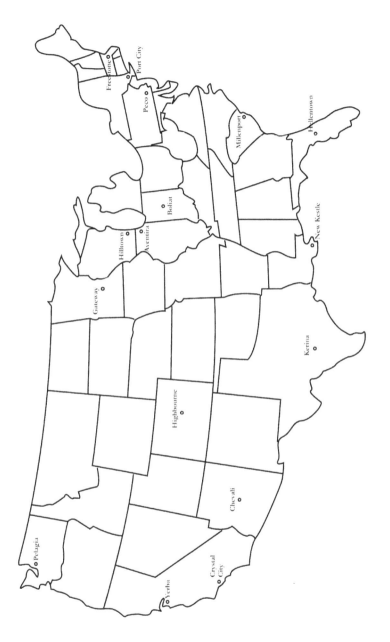

*I'm not saying the Forester Universe cities are in the United States.
But if they were, this is where they'd be.*

Foreword

Hi everyone. Welcome back to Dev and Lee's world. Please pay attention to the dates on the first few chapters.

-Ky, December 2019

Prologue 1 (Dev)

January 2014

Five years ago, around the same time I became a public figure more or less overnight, I got a brand-new smartphone from a teammate of mine, Lightning Strike. He retired last year to spend more time being photographed with celebrities, but he taught me a lot of things in the couple years we were teammates. Some of them were useful; a lot were just annoying. One of them has stuck with me, though: the difference between your phone really blowing up and just sorta blowing up.

Really blowing up means hundreds of texts, voicemails, calls. Everyone with your number wants to reach out and it's the perfect time to congratulate you. After our playoff wins, my phone really blew up.

Now I'm sitting in a Yerba hotel room alone and my phone is sorta blowing up. Was. It was sorta blowing up. It's done now, silent in my paws. The usual cluster of reporters have gotten their quotes and are busy talking to the winners or writing up their pieces. The people who felt the need to reach out have done so and don't have anything more to say.

What can they say, anyway? The usual things. "There'll be other games." "You played great." "Great effort." "Good try." "It just wasn't your day." One person unironically said, "You're always a champ in my book." Not a family member, just someone trying to make me feel better.

So here I am sitting in my boxers on the edge of my hotel bed, staring at my phone so I won't have to think about the plays that might've made a difference in the outcome of the championship game, the second one I've lost. To be fair, Yerba's probably a slightly better team, and we've been limping through the playoffs without our best receiver, Ty Nakamura, who strained a knee in the first playoff game.

If there's any silver lining to sitting here in this room, it's that I won't be alone for long. It's been a little over two weeks since I've seen Lee, since the night after that last playoff game, that Sunday night when my phone was still blowing up (really blowing up) as I was fucking him in my place in Chevali. "Championships are important," I told him afterwards, lying on my side next to him in a contented haze of lube and sex.

"That mean you want to take a break again?" he asked, rubbing a paw into my stomach fur.

"I was thinking about the way people talk about your career, but yeah, maybe that's not a bad idea."

"I don't mind giving you time to focus. It is important."

I thought it had helped. I put all my energy into football. I learned my assignments, learned the tendencies of the Whalers' tight ends and slot receivers, and we came into the game motivated to get Gerrard a title in what we all figured would be his last game before retirement. He wouldn't talk about it, but when you've played with a guy for five years, you know what he's thinking. You can tell when he tightens up even more than usual that he wants this bad, like desperate bad—and Gerrard's a guy who more or less gave up his family for football.

And then we went out and the Whalers beat us. It wasn't that we weren't good. It was that Duli Logu, their lion QB, couldn't miss. Twice I had their slot receiver as well covered as I could—which, not to gloss my own fur or anything but that's pretty well covered; I was a Pro Bowl alternate this year—and Logu just dropped the ball into his paws right out of my reach. Once that was for a score, so I felt super shitty about that.

Our guys are good too. Most of the offensive players are good if not great, but Ty was out, so there were a couple plays where I know he'd have gotten us a first down and instead we punted. In a 31-16 game, that probably didn't make a whole lot of difference, but you never know how a score in the first quarter will change team strategies.

I pull up some of the messages on my phone with the idea that maybe I can stop thinking about the game, about the ball an inch beyond my claws. There's got to be at least one or two messages that aren't about the game, some kind of reminder that I have other connections in my life.

Nope. Every message is a variation on the twin themes of pity and encouragement, so I stop looking at them and flick around the phone for other ideas. There's a match-3 game with fruits that I downloaded last summer and haven't played since then. That helps marginally more. I've played three levels of it when Lee knocks on the door.

He wraps me in a huge hug first thing, and I hug back. His breath smells of booze and he's a bit disheveled, the way you will be when you've been getting hugged and patted on the back for a couple hours after your team wins a championship, I guess.

"I'm sorry, tiger," is the first thing he says after kissing me (definite taste of booze—high class booze, too, not just champagne but also scotch).

"Why?" I pull him over to the bed. "You didn't complete eighteen of your twenty-one passes."

"No, but I pushed to draft Logu. Well, me and Jocko both liked him a lot. That's probably why Jocko's an assistant GM up in Freestone now and I got his job. One high-profile hit can define your career. But I bet he wishes he'd waited a year to take it. The job, I mean."

"You'll be an assistant GM soon," I tell him, mostly because it's true, but also so that I don't have to think about the game. "Isn't whatsisname in line for a GM position somewhere?"

"Langor." The fox settles in next to me, all warmth and curves that I've missed over the last couple weeks. "Poe Langor. Maybe. He really likes Yerba, though. He and Peter get along well too. I heard him talking about wanting to build a dynasty here. I mean, I'm sure he'll get offers now. If the right one comes along, then maybe. Who knows? Some guys want to keep moving up, get that title." He rubs his paw along my chest. "Sorry. I'm a little drunk."

"It's okay. One of us should be." I turn and kiss him again. "I'm really happy for you. We knew going into this that one of us was going to be disappointed."

"I wish it had been me. That was disappointed. I mean, we got a good team, we'll have more chances. But I'd really have liked for Gerrard to get it." His fingers slide down my stomach.

I put my paw over his, stopping it. "I dunno if I want to fuck right now," I say. "I'd rather just hold you."

"Yeah, yeah, sure." He leans against me.

The quiet is nice. Being here with him anchors me, pushes all that other stuff away. I can't forget about it, but at least I can put it into perspective. A little bit. "So I guess we're not getting married this June," I say.

He doesn't answer right away, though his paw keeps rubbing at my stomach fur. "I mean, if you want to…there's that big case coming up this summer and it could be legal everywhere by then."

"How's that going? Do you have a feel for which way it's going to go?"

He shakes his head. "I've been really busy at work. But I hired this fruit bat, Cord, he's gay and he keeps up on that stuff better than I do. I'll ask him."

I squeeze his shoulders in my arm. "It's not really important. That's not what's stopping me. Us. I still love you, fox, don't worry. But I'm okay with our arrangement."

"Besides, you told all those reporters about it."

His fingers dig in a little, tickling ineffectively under my larger paw. I squirm anyway to make him feel better. "I told them a couple years ago."

"Yeah, but they asked on Media Day and made a big deal about it and you said something about planning a wedding and it turned into," he waves his other paw around, "a whole thing."

"I remember what I said."

"Yeah, sorry. It was cute. I liked it. Everyone at the office teased me about it again. They were all like, 'don't let Lee talk to the players, he'll give them bad advice so he can get married.'"

"You wouldn't do that."

"No." His muzzle rubs mine. "The game is the thing."

"Yes it is." I cuddle him again, rubbing his paw. It doesn't seem to matter what we talk about; it all comes back to the game. "But I mean, I still love you. And I know I'll have more chances to get a ring." That's the kind of thing I have to say, even though I don't feel it right now. Intellectually I don't even know if it's true. Gerrard might stick around another season, but if he doesn't, that's a big loss to our defense. Ty's a free agent, too, and though I want him to stay a Firebird, I know he's going to get a lot of interest and so does he. He turned down a contract extension during the season—on the advice of his agent, he said, but that means that leaving is definitely on the table. Our rookies have been good but not spectacular the past few years. Nothing like Logu was this year (second-year player, not a rookie, but still).

"You will." Lee says it with more conviction than I feel.

I'm still relatively healthy, too. There was that one year I missed a bunch of games with a hip flexor injury, but that healed in the off-season and I'm back to normal. But it could happen again at any time. "You sure you don't want to come scout for the Firebirds? We could use a good fourth-round quarterback sleeper."

He laughs. "You guys have a good organization. Jo, DeVal, Dre, they're great. Don't worry, they'll find good people for you. There's no room for me there anyway. And Peter really likes me. With me being all openly flaunting my ho-mo-sex-u-ality, I don't have the options that a lot of other guys do." He sighs. "Plus I didn't actually play football and they like that. Jock culture, all that about going through the same shit. I know it's true though." He leans forward so he can look back into my eyes. "Like, I talk to you. I get it. What you've been through with Gerrard—and Carson—and, uh, Charm…"

"Kickers are different." I can't help but grin. He's drunk enough to be really earnest, which is endearing.

"Sure, sure, but you're all out there, you know, on the field but in practice too, and you see each other close up all the time."

"You see me a lot closer up."

"Right, uh." He leans back and laughs once. "But I mean, I get that, that people on the field with players, other players, they know what it takes. But that doesn't mean that they can always see it in other people. And it doesn't mean that someone who didn't play can't ever learn how to see it."

"Doc." I grab his long muzzle and kiss it. "You don't have to convince me. I think you're brilliant. I mean, look what your team just did."

"Shit, I know, I'm sorry, I'll stop talking about it."

"You don't have to. I'm proud of you. Honestly, I think this one hurts because of Gerrard, but it's not as bad as '09. That one sucked. We were so close."

He nods against me. "You'll get back."

"I hope so." I pause. "Are they still saying that Gerrard is the best player not to get a ring?"

He shakes his head. "Some people are, but there are a lot of good players who didn't win a title." His paw scritches my stomach fur. "You're not worried that'll be you one day, are you?"

"Nah." I pause. "I'll never be better than Gerrard."

We lie there silently for a little longer, and then I push his paw farther down my stomach. "You know what? Maybe I do want to fuck."

Prologue 2 (Lee)

June 2016

I've only been to three weddings in my life before today, but they were all in the past three years. This one, though, has to be my favorite.

We're in the VFW Hall of downtown Chevali, which normally is a pretty drab place that looks more like a high school classroom than anything else. But the wedding planner hooked us up with this amazing decorator, and Mike helped her out big time, and now it's gorgeous. They found a temporary hardwood floor to lay down over the 1970s linoleum, hung curtains over the cracked paint on the walls, and draped red and taupe crepe paper streamers from the ceiling. Behind the podium at the front, the officiant stands under a white wicker arch decorated with yellow and orange flowers while a little group of us fidgets in front of the arch. The hall is filled with people murmuring to themselves from the seats.

I reach up to adjust my red bowtie, and my father shoots me a look. "It's fine," he whispers.

"It doesn't feel right." I hate tuxedos, even though I look good in them. And I only learned how to tie a bowtie two days ago and it doesn't feel symmetrical.

The young coyote on my other side leans forward. "Nobody's going to be looking at you anyway."

I flick my ears back. "Pipe down or I'll start messing with yours."

Jaren grins at me. "You're not my brother yet."

Behind him, his younger brother Mike says, "Shh," and a moment later the wedding processional starts. Everyone in the audience stands.

We all straighten up and look toward the back of the room. The doors open and Angela Marvell walks in, bridal gown decorated with lace and a short train. Accompanied by her older sister, her niece, and my aunt Carolyn, she steps slowly through the hall to take her place across from my father.

I catch Aunt Carolyn's eye and we trade smiles and ear-flicks. Then I pay attention to the ceremony because I've got to give Father the rings when it's time.

While this isn't a completely secular ceremony, it's close. There's a mention of God blessing the ceremony (mainly for Angela's mom). The officiant spends most of her time talking about the journey these two have taken, from previous commitments (they felt their previous marriages should be acknowledged but not dwelt upon), through a professional relationship (my father's financial consultation sort of led to Angela's divorce, but they didn't

think that was appropriate to mention), to dating and then the careful negotiation of two families coming together (there was a big scene a year ago with Mike, but he's come around to be on board).

When Father takes Angela's paw and they recite their vows, I sneak a glance out into the audience. Wedged in between a coyote-puma couple and Angela's coyote cousins are a fox, a tiger, and a leopard, all over six feet tall and fidgeting in their suits. I'm used to seeing them in football jerseys—and the tiger, of course, I'm used to seeing in nothing at all. He's the one whose golden eyes I catch as he looks right back at me with a smile.

We marked our ten-year anniversary a few months ago. Though neither of us remembers the day he picked me up in a smoky college bar thinking I was a girl, we chose a day in April and settled on that. There have been a lot of other meaningful moments in our relationship: the day after that when he came back to my apartment; the day that fall when he sought me out after the long summer break; the day we got engaged to be engaged; the day we actually signed the papers to be domestic partners. We couldn't agree on which one matters the most, so we picked the first.

Reminiscing doesn't mean I'm ignoring the ceremony; my ears are still cupped properly toward the bride and groom. I'm experiencing the emotion of the moment and sharing it with the person most significant to me. As they conclude their vows, my full attention goes back to the couple of the moment, and when the officiant pronounces them married (they chose "married" rather than "husband and wife" as a nod to more egalitarian marriage practices), I smile and clap with everyone else.

Then I take Angela's older sister's arm and follow my father and stepmother down the aisle to the reception. I give Dev another smile as I pass him; he, Ty, and Carson all beam back at me.

The wedding party stands around and chats in the reception area while the newlyweds go into a private room to let the ceremony sink in. Angela's older sister, Beatrice, talks my ear off about what a lovely ceremony it was, and I agree when I can get a word in. We share stories from our sides of the family and laugh about how nervous they both were. Beatrice starts to make a comment about Angela's previous marriage, but cuts it short when Jaren joins in, appropriately not wanting to bash Gerrard in front of his cub.

Jaren says he appreciates how short the ceremony was and tells Beatrice how happy his mom has been the past year ("I know!" Beatrice gushes). Mike stands nearby, quiet but smiling. He and I have had a few more serious conversations in the last year, and though Jaren is more talkative and social, I feel like I know Mike better.

After about fifteen minutes, Angela and Father come out and greet all of us. They look a little dazed, and I'm sure we don't help by swarming them. Beatrice wraps her sister in a tight hug and then gives my father the same. "I'm so happy for the two of you."

I get next dibs on hugs. "Welcome to the family," I tell Angela. "I'll try to shield you from the worst of it."

She laughs and kisses my muzzle. "I've seen it. Don't worry, I've got the important people here."

That's when Aunt Carolyn comes up and takes both Angela's paws and kisses her, European style. "You sure do," she says. "Even if I'm not blood."

"Wait," I say, feigning surprise. "You're not?"

She swats at me. "Watch out for this one," she tells Angela.

"I know," Angela says, and then the wedding planner interrupts to ask if the newlyweds need more time.

They both gesture to let in the guests, so the planner shoos us all into a line and the guests come filing into the room. The next twenty minutes are shaking paws and kissing and a few hugs. Dev kisses me on the muzzle and then moves on, and I hear Angela say to Carson, "It means a lot that you came."

"Wouldn't have missed it." Carson was Gerrard's best friend on the Firebirds, the guy who played alongside him at linebacker for years until Gerrard retired. Now he and Dev anchor the line with a new guy, a wolf named Croz who's a bit of an ass, but talented enough to get away with it. Anyway, the thing about Carson is he's a big believer in family. When Gerrard and Angela split up, Carson spent a lot of time making sure Angela would be all right. He's not married himself, never had a girlfriend as far as I know (not a boyfriend either), but over the years he's gotten close enough that Jaren and Mike call him "Uncle."

And behind Dev, grabbing my paws and grinning like a young cub, is Ty. He makes up for Carson's lack of relationship: he's got a girlfriend and a boyfriend. A wife and boyfriend, actually, and the boyfriend isn't public, but they've all been together a while and they're all cool. His wife and boyfriend live together and both say it makes the long season easier, and Ty loves them both. The speedy wideout isn't on the Firebirds anymore; a few years ago he signed a huge free agent deal to go to the Tornadoes and won a championship there the next year.

"This is really cool," Ty says, and flicks his eyes toward Dev. "I mean, two more people in your family have rings now."

Dev, who's moved on from my father to Angela, turns enough that I can see him roll his eyes. Ty goes on. "I hope this year I can get one for Kella. We're favorites to repeat, you know."

Kella is their cub, born just in the last year. I grin at Ty. "You know how many times the teams favored to go to the championship actually went, the last ten years?"

"Tell me, o director of scouting."

"Two out of twenty teams."

"Hey, we have a ten percent chance. Cool." He smiles and moves down to my father.

I can't help grinning. Cocky cub—well, he's what, thirty now, but still a cub. I shake the paw of the next guest, one of the coyote cousins.

•

Dev paid for the buffet, which otherwise would've been out of the price range of this intentionally modest wedding. Father and Angela resisted most of his efforts to pay for nicer things, but when he brought samples of the food from the steak house he wanted to use, that convinced them.

The food's good, the music is good, and there's dancing and mingling. When it's time for the toasts, the waiters come around with champagne flutes and I stand up to clink mine. Eyes and ears all turn in my direction, and I give the room a big smile.

"If there's one thing I've learned in thirty…ish…years, it's that love can show up just about anywhere. That makes it sound like it's easy to find, but it isn't. When you find it, you've got to make sure to hold on as best you can. My father and stepmother…" Angela's ears flatten and she smiles as I say that. "They've been cautious and responsible for four years now. They both have families they didn't want to disrupt, children and relatives and other relationships, the things that make your lives so much more complicated the farther you get into adulthood. They're both the kind of warm, caring person who wants to make sure everyone around them is happy before they worry about themselves. I can't tell you how many times they've gone to one of Jaren's debates or Mike's soccer matches, but I can tell you how many they've missed." I hold up one finger. "One. And that's because it was on Angela's birthday and Brenly planned a surprise party without realizing Mike had a game. He had contacted all these people and finally it was one of Mike's friends' mom who told him about the game. He tried to cancel everything and move it to a different day, and Mike had to spend half an hour on the phone telling him it would be fine." I pause. My father has his paw over his eyes but is smiling. "It turned out Mike scored the winning goal at that match. So for about six months he got to do anything he wanted." Laughter. Good. "The point is, these two care as much about their families as they do about each other. I know we're a few girls short of a Beardy Bunch—"

"And a housekeeper," my father interjects.

"And a housekeeper. But I know these two are going to be at the center of a loving, happy family for a long time. So I'm really happy to see them sitting together as a married couple." I turn to them and raise the flute. "To Brenly and Angela."

The crowd echoes my toast, and we all drink and clap and cheer. Beatrice stands up for her toast and tells a story about the first time she met my father.

"Nice toast," Dev murmurs, squeezing my arm.

"Yeah," Ty says. He and Carson are on the other side of the table, all the football players hanging out together because they don't really know anyone else. "Way better than Kellen's toast."

I laugh, startled to have that memory come back. "He wasn't that bad."

Ty rolls his eyes and does an imitation of his best friend's voice. "'So, like, Ty's cool. And Tami is too. Good luck, you guys are awesome.'"

Dev shoves Ty's shoulder. "He wasn't that bad."

"Anyway," I say, "you probably shouldn't have told him about your boyfriend right before the wedding."

"I technically didn't *tell* him," Ty points out.

Carson raises his eyebrows, and Dev notices. "Ty invited his boyfriend to the bachelor party. And then made out with him there."

Ty raises a finger. "Got drunk, got a lap dance from the stripper Kellen brought, *then* kissed my boyfriend."

"See," Carson says, "I like my life uncomplicated."

The fox grins back at him. "And I like my life with a lot of sex in it."

"Doesn't have to be complicated."

Dev grasps my paw and we interlace our fingers, both grinning. "Oh hey," Ty says, "speaking of complicated, you know those Nativist assholes? A couple of them found out from my wedding that Tami and I are second-generation and now they're on me, too, even though we're foxes."

"Huh." Dev exchanges a look with Carson. I don't manage his social media anymore—he has a guy for that—but I know he'd told me that both he and Carson had over the last year seen a bump in people yelling at them to "go home," because their families are from outside the States—outside the continent, even, although Dev is two generations removed and Carson more than that.

See, all the different species in the world historically showed up in different places. Foxes were all over, but, say, raccoons were native to this continent, while fruit bats, for another example, were native to Asia. Whether you are looking at scientific and historical evidence or believing that God dropped everyone in a certain place for a reason (and there are a bunch of those wackos in this movement), these guys think that everyone should stay in the place they "came from." But there's inconsistency; red foxes aren't actually native to this continent, or rather, there were tribes of red foxes here and tribes that came over from Europe, and science thinks they were genetically distinct but similar enough to interbreed, and now their descendants—like me—are accepted as fully Native by this bunch of bullshit idealogues, for all that counts.

What it's really about is not whether your remote ancestors crossed to this country over a land bridge during the Ice Age or not. It's not even about whether you came to this country in the last few decades, though if you did, you are apparently attempting to "supplant" the people to whom this country "belongs by right of birth." What it's really about is a bunch of people who want to blame their problems on some other bunch of people rather than actually try to fix anything themselves.

It's not a huge deal for Dev and Carson; honestly as best I can tell it mostly affects new immigrants and people trying to come here. But there's always that fringe to the fringe that doesn't think we should stop at not letting new people in and agitates to get rid of anyone whose great-great-great-great grandparents weren't born here, forget the fact that a whole lot of us came here from Anglia or Gallia several hundred years ago anyway.

Usually us foxes are left out of it, because we come from here, and also there, and pretty much everywhere, but Ty's wedding had been planned by his Yamatese mother, so of course it would be obvious that they'd come here as immigrants.

"It's not a huge thing," Ty said. "Just thought you'd like to know that I'm in the 'go home' club too, now."

"Don't like to know it," Carson said. "I try not to think about it."

"Yeah." Dev reaches out to Ty. "They're assholes. Don't worry about it."

"I'm not." Ty grins. "It's just funny to me that one day I can be all cool because I'm a fox and then they find out something else and suddenly I'm unwelcome."

"You're still cool because you're a fox," I say.

He points finger-guns at me and says, "I know."

My father and Angela come up to our table on their walk around the room. "You had to tell that story," my father said, shaking his head.

"It's sweet," I say, and hug them both. Dev, beside me, does the same. "Anyway, Ty here was just telling us how it could've been worse."

"Hey, congrats again you two." Ty comes around to hug them. Carson follows him.

"Your wife couldn't be here?" Angela asks Ty.

"Ah, no, she's got work. She sends her best, though."

They move on and we settle back around our table. "What's she working on?" Dev asks, always interested in the career of Ty's video-game-making wife.

"Oh, ah." He flicks his ears. "She's got a couple mobile games going on and she's working on a partnership with StoryTime games—you know, the guys who do the, like, choose your own adventure from TV and movie stuff?"

There's something hesitant about what he's saying, so I say, "But…?"

"Ah." He smiles and finishes off his champagne. "She could've come. Kinda wanted to. But Arch did too, and I didn't know if I could bring them both, and then it'd be awkward if I was only sitting with one of them, and there'd be questions if it was both…and if it was both then they'd have to bring Kella, too, and that's a whole other hassle."

Carson lifts his glass. "See?" he says. "Complicated."

Ty shrugs. "Stuff like this only comes up like once a year. Tami's mom knows about us and Arch doesn't talk to his family so it's really just my family and then stuff like this. And I work on the holidays so I don't have to worry about that, thank god."

"And here we thought we were the last frontier," I tell Dev.

"You guys still waiting for Dev to get a ring before you do one of these?" Ty waves around the room, not making reference to his own ring this time, just asking as a friend.

"Yeah." I squeeze Dev's paw.

"We're both really busy," Dev says. "So it's nice to have an excuse not to do it."

This gets a snort from Carson, so I say, "We're keeping our lives uncomplicated."

"Yeah," he says, "good luck with that."

•

After the food is gone and the dancing has worn us out, long after the newlyweds have retired to their room for the usual post-wedding activities, Dev and I say goodbye to Ty and Carson. Dev will see Carson next week at camp, but Ty's off to Gateway, so we won't see him until they play in week nine this year. I should probably head home to Yerba, because I have a draft board to fill in for next year, but I can take a few days off to have some quality time with my tiger, so I'm staying in Chevali. I'm not allowed in his training camp, being front office for another team and all, but I'll be happy to have evenings with Dev. We've gotten used to stealing days when we can, but they never seem like enough.

He's still at the downtown Chevali apartment, even after two stalking incidents. When he signed his big deal in 2010, he paid for additional security for the building, so now we have to walk past an array of closed-circuit cameras as well as a full-time guard at the desk. Tonight it's an alert red panda who tips his hat and says, "Evening, Mister Miski."

"Hi, Grendy," Dev says.

I wave and the panda smiles back. One of the qualifications Dev insisted the private security firm supply in their guards was that they had to be okay with his relationship, and Maria, who runs the firm, said that wouldn't be a problem and even seemed a little puzzled that he was so insistent about it. Times change, even over the course of a couple years. Now, go a few miles outside of Chevali proper and you might not be so lucky with hitting enlightened residents, but here in town it's pretty progressive.

Also, being a local sports hero who went to two championship games (even if you didn't win) and has made the All Pro roster twice in eight years helps with changing people's minds. But the other part of it is that every time I walk into his building and see the security guard, I think about Dev making that demand, I think about the response, and my tail wags.

His apartment hasn't changed a whole lot in the few months since I've been here last. The new sofa's holding up well, with only a couple marks on the claw-resistant arms. Everything else is the same it's been for years, even the college poster of Mitchell Portman in his 2007 Dragons uniform. At least he put that in a frame finally.

"Long day," he says, pulling his tie loose the moment he steps through the door.

"Good day." I leave my tux intact, even though I'm panting just from the walk between Dev's parking garage and the apartment building's air conditioning.

He sheds the jacket and pulls loose the first few buttons of his shirt. "You going to stay dressed all night?"

"I like how it looks." I study my reflection in the dark TV.

"That's okay. I can work with that." He wraps a large paw around my hip. "How much of a deposit did we put down?"

I flip my tail back against him. "You can wait a bit."

He grabs the base of my tail and pokes a claw at the fabric under it. "Just a little rip here. Well, maybe a big rip."

"Weddings get you worked up, huh?" I spin away and face him, standing on tiptoe to give him a kiss.

"You get me worked up." He pulls me close and deepens the kiss.

Standing there in his arms, the kiss going on until it ends with the mutual agreement of a decade of experience, I can't help wagging my tail. I feel safe with him, but not too safe. If I start getting complacent about my life, he's there to pull me out of it, and vice versa.

As it turns out, even that sense of stability can be shaken a bit. He runs a finger down the lapel of my tux jacket and meets my eyes. "Like the tux, huh? You think maybe we shouldn't wait?"

My first thought is that he means we shouldn't wait until I get it off to have sex, and I'm halfway to nodding, deposit be damned, even on my salary I could afford it, and then I realize what I think he's saying. "Wait, you mean…"

He nods. "I'm not twenty-four anymore. I don't need the extra motivation. And…I mean, it's not like it's even all on me."

I take a breath. "I know, yeah. We've talked about it a little, right? I think if your career ends and you don't have a ring, of course I'll marry you."

"But?"

He knows me. "But…did you see how much time it took Father and Angela to plan that wedding?"

"We could hire people."

"They hired someone. They still spent every day thinking about it for months. Father called me once a week to talk about some wedding thing or another. I can't—neither of us can do that right now, honestly."

"Yeah, I guess not."

I hug him. "When we get married, tiger, I want to do it right."

"Me too." He kisses my nose. "But I think for me, doing it right just means it's you standing there across from me."

"Uh huh." I lick back at his muzzle. "But also the music has to be right and the location and everything. And the guests."

"Fine, fine." He mock-growls and starts to pull my tux jacket off. "I guess I'll have to win a ring this year, then."

"You should think that every year," I tell him.

He gets the jacket off. I work on the shirt while he attacks the cummerbund and pants. "You telling me how to do my job?"

"Weeeeeell," I say, as I shed the shirt and reach over to his, "I mean, Ty's got his ring and—aah!"

He grabs me by the sides and lifts me off the floor. "That's it," he announces, marching to the bedroom. "You need to do something with that muzzle besides talk."

Which of course I can do, having had a lot of practice. And there are other things I've had a lot of practice at too, so we go on to them in due course.

Chapter One: (Dev)

January 2017

The glow of my own climax has almost faded and I'm still all the way buried in Lee, my paw working at his shaft. "You close yet?" I ask finally.

"Yeah," he pants, but another minute later he's not squirming, he's not panting harder, and my paw is still wet only with lube. "Sorry," he says.

I stop stroking him. "You want to finish yourself?"

"Yeah. Hate to have you cramp up your paw. How would that look on the injury report?"

"Miski—Probable—Paw," I say, and he chuckles as he gets some lube on his own paw.

The game tomorrow against the Sabretooths presses on my mind while Lee takes care of himself. We're ready for them, we're better than them, and even though we're on their home field, we feel like we have the advantage. Chevali is close enough to Crystal City that on ScentBook the Firebirds Fan page has been scheduling meetups in Crystal City to support the team. Don't know how many of them will make it to the game—CC fans are pretty rabid and buying up all the tickets—but it helps to know that they're here and they made the trip.

After a few seconds of stroking, Lee sighs and works himself off me. "Sorry, tiger. I don't think it's happening."

We sit back on the bed. Outside the window, the incessant noise and light of Crystal City work their way back into my awareness. "I'm the one who should be sorry. I finished too fast."

"It's not you." He snuggles against me and kisses me. "Work's crazy and you've got that game tomorrow and I'm meeting Mike on Wednesday."

"Mike?"

"My brother? Stepbrother."

"Right. Did you tell me about this?"

"Maybe not. He emailed me a month ago. He's coming out to look at some colleges in the area."

I wrap an arm around his shoulder. "He's come a long way, huh?"

"You mean in being friends with me?" Lee asks, and I nod. "He has. Christmas was really nice. Wish you coulda been there."

"I'm amused he was still worried about me being hurt because of that thing he repeated like eight years ago."

"He really was." Lee smiles. "But more about his phase with that high school gang. He hadn't ever talked to me about it before. It was nice."

Gerrard never talks about his cubs, even though he sees them some weekends. I'd heard that for a little while Mike was with a gang and wasn't doing well in school, and then a few months later Lee told me that his father and Angela sat down with Mike and he'd given up the gang. "Cool. Did Jaren decide on a college yet?"

"Yep." Lee rests a paw on my stomach and rubs his fingers through the fur. "He got into U of Chevali, and he's going to accept. Wants to stay close to home."

"Can't imagine why he doesn't want to go to Forester."

Lee chuckles against me. "I think it had something to do with the winters."

"They're not that bad."

"That they have them at all, I mean. He might've been born in Highbourne, but he's a desert yote through and through."

"Mike isn't, though?"

Lee shakes his head so his whiskers tickle my chest. "I don't think so. He likes Yerba, even though it's a bit early to do college visits. We talked a little bit about Pelagia, too. There's a bunch of good schools up that way."

"He going for a soccer scholarship?"

"Trying. But those are really competitive and he isn't good enough to get into a top tier school. Of course, his grades aren't either. They've come back up this year, but last year was bad."

I grin and kiss his ear. "Look at us lying here talking about family."

"Yeah, that happened somehow." His dark brown paw ruffles my stomach. "You want to hear how Angela's birds are doing?"

"Not really. How's work?" Because we work for different teams, he can't be candid. We've had a couple uncomfortable situations over the years when either I figured out something he thought I wouldn't, or I mentioned something he shouldn't have known. Usually we do well at keeping it to ourselves, but it's stressful. So when he talks about work stuff, he talks in vague terms.

"There's always arguing over the draft board," he says, exhaling and resting his head against my side. "And it's the same arguments every year from the same people, and ultimately even though I know Peter takes my advice, he's the one with final authority. So sometimes I'm left feeling like, 'why bother?'"

Like that, yeah. I hug him. "They'll move you up to assistant GM soon, and then you'll have more weight."

He squints at me. "It's still the same people, just a different title."

I reach down and poke his stomach, making him jump. "I mean, you'll have more weight because you won't have time to go to the gym as much."

"Ha ha." He swats my paw away. "The title would be nice, though. Not that Poe's one of the people who's difficult, but…it's not so much a matter of weight as of having a say in lots of other things, not just scouting."

"Peter asks you about that stuff anyway."

"Yeah." His tail flicks. "But having that 'GM' next to my name, even with 'assistant' in front of it, that lets everyone know that he asks me and trusts me. Puts me one step closer to being a GM."

"You'll get there, doc."

"Mm."

He's drifting off in thought, so I nose his ear. "They're still treating you right, aren't they?"

The ear flicks against my nose. "Oh yeah. Peter's great, and we got rid of the one homophobe on my staff. Not because he was a homophobe."

"That's the guy who groped Greta at the Christmas party?"

He nods. "Took a couple weeks to put the paperwork through, which is quicker than usual because Peter expedited it. But also we got bounced out of the playoffs so there wasn't that tension over firing someone from the staff."

"Sorry about that."

He returns my grin and tickles my side lightly. "Wasn't our year. We knew that going into the playoffs. We got lucky in a few games but we're still a year or two away."

He's told me that before. So now I ask the question I'd asked him before and which he avoided answering. "Is it our year?"

Blue eyes widen with feigned innocence. "'Our' like your team, or 'our' like you and me?"

"I meant the team. Isn't it always *our* year?"

He laughs and puts his head back. "Let's see how you do tomorrow."

It always comes back to the game. "Are we taking a break again if we win?"

He yawns. "If you want to. I mean, last time it was a little more necessary. This time you'd be playing either Cansez or Port City, so we don't technically have to stay apart."

"I guess we'll decide after the game." I kiss his ears.

I love that he doesn't remind me that he has a ring from when Yerba beat us in the championship, even though I've told him a thousand times that I'm over it and he should be proud of what he accomplished. Like with his Whalers this year, that wasn't our year: we were lucky to get to the championship and our luck ran out there. But for all those years we were unlucky, it felt like karma, and I was still bitterly disappointed.

Now I've got perspective. I know I have maybe two years of starter-level play left, and I could be a good backup after that. My agent hooked me up with a nutritionist and a physical trainer who keep me healthy in the off-season and help me take care of my aging body. Feels weird to say "aging" at thirty-two, but football accelerates that. I'm good at ignoring the twinge in my hip from the injury in 2011, the ache in my knee from two years ago. Modern medicine and workouts keep them from hampering my play at all, but I know they're going to catch up with me down the line.

More concerning is the aging of my relationship with Lee. We both keep busy enough that in the precious moments we have together, we still feel young and in love—mostly. This night is the third time in the past year that he hasn't finished when we had sex. Lee, who was so ready that we almost had sex upstairs in my old bedroom at Thanksgiving when we were first dating. It's a strange development, and part of me wonders if he's found a sex buddy elsewhere for when I'm not around.

I doubt it. Neither of us has slept with anyone else (to my knowledge) in ten years, not after that time early on when he jerked off his college not-boyfriend and I almost let a groupie suck me off. So I'm left with wondering if he's bored with our relationship. That's troubling, because I can see the horizon of my football career now, and what do I do after that if Lee's bored with me?

I hug him affectionately and he hugs back. "Tired?" I ask.

"A bit."

"I gotta get up early, so…"

He grins and leans over to his side of the bed. The Sabretooths t-shirt he'd been wearing is draped over the light where it got thrown; he takes it in one paw and weighs it speculatively. "Sorry I didn't get to mess this up. Maybe I'll be more in the mood in the morning."

"I'll be here." I rest a paw on his sheath.

"Mmm." He drops the shirt to the floor and flicks the switch. In the darkness, he rolls over and presses up against me again. "Night, tiger."

"Night, fox." I push away the concerns about the future to focus on the lovely fox-scented present.

Chapter Two (Lee)

I'm hard when Dev gets me up at six-something in the morning, and he slides his body down mine until his whiskers tickle my cock. I squirm, and he purrs and holds me down while he licks up my length. When he gets his whole muzzle over it, he has to tense his muscles a bit because I'm squirming and arching more, and this time finally I come, emptying myself onto his tongue with long rasping moans.

"There we go," he says. "Just got to catch you before you start thinking about work."

"Uh huh." I feel a little bad about last night, but lately my mind skips off down tracks that I can't get it off of. And I know once Dev's inside me, he can take care of himself, so if I don't get off, that doesn't affect him. It's sweet that he's still invested in making sure I finish, though.

He reaches over the side of the bed and grabs the Sabretooths t-shirt, then brings it to his wet muzzle and exaggerates the motions of wiping his lips. "See, it's still useful for something." He weighs the shirt in one paw. "Maybe I'll send it to Aran."

I laugh. "He'd probably like that. Or…" I wink at him. "Tease your roommate with it."

"Don't even joke." Dev rolls his eyes. "If we win this game he'll probably start jerking off in front of me or something."

"Well, sure. He's been waving his cock at you all season and you haven't responded." I pause. "Right?"

"Course not." My tiger grins and tosses the shirt back to the floor. "It's such a pain. I wish he'd fucking come out already."

"You can't rush anyone," I remind him. "Wix is comfortable where he is and he has a crush on you."

"It's not a crush, it's only flirting. Anyway, it doesn't matter. I don't want a bobcat. I just want my fox." He crawls up my body and kisses me, then lies down atop me. "I should go get cleaned up and out of here."

I wrap arms around him. "Maybe you should stay here. I don't really think the team needs its defensive captain."

"Co-captain." His smile falters.

I kiss it to try to make it come back. "Both co-captains are still captains. Anyway." I can only reach down to just above his hips, so I rest paws there. "You'll do great. I'll be rooting for you."

He sighs and pushes himself up. "What about the other game? Who do you think we'd do better against?"

"Cansez." I don't even have to think about it. "Port City's built around a strong run game and your strength is your secondary. Cansez has Komell flinging the ball all over, but you could contain him."

"We did." He purrs, remembering.

"But Port City could wear you down with their running. And they have a slightly better defense than Cansez. So they'll probably win. But I have to root for Cansez anyway because of Morty."

"Oh, right."

My old boss, the cougar who brought me to my first combine and who spent a few years at the Whalers with me, got tabbed to be general manager for the expansion team in Cansez when they opened five years ago. He's got them to the playoffs twice now, and they're the first of the four expansion teams to make it to the semis.

Paws behind my head on the pillow, I watch Dev stretch and then head for the bathroom. "Join me?" he asks with a curl of one finger.

"Sure." I reach for my phone on the nightstand. "Just going to check in and I'll be in in a minute."

There are emails waiting in my queue, but nothing super urgent. Still, one of them is from Peter, about a guy we drafted last year who had a minor incident last night—drunk at a nightclub. Peter wants me to review what we have on his character from the scouting reports last year before the club issues a formal statement.

I type up a quick reply and put the phone down, but as I'm sliding out of bed, the fur drier starts up in the bathroom. I hurry in, but Dev's already brushing the damp out of his fur under the blowers. I guess that reply wasn't as quick as I thought it was. "Aw, crap," I say. "Sorry, one of the kids had a thing…" I gesture out into the bedroom where the phone is and walk over to him.

He smiles and leans down to kiss my nose. "It's okay, fox." Then as I try to hug him, he pushes me away. "Ew, you're all dirty. Go get clean."

I stick my tongue out and hurry to the shower, which is still steamy and damp and smelling of soap. By the time I'm done, he's out of the drier, so I step in and close my eyes under the warm air.

"Fox."

I jump. Dev's standing there, fully dressed in his t-shirt and slacks, with a blazer over it. Casual chic, a look he's gravitated to over the last few years and which I approve of highly. "Oh hey. Time to go?" He nods, and I step out of the drier to hug him good-bye.

"Good luck," I say. "Not that you need it. You guys are great."
"Thanks." He noses my ear. "See you tonight, one way or another."
"Count on it." I lick his whiskers.
"When's your flight back north?"

"Ugh. Stupid o'clock tomorrow. Peter wants to have a meeting at 9 and I talked him down to 9:30, but that still means I gotta land by 8:30 to have a chance of being there in time."

"Maybe we'll stay up all night." He stretches. "I won't have a game for two weeks either way."

"Yeah, but I have to be reasonably coherent at the meeting."

He waves dismissively. "Sleep on the plane."

"Go," I mock-growl. His tail flicks as he walks out.

Under the warm air of the dryer, my mind goes back to Dev as I brush the fur his paws were resting on not too long ago. He's been frank about the chronic little aches he's got, and even though none of them affect his play yet, when we're alone and he's not trying to hide them, I notice little movements and winces, things that tell me he's not a hundred percent anymore. Sure, most of the days are good days, and on good days he's fine. But every now and then his hip or his knee bothers him. I know for games he gets cortisone shots if he's feeling bad; I also know he tries not to use them and that his coaches press him to.

We've talked about his injuries. I know how much football means to him and if he says the injuries aren't at the level where he has to step away, I trust him. But that doesn't mean I don't worry.

I grab my phone before my clothes to see if Peter responded to my email, and I find a couple texts there. Hal's found a place for us to watch most of the early game before we have to head down to Sabretooth Stadium for the live game. The other text is from Mike: *Can I call you when you have a minute?*

Huh. I text back, *Anytime in the next hour*, and put my earphone in as I dig around in my suitcase for something to wear. Have to look at least somewhat professional as I'm going to meet up with a couple other front office guys from other teams for a bit.

Before I even get my underwear on, my phone rings. Mike must have been sitting right next to it waiting.

"Hi," I say. "What's up?"

"Hey." He goes quiet for a bit, which I let him do because I'm trying to decide between two shirts. I've just grabbed the yellow one and slid one arm through it when he says, "So uh. I want to run something by you. Or tell you something. I dunno."

"Okay," I say. "You're still coming up Wednesday, right?"

"Yeah. I wanted to ask about this before, because it will…you know, it might change what I bring along."

I get both arms in and button up the shirt. "This isn't about the weather, is it?" That remark gets no response, so I put on my calmer, more serious voice. "Go ahead, I'm listening."

"Yeah," he says. "I mean, it's just weird, it's something like I've been thinking about for a while and I've never really talked about it with anyone."

I drop the pants I'd been about to put on and stand up, ears perked. Is he about to come out to me? "Not even your mom?"

"Oh, jeez, no." He laughs, a weird nervous laugh like I haven't heard from him before. Mike always seems so confident, so sure of himself, but then again, I work with a lot of athletes and former athletes who have become skilled at putting up that barrier around themselves. The thing is that usually they let it down around close friends and family. So I wasn't looking for it with Mike or Jaren.

"Hey," I say, "whatever it is, it's cool. I'll still want to see you Wednesday, still want to be your big bro."

"Heh. Thanks. I mean, that's why I'm telling you first, even though…I mean, Jaren kinda knows but not really. He's so…anyway. What I'm trying to say is I don't…always feel like a guy."

"Oh." That's different, but not so unusual. The main thing is to not make him feel bad, so my first reaction has to be calm acceptance. "So you're trans?"

"No. I don't want to be a girl." He takes a breath. "Except sometimes maybe I do. But not, like, forever. So the word—I looked this up—it's genderqueer."

That's a word I've heard, because I keep at least one ear open to LGBT stuff and Dev has a foundation benefiting LGBT youth, but apart from a basic understanding of it I don't know what it means. I do know what to say to anyone revealing something intimate and personal about themselves, though. "Cool. So what do you want to do when you're up here?"

He pauses, and I think that is the "was it that easy?" pause, which is what I wanted, so I wait. "I got this skirt," he says.

When he doesn't go on, I prompt him. "Want to go out in it?"

"Kinda." He takes a breath. "Yes. But also, I want to see if the schools there are cool with it. I mean, it's Yerba, so I guess…right?"

"Should be," I say. "But we can check. You look anything up online?"

"Couple things." He's reverting back to the Mike I knew, more confident. "There's LGBT groups at all of them and I was going to wait and send an email to some of them until, ah, I knew if you'd be cool coming with me."

"Course I am."

"Cool," he says. "Thanks. I really appreciate it."

"No problem. Anything else?"

He hesitates. "You're really cool with it?"

"Sure." I walk around the hotel room, tail swishing, and I smile. "Why wouldn't I be? You know I'm gay, right?"

"Yeah, but…" He huffs. "That's, like, normal now."

"Is it? A few people might argue with you there."

"I guess not. But like, I remember when it was weird—I mean, I remember *that* it was weird, sort of, but now when I hear people say that I'm just like, 'no, *you're* weird.' It doesn't make sense to me anymore."

"Good." My tail wags. "And hey, when you're out here I'd love to hear more about what being genderqueer means to you."

"Yeah." He exhales. "Thanks."

I feel great about how I handled that after hanging up, until I've got one pants leg on and I think, shit, I didn't ask him what pronouns he wants me to use. 'They' want me to use? Should I start thinking about him—them—differently? Dammit. I drop my grade to a B+.

Chapter Three (Dev)

I found out Wixin—he goes by Wix—is gay when he told me, in the second week of the season. I knew there had to be a reason they broke up me and Carson (Charm had been my roommate for years, but when Gerrard left, Carson and I got paired up), but the coaches just told me they wanted my "steadying veteran influence" on our rookie cornerback.

When Wix came out to me, he told me he'd asked the coaches not to say anything to me because he didn't want it to be a big deal, and if he hadn't felt comfortable telling me, he wouldn't mind going through the season with me not knowing. Of course he felt comfortable pretty quickly; when he told me, I made a joke about "I hope the coaches don't think we're gonna be fucking," and his quick laughter made me think that maybe he was hoping that we would be.

But it hasn't been an issue. He is flirty—I think. Charm used to walk around our hotel rooms naked all the time, but he didn't really care whether I was there or not. Wix seems to be checking if I'm looking. He's got a nice body, of course, because he's a professional athlete, and he still keeps his fur sculpted, but I'm just not really interested.

When he's not flirting, we have good conversations about movies and stuff. It is nice to be able to talk to someone about how hot the male movie stars are, but also about the idea of being gay and out. It's different now from when I came out, Wix says, and what he means is that Aran and I held on by virtue of being some of the better players in the league, and two more players came out in the years after that, both in Yerba.

But Aran retired, and the other out gay players who aren't starters got quietly cut and are out of football now. So it's a little discouraging. But between me and Aran, we've built up a little underground network of gay players who aren't out, a dozen of them right now, and Wix says that when the season's over he'll absolutely join that list (it's a text message group at the moment). We talk about ways to make the workplace better for us, with me, Aran, Aran's ex Jay, and one of the Yerba guys as the visible arm of the group.

Lee helps with that, although he's dealing with his own issues. He doesn't have any other front office gay people to talk to except those he's hired. One owner got up in his face at an unrelated meeting and said, "I won't have faggots on my team." As much as we surround ourselves with support, that hard-line attitude has its adherents too, a lot of them, and as they feel under assault (which, let's be honest, they are), they've dug in their heels. Cutting those gay players must have resulted in a lot of back-patting around the owners meetings: *those fags think they can do anything, but we still have the power*. Again, that comes from Lee, probably through Peter, but it's matched by what scant coverage I can find in the media (not, thankfully, from the Chevali front office).

This year has been mostly about football. Aran has more time to be the public face of gay NFL players and he's been speaking and working behind the scenes a lot. Wix's orientation hasn't been a problem at all. Which isn't to say that being his roommate hasn't caused any problems.

•

The team gathers in the Sabretooths stadium visitors' locker room to watch the first semifinal game. The Port City Devils are up 14-10 on the Cansez Explorers by halftime, and it just gets worse from there for Cansez. The Devils score to open the third quarter and then Cansez's quarterback, a second-year white-tailed deer, throws an interception that's returned for a touchdown. Now it's 28-10 and the Explorers don't seem to know how to play catch-up. They run long dragged-out drives that stall, their defense is so focused on preventing big plays that they keep letting through these 10-15 yard gains underneath, and at the start of the fourth quarter it's 31-13 and everyone knows how the game's going to go.

We start cashing in bets at around four minutes left, when the Explorers settle for a field goal to make it 31-16. Down eighteen at that stage of the game you have to go for the touchdown or you've basically conceded the game. Even in the regular season that's a tough decision to justify, but in the playoffs you're basically telling your team, "We lost, pack it in, guys."

So if we beat the Sabretooths, it'll be the Devils coming to Chevali for a championship. That thought pulls my paws into fists, claws extended so I can feel them against my pads. I've been to two championships and lost both, but neither one was at home. After eight years for me, something like forty for the fans in Chevali, it would mean a lot to bring a championship home.

But first we have to beat the Sabretooths.

This city is where we lost that first championship, and for years I think we only won one game in that old stadium, no matter how good we were. For me and the other veterans of that first championship, the memory never really went away. But now that they've moved to a new stadium, we're ready to make new memories there. Last year, when it opened, we beat them, and even though we lost to them earlier this year, we didn't have our running back in that game and they got a couple lucky breaks. That's why we're playing them here even though we finished with the same record, by the way, but we can deal with that.

We get dressed and the linebackers get our pep talk from Gerrard: "We're here to play football, so let's go out and play football." He's getting better, I'll say that for him. Then the whole team crowds around Coach.

Coach Lopez joined us two years ago. We loved Coach Samuelson, but after losing the championship in 2014, the Firebirds went 5-11 the following year and ownership decided that just getting to the championship game wasn't good enough anymore. Coach Lopez got to the playoffs with the Pilots a bunch of times as an offensive coordinator and was thought of highly around the league, one of those guys about whom every off-season someone writes, "Is this the year Julio Lopez finally gets a head coaching job?"

As much as we liked Samuelson, Lopez has been great. He's also partly the reason Ty, unhappy with the new Gateway coaches, pushed to get traded back to Chevali mid-season, so for that reason alone I love him. But there's a lot of other reasons to like him, too.

The thick, muscular moose played offensive line back in the day. He's all about discipline, on and off the field, and he talks a lot about how when he played the line, if he stuck to his assignment and all his teammates stuck to theirs, they'd have a positive result. That's one of his favorite phrases, "positive result," and he pulls it out again here. "I know each and every one of you knows his job and is good at it. This staff has put together a game plan that can get us past these guys and to the championship. Execute on it and we'll see a positive result. On three, Firebirds together."

We chant, "Firebirds together!" and break to make our final preparations to go out onto the field. Samuelson was inspiring, but there's only so far you can go with the same inspirational speeches over and over again. Lopez's calm pragmatism is a nice counterpoint to that. He trusts us to get the job done, and that confidence is inspiring in its own way. I know a few of the guys would rather have the rah-rah, get worked up speech, but we've played hard for Coach Lopez and we're not going to stop now.

One of the things about this stadium is that even though it's larger than the old one, it doesn't seem as loud when we walk out. You also don't get as much scent from the crowd, though the smell of beer and sausages rolls down from the stands onto the field. Stronger is the smell of the field, that weird artificial turf, all bright green with white lines starkly dividing it into segments. I grab a cup of BoltAde and look up into the stands to see where Lee is while we're waiting through the introductions and pre-game nonsense.

This part used to seem to take forever, while the game went by so quickly when I was in it. Over the years, my perspective has shifted, and now I feel in tune with the pacing of it. All the pre-game stuff has to happen in its own time. There's the coin toss, which now I have to go out for with the other captains: our quarterback Rain Lind, a lanky dingo; the left tackle Cha Tuka, a wolverine; and of course, Colin Smith, the other defensive co-captain, our best cornerback and my least favorite person on the team. Rain and Tuke, the captains from the offense, walk out together all chummy, but Colin stays on one side of them and I stay on the other. We shake paws with the Sabretooths captains—their quarterback, middle linebacker (a buddy of mine, used to play for Kerina), center, and defensive end—and then stand while the ref shows us the coin.

As visitors, we get to call, and Rain calls, "Heads." People meeting him for the first time expect him to have an accent because he's a dingo, but his grandparents came to the States in the seventies and his dad's partner is a male wolf from Pelagia, so he sounds as native as me. He can put on an Oceanic accent and often does, to mess with people, but not here. Here, like the rest of us, he's all business.

The coin lands tails, and the Sabretooths ask to receive first, so we take the side of the field that means our kicker will be kicking with the wind.

When I get back to the sideline, I meet up with Gerrard, who's getting the linebackers ready to go out on the first series. I've got my helmet under my arm and I'm watching the special teams get ready to go out to kick off when Wix finds me in his number 22, red with gold trim on the white shirt. "We're gonna do this, right?" he says.

"Course we are." I squint across at the Sabretooths sideline, the sea of royal blue with gold numbers and helmets. "See how scared they are?"

He laughs. "Probably not as scared as I am."

Over his shoulder, farther down the sideline, Colin's grabbing some people to kneel in a prayer circle. "You got nothing to be scared of," I say. "You're good. When you go in, you'll do fine. Hey." I nod toward the prayer. "Shouldn't you be in on that?"

He turns, and when he sees what I'm talking about he makes a face. "First off, I'm not religious, and second off, come on. That guy?"

"The head of your unit and your defensive co-captain, yeah, 'that guy.'"

"Lion Christ, quit telling me that. You're my other co-captain." He shoulder-bumps me. "You trying to get rid of me? Want me to get religion?"

My tail lashes. "I'm saying you're making things more difficult for yourself."

"Not the way I see it."

I tilt my head. "Tell me the way you see it, then, because from where I stand, that's what it looks like."

"See," he says, "if I choke back who I am, go over there and play the good little choir boy—and not in the fun way—*then* I'm making things hard on myself." He taps his head. "Up here. But if I stay true to myself, act the way I feel, reflect who I really am, and he's shitty to me because of it, then he's the one making things hard on me."

There's something to that, but I also feel like there's something he's missing. Right before the game isn't the time to debate it, though, and the kickoff team is trotting out onto the field to get things started, so I say, "Just don't make things hard on the team," and I put my helmet on.

We kind of know what to expect from the first few series. Their coach likes to run scripted plays to get a feel for the defense. So there's a couple runs and some short passes, but no really new wrinkles. They can execute some of their plays, but our defense is tight, the line holding so their running back can't find gaps, and we cover the short passes well. They get one first down but then stall and have to punt, so we trot back to the sideline feeling pretty good about ourselves.

It's after that first series that Charm finds me. The big stallion handled the kickoff, but now he's just hanging around until we score, one way or another. "This new stadium sucks," he says.

"Morning to you too." I elbow him. "Thanks for pinning them back so deep."

He snorts. "Thanks for not giving up a score on the first series."

"Why don't you like this stadium?"

"Ah." He waves around. "Too shiny. Everything's new. Football should be played in old run-down smelly places, you know?"

"Yeah," I say, "but how are we going to fit both teams in your house?"

"Just because you have a boyfriend to keep your place clean," he says.

"Also I hire a cleaning service for my apartment."

"Ugh. People coming in being all up in my business? No thanks." We both turn to watch the offense run another play, this time a completion downfield to a tall, wiry fox wearing #88. That puts a smile on my face, even though I haven't talked to him yet today. "Good thing he came back," Charm says. "Really opened up the field for Rain."

"Not just for that," I say. "But a lot of it for that."

Charm gets more attentive as the next two plays don't get us a first down, and on 3rd and 3, Rain's pass floats just beyond the reach of our slot receiver, a second-year coyote. "I'm up," the big stallion says, grabbing his helmet even before the coach yells for the kicking team.

The offense comes back and I hurry down the sidelines until I find #88. "Hey," I say, grabbing his uniform. "What gives? Aren't you supposed to bring some kind of spark to our offense or something?"

Ty turns and grins wide, showing all his teeth. "You guys are supposed to be some kind of all-world defense or something," he says. "You need more than a three-point lead? Need us to carry you?"

I punch his chest. "Good catch there."

"First of many." We watch Charm hit the field goal. "All right. Go on out and earn that check."

One of the other reasons I like having Ty back is that banter. I've seen a lot of guys come and go, but the guys from that first championship game will always be special. After years of watching friends get cut or go to other teams, you stop opening up to new people. Lee says it's because I know they're going to leave, and that sounds right, but all I know is that I still text with Vonni even though he's been out of the league for years, I still would rather hang out with Carson than any of the new guys, and Charm and Ty can both bring a smile to my muzzle like nobody else.

Very little about the game is remarkable in the first half, to be honest. We go out, we do our job. They go out and do theirs. We're up 17-10 at the half, which we feel good about, but we also know we got away with a couple plays and the score could easily be reversed. Coach Lopez praises us in the locker room but says there's still work to be done. We go back out prepared to do it, and it's on my first series of the third quarter that the game changes.

Our offense scored on our first drive, so we're up 24-10 and the Sabretooths are playing a little more desperately. Lux, our defensive coordinator, calls up a delayed blitz, which means the linebackers drop back like we're in coverage but then two of us—in this case, me and Croz—rush the gaps and try to either get a sack or flush the quarterback toward the coverage on the strong side.

It works a lot of the time because Murell, their quarterback, thinks he's got time to dissect the usual pass coverage, and then we surprise him. He's not a rookie, but he's not as experienced as Rain. He sees Croz charging toward him first and tries to sidestep him, but he misses me behind two of his huge offensive linemen as I come barreling around. I wrap my arms around him and drive him to the ground.

He holds onto the ball, so we don't get a fumble, but a sack is pretty good too. I jump up and bump chests with Croz, but as we're walking back to our side of the ball, a bunch of Sabretooths hurry past us. Turning, I

stop dead at the sight of a bunch of personnel rushing toward us from the sideline as whistles blow to signal time out.

The quarterback is on his feet but holding his throwing arm with his other paw. "Hey," Croz says, "you knocked him out. Good job."

"Shut up," I say.

Too late; another Sabretooths player, a bear, gets up in his face. "Say that again, asshole," he says. "Say 'good job' again."

"Hey," Croz says, "get the fuck out of here."

"Make me."

I try to get between them. "He didn't mean anything," I said.

The bear shoves me. "You're the one who did it. That was a dirty fuckin' hit."

"Hey!" Croz steps up in the bear's face. He's not as tall but he's every bit as fierce right now. "I don't see any flags. Just 'cause your guy has a glass arm—"

Fortunately, by this time the refs have noticed, and as the bear shoves Croz, a bunch of striped jerseys hurry between them and our teammates pull us back. Carson has me by the arm even though I tell him I'm fine.

"It was a good hit," he says, even though the crowd is booing. They're replaying the hit on the Jumbotron. "He just landed badly."

I don't say anything but I feel shitty. You never want to see another player get knocked out of the game, especially a young guy. I keep thinking about the time I torqued my hip and how bad it felt not to play. And that was a fluky injury in practice; I just stepped wrong and my leg turned. What if another player had done that to me? I hope he comes back soon. But not, y'know, too soon.

The Sabretooths backup is not good. He flings the ball all over the place, once right into Colin's arms, and the fox weaves through the deflated offense for a touchdown. We're up 31-10 after Charm's extra point and even though there's a quarter and a half left, we're confident. We stop their offense on the next drive, and as I go to the sidelines, I'm greeted with cheers and slaps.

Except by Gerrard. "Good tackle." He doesn't look up from his tablet. "On Murell."

"I hope the kid's okay."

"Torn labrum is what I'm hearing." He points to the tablet where he has the game broadcast streaming in one corner. "Not coming back this game."

"So as long as we don't get cocky…"

His narrow muzzle turns my way. "Just stop right there."

"All right, Coach."

On my way down to Charm, Wix accosts me, also wanting to tell me what a great play I made. He slaps me on the back and I think his paw brushes my tail, but it's hard to tell. At least he's not happy the quarterback's injured either. "So easy just to land the wrong way," he says. "He wasn't even that old."

"Wasn't old at all," I mutter. "Gerrard says he's done, but he should be back next year. Torn labrum—they can operate on that, right?"

"I think so." Wix squints. "You think I'll get out there for more than just a play or two?"

"Probably at this point."

Their defense holds our offense to a field goal, but that's still more points on the board. We go out with all our energy knowing that the Sabretooths don't have a good option between passing the ball with an inexperienced quarterback or running the ball, which won't score as quickly as they need to do to catch up to us. We hold them scoreless in the third and through most of the fourth, until the coaches substitute in our backups to get them some playoff experience. Vic and Wix and those guys let a touchdown through, but all that means is that the final score is 37-17. Not too shabby. And we're going to the championship. Rather, I should say: the championship is coming to us.

Chapter Four (Lee)

I make a practice of never wearing any team's colors to an opposing stadium. For the first half of the semifinal in Crystal City, it wouldn't have been a problem. The crowds here aren't as fanatical, nor as drunk by half-time, as many of the crowds in other parts of the country. But when Dev sacks the quarterback and knocks him out of the game, boos rain down all around me, and every time Dev makes a play and the PA says his name, the boos start again.

I can't blame them. Honestly, I don't think they were going to win this game even with Murell, but without him the chances spiraled down. The Sabretooths aren't one of those teams that can withstand the loss of any one of their pieces. They've been lucky with injuries and scheduling, but they ran into a better team here. Losing their quarterback cinched what was going to happen anyway. The incident makes me happy I didn't accept the invitation to sit in one of the Sabretooths boxes with the front office guys I chatted with before the game. Things would maybe be a little tense after that hit.

As the game winds down, it hits me that Dev's going to another championship. I text him, *Championship!* and my tail wags against the chair. A few of the Firebirds jump up and down, but a lot of these guys have been to a championship before, and this time the thing that's really going to excite them is a win in the final game of the season.

Hal's typing up his article so I don't bother him as the game ends and the crowd starts to file out. We're in a press box, but not one of the fancy ones; about the only perk we get is that there's a table to put our hot dogs and beer or soda on, and nobody makes us get up to get in or out of the box like they would if we were in stadium seats.

Dev texts me back before we get up to leave, a very short, *Yeah! See you tonight*. Phones aren't allowed on the sideline, so he must be back in the locker room, and of course his phone is blowing up already because he's going to be playing for another championship.

The more I think about it, the more I bounce in my seat. I've been in the league almost a decade now, and I know all the things that go into winning a championship. It's a lot of skill, sure, but it's luck too, and the fact that I've seen a bunch of these games happen up close, seen behind the scenes of several of them, has made them at the same time less impressive and more impressive to me. Less impressive because, you know, you can plan and plan for years and have the best draft class year after year, and still not even get to a championship.

On the flip side, though, if you *don't* plan for years and have at least a few good draft classes, you are very unlikely to get to a championship. The point is that you get to a certain level, but there are always from three to six teams at that level in any given year. The one to win the championship is often the best one, but always it's the one that's had a bit of luck somewhere along the way. Even if it's just avoiding injuries to any of their star players, that's the kind of luck you need.

Both Chevali and Port City have had that kind of luck this year. I'm aching for Dev to have just a little bit more.

Hal wraps up his article and sends it in. "Good one?" I ask as he tosses his laptop into the shoulder bag he carries everywhere now.

"Enh. Pretty standard stuff. Had it all queued up so it was just a matter of picking the ones about the winning team. Included a little bit about Miski and Omba being the best active linebackers without a ring so far, and you're welcome for that."

"Thanks. I'll tell Dev." I grin.

"Want to hang out a bit or do you have to run off to meet him?"

"Need more relationship advice?" We're in front of a closed hot dog concession, and I put a paw on Hal's shoulder and give him a soulful look. "Just…consider her feelings, Hal."

He scowls back and shrugs my paw off. "Get bent," he says, walking on. "I revoke my invitation."

"Come on." I follow him down the concourse. "I've got a couple hours before Dev'll be free and I don't want to spend it alone in Crystal City."

"Should think of that before you run off that mouth." But he waits for me, and then as I catch up, he says, "Where you meeting him?"

We hit a place near the beach with a rooftop bar where we can sit and look out over the Pacific Ocean. I'm not a fan of Crystal City in general, but their beaches are way better than ours, even the public ones. I can't even remember the last time I went to a beach in my area.

"So," Hal says as our conversation turns to the championship, "you're not spending the next two weeks with Miski?"

I shake my head. "He wants his focus and I'm happy to step back. It's going to be—well, not as busy as it could be, but there's a lot of work for me to do. Draft is only a few months away and we want to have our board locked in as much as we can now that the college season's over. And for him, taking the relationship part of his life out of the equation for a couple weeks makes the football easier." I smile. "We've concluded that he can't just focus on football for his whole life, but for two weeks it's doable."

"Didn't work the last two times," Hal points out.

"There were other factors. That first championship…we were so on edge then, both of us, and Brian was being shitty…"

"Oh, right, the skunk." Hal leans on the railing, his ears to the breeze, fur ruffling along his cheeks. "You hear anything from him these days?"

I shake my head. "He moved back to the Midwest a few years ago, last I heard, to work with some activist organization or another. Sent us Christmas cards for a few years and we never responded, so he stopped."

"Good riddance. So two weeks apart and then the big game." Hal swishes his tail. "You think he'd mind if I hit him up?"

"Worth a try," I say. "I'll ask him tonight and I'll let you know if it's a hard no."

"Thanks." He raises his glass. "You're not driving to Miski, are you? Have a drink."

"Why's it so important to you that I drink?" I ask, but I have been eyeing one of the cocktails, so I order it.

"Cause I gotta ask you a question and I'd rather you have a drink in you when I ask it."

"That sounds ominous." But I wait until the waitress, a short chubby cheetah, brings my drink, and I take a few gulps of the pleasant herbal-sweet alcohol until I feel its warmth. "All right, shoot."

He puts on his reporter voice. "Can you confirm or deny that Poe Langor is going to take a GM job in Deleon?"

"Ah, fuck," I say.

The swift fox looks shrewdly at me. "Is that 'ah fuck' like 'you're not supposed to know that,' or 'ah fuck' like 'I didn't know that'?"

"What else are you hearing?"

"You gonna answer my question?"

I take another drink and look him in the eye. "Hal. C'mon. This is my job." My heart's beating but maybe not as much as it might if I hadn't had that drink. Am I going to be an assistant GM finally?

He shakes his head. "It's only 'cause of our many years of friendship that I'm doin' this."

"You didn't even come to my father's wedding."

He throws his paws in the air. "Game seven! FBA finals! It was a great game and I don't regret it." I wait while he stares out over the railing and then back at me. "I hear they want Dalbent Xu to replace him."

The name takes me a minute to process. "Wait, the otter? From Kerina? Shit, he's pretty good."

Hal nods. "So you didn't know?"

"No," I say, taking my phone out. "But let me see if I can get you that confirmation."

"Wait." He holds out a paw. "Don't—"

But I'm already flicking through my phone to find Peter's number. Hal sighs and settles back, looking out over the Crystal City skyline and up to the thin streaky clouds painted with red and purple.

"If you're calling to ask if we can pick up Goren for next season, we'll discuss it tomorrow," Peter says before I can even say hi.

Goren is a Port City safety, free agent-to-be. "No," I say. "What'd he do?"

"Didn't you watch the game?"

"I haven't reviewed it yet. I'm in Crystal City. Other people called?"

"Not yet. I agree we could use the upgrade at safety, but there's a bunch of other options out there. Ah, I've got another call. Talk to you tomorrow?"

"I heard Poe's leaving."

Silence. Peter must be covering the mic, because I can't even hear his breathing. Then he comes back, quieter. "Let me get rid of this other call."

He clicks off without waiting for an answer. Hal glances my way and I shrug, not even trying to perk up my flat ears.

"Lee?"

"Hi, I'm here."

Peter exhales. "Okay. So I guess you're with Kinnel. Don't know how it got out but these things always do. Yeah, Langor's gone."

"And you're bringing in Xu?"

"Fuck me." He gets control. "That's not a done deal. I was going to talk to you tomorrow, ask if you want to interview for the job. And I was going to tell you that ownership is pushing for Xu. You know what he did in Kerina, building up their audience overseas? They want that kind of reach for us. We're on the Pacific, we should be doing more outreach there."

"And that's what an assistant GM is supposed to do? Tell Michaela to harass the Marketing department."

"The players, Lee. There's interest in the game over there in Yamato and Xaiqin, and Kerina's gotten a couple useful players out of it. Those players have a huge following back home. So Ms. Martinet," he emphasizes the honorific for my benefit, "thinks that Xu could use the contacts he's made to get us some players here, as well as building up relationships within the league to get us one of those overseas games. More exposure means more merch sales which means more money to pay our guys. It's in the best interest of the club to at least investigate the possibility."

I breathe in and out. Peter fills the silence. "Lee? I was serious about letting you apply for the job. And trust me, you have a chance to get it."

"Do I? If I can bring in the kind of audience Xu can, you mean."

"You know the organization, you know the people. Everyone likes you. Don't downplay that advantage."

I sigh. "Fine." After a second, I add, "Thank you."

"No problem. Sorry you had to hear that way. Now smooth your hackles and tell Kinnel I'm going to kick him in the balls next time I see him."

That gets a smile out of me. "He wears a cup ever since that bit he wrote about Deke Danver."

"Ha ha, not surprised. All right. See you tomorrow."

I head back over to Hal. "Peter says 'fuck you very much' for telling me those rumors."

He flicks his ears back and then forward. "He should keep his employees in the loop. So it's true?"

"Xu's not a done deal yet, but they are bringing him in for interviews. So yeah, you can corroborate that."

He makes a note. "Thanks. Sorry to be the one to break it to you."

I snort. "If that were true, you wouldn't be a reporter."

"Har har. So you're just getting passed over?"

"Peter said I can interview, too, but ownership wants Xu." I finish off my drink and signal for another.

"You want the job?"

"Of course I do. I want to put my stamp on a team. If I ever want to be a GM somewhere, I kinda have to be an assistant GM first."

"Not necessarily."

"Okay, but." I wave my paws. "Who else is gonna hire the gay fox who didn't play the game? Peter trusts me, we work well together, and I love the area. I want to stick around."

He nods. "Enough to keep working for another assistant GM?"

The waitress brings my drink and I stare moodily down at it. "I guess I'll tell you in a couple weeks."

We spend a nice hour with tasty cocktails and a sunset over the ocean, a pretty lovely evening. I'm almost sad when Dev texts me to tell me he's back at the hotel, which is to say that I linger a moment between springing up from my chair and saying good-bye.

"Didn't you just see him last night?" Hal asks, half teasing, half annoyed, as I drop two twenties on the table.

"Yeah." My tail wags. "But this is the last time in two weeks."

•

The hotel room is the same as it was last night, a modest one-bedroom even though Dev can afford a suite. This one has a nice view of one of the bright city centers in the Crystal City area, newer than the actual downtown with more colorful signs and shorter buildings. Tonight is hazy, which softens the lights and gives them just a tinge of unreality, and as the last of the buzz from my cocktails wears off, I stand with Dev by the window enjoying the view.

"You did great," I say. "That sack probably decided the game."

He's in a t-shirt and shorts with one arm draped over my shoulder. "Yeah," he says. "I heard Murell has a torn labrum, might miss the start of next season."

"Not your fault," I say firmly. "You made a totally legal tackle."

"I know." He squeezes my shoulder. "It's part of the game and all. Just got me thinking about some stuff."

I wait, though I think I know what he's going to tell me. After a decade, you get a sense for it, and he's talked about his worries with injuries before. I can see his mind going through projections of the future.

"If we win the championship," he says slowly, "I'm thinking about retiring."

I nod. "I wondered. We've talked around it for a couple years but never come right to it like that."

He turns away from the ghostly city lights to me. "What do you think?"

I put a paw on his hip, the one he injured. "I think you'll know when it's time."

"Will I?"

I incline my head. "There are things even your boyfriend of ten years can't know. When it's over, you know, it's over. You can un-retire a year later, but the few times I've seen someone do that, it hasn't gone very well."

"Falua."

"Right. And others. On the one paw, you know, there's always the chance that you'll injure something that won't heal."

"Maybe I already have."

"Not like Fisher, though." That's what he's worried about, I think, the thing hanging over all of this: his former teammate and mentor who now lives a quiet, sedentary life in which he mostly recognizes his wife and cubs and on good days knows what year it is.

He lets his breath out in a hiss. "No, not yet. But he didn't know it was happening until his last year, and then it was too late. I don't want you to have to go through that."

"Me?" I'm startled.

"Yeah. Fisher, he's—I mean, a lot of the time he doesn't know what he's missing. He's happy. It's Gena and the boys who have it really hard."

"We should go see them after the game," I say. "Sometime soon. It's been too long."

Dev sits on the bed. "Yeah."

"Anyway," I go on, sitting next to him. "you have no idea what a life without football will be like."

"I could try for a coaching job." His tail flicks back and forth behind him, brushing mine. "Or announcing."

"If you want to get into announcing, you should be reaching out to networks, making connections. But the point is that football's given your life a lot of structure. I'll be here to help you through it if you give it up, but you still have to be prepared for that." The thought flits across my mind: if I don't get an assistant GM job in Yerba, where the organization has known me for almost a decade, then have I hit my ceiling? Should *I* retire?

"Uh huh." He rubs my shoulder. "So what should I do?"

"Don't make your decision hastily," I tell him. "That's the main thing. Don't go up to the podium if you win and announce your retirement. Your emotions are running all over the place there—look what Polecki did."

"That turned out okay, though." He smiles. "He says hi, by the way. He texted when we won, said he and his boyfriend will be down in Chevali to cheer me on now that the Sabretooths are out of it."

"Who's he dating now?" The coyote had been dating one of my guys, but after he retired from football it sounded to me like they both found that having each other around 24/7 wasn't the same as having each other to turn to during a busy football life. His old boyfriend, Cornwall, married a guy from his high school and moved back to the Midwest somewhere, if I recall.

Dev reaches for his phone. "Here," he says a moment later, and shows me a picture of the tall, athletic coyote kissing a much shorter red panda. "The guy's name is Mark and he's a photographer."

The picture is artfully staged. "Hal's moved on again too," I tell Dev. "How did these two meet?"

"Oh, Mark was with one of the sports magazines—I forget which one now—and went along when they did a photoshoot of 'retired athlete bodies.' He made some comment and Aran made one back and they kept in touch, saw each other a few times, and now it's steady enough to be official."

"Good for him. Life after football."

"Uh-huh." Dev looks back out to the lights of the city. "I wish I could try it out, you know? Just have a taste of what it would be like."

"That'd be nice." I smile. "Whatever happens in the game, you can try a thought exercise. Pretend you're not going to minicamps in the summer, pretend there's no season to look forward to. What would you do with that time?"

He thinks about that for so long that I nudge him. "Don't do it now. You have one more game to play and you need to keep your focus."

"Yeah." He leans down and kisses me. "So are we taking a two-week break?"

"Up to you."

He nods. "I think so. I'll text you if anything changes. But yeah, I'm going to be thinking about not much besides football starting tomorrow morning. What are you going to be doing?"

That reminds me of Mike. "Oh, right. Mike—my stepbrother Mike—"

Dev laughs, a nice deep rumble of a laugh. "I'm still not used to that."

"Me neither, but I'm making myself say it. Anyway, he called this morning." I pause for a moment, worried about pronouns again, then forge ahead. "Dropped a bit of news on me."

Dev's ears perk, so I tell him about my conversation with Mike. He scratches his ears with one free paw. "What's that mean, 'genderqueer'?"

"It means—well, what he says is that sometimes he feels female and sometimes male. But the Internet says it can also mean he might feel in between, or neither."

"I don't get that. How can you feel female if you have…" He reaches down to grab my sheath, playful.

I squirm. "Just because you can't feel it doesn't mean it isn't real. Think about how many of your teammates told you they couldn't understand how you could be attracted to…" I push into his paw's grip. "This."

"Mm, fair point. All right, hope it goes well. If anyone can guide him into a new world of gender and sexuality, it's his big stepbrother."

"Ha. I'll need to do some research on the plane flight back. I don't know if I even know anyone I could go talk to about that."

"You must. How can you not?"

"Maybe Cord. I'll ask him about it in the morning." I turn away from the city lights and kiss him back, deeper and longer. When we break apart, I say, "Do you want to talk about modern gender identities or go make the most of our night?"

By way of answer, he pulls me down to the bed, and that night, I don't think about work at all.

•

In the morning, I don't think about work again as Dev insists on getting his "last taste of fox" for a couple weeks. I point out that he doesn't have any taste receptors in the part he's using and that if he did—and at that point he grabs my muzzle and tells me to appreciate a metaphor. So I appreciate his metaphor very vocally through my clamped-shut jaw, and he buries his muzzle in my shoulder fur and does the same.

One of the reasons the two-week break works well for us is that we often go two or more weeks during the season without seeing each other. He's training, I'm working, and when I can pop in for an evening, I do, but that isn't all the time. It's been less and less over the years.

So we cherish the moments we can get with each other. Time apart makes them more special. Not that I don't want him around all the time, and seven out of the last nine years at this time he has been around all the time. But now there's one more stretch of football, and he knows that at the end of it he gets to relax with me again.

This year, I'm going to add one more wrinkle. Because we spend a lot of time apart, we are always aware that temptation might be a problem, especially with Dev and his prominence as an out gay professional athlete. So far we've been good about not cheating, but Dev has been telling me about his new roommate this year and all the flirting he's doing. Being Dev, it took him a while to recognize it as flirting, but it was pretty plain to me from the start.

So as we're in the shower, I say, "Hey. If your roommate the gay bobcat gets too flirty with you and it's distracting, you have my permission to let him suck you off."

He freezes. "I don't want to cheat on you."

It's sincere, and I kiss him for it. "I know. But right now you've just fucked me twice in the last twelve hours and you probably wouldn't even want me to suck you off here in the shower."

"Hrrr." He rubs under my muzzle. "You offering?"

I laugh. "I'm just saying, he's obviously flirting, and we've been together like ten years. I'm not worried you're gonna leave me for him. But if a few days go by and he's still waving his cock in front of you, and jerking off doesn't do it, you can do stuff. Just be safe about it. Don't pick up any cat diseases or anything."

"I'll be fine, fox. All I want is you. And I can wait two weeks."

"All right, all right."

He angles his head. "This isn't because you think you and Mike…"

"Ew." I smack his arm with a wet, soapy paw. "We're brothers!"

He laughs and grabs me. "Come on, what if he's feeling experimental?"

"Also he's eighteen. What am I, a cradle robber?"

Dev lets me go. "Wix is only twenty. He can't even drink."

"All right, but you're not related to him."

"You're not related to Mike. Technically."

I lick my tiger's wet nose. "Hush. I just don't want you to get all twisted up about things over these two weeks. If it comes down to him getting you really worked up, I'd rather you take care of it and not text me, or agonize over what it might mean, or anything. Just be safe and promise to tell me about it."

"Wait," he says. "Do you want me to do something with him?"

"Well." I slide soapy paws down his sides. "I guess not, if it comes down to it. But knowing what situation you're going to be in, I want to give you some room to make a judgment call."

"It's not going to get that bad," he says. "He's going to be as focused as I am."

I hold him against me. "I hope so. I hope you're both so focused that it's the dullest game ever and you win 51-7."

"Seven?" He pushes me against the shower wall. "In your ideal fantasy we still give up a touchdown?"

I squirm and laugh. "No, no! That was a punt returned for a touchdown! Special teams!"

"Oh, so our offense had to punt?" He pushes against me, his breath on my nose, but he can't keep up the fake indignation and we both end up laughing, clutching each other as the water cascades through our fur. It's a lovely moment, one of the ones I hold in my heart afterwards.

I don't really think Dev would do anything with his roommate. But I wouldn't have thought he'd take a random fox back to his room and almost have sex with him—honestly, by some definitions he did have sex. Depends on whether you think it doesn't count if he doesn't climax. I used to think that way but my definitions have changed a bit since then.

Too soon, it's time to say good-bye. Dressed, we hold each other and kiss, tails wagging and lashing. I rest my paws on his hips as we pull back, my gaze fixed on his golden eyes. "Go get 'em, tiger," I say. "You can do this."

"I know I can." He smiles back at me. "Just worried about my team-mates is all."

"Trust them." I hug him one more time. "All right, now I'm really late for the airport."

He squeezes me again. "Love you."

"Love you too." I half-heartedly try to get out of his embrace, but it's not until he pushes me toward my suitcase that I can get away. "Can you call the front desk and have a cab waiting to take me to the airport?"

"Sure." He picks up the phone as I open the door. "See you in two weeks."

"See you, champ," I say, and hurry out of the room.

Chapter Five (Dev)

I've got a plane to catch, too, but not until like ten o'clock, so I take my time cleaning up the hotel room, packing, and so on. I'd talked to Mom and Dad after the game yesterday, only briefly because my post-game time is short. This morning, I call back for a longer talk.

They ask how I'm going to prepare for the championship, which I tell them in the general terms they know and understand. Mom tells me that Alexi, my nephew, was so excited about my game that he jumped around their living room and fell off the couch. "Nothing serious," she said, "but he started coughing and Gregory and Marta made him sit down and gave him a shot."

"Poor cub," I say, although honestly if Alexi heard me say that he'd ask me why. As overprotective as my brother and his wife are of their white-furred cub with the lung disorder, they've done an admirable job of making him feel like a normal cub who just has to take medicine more often than others do. Exercise is good for him, but jarring blows can shake stuff loose in his lungs, so they have to be careful. "How are they doing?"

"They're good. Gregory is very busy and Marta will graduate with her nursing degree this summer."

"Good to hear," I say. I don't talk to my brother much, but we stay cordial and he comes over to watch my important games with Mom and Dad, though I think that's more because they dote on Alexi than because he wants to watch the games.

I tell Mom that Lee is going through some stuff at work but not sure how it's going to end up yet, and she tells me to wish him luck. Then she says they all know I'm going to get a ring this year, and I thank her, hoping that she's right.

Lee left his toothbrush in the bathroom. I text him about it since it's early enough in our two weeks that it doesn't really count.

He texts back "hold on to it," so he's not on the plane yet, or maybe he is; he's gotten yelled at more than once by flight attendants over the years. I don't ask; I toss the brush into my bag and get everything arranged in the suitcase.

I am wondering, though, what Lee meant by telling me I could have sex with Wix. He said he didn't really want me to, but he also didn't want me to be confused about it. So did he think I want to? Or did he think I was going to be tempted? And what should I do with that information? Should I encourage Wix? I don't think anything will happen if I just keep going on the same way we have been, though admittedly he's been a little more direct lately than he was at the start of the year. Maybe that's just getting comfortable with me.

Maybe I should start walking around him naked and fondling myself. No, no, I remind myself, you're thirty-two years old and he's still a kid. You need to be the one to set an example.

So I'll be the mature one, and nothing will happen, and then I can tell Lee that in two weeks and everything will be fine.

•

My flight experience is very different from Lee's. The team bus gets to the airport, where we go around security and to a small hub where chartered flights take off from. There we board our plane, by far the largest in the area, and get settled comfortably in wide leather seats while we prepare for takeoff. We can use our phones throughout, and there's WiFi on the plane so we can turn the cellular off.

"I've been thinking about it." Ty plops down next to me. "I must be the good luck charm. Check it: My first year—we make the championship game. My last year with Chevali—we make the championship game. My first year with the Tornadoes, well, you know what happened. And now I'm back with Chevali and hey!" He spreads his paws wide. "Back in the championship."

"What about all those years between your first and last with Chevali?" I love Ty, but sometimes his "everything works out for me" attitude grates on me. In a friend kind of way, you know, like the way Lee always has to be right.

"Ah," Ty says, "you can't make the magic happen all the time or it's not special anymore."

I wonder if Lee would care if I slept with Ty. I know for a fact he sleeps around on the road, guys and girls, though he's more discreet about the former. But I also know his boyfriend and wife, so I think it would make things pretty awkward. Not to mention I have no idea how to go from "friends for eight years" to "fuck buddies," so it's probably better to leave that alone.

Still, part of me wonders what it would be like. He's still in great shape, of course, even by the high standards of football players. Better than Wix, and definitely more experienced by this point. We're not going to talk sex on the plane, but over the years he hasn't been shy about sharing experimental things he's done with his partners, a couple of which have almost made me ask Lee about finding a third sometime. Funny how back in college, I was reluctant to sleep with two girls at once even though my teammates and I talked about three-ways a lot, and now that I know someone in a three-way relationship, it's not so weird to me.

That's the way things go, Lee would say. That's how gay marriage became legal: gay people coming out and talking about their lives. Once people know that they know a gay person, or a couple, the issue becomes more personal for them. Ty isn't an evangelist for threesomes ("poly relationships," Lee would remind me), but just knowing him and seeing his relationship remain stable for years has made that arrangement feel less weird to me.

Not that there's anyone in my and Lee's life I would consider as a third, nor do I think Lee has anyone in mind.

"Hey." Ty nudges me. "Come back from Dreamland."

"Yeah, yeah. You think your luck can win us the game this time?"

He puffs out his chest. "I'm actually going to play in the game this time, so…yeah. Plus I'm better than I was then."

I like to think that's true of me, too. I'm as fast as I was a few years ago, and I'm smarter than I used to be. I can read offenses better, and Gerrard trusts me to make snap decisions mid-play. But there was that hip injury, and even though I haven't lost a step, the kids coming into the game just keep getting bigger and faster.

"Big deal," says a voice beside us, a sharp one I know well. We both turn and see Colin leaning on our seat. The plane isn't taking off yet so nobody's yelling at him to sit down. "Who isn't better than three years ago?"

He glares at me, somewhat reinforcing my own doubts, but Ty answers before I can. "Aston, for one," he says mildly.

"It's not all a ride up," I say to Colin, miming a roller coaster hill with my paw. "Eventually it starts going down again."

"Funny," he says, "that's what I was going to tell you about the movements to normalize perversion and dilution of our country's heritage."

Ty has heard about this from me, but because he joined us midseason, he's missed most of Colin's rhetoric, and even managed to miss the gloating after the recent election because that was in a meeting of the defense. He knew about Colin hating gay people, of course, but the "heritage" is a new addition the last couple years. So now Ty turns to me as he reaches for his phone. "Wow," he says, "you were right. I didn't know people like this actually existed. I thought the media was making them all up."

He brings his phone up and Colin pushes it aside with a snarl. "What are you doing?"

"Taking a picture." Ty leans back out of reach and snaps some pictures with his phone.

Colin rolls his eyes and shifts his attention back to me. "I came over to tell you that you're changing roommates. I'm taking Wixin and you can have Dublovic."

"Wait, whoa." I sit up. "I didn't agree to that."

"It's not up to you. I told Coach that I thought our rookie corner should be bunking with another corner this season, and since Dublovic is a safety, it made more sense for him to room with you."

Dublovic is also one of Colin's prayer group, a puma who wears a cross around his neck during games and who, when he came to the team, asked for a locker as far from mine as possible. He's never confronted me directly, not that anyone has over the past few years. In fact, this conversation with Colin is as close as anyone's come in a long time. And it's pissing me off.

So I unbuckle my seat belt. "I'm going to talk to Coach," I say.

"Be my guest." Colin hurries back to his seat.

I think I've scared him away, until a moment later the announcement comes that we have to take our seats. Coach is up at the front talking to our offensive coordinator anyway, and just because I'm all worked up about the issue now doesn't mean he's going to care about it the same way. Anyway, nothing's going to change between now and the time we land in Chevali.

So I sit down and buckle in again. "Hey," says Ty, "Didn't he have a cub?"

"Yeah."

"I'd have thought that would mellow him out, but somehow he's even more of a dick. What's the big deal with Wix anyway?"

Certainly Ty wouldn't care, but Wix's secret isn't mine to tell. I'd encourage him to come out to Ty, but he doesn't really know Ty and while he doesn't care if the coaches know—they're his bosses—they also don't interact with him socially the way the other players do. At least, that's my guess as to why he was open with the coaches but private with everyone else.

I settle for, "He's a good kid. Colin's worried I'm a bad influence on him."

"What," Ty laughs, "like he thinks you'll turn the kid gay?"

To forestall the rest of this conversation, I shake my head. "Hey, how's Kella doing?"

"Omigod." He pulls out his phone. "Arch got her the cutest outfit. Here, look at this."

He passes the phone over as the plane's engines spin up and we roll forward. "There's a bunch of pictures there," he says.

"Of course there are." I take the phone and flip past the pictures of an adorable fox cub in a sunshine yellow jumper with a gold-embroidered sun on it. Her smile is as bright as Ty's, and then there's one picture where she's trying to figure something out off-camera and I can see her mother in her too. Tami and Arch are by turns in the pictures holding her paw, guiding her, laughing with her.

Ty leans in to point out things in the pictures as I flip through them. There are a couple out on his deck overlooking the coast near Pelagia on a bright sunny day, the water sparkling with light. "She loves the ocean," he says. "She could swim before she could walk."

"In the ocean?"

"No, no. Well, sort of. There are tidal pools, but no, we have a covered pool and she loves it. Here, look."

He takes the phone back and flips to another album. There's Kella in an adorable baby-blue swimsuit paddling in the pool, Arch holding her in most of the pictures with as tender an expression as if he were her father. And I suppose he is, come to think of it.

"You miss being there for her?" I ask as we come to the end of the album.

"I'm there for a lot of it." He lingers on the last image, Kella looking right into the camera. "We vidchat most mornings, and I make the most of the time I'm there. Anyway, she's only just started really talking in sentences. By the time she's a person who can have conversations I'll be there."

"Cub pictures?" One of the offensive line guys leans around on Ty's other side from the seat behind.

"Yep." Ty passes his phone back. "How old's yours?"

He gets a phone in return, along with, "Six and three."

Together he and I flip through the album of pictures, two little bear cubs out on a hike in the woods with their mom. They pose with flowers, wade in a stream, climb partway up a tree. The older shows her little brother (I'm guessing at their genders from the clothes) a pine cone; he shows her a rock he's found.

He and the bear swap phones back. "Who's the wolf?" the bear asks.

"Caretaker," Ty says casually. "Helps Tami out with the cub since she works full time."

"Like a male nanny?"

"Kind of."

"Heh. Not worried he's fuckin' your wife on the side?"

Ty winks at me where the bear can't see it. "She don't ask what I do on the road, I don't ask what she does at home."

The bear wasn't expecting that. "Huh. If my wife fucked around on me…" He punches the back of the seat.

"I'm sure she isn't," Ty says.

"How modern and progressive," I mutter, but it's not the bear that's on my mind as the plane levels off. I glance back to see him putting his earphones on—the big noise-canceling kind—and still I keep my voice down as I mutter to Ty, "Caretaker?"

He gives a flick of his ears and his smile doesn't budge. "It's factually more or less right."

"Doesn't he have a full-time job too?"

"Yeah, but Tami can work at home a couple days a week and his work actually has a daycare, so he takes her in there when Tami doesn't work at home."

I nod and settle back. Of course Ty doesn't want to have awkward conversations about how his wife lives with his boyfriend and they do fuck when he's away, and also when he's home. I'm sure he especially doesn't want to have that conversation with a guy who thinks it's okay to punch his wife if he suspects her of cheating on him. But I feel bad because Arch is being minimized, if not erased, from Ty's life. When I've visited them with Lee, we've been impressed by how close all three of them are, a real family. It just feels shitty to me that Ty has to hide that, and more so that he doesn't seem to mind hiding it.

Not my problem, I remind myself, but that doesn't make me feel better about it.

Chapter Six (Lee)

All the way in the cab to work, I rehearse ways to talk to my boss about the Assistant GM position. I don't want to come off too pushy, but when you're in an office full of ex-jocks, you can't sit back and play the finesse game either. I've already set a precedent with the phone call, so I'm trying to figure out whether I'm going to build on that or walk back from it when my phone rings.

I check the number as usual and double-take when I don't recognize it. Weird area code, too. I get calls from agents sometimes, though usually it's closer to the draft, and often I don't have their numbers. So I pick up the call and say, "Lee Farrel."

"Mister Farrel." An unfamiliar voice on the other end, a little bit of a growl to it, so a larger predator, I'd guess. Wolf, bear, wolverine maybe. Too nasal to be a tiger. "Hi. Please hold for Mister DeWitt."

DeWitt? Oh, shit. Morty?

Sure enough, when the line clicks, it's the old cougar's voice I hear, thick with the residue of decades of smoking (he finally quit a few years ago). "Lee. Catch you at a good time?"

"What the hell, Morty?" I can't help smiling. "You've got a secretary placing your calls now?"

"Ah. I got a lot on my plate," he says. "Wasn't sure when to get you so he was gonna try 'til we got through. Lucky first time. You ain't in the office yet?"

"On my way there now." I hesitate, because of all the people I'd love to ask advice from, Morty is at the top of my list. But telling him what Yerba's doing with the assistant GM position might not be a great idea, given he currently runs a rival team.

Turns out, though, he already knows. "Heard you guys lost your assistant GM," he says. "You going to replace him?"

"I've got a meeting about that this morning," I say.

"Good. Well, listen. If it ain't a done deal, I'd like to fly you out here."

"Um, I've got a friend coming in Wednesday I have to show around—wait, why do you want to fly me out?"

He laughs. "To interview for the same position here. Want to work with me? Get the ol' team back together?"

Whoa. I can't say anything for a minute. Honestly, of all the people I'd love to work with, Morty is probably a close second to Peter. And Cansez just went to the semifinals. They're returning a good core of players, couple free agents might leave…I don't know what their salary situation is off-hand, but I'd guess they can afford to pick up at least one decent free agent. "Assistant GM?"

"That's right."

"Wow." Collect yourself, fox. "Could it be, like…this weekend? Early next week?"

"If you're available to do phone interviews before then, sure. Miski's busy, right, so who's this coming in?"

"My stepbrother. He's looking at colleges in the area." And dealing with a bunch of other issues. "Sorry, I'd put it off, but he's got his flight already and we've made appointments at a couple schools."

"Sure, no prob." He coughs. "But you're interested?"

"I'm at least interested in interviewing." I pause. "Who else ya got?"

"You just worry about your own interview," he says.

"Come on," I say. "You want me to ask my reporter friend to find out?"

He laughs. "Let him try."

"He found out who else Yerba's looking at for the position."

The laughter stops. "Oh yeah? Who's that?"

"Not telling." I can't help a satisfied grin. "Maybe you should ask one of your reporter friends."

"All right, I got a lot on my plate here." Morty growls a bit. "Get to your office before I change my mind about working with a smart-ass fox. Glad we got to you before they could lock you up, though. I'll call your agent, let him know we're interested."

That brings a little more perk to my ears. The conversation with Peter made me feel, not undervalued exactly, but not quite sought after. Now here's Morty, the guy who gave me my first break in the business, giving a little boost to my ego.

Cansez is a team on the rise, that's for sure. I call up some articles on my phone and spend the rest of the cab ride and a little bit of the walk into the office reading up on their financial situation and free agency worries. I scout college teams for my job, but still keep half an eye on the pro teams, so most of this isn't new to me, but it does give me a level of detail I hadn't had before.

Their situation, if I'm being honest, is a little better than ours. We lost a bunch of players after our championship and have been trying to rebuild through the draft, with mixed results. Not my team's fault in most cases, although there's always the guy you recommended who's a bust, and the other guy some other team got two picks later who turns out to be a star. But Peter understands what a crapshoot this is, and he also understands that a significant part of whether a college player makes it in the pros is the attention and skill of the coaching staff. Even knowing that, it's not easy finding a coach who's great at developing all players. Our coaches are great—with some players. Others don't find common ground, and most commonly when a player's a bust, you hear his position coach say some variation on "I can't get through to him."

(Hiring coaches is definitely out of my purview, but when I run into a college coach who impresses me, I mention him to Peter and Peter keeps tabs on him. In my eight years with the Whalers, we've hired exactly one coach I recommended, a strength and conditioning coach from Tall Valley College, and he's still working for us, so I guess he was good.)

Cord, the gay fruit bat I hired, is the general assistant to the scouting department, in charge of the interns we have running around here come draft time. Right now there's only one, a female fennec named Jess who comes in from eight to ten every day and then goes to her classes. When I get to the office, both Cord and Jess are watching a video about the previous day's game.

"Hi, Mr. Farrel," Cord says, and Jess waves too. "You excited about the championship?"

"More important," the fennec chimes in, "is your boyfriend excited? Third time the charm?"

"Fingers crossed." I hold up a paw with crossed fingers, redundantly. "What'd you guys end up doing?"

Cord and his boyfriend went out to a bar, he says. Jess got together with some of her rugby team to watch at home. "We made seven-layer dip and nachos," she said. "I brought in some of the dip. We made a ton. You guys should break it out over lunch."

I pat my stomach. "I'll just take a taste, thanks."

"I keep telling you, you got nothing to worry about," Jess says. "You're in better shape than half the ex-jocks around here."

"Thanks." I wave and head on into my office, where I retrieve one of my Whalers ties from my desk drawer and put it on my collared shirt to look even more business-y.

Over the last few years here, I've put together a pretty good team. I've got five college scouts working for me, four ex-players and one statistics nerd, a rat who, like Cord, is gay. I haven't turned down qualified straight people for these positions—I have to be clear on that to Peter and to our owner. But the fact that I'm here brings in gay people who love football but wouldn't feel comfortable in an environment where there wasn't a gay person in a position of power. Some power. Moderate power. I fiddle with a pen on my desk and think about that.

Of course, in Cansez I could build a team, too. But that's in the middle of the country, right in the Bible belt, next to the state with the batshit crazy religious compound that pickets funerals and shit. Would they even accept a gay exec on their football team? I draw little spirals on a folder on my desk. Morty must have run it past the owner before he called me, and my identity is pretty well known in football circles. I've attended a couple owner meetings and had people there flatten their ears and hurry away from me, like I was contagious. So that's always fun.

I don't know much about the Cansez owner, Harley Devereaux, so I check him out (of course it's a him). Not as old as I would've thought, an Internet billionaire who made a website I only vaguely remember having heard of and then sold it to a big company right before the economy went to shit. He's a red wolf, which I would usually associate with Southern good ol' boys, but if he's down with hiring a gay guy then maybe I need to set that stereotype aside.

Cord knocks on my door. "Hey, I'm hitting Starbucks. You want the usual?"

"Sure," I say.

"And Mister Emmanuel put a meeting on your calendar for nine-thirty and wanted to make sure you'd seen it."

"I saw it. Thanks."

"Cool." He rustles his wings, gives me a smile that shows his one broken fang, and heads out.

Between Dev and the job here and the job possibility in Cansez, I'm finding it hard to concentrate on anything else, so I waste half an hour staring at more info about Cansez's team and then it's nine-thirty and my calendar reminder jolts me out of my seat and down the hall.

I knock, and Peter gestures me into his office. He's a red fox, taller than me and with lighter fur that offsets his maroon Whalers polo shirt better than my darker fur does, which is why I rarely wear mine. The gold t-shirt works for me, but to keep my clothes at least somewhat office-appropriate, I usually toss a dark blazer on over it.

I generally feel really comfortable with Peter, not just because we're the same species (that's part of it) but because from the beginning he's always treated me fairly and well. So my tail's a little twitchy as he steeples his paws together, elbows on his desk, and looks at me over the tips of his fingers.

"First off," he says, "I'm sorry you had to find out from the reporter. I promise I would've told you we have other candidates for the position this morning."

"Thanks." I shift in my seat. I can tell he's upset because he only calls Hal "the reporter" when he's annoyed at him. "Sorry if I overreacted a bit."

His ears flick. "Understandable. So let's talk about this assistant GM position. Interviews will be this week and next, and I'll want you to sit down with me and with Ms. Martinet. You should also probably talk to Andy."

Michaela Martinet, the Whalers' owner, I've met on a few occasions. She's a tanuki whose parents made their money from bringing Toyota to the States in the eighties and settled here. She convinced her parents to buy the Whalers fifteen years ago and she's been running the team since then. Andy, the Director of Player Personnel, is a cheetah I work with a fair amount, though I don't know much about him outside of work. "Cool."

We talk for a while about the direction the organization is going, all stuff we've talked about over the years. I take notes, condensing the conversation and making sure I have all the finer points sorted out. And then at the end of the meeting, Peter asks if I have anything else to tell him.

I debate for a moment. I'm not obligated to tell him anything about my outside job possibility this morning. I want to tell him, though. I take a moment to make sure I'm not doing it spitefully—look, these guys went out of their way to interview me! It doesn't feel like I am, so I go ahead, trying to be casual about it.

"Oh yeah," I say. "I heard from Morty. He wants me to interview for the assistant job in Cansez."

Peter nods. "Thought he might. You interested?"

"Thinking about it. It'd be a big change, moving to the Midwest and all."

"Aren't you from the Midwest?"

"A different part." Saying it out loud reminds me how different my liberalish hometown is from the hyper-conservative Cansez. Though in the city it would be better, wouldn't it?

"For sure. Hey, I'm not gonna lie. It's a great opportunity. They've got a good future and I think there's a good chance you could get another ring with them." He smiles a long smile. "Also a chance you could get another one if you stay here."

"I know."

"When's he want you to go out?"

"Next week. I've got my stepbrother in on Wednesday to look at colleges so I'll be in and out the last half of the week."

"Mmm." He brings out his phone and checks it. "Let me know if you decide to fly out there and when. Pretty light on the calendar early next week, but I'm kicking off Thursday draft meetings again."

I bring out my phone to look at my calendar, too. "I scheduled the first meetings to go over our incoming rookie program." I look up. "Can we change—"

He laughs. "No."

"What other kind of rookie is there? Why can't we just call it our rookie program? 'Incoming' is redundant."

"See," he says, pointing at me, "this is the kind of insight you can't get from ex-football players. Be sure to nitpick titles in the Cansez interview."

"Ha ha." I check the phone. "Anyway, I've got that, got a couple calls with colleges lined up. And I'm sure you'll have other things to fill my week with."

"As a matter of fact, I'm going to forward you this email from Remington's agent. He hurt his ankle, it turns out, and the agent's being coy about the injury and how he got it. Don't know any more about it, but it'd really help me if you could give him a call."

That's the guy who was drunk at the nightclub, the one I was looking up reports on for Peter yesterday. Not a critical player, so what Peter's asking me to find out is whether this injury is the kind of thing that will make him a liability to keep, either because of the severity or the circumstances. "Can do."

"Thanks. And one more thing before you go." He gets serious. "It might be awkward, but I'd like for you to interview Xu when he comes in tomorrow."

My fur bristles, but I keep my demeanor pleasant. "Sure," I say.

"I trust you to be at least somewhat objective." Peter smiles. "I know you too well to ask for 100%, but I'll put it on myself to figure that out. Anyway, if we do end up hiring him, and you stay, you're going to have to work with him too. So if he's a huge asshole and somehow the rest of us all miss it, I'm counting on you."

"I'm an asshole, and you hired me," I say.

His ears flick back. "You're not a *huge* asshole, though. Besides, I need all our assholes to get along with each other."

I resist the temptation to make that a sexual remark, mostly because nothing easy comes to mind. "I'll interview him," I say. "And I'll tell you what I think. If he'd be better than me at the job, I won't lie."

"I trust you," he says again, to drive it home, and I leave the office cursing him for appealing to my better nature.

Chapter Seven (Dev)

The first thing I do when we land is corner Coach Lopez. He's talking to another assistant, but they put their conversation on pause when I walk up. "What can I do for you, Miski?"

"It's about my roommate."

"Right," he says. "Smith told me the backs coach wanted the change, so I approved it. Something wrong?"

"Not exactly." I fidget. "I mean, yes. I'd rather things stay the way they are."

The moose turns to his assistant coach, a tall black wolf, and then back to me. "Superstitious?"

That'd be a good out. Why mess with a winning streak, I could say. "No. But Wix and I were getting along well, and Dublovic is an idiot."

"We can see about swapping someone else in," Lopez says.

The wolf speaks up. "Or give them separate rooms. It's just for a couple weeks."

I could also just go home, but Coach has said he wants the whole team staying together in a hotel by the stadium so we bond over these two weeks, and the owner has paid for the hotel already. "It's more about…personal issues," I say.

We're surrounded by players, so I don't want to give away Wix's secret. But Coach gets my meaning right away, and he heaves a sigh. "All right," he says. "Come to my office this afternoon and I'll bring Smith in and we'll see what we can do."

"Does he have to be there?" I ask before I can stop myself.

Coach flicks his ears. "He requested the change, so we gotta work it out with him."

"Can't you just issue one of your Team Rules?"

That loosens him up and he laughs. "I don't want to waste a Team Rule on a minor disagreement. Now go home and come back to my office at one. I'll talk to you guys then."

He fingers the silver cross he wears around his neck as if to remind me that he's got a paw on Colin's side of the debate as well. Despite his religion, Coach Lopez has never talked down to me nor treated me as anything other than a good player and a good person. I'm not really friends with him like I became with Coach Samuelson, who texted me congratulations when we won the semifinal, but coaches aren't always going to be your friends. I'd thought my first linebackers coach, Steez, would remain friendly with me, but I haven't heard from him since the team fired him years ago. So you never know.

Ty's already gone, and so is Carson, but Wix (of course) is hanging around. He corners me even though I try to get out without seeing him. "Hey," he says, "Smith said something about changing up rooms. What's this about? I don't want to change."

"Me neither." He falls into step beside me as we walk out of the charter terminal. There's a small crowd of fans, so I stop to sign some autographs. Wix stops with me, and a few of the fans give him something to sign too, though none of them recognize him.

There is a group of two coyotes and a skunk at one edge of the crowd who stare at me but don't come forward as I get close. That's fine; not everyone is a fan of everyone on the team. And over the last year, there's been a resurgence of people yelling hateful things at me, more than I can recall since the first year I played with Chevali.

So it's no surprise when the skunk says, loud enough for me to hear, "Keep walking. Nobody wants you here."

The comment appears to bother Wix more than it bothers me; he folds his ears back, while I put it away into the space where I've grown accustomed to keeping such things.

Then one of the coyotes says, "Hey, bobcat."

Wix stops for a moment, an involuntary reaction to being addressed. Then his thoughts catch up and he keeps walking. The coyote takes a step forward. "Why you hangin' with outsiders?" he asks as we approach the building we have to walk through to get to our cars.

I hold the door open there and Wix hurries through. "What's he mean, 'outsiders'? You were born here, right?"

"Born and raised," I say. "But my grandparents came over from Siberia. I guess that's what they mean."

He huffs. "That's dumb. Is that about jobs? Like there's another linebacker who's waiting to take your job. Don't they want us to win games?"

I glance back, even though I can't see the crowd anymore. "I don't think they were actually fans," I say. "I think they just showed up to yell at me. Maybe Carson too, and Rain for that matter."

"People do that?"

"Well." I shrug. "They used to yell at me because I'm gay, so maybe this is progress? Anyway, it's only happened one other time."

"Still." Wix puts a paw on my arm. "They're assholes. Who cares where someone was born?"

"Ask Colin."

Wix's ears go back. "Him too?"

SEND
THEM BA

"Honestly, I don't know. He says things, but it's only really to me, and he hates me anyway. I don't think he's said anything to Carson. But there's been one or two of his friends who make comments just loud enough for us to hear." Like Dublovic, asshole safety. "It's not a big deal."

"Not a big deal? What if they were being homophobic?"

"They do that too." I grin. "One of the things you learn in this business is that there are a lot of assholes out there. You can't let them get to you. If you do, they win."

We walk out to the parking lot in silence, and when we get to my truck, I clap him on the shoulder. "See you over at the facility in a few hours."

"Yeah," Wix says. "I'm gonna take the last good nap I'm going to get for two weeks."

"Good plan," I say, and I watch him walk away to his car.

I'd like to do the same, but all the way home, I find myself thinking about how I'm not attracted to Wix even when we're talking about being gay, and that leads me to thinking about Lee again.

After a decade, you'd think we'd be more stable and sure with each other, but I still have moments when I can't be sure what Lee's thinking. And maybe part of this is my self-doubt, that I'm still amazed sometimes that this bright, wonderful fox wants to be with me. Even though intellectually I know there are a lot of reasons for that, I can also discount all of them. Sure, I have a great body. So do a lot of other guys, including a bunch he works with. I'm a successful football player? Same. He lives in a city full of gay guys and our relationship is a lot of work, and sometimes we get frustrated with each other. Sometimes I feel like there's got to be someone else out there he could spend more time with and get closer to.

And the thing is that that's not true of me. All of us here on the team who have partners of any kind have a long-distance relationship at least part of the year. There's not many options other than "patient partner willing to take on a lot of the work of building a life" for someone like me. So while he could clearly trade up to a less complicated relationship, I definitely couldn't. Not that he's ever given any indication that he wants to, but it's always there in the back of my mind.

Besides that, we've had conversations about me playing around on the road, and he's said several times that if anything happened and I told him about it, it wouldn't be a huge deal. It's a matter of pride to me, though, to be better than that. Knowing that I have the leeway to slip up is nice, but I also know that "slipping up" isn't just a matter of, say, stumbling into the wrong hotel room. It's a series of decisions, usually involving hanging around people who want to fuck you, drinking so your judgment is impaired, and then not going back to your room when they start taking off their clothes, or yours. I've made one of those decisions many nights, two occasionally, but never gotten all the way to the third one.

So yeah, we've talked about it, but Lee's never been this specific with his permission before. I told him about how Wix has been all season, getting bolder as the games go on and he got to know me better, and Lee said that for sure the guy was flirting with me. I took his word for it, though I was never good at picking up on that from guys. Now it's pretty darn obvious—walking around naked and half-hard after his shower is a sign even thick-skulled me can pick up on.

In the elevator on the way up to my apartment, another thought occurs to me: if I'm sure I'm not going to do anything with Wix, wouldn't it be best if I let him room with Colin? It's only for two weeks, and it's not going to kill him to spend two weeks with a Jesus-freak. Is it?

I go over to the window and look down at the view, my thoughts turning in another direction. It won't be too long now—if we win—that I won't be such an inconvenient boyfriend anymore. I'll be able to move to Yerba and live in the house we bought, maybe even get a job with the Whalers if I still want to work. Though let's be honest, I probably won't. I'll enjoy being home when Lee comes home every day. Maybe I'll learn to cook better or pick up some hobby, or just play video games all day and once in a while go do appearances for the foundation.

I've been playing football for over fifteen years, since high school. Never got to a championship game in high school or college, but three times I've made it in the pros. That fire to win still burns in me, but when I imagine holding the trophy, standing at the podium, I can imagine walking away afterwards. The game still holds appeal for me, and it's scary knowing that once I walk away I can't go back, but after a decade in the pros, I don't have a lot of excitement for the new year starting up again: the camps, the new crop of rookies, learning new plays that are like plays I forgot three years ago, and then the games, getting beat up eighteen times a year. For a championship, to stand up on the biggest stage a winner, I can continue to motivate myself. But having won one, I don't know. Maybe that would be enough. There are more important things in life.

•

Dreading going back to the stadium that afternoon has nothing to do with football. I'm fine at confrontation on the field, and I'm sure not afraid of Colin. But he's got a way with words and I'm not so great that way, and

I'm worried he'll make a case and I won't have any response for it. I think about texting Lee for help. It's not that far into our two weeks, after all. But I don't want to type out the explanation of the situation, and anyway I know Lee well enough to have a pretty good idea of what he'd tell me to say. Or at least what advice he'd give me: keep your head and speak from the heart.

What I've learned over two years with Coach Lopez is that he's football-focused. Not quite Gerrard-level, but he definitely doesn't have Coach Samuelson's knack for talking players through personal issues. Since he's been here, the team has been less like a family and more like a professional organization. Which is maybe what we needed, but there are times when I miss the family aspect.

When I walk into his office, Colin's already there, along with Javy, the fox who coaches the defensive backs, the two of them taking up both chairs in front of Coach's desk. I don't know the backs coach all that well, but I don't think he's part of Colin's prayer group. Likely just taking the side of his star corner.

They're talking about one of the Port City wideouts as I come in but stop at the creak of the door. Both foxes' ears flip back, and Coach Lopez raises his head and gestures for me to stand to one side. "Miski, thanks for coming in."

Colin leans over to the coach and his lips move. I've seen Lee and his father do what they call, "fox-whisper," talking in tones so low that only a nearby fox's sensitive ears can pick out the words. Lee knows it's rude, so he only does it at parties or in restaurants—places where he's surrounded by a lot of people he doesn't know. I'm sure Colin knows it's rude, too.

"All right," Coach Lopez says. "Let me see if I understand this. You," he points at Colin, "want his roommate," he shifts his finger to me, "to move in with you."

"I think," Colin says, smooth as butter, "that Wixin would benefit from the company of another cornerback during non-practice hours. A little bit of extra coaching could mean the edge that would give us the championship." It's a good line. Coach likes "edges."

"And you," Coach points at me, cutting off my retort, "want to keep things the way they are."

Do I? My hesitation over Wix could be solved if I just told Colin he could have the bobcat. But one, I don't want to room with that asshole Dublovic, even for one night, and two, I don't want to let Colin win. It's petty, but there it is. So I stand up straight and make my argument. "We've developed a good rapport over the season," I say. "The linebackers and cornerbacks have to work together. Anyway, I was a corner in college, so I know some of that mentality too."

"But you're not a cornerback now." Colin's smugness ratchets up a notch.

"Because of my physical limitations," I growl. "Not mental ones."

"And you haven't studied a cornerback play in, what, nine years? Ten?"

"I'm not saying I'm going to be his coach. I think that position is taken." I nod toward the other fox. "What I'm saying is that messing up team chemistry right before the championship could be that one little disruption that costs us the game."

Team chemistry is another of Coach Lopez's things, and Colin's flattened ears show his annoyance that I hit on that. Coach, sure enough, goes, "Mm, yeah," and turns to Colin. "Why do you think it's so important to switch up the rooms now? The kid's been okay this whole season. He's not going to start."

Colin's smooth, and he's got charm to a point, but he's not actually the quickest of foxes mentally, I've found. Below-average fox still puts him at an advantage to much of the population. "Of course we could change things up next season," he says. "I'm happy to revisit this discussion in June. I'm just thinking of the team and the championship game."

Coach Lopez turns to the defensive backs coach. "Javy, what do you say? You think Wixin could use a little extra training?"

That fox doesn't even look at me, but he does give Colin a glance before answering. He's got a deep, drawling voice with just the hint of a Sonoran accent. "Sure, everyone could use more training. But I don't think he's gonna get it from rooming with Smith."

"Coach, I—"

The fox—Javy—holds up a paw. "My feeling is that there's a moral concern here. Smith is worried about a corruption of young Wixin's character by our gay football player. Only that's not politically correct to say."

Coach Lopez stares intently at Colin. "Is that true?"

"First of all." Colin doesn't look at me. I'm starting to feel invisible. "I want to make it clear that I'm not accusing Miski of any harassment or unprofessional behavior."

"That's nice," I interject sharply.

Nobody pays attention. "But I do feel that Miski's lifestyle normalizes—normalizes his lifestyle." Colin stumbles but recovers quickly. "And Wixin is showing some of the effects of it."

Ah, fuck, what did the kid do? I want to ask but I'm smart enough not to. And anyway, Coach asks for me. "What effects?"

Colin shifts, and Coach Javy's confident ears sweep back as well. "It's—" Colin clears his throat, but his voice remains rough. "He's beginning to voice opinions that he didn't at the beginning of the season."

Coach's eyes narrow. "Opinions?"

Colin looks to Coach Javy for help, but the other fox isn't going to get him out of this one. So Colin clears his throat again. "He's made it clear that he doesn't want to be part of our group discussions."

"The prayer group?"

"That too." Colin's tail flicks.

Coach Lopez shakes his head. "All right, listen. We're not going to change anything two weeks before the championship because a rookie's getting more comfortable opening his yapper. Wixin stays with Miski. Smith, it's your job to keep him integrated into the unit on the field. Javy, you keep your corners together. And Miski, don't talk shit about your fellow players to your roommate."

"I don't—"

The moose holds up a hand. "I didn't say, 'stop doing it.' I said, 'don't.' If you were going to after this meeting."

"He already knows Colin wants him," I say, unable to resist teasing Colin a bit. And it works; he flattens his ears and snarls.

"Hey." Coach Lopez's voice sharpens. "We can't win a championship if there's friction on either side of the ball. Now I know you guys don't get along, but you're going to have to work together if we're going to win this game."

We look at each other uncomfortably. In the silence, Coach Javy stands up. "I'll go tell Wix there's no changes."

"Hang on," the moose says. The fox stops partway to the door. "Listen, you're right about not making changes, not rocking the boat. But where there's already a problem, making a change won't make it worse. So Miski, I want you to practice with Javy's group Wednesday. Smith, you practice with Marvell's group on Thursday. Next week, same thing, Wednesday-Thursday. Clear?"

Fuck. If I'd just shut up… Colin opens his mouth to protest and sees my mouth open at the same time I see his. We both snap our jaws shut and mutter, "Clear," because when Coach asks you a question you better answer it.

Coach Javy says, "I'll tell Marvell," and heads for the door.

As he leaves the office, Coach Lopez tells me, "So you don't have to say anything to him about this. Thanks, Miski. Close the door on your way out."

My triumph at keeping Wix is tempered by the idea that I'm going to have to practice with Colin for two days this week and next. As I leave the office, I think about telling Coach that I need the time with my unit, that Colin needs the time with his, but I know he's already thought about all that.

I turn right outside the office, and Colin turns left, and that's the end of any chance we'll talk about it before tomorrow.

•

Of course, now I want to be able to tell Wix not to be so vocal around Colin, but I know I might as well tell him not to walk around naked in the mornings for all the good that'll do. And Coach told me not to say anything to him anyway, so it's not even up to me.

Wix isn't in our hotel room yet, so I claim the bed nearer the window and toss my stuff to one side of it. As the senior player, I get my pick of bed anyway, but the last few weeks he's been a little more pushy about it. Claiming he's "not really a rookie anymore," that kind of stuff.

I check the schedules we've got and see that I've got practice in forty minutes. So I lie back on the bed and try not to dwell on Lee's words. He was probably just trying to save me some stress in case Wix got too pushy, or I got too pent up, because my fox loves me. That's what's important. What is only slightly less important is that in two weeks I've got a chance—maybe at this point in my career, my last one—to be a champion. All that talk about team chemistry and tiny edges wasn't just jockeying for advantage in the fight for Wix's soul; it reflected truthfully what is on all of our minds. So: football now.

My phone rings.

I grab it and look at the number. But it's not my agent or my social media person; it's Lee.

"Hi," he says when I answer. "Sorry to break our two-week vacation, but it's only just started and this is pretty big."

"Shit. What happened?"

"No, it's good. Cansez called. Morty's there and he wants me to apply for their assistant GM position."

That takes a moment to sink in. "Holy shit, fox, that's awesome." Then the penny drops. "But oh shit, Cansez."

"Yeah. Team's great, Morty's great. But."

"Okay." I try to work through this. "But if they want you—the owner must have signed off, right? So he's not one of the asshole owners?"

"I guess not." He doesn't sound super confident. "Youngish Internet billionaire. Morty says it's cool, but I dunno how much I could do there like I do with the college students here."

"You won't be working with the college students directly anymore, though."

"That's true." He says it slowly, pondering. "But I'll be working with the guys who are."

"It's a good thing." I stay firm. "They've got to know it'll be a challenge and they want you anyway. And they're positioned to go to the championship soon."

"I know." He exhales. "So you think I should pursue it?"

I laugh. "Doc, when have you ever needed my advice for your career?"

"Whether I need it doesn't matter, stud." His tone recovers some of its sharpness along with humor. "I always want it."

"All right then." I think for a second, but I can't see any reason not to tell him to go ahead. "Yeah. You should do it."

"There's the townhouse…"

"Hey. I bet you can buy a nice house with a yard in Cansez with what you have in the Mercer account." We have our savings diversified; Mercer Financial is Lee's second savings account, for "fun stuff." I am exaggerating a little, but houses in the Midwest are really cheap.

My exaggeration works; he laughs. "If we wanted a nice house with a yard, we could have one."

It's not like we haven't talked about that. It's mostly that we travel a lot and we like a whole lot of different places, too many to settle down to just one. My teammates have bought houses for parents, grandparents, and siblings, but my parents like their house a lot (I did pay for an addition, which is where Lee and I stay when we visit) and my brother barely talks to me, let alone accepts gifts. Lee's family is similarly pretty well off and his father, who handles finances for me and a lot of my current and former teammates, says he's gotten plenty from the Firebirds without taking a house from me. "All right," I say. "Maybe Cansez is really nice. We only played there once." I try to remember whether there were more homophobic signs there than anywhere else.

"You think they're ready for me?"

"Doc," I say, "I don't think anyone's ready for you. The question is, are you ready for them?"

"Fair point. Thanks, tiger."

"Hey," I say, because he's getting ready to hang up, "you'll never guess what I've been dealing with here."

It takes me only a few minutes to tell him about the whole minor Colin kerfuffle. "What an asshole, huh? And now I have to practice with him."

He's thoughtful. "Practice is fine, right? Shouldn't be a big deal. You going to talk to Wix about watching what he says?"

"Yeah. I mean, I'm not supposed to say anything about Colin but I feel like I need to say something."

"You should." He sighs. "I don't like what that says about the progress we're making toward acceptance within teams."

"Oh, and there were a bunch of Nativists booing me when we landed."

"Ugh."

"Right? Remember when I just got booed for who I sleep with and not where my grandparents came from? At least you're not an 'outsider.'"

"They're also against mixed-species couples. And since gay couples can't have cubs they're not thrilled about me in general. If I'd marry a nice vixen and have nice fox cubs…"

"Same shit, different mouths."

"You said it. All right, tiger. Glad you're going to be there for Wix. Maybe drag him along with Ty and Carson on one of your wild nights out."

"I think he'd like that. He keeps telling me he's not a rookie anymore. Oh, and speaking of Wix, uh…" As I'm trying to think of how to ask Lee if his comment had anything to do with our relationship, the door opens and the bobcat himself walks in. "He just walked in."

Wix's ears flick. "Talking about me?"

"Tell him you're telling your boyfriend about him showing you his cock."

I clear my throat. "Lee was asking how you're doing."

Lee snorts on the phone. "Love you, tiger. Talk to you later."

"Tell him I'm fine." Wix throws his bag on the unoccupied bed and unzips it, grabbing a pile of clothes and heading for the dresser.

"Talk to you in a couple weeks, fox." In my head I play out a little fantasy where I say loudly into the phone, "Did you mean it when you said Wix could blow me?" I'm mostly curious to see Wix's reaction. But then the connection's broken and the moment's over.

"Hey," I say to Wix, busy arranging all his clothes in the drawer. "I need to talk to you."

Chapter Eight (Lee)

The first few minutes after I hang up the phone, I worry about Dev talking to Wix. I think about what I was like at twenty and how I would've reacted to someone telling me to tone down my progressive words. I would've told them to fuck right off. But Wix isn't doing the out and proud walk either, so he has at least some measure of discretion. When I was at the Dragons, I kept my sexuality hidden—until my boss made one too many gay jokes and I blurted it out for the satisfaction of seeing him shocked. In retrospect, it probably wasn't worth losing my job over, even though I got a better one and it worked out.

That hasn't been an issue for me for a while. For one thing, my whole office—the whole world, as many of them as care—knows my sexuality. For another, I'm mostly focusing on football these days. Gay players and sometimes coaches reach out to me, and I help them as much as I can, and I read up on the issues, but I grew to rely more and more on Cord after I hired him to keep me posted. Our morning discussions about the LGBT topics du jour slowly turned into him informing me. Not that they're one-sided; I still have plenty to say. It's just that he's the one bringing the headlines to the water cooler, as it were.

After I hang up with Dev, I research Xu's career looking for any holes I can poke into. I'm just starting to get depressed about how solid his resume is when Mike calls. I try to remember if I'd promised to call back after our last call, but there's no accusation to start with. "I was looking up stuff in Yerba," Mike says, "and there's a film showing Thursday night at the Sexuality and Gender Spectrum, um, symposium at the Wright Center. Is that close to where we'll be?"

"Close as anything," I say. "I'll put it on the schedule."

"Thanks." Relief, as if I might've shot down the idea.

"Hey." I pause, not sure how to bring this up, and then I decide to just dive in. "What, ah, what pronouns are you using now? I forgot to ask before."

"Oh." There's silence for a moment. "I'm still Mike. I guess call me 'he.' Anything else sounds weird, right?"

"It's up to you. I'll adapt to whatever makes you feel better."

Another pause. "Yeah, just stick with 'he' for now."

"You got it." I don't let the silence stretch into awkwardness. "So we've got Laurel on Thursday afternoon, the film Thursday night, UG on Friday, and Bautista State Saturday. You fly back Sunday, right?"

"Uh huh."

"Anything else you might want to do while you're here?"

He clears his throat. "Maybe, uh. I was reading a bit about Korsat Street?"

Korsat is the gay hangout street in the city. The first couple years I lived here, I went there a bunch to dance and drink and be gay out in public. Now you can be gay pretty much anywhere, so hanging around a community that was very important years ago but now feels less relevant to me doesn't appeal so much. But it's important for queers of all stripes to know and appreciate our history, and even though Mike probably just wants to wear something outrageous out in public—strike that. *Because* he probably wants to wear something outrageous out in public, it'd be good for him to go.

"Sure," I say. "Friday night after UG would be most convenient. Sound okay?"

"Yeah." Again the relief.

When he hangs up, I fight the compulsion to call Father or Angela to let them know what their son is getting up to. I can't reveal his secret, though, and telling them there's a secret to reveal would be giving away too much. Saying nothing doesn't sit right with me either, so in the end I call Father even though I don't have anything to say to him.

"Did you get tickets to the game?" he asks.

"What? No. Sorry, I haven't tried. Was I supposed to?"

"I thought Dev would get you some. Angela's working her connections but so far we only have two, and the boys really want to go."

"I'll see what I can do." I lean against the window of my bedroom, looking out at the quiet suburban street. "Speaking of the boys, Mike's coming out here in a couple days."

"Good to hear he won't just be hanging around the airport when we leave him there Wednesday."

"Har har. I wanted to let you know that if you're worried that he's going to ask me to do a lot of…you know, college-kid things…that I'm going to watch out for him."

Father doesn't signal his jokes with chuckles. "Okay, but if the Deltas try to rush him, make sure you get him out of there."

"Don't worry, I don't plan to take him to any colleges in the early 80s."

"Good choice. He'd graduate into a recession."

"You did okay."

"I graduated with a finance degree in the third greediest decade of the past hundred years. I'm actually ashamed I wasn't a millionaire by the time you were born."

"You weren't?" I smile at my reflection in the window. "I assumed you lost it all to poker out on Boardwalk Beach."

"No, the only thing I lost there was your older brother. Someday, Wiley, we'll track him down."

The window is a little chilly on my nose. I like the way my smile looks in it. "Give my best to Angela and Jaren."

"Best to Devlin."

"We're taking a two-week break so he can focus on football. I'll pass it along after the championship."

"Never mind, then, I'll tell him myself."

"Oh," I say. "And…"

I tell him about the Cansez possibility. He's not as enthusiastic as Dev, but he does tell me I should give it careful consideration. "It'd be a challenge," he says, "but challenges aren't positive or negative by nature."

"I feel like this one might be both. The team's great, but that city…that part of the country…"

"What I mean is, you shouldn't automatically turn something down or seek it out because it's a challenge." He covers the mic and calls, "Just a minute," to someone else. "I do think challenges help you grow, so if it's the right kind, it'd be a great experience. But you're very aware, too, of all the ways in which it could be not so great."

"Very. But hearing you say it's worthwhile helps me decide to put some energy into it."

"Glad to be of service. Keep me posted."

I let him go after that. I want to keep researching Xu, but my mind is scattered, so I call up Netflix and watch a couple episodes of a dumb science fiction show that doesn't require me to think (in fact, it actively discourages it). Almost all the way through the second one, I start dozing off, so I force myself off the couch and up to my bed. The phone call makes me miss Dev, and there's a pillow on his side of the bed that still smells like him so I bury my nose in it for a moment, inhale, and then roll over and close my eyes.

•

In the morning, I've got a pile of emails in my inbox. Having determined that they can all wait until I get coffee, I proceed to my corner Peet's and respond to a few of them while waiting for my order. The one that doesn't need a response is the one I spend the longest time staring at: the meeting request from Peter for the interview with Xu that afternoon. The team can move glacially slowly, but when they sense there's an opportunity they might miss out on, they pounce. Which means that there must be other teams interested in Xu as well. The fact that he's come here is a good sign—for the team, anyway.

On the walk from the coffee shop to the office, a brisk half-mile, I call up Remington's agent and ask about his client's broken ankle. Right away I know it's not going to be good news, because the agent's evasive. "It's nothing to be concerned about. He was out with some friends and it's just an accident."

"Out with friends doing what?"

"I don't see that that's pertinent to the discussion. And why is the director of scouting calling me and not an assistant GM?"

"Because the GM asked me to call you." I can't tell him we don't have an assistant GM at the moment, because that's not public. "I scouted Remington, I've interviewed him, and I'm the one asking you again, out with friends doing what?"

"Listen, Mr. Farrel. Mr. Remington is being examined by a hospital, but at the current time we're confident that the injury will not impact his attendance at the first minicamp in June."

I don't deal with agents a whole lot, but there are a few I know and trust. In general they work hard in their clients' interests. It's mostly when those interests conflict with the team's or when their client does something stupid that they become harder to work with. This agent is not one of the ones I know well. "Listen, Mr. Vespry. I'm not a reporter. I'm a representative of your client's employer calling you on behalf of his boss to ask you for full details of his situation. So how about you drop the lawyer act and tell me how bad it is."

The agent sighs and comes back with hope in his voice. "If he's healthy by the time he has to report, then it isn't any of the team's business?"

I don't say anything, and after another sigh, he goes on. "It was nothing. He wasn't engaging in any of the activities forbidden in his contract. No motorcycle, no jet ski, nothing like that."

"I assumed he didn't ride his jet ski into a bar. So what's the problem?" When he still doesn't answer, I say, "Do you think we're never going to find out?"

"All right," he says finally. "Look, these are just friends of his from college and I'm trying to get him to stop associating with them. We kept his name out of the police report, but I'd rather it not leak out later."

"Unsavory friends. Check."

"These friends were a bit intoxicated and were at a bar, things got a bit disorderly, and there was a little brawl. Remington didn't get arrested—he didn't throw a punch or anything."

"But he was drinking."

"He's legal age."

"Okay, so…" I'm outside the office now, but there's a secure little alcove where nobody can hear me. "Why the big secrecy about it? Drinking with friends?" I lay my ears back. "What was the brawl about?"

"Nothing's proven." The lawyer-voice comes back. "But the allegation is that Remington's friends were yelling pro-Native slurs at a group of tanukis."

In my head, the incident shifts, like when the light in a room changes and you see the shadows behind everything. I'd thought this was just a dumb kid getting drunk with friends, twisted his ankle when he stepped on a bottle during a fight, and that was it. But now it turns out he's hanging out with Nativists, and the agent's been trying to get him to dump those friends, but he hasn't.

The agent coughs. "Mr. Farrel?"

"Was he?"

He pauses. "Listen, Mr. Farrel, they weren't anti-gay—Remington is fine with his gay teammates. He had a gay teammate in college. And he's not—I mean, that's not why he's friends with them."

"Was he yelling pro-Native slurs? At the species of the person who owns the team he plays for?"

Vespry sighs. "How do we make this better?"

"There we go," I say. "Let's talk to our public relations department and see if your client will issue an apologetic statement. Then you have a talk with him about hanging out with those friends and the possible long-term effect on his financial situation."

"And that'll do it?"

"Let me get back to the GM. I can't promise anything myself, but those are things that should happen anyway, regardless of his future with the team. Okay?"

"Fine." He's not very happy about it, but he's resigned. I wouldn't be surprised if he's got a little pro-Native sentiment himself. He doesn't have a predator's growl, but with his deep voice maybe he could be an elk.

I feel like that got resolved well enough as I walk into the office. See, I could totally be an assistant GM. I go in and report to Peter, and he thanks me, but he gets a call and has to cut our conversation short. So I write it up in an email and I get a quick "good job" back from him two minutes later.

Cord and I go out to lunch and talk about Xu. Like a good employee and friend, he staunchly maintains that I'd be a better assistant GM. I don't argue much, but the conversation makes me a little uncomfortable, so I turn it around to ask him what's new with the Nativist movement. I only know a little, what I've been reading in the papers. There have been more than a few articles online talking about their growing political clout, especially their influence in the recent presidential election, but as much as I don't like the direction things are going, I haven't had the stomach to read all the repetitive articles dissecting it, attributing it to economics or speciesism or whatever, every writer claiming priority for their own personal crusade.

That said, my conversations with Cord have been more instructive than most of the articles I read. As a fruit bat, he's way more affected by it than I am. Here in Yerba his species isn't such a big deal, but his family's from Taysha and mostly still lives there. "We haven't had, like, shit thrown at us or nothing," he says now at this lunch, "but just in the last year or two my sister had some armadillo yell, 'Go home,' and one of the guys my dad works with didn't invite him to the yearly barbecue that he had been going to for years. So...shit's changing, and not for the better."

"I never heard of it hitting out here, or, like..." I stop myself from saying something about Dev being famous. "Football teams. A bunch of guys were calling Dev 'outsider' when he came back."

Cord's ears go back at the word. "Harassing random fruit bats is one thing, but an All Star player?"

"Not that that's any worse."

"No, course not," he says, "but it's more ballsy. Fewer people are gonna come after you for harassing randos."

"That's sad too," I point out. "So why is this getting so much more popular?"

He shrugs. "If I knew that...I mean, where my family lives, the economy's not great. People like to have someone to blame, and the real answers aren't very satisfying. It's better to have a whole class of people you can pin your problems on."

"Of course." I rub my whiskers. "So first off—have you been treated badly in the office, or anywhere here?"

"Nah." Cord smiles and shakes his shoulders, rustling his wings. "I'm trying to get my family to move out here but it's expensive."

"Okay, good." I tap my glass. "Can you draft an email to all the athletic directors on our list, tell them that we are aware of growing Nativist sentiment and that we will not tolerate any players associated with it. In the name of team chemistry, blah blah, you know what to write."

He nods. "Yeah, got it." He smiles. "That's good. For all those fruit bat football players."

"If you want," I say, "we can shoot a letter over to the Thrust for them to send to their basketball recruiting contacts. That'd cover your fruit bats. In fact, I know one of the scouting guys over there."

Cord laughs. "Really?"

"Sure. You ever want to go to a game, let me know."

"Thanks, boss."

I run through our roster in my head. "I'm gonna send an email to Peter too, see if he wants to say something to the team."

"That's something an assistant GM would do." Cord winks at me.

"Yeah," I say. "Let's hope."

We get back to the office and I have half an hour to prepare for the interview with Xu. Even though I'm the one conducting the interview, I'm nervous as I walk into the conference room.

They've given the otter the room with a view of the Bay, but he's looking down at his notes as I walk in. My first impression of him is his sharp charcoal-grey suit and maroon and gold checked tie, Whalers colors. Nice touch. He's immaculately groomed down to the whiskers, and even to my fox's nose he smells good, a designer fragrance but not overwhelming.

He's intent, so he doesn't notice me until I reach the table and pull out a chair. "Oh," he says, standing. "Mister Farrel, sorry."

I extend a paw to his and we shake. Firm grip, good shake, releases in time. We sit, make a little small talk, and then I get right into it. "Tell me about one of the most challenging things you handled at Kerina," I ask.

He launches into a great story about dealing with a higher-up who wouldn't buy into his vision because he hadn't played football, and the work he had to do to convince this guy, and how he eventually did. It's the kind of story that could come off as phony, or artificial, but he sells it. And when I say "sells it," I mean that I don't think he's actually selling it. I think he's telling me a true story. Sure, some details probably changed, but I know at least one of the guys in his story (not the main one) and it rings true.

And the worst part of it is that I don't even get the feeling that he's boasting. He's just telling me a story that is exactly what I asked him to tell. I realize that in all the preparation to interview Xu, the thing I hadn't been prepared for was that I might end up liking him.

Chapter Nine (Dev)

Tuesday's practice (with my own unit) goes fine, but I'm a little off in practice Wednesday, and it's not just because I'm doing drills with the cornerbacks and safeties. They're good guys for the most part, but my mind is on Wix and the reason I'm here, which means I'm thinking about the few who aren't good guys. Colin has three close friends on the team this year: Dublovic the puma, Marshall the black bear, Lukos the coyote (a new addition). They don't practice together—Lukos is a backup linebacker so he's in my group, and he's the most polite of the three. He's figured out that he can disagree with someone and yet still perform on a team with them. Marshall, part of the defensive line, mostly ignores me, as does Colin himself. Dublovic, the safety, peppers his conversation with talk of God and talks about our team redeeming themselves and earning God's favor and stuff like that, often with an eye on me. I've grown inured to it most of the time, but today he shoots me one sneering look and touches the cross around his neck and my hackles rise.

We start with callisthenic drills and go on to station drills, the same as the linebackers do. We also have pass defense drills, and I do okay in those, but when we get to comeback/hitch breaks and 45-degree breaks, Coach Javy puts me with the backups because I'm not preparing for a specific wideout on the Devils. Colin and the other two starters, a talkative weasel named Pock and a rat named Haluamma, get specific drills based on the patterns their assigned wideouts like to run.

I try to keep an eye on those patterns, but to be honest it was hard enough keeping my mind on the cornerback drills, which aren't nearly as advanced. I've done corner drills since my college career, usually in summer workouts with Gerrard, but not for Coach Javy and his staff.

At first they only correct the other backups and leave me alone, but then Javy comes over and says, "He's on our squad today, so give him the same as everyone else." Colin smirks across the field, but I keep my temper under control. We move on to post breaks and open-hip post breaks, and here the assistants correct my form when they need to, which still isn't often.

As a linebacker, I drop into coverage sometimes. I'm not going to be covering the other team's fastest guys, but if one of their receivers is in the slot (short routes near the line of scrimmage), I'll keep an eye on him. I get more tight end assignments as the middle linebacker than I did on the weak side, so sometimes teams will mix up coverage and I'll end up on a guy who's streaking up the field with speed I can't match (especially with these fucking speedster tight ends who are basically wideouts these days).

That's when the safeties are supposed to help out, or the corners. One of the elements of my ongoing beef with Colin is a list of games over the years in which I've been stranded in a situation like that and he hasn't come over to help and we've been burned on the play. I can't ever prove that he did it on purpose—he always has an assignment of his own—but I feel like with the football instincts we're all supposed to have, he should figure out where the play's going faster than he does.

(He said once when I brought it up, "If I left my assignment to help your slow tail, the play would go to my assignment and I'd look stupid.")

For his part, he's said a couple times that I'm too slow in my coverage, that since I took over at middle linebacker our defensive schemes give the QBs too much time to sit back, too much time for receivers to shake free. He doesn't say this around the coaches, just makes comments like, "Marvell would've gotten that sack," or "Marvell wouldn't have left us hanging out there for eight seconds."

None of my linebackers ever say anything like that. Gerrard has worked with the defensive coordinator to improve our coverages and we rarely let the opposing QB feel comfortable, especially this year when I'm really getting the hang of the middle linebacker position.

Which doesn't do me any good in the cornerback drills. It's worse at the end, because we do one-on-ones, where one of us plays the wideout and the other defends, and Coach Javy matches up me and Colin.

No surprise, Colin defends me really well. I try a lot of moves but only get my paws on the ball once, and I can't complete the catch. When it's my turn to defend him, I do pretty well, but he gets three good catches off me and waves the ball in my face in a move that would definitely get him a taunting flag in a game. "Not so easy doing this job, is it?" he asks.

We take a break, and I try to chat up Haluamma. I don't think the rat is too friendly with Colin, but when I say, "I know superstars are supposed to have attitude," he makes a small "hmph" noise in response.

I try again. "I'm doin' my best out there."

"Look," the rat says, a little accented, "I don't wanna get between you two, but if I gotta take sides, I'm goin' with my corner. You barely ever come over to talk to the backs."

Which isn't true; I talk to the backs a lot, but mostly the safeties and backup corners. I guess I do avoid the starting corners because of Colin. "Sorry," I say. "I'm not trying to put you between us."

"You seem like an okay guy," Haluamma says, "and a damn good line-backer. But things are working okay so let's just keep 'em that way."

"Sure," I say.

Wix comes over as I walk away. "They don't hate you," he said. "They're just afraid of Colin."

"I got that." I breathe. "This whole scheme of Coach's is dumb. I'm more stressed out than I would be just after a day of practice."

"You're doing great," he says. "Colin usually gets more than three catches off most of us."

"I don't want him to get any catches," I growl. "We're doing open-field tackling next?"

"I think so."

"All right." I pound a fist into my paw. "Let's do it."

So we move into the open-field tackling drill, where I'm determined to show my merit. Again, Colin's my drill partner, and I only allow him two good tackles out of a dozen tries. Then he tries to elude me, and as slippery and fast as he is, I get two good tackles on him, too. Panting, we glare at each other at the end of the drill, but neither of us says anything.

The rest of our day is spent in more coverage drills, but against the practice squad, not each other. I escape as soon as I'm allowed and hurry back to my locker, where I slam the door open.

"Hey." Carson pats my arm. "Chill."

I hadn't even noticed him sitting there. "Sorry."

"What's in your fur?"

I shake my head. "Not worth it."

He pulls his shirt off and ruffles up the fur on his chest. "Is it the Jesus guys?"

"It's fine," I say. "Colin tried to pawn Dublovic on me and get Wix as his roommate."

Carson narrows his eyes. "Dublovic?"

"He's worried about the moral character of the team. I'm a bad influence on Wix and I guess he feels like Dublovic would be safe from my evil gay wiles, whatever. There's no reason for him to do it except to mess with me."

"Why mess with you?"

I wave a paw. "Because it's Colin."

The leopard shakes his head. "He's left you alone for years. Why now?"

"He hasn't exactly left me alone for years. Remember in the playoffs in 2010 when he kept putting Bible verses in my locker? And a couple years ago when he kept going on about freedom of speech?"

Carson frowns. "I broke my leg a couple years ago. That playoff game?"

"Yeah, there was that whole case going on about laws that let people discriminate against gays if their religious beliefs forbid it, or something, and he kept talking about freedom of speech and how we should all be free to say anything we want even if it's not politically correct."

"How'd that end?"

I shrug. "We lost. The game, I mean, not the fight for—whatever."

"Maybe that's why he does these things over the playoffs." Carson flicks his tail back and forth. "Knows it'll be over soon."

"Or it's because this is the highest-stress part of the year." I breathe out, make fists of my paws and flex them again. "This is the time when everything gets amplified and people are afraid to make waves. He's the one who's not afraid to mess around with things, so he can get away with more. Maybe."

Carson shakes his head. "Don't let him get to you."

"But that's what he wants, is for me just to ignore him. That's what I did those other times. That lets him say whatever he wants and nobody argues…"

The leopard stands and pulls his pants off, then grabs a towel. "Nobody pays attention to him anyway."

"Enough people do," I mutter, but he's right, and our break is about over. "I just wish he'd stop doing this."

Carson flashes a grin at me as he heads to the shower. "Then let's not lose."

He's right, of course. If we win, I can retire, and I won't have to deal with Colin ever again. That tantalizing thought calms me down through my shower, and then over the course of a strenuous film study meeting with Gerrard, I manage to forget about Colin and his right-wing crusades. That lasts all of five minutes, before Coach Lopez grabs me and Gerrard coming out of our session.

"Just a quick word, if I could," he says, and leads us to his office, where Coach Javy is leaning against the wall, tail swishing as he reads something on his phone. His big black ears perk toward us, followed a moment later by his eyes and muzzle as he finishes whatever he's looking at.

"Close the door," Coach Lopez says, and I as the lowest ranking guy there push the door closed. Outside in the hall, a couple offensive line players give me a puzzled look through the door; I meet their eyes and shrug, then turn back.

To my surprise, Coach Javy is the one to speak. "This probably isn't a big deal, but I thought we should all be aware of it," he says, and holds up his phone. "Guy from Wixin's college claiming he dated him. Made a video about it. Got a couple hundred hits."

Coach Lopez shakes his head. "We already know about his orientation and these rumors aren't getting much play."

"That's why Colin wanted to switch rooms," I say. "He heard this and figured out Wix is gay."

"Honestly," Javy says, "the kid runs his mouth off a bunch. Woulda thought he was a veteran the way he yaps out there. Plus just the last week or so he's been makin' fun of the prayer group. I told him to cut it out, but he probably still does it when I'm not around."

"Making fun of religion is not okay." Coach Lopez looks surprised. "You should've disciplined him."

"He wasn't making fun of their religion." The fox puts out a paw. "Called them backwards thinkers. Just happened that it was the prayer group."

"Still." Coach Lopez exhales.

The fox cuts off whatever he was about to say. "You gave us authority to discipline how we want."

"I don't want players making other players feel unwelcome."

I open my mouth, 'cause I got a whole list of things Colin has done, but then I snap it shut again because I figure this isn't the time. Coach Lopez sees me, though, and the moose points in my direction. "You got something to say, Miski, say it."

"Nah." I shake my head. "I mean, a lot of it was before your time. Doesn't happen so much now."

"You come to me if there's a problem." He turns to the fox. "Javy, call Ellery and make sure he's prepped in case this story gets bigger."

"Yes sir. Should we talk to the cat?"

"Wixin? Your call. I don't think you need to yet, but maybe if he's aware that this thing is out there…" Coach Lopez looks my way. "You went through this, didn't you, Miski?"

I nod. "What, people outing me publicly? Yeah. Kind of. It was different then."

"Seems like the important parts are mostly the same." The moose taps fingers on his desk. "If Wix needs help, you'll be available for him?"

"Of course."

"All right. Hope we don't need any of this."

"Also." Javy holds up a finger. "In the championship game, you know, Miski, when we dialed up that corner blitz, you told him he was too slow running the route."

"He was too slow." I barely remember the play, but I know Colin was about half a second behind where I expected him to be. "And you already told me not to do that again. I'm sorry about it, it just came out in the heat of the game."

"That happens," Coach Lopez says.

"It does." Javy shakes his head and puts a paw on my shoulder. "I'm asking you for the good of the team to try to keep it in."

"If I say yes," I ask hopefully, "can we go back to practicing with our own units?"

"Ha." Coach Lopez shows me a row of moose teeth. "Nice try."

•

I grab dinner with Charm that night and we talk about the playoffs we've been through and how this team is different. "I still think the '08 team is the best one we've had," he says. "Remember Aston?"

"Rain's better than Aston."

"Got a better arm for sure, but he forces it a lot. He'll be better than Aston in a year or two. Probably."

I laugh. "Gonna try out for quarterback coach?"

"Sure, if they're looking for a 40-year-old one in another decade."

It's nice to relax with Charm and not have to think about Wix or about the game or about any of it, talking about the Firebirds of past and current years like we're not part of it. "What else do you see while you spend most of the game on the sidelines?"

He snorts into his beer, spraying me with foam. As I wipe it off, he says, "Defense is better this year than it was then, but not by much."

"There's a dropoff from Gerrard to me."

"Not just that."

"Thanks."

He grins. "Defensive line is a bit shakier. You're doing good and Colin's fantastic."

"How's our kicking game?"

He makes a level motion with one huge hand. "Exactly the same."

"Great." I laugh and lean back in my chair. His comment about Colin brings back all the stuff about Wix, much as I'd prefer not to think about it.

And Charm notices. "What's the deal? Not that fox being a shit again?"

"Kind of." He knows about Wix—come on, he's my best friend on the team, or one of them—so I don't have to explain much.

When I'm done, he takes another long drink of beer and signals to the bar for a refill. "You gotta talk to him."

"That's what I think. I'm probably putting it off by talking to you."

"Nah." He grins. "You're consulting with a friend. Doesn't matter if you talk to him now or in an hour. But you gotta do it soon, because what if this shit gets bigger?"

"It is going to, isn't it?" I fold my ears back. "Maybe I should call Lee."

"If you need to." Charm grins. "But hey, who's gonna give you better advice than me?"

"You make a compelling case." I gulp down the rest of my beer. "How's your practice going? Ankle doing better?"

"Ankle's fine." He glares at me.

The waitress, a tall wolf, brings his beer. She lingers a moment over it, in a way that I've learned to recognize over the years, and when she says, "Is there anything else I can get you?" she's looking at Charm, not me at all.

"Not right now," Charm says, "but maybe hit me up when your shift's over, Luciana."

She smiles and wags her tail. "I'm here 'til one."

"That's cool." The big stallion raises his beer. "I'll go slow."

When she leaves without asking if I want a refill, I get up. "Looks like you've got your night planned. I'm just gonna get back to mine."

"Mine's gonna be more fun." Charm lifts his glass and takes his phone out.

I check my own phone. "You're gonna sit here for two hours on your own?"

"Ha ha, no." He leans back and grins up at me. "She'll take a break sometime in the next hour."

The wolf waitress seems pretty busy in the bar. "She said one, though."

"That was to see what I'd say. If I wouldn't wait that long, I'm not worth her time. But since I am willing to wait…" He took a gulp of beer. "I won't have to."

I shook my head. "If you say so."

"Bet you."

Charm nearly always wins this kind of bet, but the few that he loses give me enough ammunition to tease him for months. It's been over a year since he lost; I remember because that was during last year's playoffs. "You're on."

He extends a hand and I clasp it in my paw, shaking firmly. "Good luck. See ya tomorrow."

"Good luck to you."

He laughs and waves away my wish. "Get some rest," he says, unnecessarily loudly. "We got a championship game in a week and a half."

Heads turn in the bar, following me as I leave and then looking back at him. I shake my head as I leave. If he doesn't have the waitress, he'll probably have his pick of girls—or guys, come to think of it, but though he once confessed he'd gotten a blow job from a guy, Charm doesn't swing that way.

On the way back, I call Hal and text two other reporters. The requests for comments about everything get intense this time of year, so I manage them by keeping them to a short window once or twice a day. Nothing's really going on, but people are always working on new stories with new angles when a championship game comes around. Some of my teammates don't respond to every request, but I try to. It's courtesy, and if these guys like me, they'll write better things about me.

Wix is back at the hotel room when I get there, lying back on the bed with his tablet in his lap. I think he's studying film, but when I crane my head around to look, I see bright colors and dragons. He pops his headphones out. "I did a bunch of film already this evening," he says. "I wanted to go out, but everyone else is studying or spending time with family."

"You've looked over all your film?" It slips out before I remember that I'm not his coach, and I'm not Gerrard either. The kid has a right to relax.

He shakes his head. "But I can't focus after a couple hours. I need to chill."

And they used to call my generation the short attention span generation. I stifle a mental chuckle and remember what I have to tell Wix about. "Hey, you never told me you had a college boyfriend."

He sits bolt upright in bed, ears back, eyes big. "Who told you?"

"Coach. I guess he made a video about you."

"Ah, fuck that guy. I can't believe he'd do that." He puts his headphones back in and taps his tablet.

At first I think he's watching his movie again. "Coach says it hasn't gotten out very much and it's probably not worth making a big deal about." He doesn't answer, so I shut up and go over to sit on my bed, calling up my messages.

After a minute, though, Wix calls, "Hey. Is this another prank or something?"

"What?"

"Mack swears he didn't do anything."

Oh, he's texting his college boyfriend. "No. I mean…" I think about it. "If it is, it's a really good one. Coaches all committed to it." I imagine Coach Javy and Coach Lopez huddled in the hallway outside our door, listening in and snickering to themselves. I resist the urge to get up and check. "No, it's real. Search the Internet or something."

He pokes at his tablet, then stops and listens. "Oh, that fuckin' asshole. Goddammit." He types a bunch more.

I clear my throat. "So…you had two boyfriends in college?"

"No." He doesn't look over at me. "Mack and me just hooked up a bunch for a few months. He's a fencer so I knew he'd keep quiet about it."

I can't resist a little teasing. "So you were hooking up with other guys at the same time?"

"No."

"So he was?"

"No."

"So…you were boyfriends."

"Hrf." He still doesn't look up from his tablet. "I mean, he said that once or twice, but he knew it wasn't gonna go anywhere."

"So who's this other guy?"

Wix pauses and stares at his screen. "Fuck. I can't believe this." He shakes his head again. "He's just some asshole. He's how I met Mack. But we never even fucked."

I raise my eyebrows. "Not even blow jobs?"

"Blow jobs don't count." He says it automatically, without thinking. "It was just at this party they were throwing for the freshmen and he was one of the guys serving drinks or something, and somehow we ended up in the closet feeling each other up, I dunno how this shit happens."

I know how those things happen and I suspect Wix does too. Decision points, one two three. "But you didn't get caught?"

"Nah."

"Hey," I say. "You know, from my experience, it's best not to make a big deal out of this shit."

"Oh yeah?" He's still typing.

"You know how I got outed, right?"

That gets his attention. His paw stays hovering over the surface of the tablet. "I thought you came out yourself, at that press conference."

"I did, but I didn't have much of a choice. My agent at the time was— ah, let's just say 'inexperienced,' and when some idiot blogged about me being gay, he made me call a big press conference to deny it. He got me a fake girlfriend and everything."

Wix leans back on his bed and pulls a pillow up to prop up his back. "But you didn't deny it."

"Nah. My boyfriend was in the audience and I remember looking at him and thinking how disappointed he'd be if I did."

He snorts. "Lucky you didn't lose your job."

"Sort of. But also, I was a good player and they couldn't afford to get rid of me."

Wix's ears have come back up and he brushes his cheek ruffs thoughtfully. "You really think this'll just go away if I ignore it?"

"Let me put it this way," I say. "If you make a big deal about it, it sure as hell won't go away."

He thinks about that and then tosses his tablet to the floor. "All right. Thanks for the advice."

I'm ready to get some sleep too, so we shut off the lights and I lie there thinking about how much of my life is luck. Being in a bar at the right time, being in the right spot when Mitchell got injured, being part of a team that went to the championship the year I came out, playing Polecki which diluted the impact of my revelation. What right do I have to give this kid advice based on my life? What if the breaks don't go his way like they did for me?

I wish I'd called Lee.

Chapter Ten (Lee)

At the end of the interview, I ask the otter, "Why are you leaving Kerina?" It's a standard question; his contract is up and he wants another opportunity somewhere. All he has to say is some variant on that bland response and it'll be fine. But—and this is one of the reasons I'm starting to like him, against all my preconceptions—he nods thoughtfully and considers the question.

"It's a great organization," he says. "They've been nothing but kind to me, and they've embraced their Xaiqinese fans wholeheartedly. The problem was more mine. Kerina is a great city, and like most good cities, it's becoming more diverse every day. But Yerba…" He smiles and for a moment his eyes look dreamy. "When I got to the stage where I could choose my job, I knew I'd want to be in a place like this, or Port City, or Pelagia. These are the places where you can walk down the street and see people from all over the world living side by side, helping each other. That's the future I want to see and the world I want to live in."

I'm taken aback by the passion underlying his gentle words, and when I don't say anything, he coughs, his smile remaining. "I probably shouldn't tell you that that's so important to me."

"No, it was great," I say. "Why not?"

"I lose leverage this way. Now you'll report back and say, 'he really wants to live here,' and your bosses will knock a hundred thousand off their offer."

I laugh. "I won't tell them. I totally get where you're coming from. This is a great place to live."

Peter doesn't want my report until the next day, when everyone's finished interviewing Xu. So I spend the afternoon following up on all the other stuff on my plate, and around three o'clock Cord comes over to my office.

"Hey." He's holding his phone and he taps a couple keys. "I wrote that letter you wanted, aaaaand just sending it to you now."

"Thanks. You going to stay while I read it?"

"If that's okay."

The letter's pretty good. It strikes a tactful tone—too tactful in parts. But I know why Cord wanted to be here when I read it. He's dancing around the point of the letter like someone who knows what he wants to say but doesn't want to offend. What he wants to know, badly enough that he wants immediate feedback, is where the line is.

I appreciate that. We spent a lot of time arguing about just this sort of thing in college, back when we were upstart cubs trying to shout our truths. Then, we wielded those truths like knives because we believed we had to cut through tradition and establishment. Now I'm trying to shape an existing structure, to smooth rather than slice. Even so, Cord's too far on the smooth side of the line.

"We can strengthen this here, and here." I change two of his sentences. "The colleges are aware of the Nativist movement, so you don't have to spend so much time introducing it."

"I thought it might be useful to have some context. I mean, would it be helpful to maybe talk to some Athletic Directors before we send it out to all of them?"

I think about it. "We could run this by Jody Dornheiser over at UG Emery. I'm visiting there later this week."

The fruit bat nods. "I was thinking of her or of Al up at U of Columbia."

"That's a good one too. I could get him on the phone tomorrow maybe."

We go through the letter for half an hour and then I say, "Hey, I remember you talking about the Ace of Hearts a few months ago."

His ears flick around and he tilts his head. "You mean the drag bar?"

"Yeah. Is that still around?"

The headtilt stays. "Coming up with new ways to relax your boyfriend before the championship?"

I laugh. "No. My stepbrother's coming into town and he was asking about Korsat Street. I don't really want to go dancing with him and that seems like it'd be fun."

"Yeah, it's good. Hang on, I'll check what the shows are this weekend."

He messes around on his phone for a bit while I read through the letter again. With my changes, I think it'll be good, so I send it on to Peter to approve before I send it to some of our connections. And my mind drifts on to my decision about Cansez. I wonder how many drag clubs there are out in Cansez City. On the other side, though, I never go out to drag clubs here anyway, and I could fly back to Yerba whenever I wanted. We'd keep the townhouse for sure.

"Here, Ace of Hearts has a show Friday and Saturday night, the Foxxxy Girls." Cord holds his phone out to me. "They're not all foxes. And there's three X's in the name."

"I see that." There's a lineup of a half dozen drag queens, two red foxes, a wolf, a white-tailed deer, a rabbit, and a porcupine, wearing glittering dresses and variously colored blushes on their muzzles. I nod and hold the phone up to him. "Looks like fun. I used to do drag, you know."

He takes the phone back and squints at me. "I guess I can see that. Doesn't seem like you'd have the voice for it, though."

"Oh, I don't—I didn't do shows. I did theater in college and I sometimes went out dressed as a girl." I debate telling him that's how I met my boyfriend and decide that maybe another year of getting to know him should precede that story. "Just for fun. Haven't done it in years, though."

He chuckles, slides his phone into his pocket, and rattles his wings. "Never cross-dressed myself. When I came out to my family, though, that was one of the things they asked me. My mom said if I needed fur care tips I could ask her. It was kinda clueless and sweet all at the same time."

Cross-dressing, that's what it was, not drag. Drag is a performance. I curse myself for not having thought of this stuff in years. "That's cool, though. You should take her up on it."

He laughs. "They're all cool with me being gay in the abstract. I don't know how they'd react if I actually showed up in makeup and a dress. Well, Mom would probably be fine with it. She's the only one who's met Alai."

"Yeah, I was gonna say, she came out here, right?"

Cord leans back against the wall. "Yup. She liked the area, even the parts that smelled like fish." He rattles his wings again. "So, uh, what'd you think of Xu?"

I think about that for a moment. "I need a coffee. You want to go to Peet's?"

So we walk out of the office and into the temperate January afternoon, sunlight glaring off the blue glass around our office complex. Starbucks has a location beside the lobby of our building, but that's where everyone from the Whalers goes, so if I'm going to be saying stuff I don't want to get back to Peter immediately, I usually walk the two blocks to the Peet's. Not to mention their coffee's better.

Sipping lattes, we find a little metal table outside at the edge of the patio and sit down there. Cord drapes one wing over the back of his chair. "So?"

"I like him." I breathe in the smell of my latte. "He's smart, he'll get along well with people, and he knows his football."

"Uh-huh." Cord leans closer. "Would he be a better assistant GM than you?"

I know what he wants me to say, what he believes, but he's also asking me not as assistant to boss but as friend to friend. So I'm honest. "He'd be different. He's got a lot of strengths in different areas than I do. I know player evaluation and I'm learning how to deal with players and agents and so on. He's got a good feel for dealing with agents, from what I can tell, and obviously he's done a pretty good job in Kerina. So I don't know."

He nods. "As long as they don't hire some asshole."

"Right." My latte is cool enough to drink more than just a cautious sip of, so I do. "But also…don't spread this around, but I have an interview for an assistant GM position."

He stops, looks warily at me. "Where?"

"Cansez. My old boss is the GM there and he'd like to work with me." My tail swishes back and forth, as restless and unsure as I feel. "It'd be a good opportunity."

Cord shakes his wing free of the back of his chair and hunches his shoulders forward, staring down at his latte. "Yeah, I guess if it doesn't happen here…"

It takes me a moment to understand the shift in his demeanor. "Your job's safe," I say. "I tell Peter all the time what a good job you're doing, and I'll tell whoever takes my place. If I take the Cansez job, which they haven't even offered me yet. And which I don't know if I'd take if they do." I'd take Cord with me, of course, but I know he won't want to leave Yerba.

"How can you think about going there?" He keeps his voice low, still staring down at his coffee. "Jeez, if you tried you couldn't pick a more backward place in this country to go. I know this city isn't perfect, but it's a damn sight better than most other places, and that goes double for Cansez."

"We'd be in the city," I point out, "and the urban areas are way better." I don't want to move to Cansez, but Cord's acting like I've already decided to, and I'm somehow annoyed enough to defend the decision.

"Your base, the people who follow the team, those are the farmers and religious cranks. You know that shitty church is out there, right? Those are the people you'd be building a team for."

"I don't think that church are football fans."

My attempt to keep the talk light fails. "I get it," he says with some sourness. "You want to move up in the league."

"I'm not going to have many options. There's maybe one or two people who'd hire me, and one of them works here, and another is in Cansez. I guess Jocko might if he ever gets to a GM position, but I wouldn't be first on his list."

"They're not gonna let you keep bringing gay people in."

"Maybe Morty actually wants me for my football experience," I say. "I have been scouting for almost a decade."

"Maybe he just wants to poach Yerba's secrets," Cord counters. "Or maybe the owner is one of those hard-liners who wants to stop you bringing 'fags' into the league and figures he can control you better if you work for him."

"That's kind of paranoid."

"It's how these people think."

"Well." I try to stay reasonable. "Is the owner a hard-liner? I've never met him and don't know anything about him except that he's a red wolf who made his money in tech. Is he hardcore religious?"

"I don't know," Cord admits.

"Then maybe I'll wait to get more information."

The bat looks away from me. "Regardless, I don't know if living in Cansez for years is worth it."

I can't help the annoyance. "I guess I shouldn't try to convince you to come out with me if I do get the job and decide to go."

He snorted, and then his ears go back. "Sorry. I'd really appreciate the offer, but yeah, I don't think I'd take it."

"I guess we'll see what happens then. I've enjoyed working with you."

"Yeah, me too." He pushes his chair back. "Okay to head back? I've got some stuff to take care of."

"Sure."

We walk back in a less comfortable silence, and when we get to the office, Cord disappears to his desk, leaving me to mine. And in my personal email is a message from Morty asking if I'm free for a preliminary phone interview with him the following morning, Wednesday. "Don't know when your stepbrother gets in," he writes, "but if you can do nine a.m. your time, let me know asap."

I push aside the annoyance with Cord and tell Morty that'll be fine, and then I have plenty of work to keep me from thinking about that interview until about six-thirty. Cord takes off at six (without saying anything to me, just a quick wave with his head down), but Peter's still in the office. I check to see if he wants to talk about Xu, but he's busy and says he'll circle back tomorrow morning before I go. I mention the letter I want to write about the Nativist stuff, and he says he's on board with it and to shoot it over to him when I've got a draft I like.

All the way home I think about dealing with Mike this week and making a decision next week about the job, and I can't talk to my father about the first thing, and I can't talk to my work friends about the second. The house, when I get there, feels large and quiet, so I call up Netflix on the TV and throw on one of the big set-piece action movies from last year, the League of Canids one called "Vixen."

(Her original name was Vicious Vixen, but the studio didn't want to use "Vicious," and then there was a backlash online because some female foxes don't like being called "vixens," and another group—maybe some of the same ones—said that there was nothing wrong with a heroine being vicious in defense of her friends. So she still wears her "VV" logo but they don't call her "Vicious" in the movie, and it's an origin story so the writer weakly said that they might address the name in the sequel. Whatever they called it, it turned out to be a pretty good movie.)

The movie helps distract me only a little. Usually I find work tasks to do in the evening if Dev's busy, or I'll go out with some of the guys from work. I haven't made many other friends in the area, and honestly I don't mind staying in, watching movies or TV while I work. I've lost myself in my job and the world of professional football over the last several years, and maybe that's why it feels like a betrayal that I've put in all that work and now the team I want to stay with is looking seriously at someone else rather than reward me for it.

Focusing on work is impossible, and the loud, shiny battles of the movie aren't much more help. I pace up the stairs, back down, take out some things to make for dinner and then decide I don't want to go to that much trouble and put them away again. I order a healthy salad with chicken from Green Pieces and force myself not to call Dev.

•

Wednesday morning when I check my phone before hopping in the shower, there's a request from Peter for a 9:30 meeting to talk about Xu. So

I have to tell him that I have a phone interview with Morty at nine, and he must've had a bad night or not gotten much sleep because his email reply, when I get out of the shower, is not an actual email but just a reschedule for ten. I feel bad about it, but I don't want to lose out on the Cansez opportunity because I jerked them around. If I'm not going to go, it'll be a decision, not a blown chance.

But if I'm going to meet with Peter at ten and I have this other call at nine, I'm going to need to be near the Whalers offices when I take the interview. So I head for the same Peet's where Cord and I had the chat and get seated with a coffee by 8:57.

"Hey, Lee," Morty says when we get on the phone. He sounds like he's on speaker.

"Hi."

"Hey, I've got Devereaux here with me."

There's a moment where the sun and the umbrella over me and the metal of the chair and the table feel surreal all of a sudden. What? The owner?

I take a breath and remind myself that they want to interview me. I got this. Everything snaps back into place. "Hi there," I say. "Nice to meet you."

He's got a baritone voice and a lupine growl. "Hi, Wiley. Sorry to jump in. I know Morty didn't prepare you to talk to me. I don't have an agenda here; I want to listen in on the interview and be available if you have any questions Morty can't answer. But I don't want to lurk in the background. Not my style."

"Okay." I clear my throat. "Uh, thanks."

His laugh is one of those laughs that puts me at ease. "Trust me, you wouldn't be on this phone call if I weren't already very interested in you. I know your record and everything. I just want to get a sense of who you are as a person."

"Sure," I say. "Well, I appreciate that actually, because I was worried I'd be a bit too relaxed on this call, what with having breathed in Morty's cigarette smoke for a couple years."

Devereaux laughs again. "There we go. Okay, Morty, carry on."

"For the record," the cougar says, "I gave up smoking."

"He vapes now."

I grin, but I can't muster a laugh. "Of course he does."

"If we're done discussing my personal habits," Morty says.

And we get on with the interview. Morty does a quick review of our time at the Dragons, asks me what I learned from that. I run down the football stuff and resist the temptation to add, "and I learned not to have a secret boyfriend." Morty knows that, Devereaux knows that, and it's ten years in the past now.

Then we move on to the Whalers. I've made up a spreadsheet listing the public events that marked my time here and I keep an eye on it as I talk, making sure to stick to these events and not give away too much of the internal workings of the organization. A couple times Morty presses for details and I have to make a decision about whether to expand my story or not. On the whole, I do pretty well. I think.

The trickiest part is at the end, when Morty asks, "So what would you change about our organization?"

I'm ready for this one, but it's still hard to navigate in the moment. You don't want to come off too critical, but you also can't say everything's fine, but you also don't want to spill all your ideas. "Let me start," I say, "with what I think you're doing right."

This is the longest part of the interview. I talk for a while about what I like about Cansez, what I've heard of their philosophy and what I've seen of it. I make a few suggestions and talk about league-wide trends I've observed, why the clamp-down defense that won last year's championship won't necessarily be replicable for other teams. Somewhere along the way, Morty and I slide into the familiar banter we used to have back at the Dragons, when we'd watch film and argue about whether such and such player would fit into our scheme, whether he had the tools to adapt, whether our scheme was going to change over the next couple years and whether it even should.

We get so involved that it's a little bit of a shock when Devereaux jumps back in. "Sorry to interrupt," he says, "but I wonder how you guys view what Gateway's doing right now."

Morty lets me answer first, and that sends us off on another fifteen minutes of discussion, until my phone buzzes with the ten-minute alert for my meeting with Peter. I don't want to cut this interview short, but fortunately Morty says, "I guess we should wrap this up," and I imagine that he's just had a ten-minute alert pop up as well.

I feel really good about the interview, not only my chances but also about the team I'd be going to work for. I didn't ask them about hiring gay people or how my hire would go over with their base, but I'm going out there next week. I can ask about it then.

Chapter Eleven (Dev)

Thursday, it's Colin's turn to come work out with the linebackers. Again, most of the drills are similar, but here he's among my friends, and most of them know about the bad blood between us. So Colin's knocked around a bit even in the low-contact drills, and he doesn't do well in our blocking drills (corners don't block a lot, not nearly as much as we do). Gerrard doesn't pair me with Colin, so either it was Coach Javy's idea to pair us up yesterday or (more likely) Coach Lopez suggested it and Coach Javy listened while Gerrard did whatever he thought was best.

Colin says he wants to work with Lukos, his buddy, but Gerrard doesn't acknowledge that, pairing him instead with even-tempered Carson while I work with Price, the big wolf. I like working with Price because I've only been a middle linebacker for a couple years—since Gerrard retired—and he's been doing it for his whole career. He's taught me a few things that Gerrard didn't, and he's chill enough to take tips from me as well.

He didn't know about me and Colin until a couple months into the season, when he finally picked up on the tension. "Don't pay attention to him," he says when he sees my eyes flick over to Colin. "Pay attention to the guy in front of you."

We're doing a weave-and-tackle drill, where I have to get between two obstacles to get to the tackling dummy. This is another one Colin doesn't have experience with, and I was enjoying watching him be frustrated while not paying attention to Price, who was trying to stop me from completing my drill. "Hey," he says, "I know you hate the guy, but it's not funny if someone on the team can't do the drill."

I'm panting with the effort of getting past him, even though I did it instinctively. "He doesn't have to avoid blockers to tackle that much. All his tackling is open-field."

"Corner blitzes happen. Not much under Lopez, sure, but they could. He needs to know how to do that."

"When we rush the passer, he'll learn."

I reset and do the drill again and again. Price gives me a few tips, but not many, and when we switch, I'm more effective at stopping him. I give him a few tips back, and like the veteran he is (we both are), he takes them gracefully.

I may not be watching Colin as closely, but I can still listen, and Carson isn't giving him many tips at all. I think about what Price said and about all the years of enmity between me and Colin. I've never been in a situation like this with him, though, and since he mostly mocked me yesterday, won't it put me one up on him if I help him out?

That's what I call the "Lee voice" in me, the voice that tells me the better thing to do in cases where my instincts are leading me to be mean or selfish. I know I should listen to it, but I don't always. In this case, I can't imagine a way for me to give tips to Colin that he'd accept, unless maybe I could couch them in Bible verses or something.

But Price is an old vet, and he doesn't have any ties to me specifically on the team. So when we take a break before the rushing the passer drill, I ask him to go over to Colin. "Just tell him about keeping his eye on the ball, because he's usually tackling people who have it tucked away. And he's reacting to his blocker instead of determining his own path. I know that's how he's trained, but just…maybe point it out to him. That was something I had to learn when I transitioned from corner."

He squints at me. "I can barely remember what coaches were telling me ten months ago, let alone years."

"Ha ha."

"No, seriously. I remember it here." He points at his legs and arms. "But the words they said, shit like that…week to week, month to month, sure. Maybe you should be a coach. Got a good memory for words."

And he goes over to talk to Colin. I deliberately don't look at them, so that if Colin looks over he won't think I sent Price. I think instead about what Price said. Would I want to be a coach? Nobody's approached me about that, and when I compare my football knowledge to Gerrard—the only player I've known as both coach and player—I feel like a first-grader. But maybe I could be an assistant for a couple years, see how I liked it.

I've thought about trying out for broadcasting, too, but nobody's come to ask me about jobs. I did sit in on a local sports show a few times, years when the Firebirds weren't in the playoffs, and commented on the playoff games. That was a little bit of money and publicity, and everyone in the studio was nice to me, but I never got a sense that people thought that was a good path for my future. Hal said diplomatically that it takes a certain kind of person to have the right way with words, and I guess he should know.

"Well," Price says, coming back to me, "that guy certainly thinks his shit don't stink. And he's a fox. Oh, sorry, dude."

I laugh. "The smell was a bit weird when I started dating Lee, but I like it now. Just don't say that in front of him. Lee, I mean. You can tell Colin he stinks. How'd he take the tips?"

Price shakes his head. "I dunno. He looked at you a couple times and then he said he's been in the league a long time, but he didn't tell me to fuck off, so I guess with a guy like that, that's something."

"Best you can hope for," I say, and finish off the BoltAde just as Gerrard whistles us back. "Let's kill this second half."

We do, I think, though Gerrard cautions us not to be too hyped. The game's a week and a half away, plenty of time to get lost in our heads about it. "It's a simple game. Learn your moves, execute on what you know."

Colin doesn't say anything, but I see the fox roll his eyes. Even Croz knows better than to disrespect Gerrard that openly. My fists tighten, but I keep control. Carson sees it too and makes a low growl in his throat that I've only heard him make on a few occasions. Like when the Whalers' running back beat him in the championship game for a first down.

Price rests a paw on each of our shoulders. "Don't get in your head also means don't let other guys get in your head," he murmurs. "This guy wants to be an ass, let him. He knows how to do his job."

It's advice I've heard over and over many times, specifically regarding Colin, and it makes me shake my head. "Eleven more days," I mutter. Then the game will be over, and maybe my career, and I won't have to deal with him anymore.

Still, when we break for lunch, I'm wound up and so I think, hell with it, and I walk outside and lean against the wall of the facility in the chill January sunshine. I close my eyes and then I pull out my phone and I call up Lee. He sounds surprised when he picks up. "Hey. I'm grabbing lunch at Laurel. Mike's talking to people, so I have a couple minutes. What's up?"

"Sorry, I know, the two weeks thing, but I'm just on edge." So I tell him about Colin and I switching practices yesterday and today, and about Colin disrespecting Gerrard. "I don't care when he says shit about me, whatever, but Gerrard's a coach. Colin would never act like that with Coach Javy or Coach Lopez."

"Doesn't he dislike Gerrard because of his divorce?"

"He doesn't care about that. I mean, maybe for a bit. But I think it's more that Gerrard's always been my friend. Ugh. That guy."

"At least you helped him out with the practice," Lee says. "That was the right thing to do."

"Yeah, thanks, doc." I grin despite myself.

"'Me' voice?"

"Yup."

He sounds fox-smug on the other end. "Good to know I haven't lost my remote touch. Say, if you really want to get under his fur, you could be even more helpful this afternoon."

"I'll keep that in mind. How's stuff with you?"

He tells me about how he has to evaluate this guy he interviewed to his boss. "Sounds like this guy's pretty good. You think you can beat him out for the job?"

"They haven't gotten around to interviewing me yet, so I'm not holding my breath. The Cansez guy sounds sharp, though, the owner. He was on the call with Morty." He exhales. "I'm gonna go, because I can't just say no, but it's so hard to see myself moving there."

"You're flying out there, what, next week?"

"Yeah."

"So check it out."

"I'm planning on it, stud. But I don't want to be swayed by a shiny presentation. You know—well, maybe you don't—guys will promise a lot when they want you to come work for them. Doesn't mean they'll follow through once you're under contract."

"What does Damien say?" My agent also agreed to represent Lee a couple years after I signed with him, when Lee was negotiating a contract extension with the Whalers.

"Haven't talked to him yet. Morty called him and he sent me an email telling me it all looked good and to keep him posted. He's got a lot of irons in the fire with his players and I know he'll be there when I need him, which at this point is only to compare numbers."

"Right." I exhale. My tail uncurls and swishes against the chilly concrete wall. "Thanks, fox. It's good to talk to you."

"Good to talk to you, too, tiger. Thanks for calling."

"I guess…week and a half off now."

He sounds amused. "Love you."

"Love you too."

In the afternoon, I decide to be a little more hands-on with Colin. Lee's actual voice isn't always as helpful as the voice I hear in my head, and part of me does recognize that this might just be a good way to cause trouble. But I figure the coaches can't fault me for it if I look like I'm helping. So I ask Gerrard to pair me up with Colin.

He stares steadily at me. "That's what Lopez said to do. I thought I'd spare you the hassle. You and Price have been helping each other out."

"Just for the afternoon," I say. "He's back to his own unit tomorrow."

"What about next week?"

"Next week is next week."

That's one of the things he used to say to me. If I'd pulled that on Steez, he'd have laughed and said something like, "You learning well," but Gerrard doesn't smile for jokes. He just goes, "Huh," and snorts through his long coyote muzzle. And when he calls out the assignments, he pairs me with Colin.

The fox, predictably, complains. "The matchups this morning were fine. Why do we have to change them up?"

The rest of us go quiet. Gerrard fixes Colin with a glare. "Because I'm the coach and what I say goes."

"I know you and he are tight," Colin says. "Did he ask for this?"

"I'm gonna tell you one more time and if you open your muzzle again, you can come back tomorrow and practice with this unit again."

Ah, shit, I think. I don't want that. But Colin is not used to being challenged, clearly, and he takes a step forward. "You don't have the authority to do that."

This is one of the times when Gerrard smiles, fangs showing. "I guess we'll see," he says. "Now get going."

Colin opens his mouth to argue again, and as his workout partner I feel the need to caution him, so I step between him and Gerrard. "You're not gonna change his mind. Better get to it."

He switches his glare to me. "If you want to be close to me because—"

"I don't. I just don't think it's fair for Carson to have to deal with you for a full day when you're here because of me. Besides," I do my best shot at a grin like Gerrard's. "We're doing hit-and-shed first. You get to run into me."

For as much as we dislike each other, we haven't spent a lot of time talking. Mostly we exchange disgusted looks across a locker room. He talks about me, sure, to his friends. I talk about him to mine. We're all business during games; we talk on the field when we need to, and we play together well. Coach Samuelson was worried in those first few years about our beef spilling out on the field, but let's be honest, we weren't the only guys who didn't like each other on those teams, and we're not the only guys who don't like each other on this one. Rain, our QB, doesn't get along with Carlos, a cheetah who's our #2 wideout, calls him a fame-fucker, and Carlos says Rain is a plastic marketing product, but when the coach calls Carlos's number, he gets to the right spot and Rain throws him the ball and they both look good.

So this thing between me and Colin isn't generally a big deal, and we haven't been made to confront it yet. These two days are probably the most time we've spent in close proximity ever. Can't say it's endearing me to him.

Carlos might be a prima donna—is a prima donna—but that's much more common among wideouts than it is cornerbacks. Wideouts catch touchdowns; cornerbacks have to get interceptions, ideally pick sixes, to get noticed, and that's hard and rare. Colin's led the league in interceptions twice, he's had a pick six in six of his eight seasons. So among corners in the league—and I know most of the good ones at this point—he's earned his prima donna status.

That doesn't make it easier to live with. But it does make it easier to needle him while we're working out. "Set your feet differently," I tell him as we get ready for the hit-and-shed drill. I'm standing in front of the ball-carrier dummy that Colin has to get to, set up like a defender. "Come on, I'm letting you hit first."

"I know how to set my feet."

"Don't care if you know, you're not doing it. Shoulder-width apart."

"They are."

"If your shoulders are four feet wide…"

He growls and moves his feet in about six inches. I nod. "Bend your knees, keep your center of gravity low."

"This is pointless," he says, not doing it.

"Suit yourself." Gerrard is about to blow the whistle, so I get in position and wait.

Colin's used to backpedaling off the line, reacting to a wideout. He sometimes bumps wideouts at the line to disrupt their timing. He's not necessarily used to defenders trying hard to block him. So I go easy on him at first, a side block that he still struggles with.

"Hey," Gerrard yells in my direction but to the whole team in general, "remember, blockers, we're doing cut blocks. That's what we're going to see on the field, that's what we gotta learn to avoid."

A cut block is when you block low, around the knees. There's all kinds of rules around it because you don't want to wreck a guy's knees. To start, you can't cut block if someone else is already blocking the guy; for another, the cut block has to be in the direction of the play, so you can't come at someone from the opposite direction and use their momentum against them. Of course, in practice, we're not supposed to actually target the knees. We're supposed to go low but not actually make contact.

So for the next few times I play-dive for Colin's knees and he jumps out of the way and tackles the dummy. I try to be more and more aggressive so that eventually I'll approach the level I'd use with Carson. It's not like Colin is bad exactly, but he's not reacting quite as quickly as someone who's done these drills a thousand times.

And then he jumps the wrong way, or mistimes his jump, or something, and he bangs into my shoulder. He stumbles, gets up hopping, and for a moment I'm seeing that quarterback sack all over again. But he puts weight on the foot immediately, so I'm sure it's fine, just surprised him is all.

Of course, being Colin, he can't leave it at that. "What the fuck are you doing? Trying to lose the championship for us?"

I stand and put my paws on my hips. "I did a cut block, and your knee is fine. You never banged your knee in practice before?"

"Get set," Gerrard barks.

Colin and I glare at each other as we get back into our sets. He rubs his knee. "Still hurt?" I say. "Suck it up, glass-bones. This drill is about avoiding blocks."

He leaps at me at the whistle and tries to wrestle me out of the way. He gets me to stagger back because he's taken me by surprise, but I recover and shove his hips. He's supposed to run at the tackling dummy, but he tries to shove me over again. I push him toward the dummy until he runs at it.

It's clear that something's going to happen. We manage to stay focused until we switch places. The first time I run at him, he takes a shot right at my knees, which I manage to dodge on my way to the dummy. "Hey," I yell as we get back to our set, "you're not trying to hurt me."

"Don't like it when it happens to you, do you, priss?" He sneers and gets back to his set.

I clamp my muzzle shut and get back, focusing on my footwork and drills. But on the next run, he jumps at my knees again and this time I don't worry so much about getting out of his way. I clip him on the shoulder and he falls backwards, letting me go unimpeded to the dummy.

I'm straightening up from the tackle when he slams me from behind, pushing me into it. "You think this is funny?"

I stumble, and then without thinking I run back at him. We're too smart to throw punches, but we grapple with each other. I outweigh him, but he gets the dummy at my back and I can't quite get the right leverage. Anyway, Carson's there a moment later to pull us apart and we stand there, panting, while Gerrard walks over.

"Can you guys put your differences aside for the sake of the team?" Other coaches might say it sarcastically, but Gerrard is one hundred percent serious. "This is important stuff. I'm not going to split you up. You have to learn how to play through anything."

I fix my eyes on Colin. "I can do it."

"I don't see why I should have to…" Gerrard's already walking away yelling at everyone to go again. Colin trails off, glowers, and gets into his set. I notice that he's in a proper crouch and his feet are shoulder-width apart.

Chapter Twelve (Lee)

I'm not sure what to expect at the airport. The last time I saw Mike was over the holidays when we were all together for Christmas. I remember him wearing a Cheltenham FC shirt and asking if he was getting into pro soccer, and he said someone had given him the shirt. But I didn't think anything of his appearance at the time, nor of his attitude. Mike and I have never been the closest, to be honest, so I was glad he came to me, even if it was because I'm his gay stepbrother. Jaren, getting ready to go to college, was the one who'd previously come to me for advice.

Normally, when I meet Dev at the airport, I show up and pick him up at the curb. For Mike, though, I figure I should park and go inside. It seems a lot politer, not to mention brotherly.

It's a long walk from the garage to the waiting area, giving me lots of time to think. At the wedding, Mike and Jaren became my brothers. I saw them over Thanksgiving and Christmas, but I've been busy with work and I haven't had a lot of time to think about what my family's become. I call them "brother" and "stepbrother," but it's playful. I'm a good dozen years older than they are, and I never had a brother growing up. Dev's estranged from his brother and has been for the better part of a decade. So I don't really know how brothers relate except from watching the two of them with each other. But they're family, and I know about family.

I lean against the wall of the passenger meeting area and check the email on my phone. There's a small amount of spam, and everything else is from my job. Of course, I'm not talking to Dev, except on the phone, and my father generally waits for me to call him these days because of all the times I've said, "I'm in the middle of something, can I call you right back?" He forwards articles to me every now and then, but not much more. And Hal writes me too, he just hasn't lately because he's been filing his championship stories.

A text comes in from Mike: *Here got 1 bag.*

I text back that I'm waiting outside security, but as I send it, a sense tells me to lift my eyes, and I see Mike coming through the doors.

He's wearing a loose Chevali Firebirds t-shirt that hangs down over a pair of cargo pants, tail swishing as he walks. His ears perk up when he sees me and my tail wags just like his does. "Hey," he says with a smile, hefting the backpack he carries and reaching out to clasp my paw.

Still got the firm grip I remember. "Good trip?" I ask as we head down to the baggage claim. Every time I say something I'm scanning it in advance to see if it has a gender pronoun in it. I know he said 'he' was still okay but I feel weird saying it.

"Ah, it was fine," he says. "I spent most of it watching the latest 'Parktown.'"

This is a new one on me. "Parktown?"

"It's, ah, it's like a sports soap…kind of like Dillon Lights, but…" His ears go back. "It's kinda dumb."

"Dumb TV is the best sometimes," I say.

He doesn't answer, so I don't press. I never watched Dillon Lights, but I heard a lot about it. Good show about high school football the first two seasons, went off the rails in the next two. It's on that list that Dev and I keep saying we should check out when we have time, but of course that list is longer than both our tails combined.

When his Firebirds duffel comes down onto the carousel, I offer to carry it. He shrugs the backpack on over his shoulders, grabs the duffel, and says, "It's not heavy."

For as much as we were talking on the phone, we don't seem to be able to make conversation in person. I really want to show him that I'm interested in his recent self-discovery and that I'm cool with it, but he hasn't brought it up so I don't want to say, "Hey, so, genderqueer, huh?" Pulling onto the highway, I wonder if this is what my dad felt like when I was trying to tell him I was gay. Oh god. Am I my dad?

No, I think. No. He's just tired from his trip. So I try again, asking how his trip was, and he says it was fine; I ask if he's hungry and he says he's not yet. I list off some of the good restaurants around me and ask if any of them sound interesting to him.

He says some of them do, and then as I make the turn to the street I live on, he asks, "You nervous about the championship? For Dev, I mean."

I think about that. "Not especially. I mean, I know he's going to do the best he can. I want him to get it, but also I think if he doesn't…I don't think it's going to hurt as much as it did the last couple times. He knows that it's not down to one person, that championships rely on teammates and luck and all that."

He nods, taking that in. As I park in front of my townhouse, I ask, "Are you nervous for your dad?"

"Yeah. I don't think he's gonna be happy until he has a championship. The last time—the first one he played in, I mean, because…" In the space between sentences, I fill in, because after that he was separated and then divorced and we didn't see him as often. "After that one he was so distant for a while. Jaren went off with his friends a lot. Mom and I kinda only had each other for a bit, and she was working out all kinds of stuff, so I had to learn stress techniques."

"Oh, is that when that happened? I know you had a, what, a mantra?"

He slides a sardonic coyote scowl my way. As athletic as he is, taking after his father in that way, he's got Angela's expressiveness. He explains with a recitation most likely learned from a counselor: "I had a formula for deconstructing stress so I could better cope with it rather than acting out."

I see my step-family mostly on holidays, and Mike is the quieter of my stepbrothers, at least for the last few years, so I still think of him as a cub of about twelve or thirteen, from that Christmas when my father and Angela first started dating and we all shared an awkward holiday. Mike stayed quiet through most of the dinner while Jaren talked incessantly about sports, both of them clearly trying, as I was, to parse the possible new family configuration. Jaren never talked to me one on one there (he did later, but again, mostly about sports—I would learn that that's how he prefers to communicate), but Mike met me on my way back from a quick email break and said, solemnly, "I'd be okay if you were my brother."

"Me too," I said. "I like you guys."

He nodded and then said, with the gravitas that only a focused pre-teen can summon, "As long as my mom's happy."

"And my dad."

He gave me a quick nod and then went back into the house.

At the time, I didn't know for sure he was going through therapy for his parents' divorce. Father told me a couple years ago, when Mike and Jaren and Angela stopped going. He said it had helped them and I could talk to them about it if I wanted to. I never have.

We get out of the car and again he takes his bags without letting me carry one. "Nice house. I've only ever seen pictures."

"Yeah, it's not bad." I'm aware of the patch of faded paint under the front window, the scratches on the door handle, and the ragged edges of the lawn that the HOA is supposed to take care of but it's been raining so they haven't. The frame around the front door doesn't quite fit; the wet winter expands the wood and warps it enough that I notice. Unlocking the door, I race through all the problems inside, even though I cleaned the night before. It'll be fine, I think. He's a high-schooler, probably just wants to plop his stuff down and watch some videos on his phone for a while, or text his friends.

So I show him the office where I've set up the futon, point out the towels and the bathroom, and he thanks me. "I'm just gonna chill for a bit," he says, "if that's okay."

"Sure." I sit down at the dining room table with my laptop. "I'll do some work here."

I'm deep into my email when I notice Mike standing at the entrance to the kitchen. "Oh," I say, getting up. "You want something to drink?" It's only when I'm on my feet that I notice that he's wearing the skirt he'd talked about. It looks good on him, but also a little weird. I'm not sure what my reaction ought to be, so I go to the fridge and get him a Coke.

He leans against the door and asks me, "You got a lot of work to do?"

"Always." I gesture at the laptop. "But it's a little slower now. I have a couple other things going on around the job, but they're not going anywhere."

"Cool." He takes a drink.

Now I feel like he's inviting comment, so I say, "That looks good on you."

His ears lay back. "It doesn't look good with this shirt."

"Hmm. You got a different shirt?"

He shakes his head. "All my t-shirts are too tight and then it looks worse."

"You want to go shopping for a better shirt?"

That perks his ears up. "Really?"

"Sure. I know a couple places. Won't be too busy this time of day."

"All right." His tail wags under the skirt. "Lemme go change."

He turns quickly, so I call after him. "You don't have to."

His ears swivel back toward me. "What?"

"You don't have to change. You want to go out like that?"

He hesitates and then exhales. "Not yet."

"Okay. But you can bring it if you want. Put it on in the fitting room."

He thinks that over for a few seconds. "Yeah, okay. Sure."

So we go out to a few of my favorite department stores. I try to steer him toward some slightly fancy button-down shirts, but he gravitates over to the plainer, more casual ones. More than once I remind him that the shirts are on me, to make sure he's not just going for cheaper ones, but after the second time he rolls his eyes and says, "I *know*," so I leave it there.

He is picking conservative colors, and his skirt was a nice basic chocolate brown, so I suggest some flashier colors that I think will go with it. He doesn't say anything at the first one, but he takes the second one back into the fitting room to try it on.

I don't get to see any of the outfits. I don't know whether it's too intrusive to ask, so I lean against a wall and check work email on my phone while Mike tries on everything. Peter's asked if I can join a meeting tomorrow, by phone if necessary, to talk about Xu. I tell him if it's early morning I could come in, but I'd prefer to join by phone because Mike and I are going to visit schools.

Mike comes out after a while and holds out two shirts. "I like these," he says, and goes to put the other two back.

We visit a couple other stores after that first one even though he says, "That's probably enough," and he ends up finding a few other shirts he likes. At the last store, I wander over and look at skirts myself, like I'm interested in them, and when he comes over he gets this guarded look on his muzzle, like I'm going to make fun of him. "What are you doing?" he asks.

"Oh," I say, "I used to cross-dress a bit. I was just looking at how the fashion's changed."

The first thing he does is flick his ears around and back to scan the room for anyone nearby. There's an old possum going through the clearance rack, but her little ears are focused on the headset and the conversation she's having in a low mutter. And the two salespeople, a jackal and a fruit bat, are deep in their own conversation, though they are keeping an eye on us.

So Mike says, "You used to—seriously?"

"Oh yeah." I try to stay casual about it. "Didn't I ever tell you how Dev and I met?"

I know I haven't; it isn't a story I've told any of my step-family. I haven't even mentioned it to my father in years and I'm not sure how much he remembers. Dev and I are an established couple now, and when people ask how we met, we say, "In college," and that's far enough in our past that nobody asks further questions. We both work in sports, so they assume I was an assistant on the team and he was a player.

His eyes get bigger and he shakes his head. "Over dinner tonight, then," I say.

"Uh, yeah, sure."

I grab one of the skirts almost at random and say, "What do you think about this one?" When his ears flick around again, I say, "Hey, you're in Yerba. Nobody's going to blink at two guys comparing skirts. If you asked the salespeople over there, they'd probably happily make recommendations."

He shakes his head quickly, violently. "No, that's okay."

I keep my expression serious, but inside I smile, remembering a brash eighteen-year-old fox who pushed his sexuality in people's noses, who went out in public in a dress—and still was worried that people would find out.

He does pick out a skirt he likes and I grab another one over his mild protests. "I'm getting this for you," I say. "You don't have to wear it."

His ears go back, like they seem to do often, but he doesn't object. I hope this is earning me "cool older brother" points. You'd think winning a championship with a sports team would do that, but he hasn't said anything about the ring display in my office. That championship was just after our first Christmas dinner as a potential family, come to think of it, because I remember taking a few work calls from Peter asking me to handle some of the lower-priority things on his plate.

And now he's asking me to evaluate someone else for the assistant GM position. The reminder makes me scowl, not a good look when I'm checking out, so I compose myself and smile at the checkout clerk.

Over dinner at a Bharatian restaurant (Mike's choice; they don't have many of them down in Chevali), I tell Mike a mostly-sanitized version of the way we met. I mean, first off, he's my brother, and secondly, he's sixteen. Any story that starts with, "I was dressed as a vixen in a college bar and Dev walked me home," doesn't leave a lot of room for interpretation about how he figured out I wasn't really female.

Still he asks. "So did you guys…" He plays with a fork in his tikka masala chicken. "Uh."

I chuckle. "Well, uh, yeah. I mean, you get guys worked up at that age, and they'll do a lot before they stop themselves. In retrospect, it was really not smart of me, because Dev could easily have punched me or—or worse. I was lucky."

"But, um." His ears fold down and I can see the question in his mind, the how did it work, did you trick him into fucking you in the rear or did you tell him and then he did it anyway, and then the question around that one, do I really want to ask my stepbrother this question?

I let it go, because it's cute and because I'm not sure if I want to talk about it either so I'm leaving it up to him. And I'm honestly not sure whether he'll ask or not, or if he'll just change the subject.

Then he clears his throat and looks across his plate at me. "When you were dressing up," he says, "did you feel like it was right?"

I keep my ears up, my expression carefully not betraying any of my confusion. "I enjoyed it," I tell him, "but I haven't done it in years."

"Because you didn't want to, or…"

I shake my head. "It wasn't really important to me. It was…" I rub fingers over my whiskers. "It was a way to be able to be with Dev in public that we couldn't do otherwise. There was an element of danger to it, too, and I'll admit that was kind of fun." Except when it wasn't, but he doesn't need to hear about the time I was scared I might get beat up by some football players in the locker room.

He nods, his ears lower, and he takes a bite of his chicken. We eat in silence for a bit until he asks me whether I think Dev can stop Tallaman, the Port City running back who is also a tiger, and we talk football through the rest of the meal.

As we're nibbling on gulab jamun, he goes quiet again, thinking, and then he says, "You still have any of your, uh, vixen clothes?"

"Mmm. Probably. We have a ton of storage space and I definitely moved them out of my parents' house." I make a face, then hurriedly regain my composure. "I mean, Father's come a long way. I'm sure he'd be fine with it now."

"I only met your mom once," Mike says. "She seemed nice."

"She's a good person, or she's trying to be. I don't see her much since she remarried, but we talk on Christmas and Easter." He nods, and I smile. "I like your mom better."

He fidgets in his seat and doesn't look right at me. "But hey," I add quickly, "you don't have to say you like my father better than yours. I mean, your father didn't burn a bunch of your childhood toys."

That story I've told him; he nods and folds his ears down. "I know I'm not supposed to take sides between my parents. I heard that a lot. But they didn't tell me everything when it happened. Like, it was only a couple years ago that I found out about our sister. Half-sister, I guess."

I take the last bite of the dessert. Extra ten minutes at the gym, I promise myself, even though I don't know when I'll go next. Mike sighs and rubs his paws together. "I tried to contact her, did I tell you?"

"You mentioned it once, but you didn't say what happened."

He holds his paws up as though he's getting ready to catch something, then spreads them to either side. "Her mom shut it down. Not much to tell. I mean, I talked to her once, the mom, I mean, and she said it would be okay, but when I called back, she told me to stop bothering them. I found her mom on ScentBook, but Charmaline doesn't have an account yet. I think she's on Insta, but I'm not a hundred percent sure, and I was going to send her a message but then I thought, what am I going to say to her? What do I want her to say to me? It felt like it might be, I dunno…"

"Unproductive?"

He nods and licks rosewater off one of his fingers. "That's a good way to put it."

We don't mention her again, switching to basketball on the way home. Neither of us follows it closely, which leaves us at about the right level to talk to each other. There's a game on that evening, so I put it on in the living room and sit there with my computer handling a few more work things. Mike sits with his phone on the couch for a while and then says he's tired from the day.

When he's in the office with the door closed, I think about our conversations over that night. I call Dev with an idea, a question, and an apology ready, but he doesn't answer. Turning his phone off at night—good tiger. I put a reminder on my phone to call the next evening.

•

Thursday we go to Laurel and spend the day talking to college advisors. One thinks I'm Mike's father, the others wait for me to confirm my relationship before saying anything. While Mike is being shown around Laurel with a few other prospects by a chipper, wagging arctic fox, I hang by the car to talk to Peter about Xu and I do my professional best to keep the remarks objective. Most of it's positive anyway; I have to reach to find negatives that aren't "he's not me."

After the call, Peter asks me how my interviews with Morty are progressing and I tell him I've had one and they still want to fly me out. "You know," he says, "how when we're trying to decide between two draft choices and we say, 'if only there were a way we could have them both'?"

"Sure."

"That's the position I'm in here."

I sigh. "Wish in one paw."

"I know, I know. Think about whether there's anything I can do to sweeten your current position."

"I will."

He pauses. "When I gave you a chance after the Dragons fired you, I thought we were going to build something great here."

My fur prickles. I'm standing outside in the sun, so even though the air is cool, I'm warm. "True," I say. "I appreciate that. And your charity is going on, what, nine years now? Ten?"

"That's not what I meant, Lee."

"You think if I get fired by Cansez in a couple years I won't be able to find another job? You saying I won't be able to come back here or that you wouldn't work with me again?"

"No. Of course I'm not saying that." But he's a fox like me, and it's pretty clear what he was saying. "All right, listen, just come in and see me before you make any decisions, okay?"

"Yeah, of course I will. I wouldn't just quit on you."

"Thank you."

"Sure." I feel bad now that I snapped at him, especially because I don't want to leave. It's not like I haven't lost my temper before, but only about once a year on average, and he's snapped at me plenty. It's our ability to put moments behind us and focus on the relationship that I really appreciate about working with him.

Of course, the only other person I've had a working relationship like that with was Morty. So that doesn't really help me make a decision in this. When I get a call from Dev over lunch, it helps distract me from the problem because he has issues of his own to talk about with Colin and practice and everything. I like knowing that he thinks I have good judgment. I wish I thought the same sometimes.

Chapter Thirteen (Dev)

We get through the rest of the workout without another incident between me and Colin, though at the end of the workout, Croz comes over with his big wolf swagger and grabs Colin's shoulder. "Hey, fox," he says, "what's your problem with my mike over here?"

"It's cool," I say before Colin can answer. "We worked it out."

"Don't answer for me," the fox snaps.

I arch an eyebrow at him. "Did we not work it out?"

Croz is trying to supportively loom over Colin, but the fox is pretty tall and clearly not intimidated. He doesn't even look at the wolf, just at me. His muzzle drops open to say something, but then he snaps it shut and walks off to the locker room.

"Nice guy," Croz says. "Looks like he made that face as a cub and it froze that way. My ma always used to tell me that when she made me eat broccoli."

I shake my head. "I wish he'd just…lighten up. It's been years."

"Seriously, dude. It's twenty-fucking-seventeen. Are you still hung up on gay people? Get the fuck over yourself."

I wish Colin could hear that message—literally and figuratively. "He's been that way for a decade," I say. "Don't think he's about to change now."

"Eh, his loss." Croz dismisses the fox with a shake of his head. "Hey, we doing linebackers dinner tonight?"

"Yeah, that's what Gerrard said this morning."

Gerrard started this tradition of going out to dinner with the linebackers. At first he tried to make it every Thursday night, but we skipped it during the bye week and then again during our playoff bye. Since we're practicing this week, even though there's not a game, he said we're doing dinner again. Of course, Croz was on his phone or late or something and missed it.

The wolf, as always, doesn't give a shit. He wags his tail and says, "Cool, let me tell my guys I can't raid tonight."

He goes off on his phone, texting, and the rest of us follow to the film room. Carson comes up beside me and pats my shoulder. "Good workout."

"I'm glad it's over." I shake my head. "I dunno what Coach is hoping to do. If Colin and I haven't become friends in ten years, it's not going to happen magically over a week because we have to practice together."

"Focus on the game." The leopard shrugs. "Think of it like game conditions. Making practice harder."

"Great." I punch my fist into my other paw. "At least I don't have to worry about it until next Wednesday."

The other linebackers get that it was a tough practice too; they all make a point to give me shoulder-punches or backslaps and a few words of encouragement, all except for Colin's friend Lukos (but even he gives me a nod). When we get to the door into the facility, Carson stops to say to me, "Being the leader of the group doesn't just mean relaying everything Coach says."

That stays in my head as we change and start watching film. When Gerrard retired and I took over the middle linebacker spot (the "mike"), I also became the de facto leader of the linebackers. Gerrard had been the leader of our defense, too, and I took over that spot in that I relayed the plays in from the sideline, but I never really stepped up to speak for the whole defense the way Gerrard had. For one thing, we got a new defensive coordinator in who went out of his way to go talk to all the different position groups, so there wasn't really a need for someone to speak up.

Do we need that now? Ideally there would be a player to mediate for me and Colin, but as much as I'm leading the linebackers, he's leading the defensive backs, so if the defensive line (the third of the three defensive groups) had a position leader, that'd be the person to do it. But they're pretty insular, and Doca, the bear nose tackle who's got the most seniority on the line, takes care of his guys and doesn't worry about much else. He's certainly not going to get in between me and Colin, both of whom have been on the team longer than he has.

So I need to get through this on my own. Coach mandated it, so Gerrard's going to go along with it, which means I need to do some work to make it through the next cornerback practice without embarrassing myself.

Out at dinner, I'm looking forward to relaxing and forgetting about Colin, but Croz, once he gets a couple beers in him, doesn't seem inclined to let that happen. "Has that guy always been a shit and I never noticed?" he asks the room at large.

Paxi, a cougar who hangs out with Lukos a lot, is good at helping the coyote ignore when the linebackers talk shit about his friend Colin. The two of them, down at the end of the table, have their own conversation while everyone else replies in the affirmative, which Croz misses because he's texting someone. When he looks up, Carson rolls his eyes while Vic, the coyote who's his primary backup, says "Yes" again very clearly.

Croz sets his phone on the table. "Well, that's his deal."

"We know," Price says. He usually sits next to Croz, wolf with wolf. "You think we all ain't got Miski's back?"

"I know we do." The big wolf tosses back the rest of his beer. "Because you got mine too."

The table goes quiet. "Uh," Price says. "Are you saying you're gay?"

"Did you tell us?" Carson asks as we all consider the possibility that Croz might've come out and we all missed it somehow, like maybe he just texted everyone.

"What? No, but I'd tell you guys if I was. No, I mean, because I play SimEpic and Dungeons. You know I got so much shit for that in college, and I still get tweeted at about it, but you guys are cool with it. Totally appreciate that."

Price and I exchange glances and smiles. "Dude," I say, "don't pretend like it's not weird. But you like it, so whatever, not going to judge."

"Also," Price says, "don't fuckin' look at Twitter."

"Hey," Croz says, "You should try it sometime. I'll get you totally set up with an account. Not Twitter, I mean, Dungeons."

He offers this every week and every week we all laugh and nobody takes him up on it. This time, though, Price says, "It's cool that it's your thing. I don't get it though."

"I'll get all of you in. Just like, a couple days," Croz says. "After we win the championship."

Vic, sitting next to me, pipes up. "Dude, Dev likes dick and that's cool, but you don't see him trying to get us all to try it."

"Sucking dick isn't a hobby." Price leans in to stare down at the coyote.

Unfazed, Vic shrugs just as Croz says, "Ah, don't get him started on his 'sexuality is fluid' shit."

"Sorry they didn't teach you that in the one class you took your one year in college," Vic shoots back.

Croz points at me. "Gay." Then at himself. "Straight. You can't be, like, half-gay."

"You can be bisexual," I say, thinking about Ty.

"Okay, but I heard bisexual guys are just gay guys afraid to commit."

Vic snorts. "That's not true at all."

"Look." Croz is full up now, both of beer and Vic's attitude. "Sexuality's so fluid, why don't you just go out and put your money where your mouth is—put your mouth where your money is—where your words are…" He stops grasping at the metaphor, shooing it away as if it were a fly buzzing around his head. "You ever suck dick?"

I tense, but only slightly. When you're gay and most of your friends are straight, this conversation comes up every now and then. They're all very convinced that they're one hundred and ten percent straight, only they're super-curious about what it's like to have a cock in your mouth, or your cock in a guy. Usually they draw a hard line at having a cock under their tail, and are surprised when I tell them that my relationship with Lee has pretty defined top/bottom roles. If I choose to tell them that. So I know what to expect from this conversation, down to the "revelation" that one of them has had a gay experience. I already know about Carson's, but for a number of reasons I also know he won't talk. Because Vic is the subject of the questioning, it's not a surprise when he speaks up, calm, ears perked, not showing the effects of his beer nearly as much as Croz.

"Once, in college."

The one thing that has changed over the years is that the reaction of my straight friends has gone from pearl-clutching gasps to simply perking their ears in interest, which the coyote basks in. "Sure," he says. "Friend of mine, gay deer, got drunk with me one night and wanted to blow me, and then he was gonna just jerk off. I was curious…" He spreads his paws and grins. "Wasn't no big deal. He pulled out before he came. We didn't do anything after that."

"Hell, I mean, I messed around with a dude in high school," Croz says. "But it's not the same."

I clear my throat and look down the table at Lukos, Colin's friend, who is studiously staring down, ears back. "It's cool, guys," I say. "I don't really need to know how many dicks you guys have touched. I appreciate the support. And if you want, you new guys don't know that when we go to Yerba, my boyfriend takes us out dancing at a gay club, and you're all welcome to come along."

"We didn't go last year," Croz says.

"No, he was busy, but he promised next year."

"I'm down," Vic says, and Price chimes in as well.

"All right, it's set." I wonder, though, whether I'll be on the team next year. Just a week of practice makes me aware of nagging aches that will take months to vanish, if even then. How long before they don't go away ever? "So who else has hobbies we can all share in? Everyone going to leave dirty shirts in their locker for a month like Price?"

"What I want to know," Price drawls, "is if Vic's going to buy us all motorcycles if we win the championship."

"I'm a backup," Vic says. "Buy your own fucking motorcycle, mister ten year vet."

"You're not allowed to ride motorcycles by the terms of your contract." Gerrard gives me a look like, *fucking kids*.

"Who said anything about riding them?" Price shields his face from Gerrard and broadly winks at the rest of the table.

"Can't say I didn't warn you when you break your arm and void your contract," the older coyote says and leans back, shaking his head.

I really enjoy these dinners, sexuality conversations and all. Gerrard talks about some of the people he's played against, and over the course of the season, I've realized that I have some stories, too. McCrae isn't in the Hall of Fame, but he's building his case, and my sack of him in the championship game is a story that's worth a drink or two. But often we don't even talk about football. We talk about movies, about families, about video games, about politics sometimes. Croz is a conservative on most issues, but we can have reasonable discussions even though I'm a moderate (he considers me liberal, and maybe I am now), and he came around quickly to be more progressive on gay rights. I make sure that conversations about politics or religion—Lukos is devout, and so is Carson and I think Price, but neither of them make a big deal of it usually—don't get out of control.

We all get a little buzzed, and Croz more than a little, but though he's a loud drunk, he's not obnoxious, and he knows his limits pretty well. More importantly, the rest of us know them too, and if he orders one drink too many, we cut him off. He grumbles, but he listens.

So I'm still buzzed and happy when I get back to the room and find Wix there, lying on his bed with his tablet and wearing nothing but his shorts. He puts the tablet down when I come in and props himself up on his elbows. "How's it going?"

"Good dinner," I say, pulling my shirt off. "Good beer. How was your night?"

"Ah, whatever." I'd thought he was looking at porn on his tablet, but to my surprise there are actual football plays there. "Same old, not worth talking about. What'd you guys talk about?"

"Same old." I pause the conversation long enough to hit the bathroom and get rid of some of the beer, then come back out. "Whether we should be feeding poor people, who sucked a dick once, shit like that."

His ears perk up. "Who sucked a dick?"

"Hey now," I say. "That's just linebacker talk." I throw my shirt at him. "You want to hear linebacker secrets, you gotta do linebacker laundry."

He doesn't laugh, doesn't throw the shirt back at me. His ears go down and he drops the shirt off the side of the bed. "Already did enough laundry," he grumbles.

"Life of a rookie," I say. "You know, I did plenty of laundry."

"Did you do it the week before the championship game?"

"Well, no." I spread my paws. "I was a rookie with the Dragons, so about ten games into the season everyone knew we weren't going to the playoffs and the team basically shut down." I don't like to remember that year; when we have rookies carry bags and do laundry here, there's a sense that they're going through a ritual to become part of something great. We've been to the championship three times in ten years, which is tied for second best in the league, and generally the rookies have been happy to do rookie stuff. With the Dragons, though, all of us rookies were assigned chores without enthusiasm or joy, because it was the way football worked, and some of the vets took out their frustrations on us. I promised myself I'd never do that with any rookies I worked with, and I haven't.

"Ugh." The bobcat lies back and looks at the ceiling. "I wish the game was tomorrow. This waiting sucks."

I sit on my bed. "Who made you do laundry?"

"Who do you think?"

I sigh. "I'll talk to him. Whatever's going on between us, he shouldn't take out his frustrations on you."

"Don't talk to him, you'll make it worse." Wix shakes his head. "Just another week and then we'll be playing the game and it'll be over."

"He needs to get laid," I say.

"Doesn't his wife live in town? Or he can take his pick from the crew hanging out in the street." Wix is in a mood tonight. "Half tempted to go down there myself. Blow job's a blow job, right? Doesn't matter whose mouth it is."

It's funny to hear the same argument I'd just been hearing from a bunch of straight guys turned around. "You've done it before," I say. "If you want the room, go ahead. I'll go play video games with Charm or something."

"Nah, it's fine." His claws are out, pricking the bedsheets, and then he retracts them and rests one paw on his shorts. "There was a guy hanging out with the girls a month or so ago, did I tell you?"

"Yeah."

"I kept trying to corner him, but he had someone else to go off with." He rubs at his sheath a bit.

"I know."

"And then he just stopped coming around."

"Yeah, I feel bad about that."

The words come out without me thinking about them, because I'm thinking about a bunch of different things at once and because I'm still a little buzzed. Wix sits all the way up, his paw dropping back to the bed. "Wait, you know why he left?"

"No." I stumble. "I just mean, I feel bad—all those groupies, they're kinda—you know, it's not a great life—"

"Sure, sure." He leans toward me. "But you weren't just talking about random groupies. Did you warn that guy off? Are you, like…trying to be a gay dad or something?"

"I—"

"Because that's kinda hot, so you know." He's smiling, but there's also sparks in his eyes.

I ignore his come-on and shake my head. "It's no big deal, I just sometimes talk to the guys who show up and see what their deal is. I mean, a groupie wrecked Gerrard's family, and most of the guys who are married and fool around know what they're in for…" I'm not making sense but I can't tell him the central premise of my actions. "But like, a gay guy with a closeted player, that could ruin the player's marriage, and the guy's never going to get anything out of it more than a story."

"A closeted player—so you know who it is?"

There I'm caught. I'm not so drunk that I'm going to spill the secret, but I'm also not sober enough to think of a response other than to shake my head and say, "Uh, no."

"You do." Wix stands up and paces, keeping his eyes on me. "Who is it?"

"Look, I—even if I did know—it's someone else's secret. Like—would you want me telling the rest of the team that you're gay?"

The bobcat waves a paw. "Whatever, that shit's out there, it's gonna happen sooner or later. But look, I'm closeted and I get that that means I do my shit on the DL and that means I don't go diving for groupies. Guy who does that is desperate and that's—"

"None of your business," I say. "Or mine."

"Except." He walks over to my bed. "You're making it your business. You're trying to get the gay groupies to leave so this guy won't have any other outlet. You want him to come out? I mean, that's a pretty shitty thing to do to someone."

"It's not great, I admit. But…" I search for the words. "These guys who come here, they're just kids, and they're chasing this idea that, I dunno, they're going to find a sugar daddy to keep them on the side."

He sits next to me on my bed. "How's that different from what the girls want?"

This is not a great conversation to have while I'm buzzed. "I guess it's not, but I mean, that's a more…um, accepted thing? Like, a lot of the guys have regulars in other towns and at least a few of them were girls they met at the hotel or in a club or something. But I know with this guy that that's not going to happen. Basically he wants to use these guys for as long as they'll put up with it and then move on to the next one."

"And if they're okay with that?"

"I mean…" I scratch my ear. "There was one guy I talked to a few years ago who was totally fine with it. He knew what the deal was and like it was cool and all. But—the other thing is that a lot of these guys come hang around because they think they've got a chance to get with me."

Wix's eyes widen and he nods. "Oh, shit, okay. Yeah, so it's like you're accidentally bait and this guy's the trap."

"That's…one way to put it, I guess. I feel responsible for them."

"Yeah." He stares down at his paws. Then he looks up. "It's Colin, isn't it?"

"Uh—what? I mean—no."

He grins and flops back, almost hitting my tail. "It's cool. You didn't tell me. But it's someone you don't get along with and this has been going on for years, so…not many guys fit that profile. And he's a classic closet case. Shit, I was already wondering that about him. Pock said something once—and Haluamma too."

"Wix. Listen, you can't go doing anything—don't go talk to him or anything."

"I won't tell him you told me." He says it like I told him not to punch an opposing player in front of a ref, something so obvious I didn't have to say it.

"I'm the only one on the team who knows! You're my roommate!"

"You're not the only one who knows, I bet." He turns his head toward me. "Didn't you hear me say that the other corners have made comments? I didn't get them at the time, but if he's gay and hooks up on the road, yeah, it makes sense. Anyway, he knows I'm gay, or suspects, so maybe I talked to that groupie during the season and *he* told me?"

I'm much closer to sober now, but even so I can't think of a good answer to that. "Just don't get in the middle of this," I plead, knowing that it's already too late for that. And of course it's right then that Lee calls.

Chapter Fourteen (Lee)

Mike comes back from the tour while I'm still stewing about the phone call, both Peter's action and my reaction. Glad for the distraction, I ask him what he thinks of the school and he says it's really pretty. He has appointments with an assistant soccer coach and then he wants to go meet with someone from their Queer Life club, which sounds a lot more inclusive than the Forester Lesbians and Gays club I belonged to in college. I debate offering to tag along, but there's really nothing I can say to the soccer coach. I guess he might be impressed that Mike's stepbrother works in professional sports, but more likely he'd view me as a peer and would tell me that there isn't much chance of Mike getting a soccer scholarship. Which Mike knows but is meeting with him anyway, I suspect because Gerrard insisted on it.

As for the Queer Life people, I can't deny that I'm interested in what they might say, but this is Mike's visit and I trust him to evaluate whether they'll be a good group for him. He'll likely be more open without me around anyway. So I tell him I'll wait in the campus coffee shop and he gives me a thumbs up, heading off to his appointments.

This is a good time to work on Cord's Nativist letter, I think. So I grab a latte and start looking up the movement online. It distracts me from being annoyed at Peter—rather, reading all of this stuff makes me actually angry, which make me realize that I'm not angry at Peter but only annoyed. He's a good guy overall, and he doesn't want to lose me. But these Nativist people…

The basics of the movement are the same as any outgroup fearmongering—"stranger danger" hysteria, to simplify. Why are you struggling to make ends meet? Why do you feel like our culture's values are declining? Why, it's not because the rich people who own the companies you work for keep finding ways to take more and more money from you. It's not because you haven't opened your minds and hearts to people who don't live the way you do. It's because of immigrants! They don't look like you! Our world has always had speciesism, and it keeps coming back in different forms.

I also find a few hints of darker areas below that, people warning that demographic trends move toward the "apocalyptic" end of "Native" people becoming a minority, sometimes mentioning specific species (most often bears and elk in my research). I have to read a few of these to understand the convoluted logic of it, because it's not like "Native" people vote as a bloc or have the same concerns across species even. Politicians will usually get a majority of the votes of their species, but those groups aren't enough to win elections on their own, which is why you don't get a majority of rabbits, mice, foxes, and deer in the government.

But electing those kinds of representatives is exactly what some of these groups want. And others, when you slide down into the darker depths, hint that legal measures may not be enough to protect our homeland.

I feel gross after all that research, but I have to know what's going on in the worst parts to be able to justify the memo. So I make up a few internal links for Peter's reference and then review Cord's letter.

We want to say that the Whalers support each of their players of every species and that any involvement with the Nativist movement will be viewed as detrimental to the team. Short and to the point, but I spend half an hour thinking over every word in every sentence, strengthening and weakening the same line four or five times sometimes. I add a line at the end saying that past activities won't be held against players if they sever ties with those groups.

I feel good writing this letter. In my younger days I wanted to punish people who knowingly helped hate groups and the nearest I came to that in this job was when the league as a whole condemned a certain group, which almost never happened. You can't stop players from donating to a church or a political cause because that's limiting their free speech or freedom of religion, even if it's a church that actively crusades against gay marriage—politically—or a political cause that seeks to strip away civil rights.

But the Nativists are a bigger problem, and Peter sees, as I do, the danger they pose to team chemistry. Every single team has "outsider" (non-Native) players. If you have guys who believe that those players are worth less because of their species, then that's a problem. Football is a great equalizer, teams made up of players of different faiths, a few of different sexualities, different moral codes, but we manage to make it work. Most of the time.

One of the things that I find to support this letter is that there are already a number of prominent athletes speaking out against the movement. A lot are from basketball, but there are a few football players as well. I spend another half hour compiling all of their tweets, insta-posts, etc. into a supporting document for Peter so he knows there's broad support for this move.

Honestly, the fact that Remington's agent spoke so reluctantly about it means that people in the industry already think of this movement as toxic, and that's a good place to start from. I'm adding a note to that effect when Mike shows back up.

"How'd it go?" I ask. "Want a coffee?"

He nods, so we order him a latte (with soy milk, what?) and then sit down. "It was pretty cool, I guess," he says. "They talked a lot about their activities and protests. I guess they went to Potomac a couple weeks ago for the inauguration protest. They kept talking about meeting people from other schools and all the connections they'd made."

"Sounds pretty cool."

One thing coyotes and foxes have in common is that our large ears make it hard for us to hide emotion. As we get older, we get better at controlling them, but Mike's not there yet. His ears aren't perked all the way up. "It was, I guess."

"But the idea of going to Potomac to protest isn't really your thing?" He shakes his head. "You know, when I was in college, I fought so hard for us to go protest, but they said we didn't have the numbers. They didn't want to show up with under a thousand people and they weren't sure other people would back us."

"When was this? Back in the nineties?"

"Uh, the oughts, thank you very much." I fold my ears back. "How old do you think I am?"

Now he grins at me. "I dunno, you were like thirty when you came over for the first time, right?"

"I'm thirty-one now," I snap.

"Seriously? You've been working here, like, forever."

I roll my eyes. "God, you kids."

"So it was, like, the early oughts, right? 2001 or something?"

I clear my throat. "So they focus a lot on activism. What would you rather do?"

He drinks his coffee rather than answering. I wait, and when he looks out the window, I make sure all my documents are saved. Finally he says, "I dunno really."

"Something more chill?"

He turns back to me with a wary look that I'm not sure how to interpret. "Yeah. Maybe."

"Someplace you could meet people and talk about what this all means, hang out in your skirt and all?"

He nods slowly. "That'd be cool."

"Okay," I say. "That's not a bad thing to want. I'm sure they have social functions here. They're probably just jazzed about their trip."

He doesn't seem inclined to say much more, so I suggest we head out. We're supposed to go up to the city for that film he wanted to see, but as I get on the freeway heading north, he says, "Wait, isn't your place the other direction?"

"Yeah." I point to the traffic. "It's rush hour. It's going to take us an hour and a half to get there, according to the maps, so we can't go back or we won't make it in time."

"Oh." He stares out the window as we drive and doesn't say anything.

I work out finally that he (probably) wanted to change into his skirt to go out to this LGBT film in his genderqueer outfit. But if he wanted to do that, he should've told me. I thought I said we were going to have to go directly from Laurel to the film. Maybe I didn't. But he should've—well, we should've laid out our plans more directly. Oh well. Something to remember for the future. I'd say something to him about it, but I'm fighting with traffic and still going over that Nativist stuff in my head.

We pass most of the drive in silence for those reasons, lost in whatever thoughts are in both our heads, until we get to the city and I ask him what the movie's about. He looks it up on his phone.

"This one's about a lesbian couple and their gay best friend trying to keep their apartment building from being demolished."

"Ah. Sounds like a…comedy?"

Mike snorts. "The review quote is 'an unflinching look at the housing crisis facing our minority populations today.' So I'm guessing no."

It is not, in fact, a comedy. The acting is pretty good, but the movie is way too preachy for me and I think also for Mike. The evening is pretty well salvaged by the excellent burritos we get at a local taqueria. Mike gets good Sonoran food there in Chevali, but the taquerias in the city have a different flavor to them, different spices and ingredients—he tries one with avocado because, he says, he has to have avocado in Goldenwater, it's a thing.

He talks a little more on the way home, but I don't bring up his disappointment. We talk about going over to UG tomorrow and what he expects and what to talk about. "If you want to go to the clubs on Korsat after that," I say, "better bring a club outfit, because we probably can't go all the way back to my place and up to the city again."

"Yeah," he says, his ears back.

"You have an idea of what you want to wear to the club?"

"What sort of club is it?"

"Well, there's a couple different ones. The all-ages ones I know are pretty casual."

"Okay," he says. "I'll pick out something."

"If you want some help…"

"Nah, I can manage."

So I leave it there and talk about the movie the rest of the way home. As much as neither of us can say we enjoyed the movie, we both learned something. Mike thought the discrimination was exaggerated in the film, and I told him that sadly, no, there are a lot of cases where landlords preferentially evict gay tenants, especially in conservative areas where the gay people might not want their sexuality made public in a court proceeding.

"I guess that could happen even if you're not gay but maybe you don't want your private life in all the papers," he says.

"Yeah. I admit, I didn't know it was still happening. I remember that from back in…" I glance at him. "The nineties."

He doesn't get it at first, and then he grins. "I don't really think you're as old as my dad."

I feel a little better about the evening when he gets back and asks if I have any streaming video and do I want to watch something. I say he's welcome to put something on but I need to get this letter to Peter tonight and I want to put a little more time into it. So he goes off and watches something with a lot of explosions that I eventually find out is one of the latest superhero films, while I spend forty minutes putting together a note to introduce the letter to Peter and tell him I'm planning to run it by Jody at UG tomorrow, and then remember that I was going to call Dev, so I do.

"Hey," I start with. "I'm sorry, I know about our week and a half and I know we just talked this afternoon, but I had an idea and you're the only one who can really help me with it and I don't know if it's a good idea."

"It's fine, fox," he says. "I'm glad you called. You would not believe what's been going on."

"Also I miss you," I say. "What's been going on?"

"What's your idea?"

"You first."

He sighs. "Hang on." A bed creaks, a door closes. He settles onto something, can't tell what, and then says, "I just kinda outed Colin to Wix."

"Why? How?"

"The guys were talking about gay shit at the bar again, like who's ever touched another dick in their life, and I was getting buzzed and talking to Colin—shit, I mean, talking to Wix about the groupies and he—he figured it out."

Even as buzzed as he sounds, I'm a little surprised. Dev is usually pretty discreet. Wix must be fox levels of clever, or close to it. "Okay, well, just another week and change, no harm done, right?"

"God, I hope not. I told him not to do anything, but who knows? Cubs."

"Yeah, tell me about it."

"Oh, right. How's things going with Mike?"

So I tell him about our shopping and the college visit. "But I have this nagging feeling that I'm…how to put this. If my father had been supportive of me being gay when I came out to him, that's how I feel like I am to Mike right now. I want to help him and be cool and everything, but I can't tell if I'm doing it right or not. He wanted to dress up for the film tonight and I messed that up. Though also he should've told me. But I know it's touchy for him, so he can't be expected to tell me. Ugh, you see how I'm going round and round on this."

"Making me a bit dizzy."

"Or else that's the beer."

"I didn't have that many."

I lean back in my dining room chair. "So anyway, Mike was talking about wanting to get in touch with Charmaline, Gerrard's daughter. And I think Gerrard is probably the only one who has her number."

"Shouldn't you ask your father and his mother about this?"

"I will, but I wanted to make sure you were okay trying to get the number first."

He takes a while to think about it. "I'm not really that buzzed anymore. I'm just saying that so when I say I'm not sure it's a good idea, you'll know I'm sober."

"I know, I know. Listen, just ask Gerrard for me, okay? I'll talk to Father and Angela, I promise."

"All right, fox. But maybe after the game?"

"Yeah. Thanks." I rub my eyes. "So what else is going on with you? Done your practices with Colin?"

"For this week," he says. "I have to do it again next week."

The practices sound frustrating as all hell. "If Coach says you have to do them, you gotta do them."

He growls. "I know. And I feel like if I go back to Coach, I'll be a 'complainer.' I think he's waiting to see if me or Colin complains first, and it sure isn't going to be me."

"This is a dumb game that nobody wins."

"Wrong. I win it."

I can't help but smile. "All right, tiger. You know your team."

"Damn right. Now I just have to figure out what to do about Wix." He pauses. "You think I should let him blow me?"

The question seems to come out of nowhere and startles me, until I remember that I told him that almost a week ago. "Stud, I mean, if you think it'll help. Or if you're really curious about it. I said that so you wouldn't feel pent up or anything, not because I was trying to make it happen."

"Oh." He sounds either relieved or disappointed, or maybe a little of both.

"Seriously, tiger, if the situation comes up or whatever, I won't be mad. Just tell me about it."

"Okay." He exhales. "Thanks, fox."

"And as for the Colin thing, you know, make the best of it?"

That's a little joke between us, when bad things happen, because the second time Dev lost the championship, one of his uncles said, "Make the best of it."

He laughs. "Yeah, I'll do my best. It's only two more practices. What's the worst that can happen?"

"Don't make me think about that."

He laughs again, this time even more relaxed, and asks me what's going on with the Cansez job, so I tell him a little. "But I'm not so worried about that until I get Mike's visit over with. I argued with Peter because he wants me to stay, but I don't think he'll give me the assistant GM job."

"Want to talk about it?"

I lean back in my chair. "There's not a lot to talk about. I mean, I'm gonna do the interview, but…can you see me living in Cansez?"

He doesn't answer right away. "I can see you with an 'assistant GM' title next to your name."

"What if I'm only succeeding because of the people around me? Maybe they're not hiring me for the position here because I'm not ready." I stare out my living room window into the bushes starkly lit by the streetlight. My suburban street is quiet. It could be the Midwest, except for the smell and the air and the confidence I feel about things like taking my stepbrother out in a skirt. "I think about that sometimes. Am I really that great?"

"Of course you are."

"I appreciate you saying that." I smile. "I know you have to, but I also know you mean it."

"Course I do."

"You're great too."

He snorts. "I know that, fox."

"Yeah you do. So don't let Colin get under your skin." I pause. "Or your tail, or whatever else he wants to do."

Dev laughs. "I don't even let you do that, I'm sure as hell not gonna let him."

"All right, tiger. Sleep well. I'm gonna send off this letter and then I'll sleep too."

"What letter?"

So I tell him about it, and to my surprise, he's not that excited. "I know these guys are bad, but isn't this making a big deal out of it? I don't like 'em, but me and Carson ignore them and…"

"Am I doing the activist over-reaction thing?" I dredge that question out of my memory.

"Your boss doesn't think so, so no. I'm just talking out loud, fox. Ignore me."

I laugh. "Never, tiger. I think for you it's different because it's all outside the team. Colin's shitty about it but it sounds like it's more to needle you than because he believes it."

"I guess."

I shift the phone against my ear. "Tell you what. Let's solve the Nativist problem after the championship. Get some rest and I'll talk to you in a while."

"Not going to commit to keeping our two weeks?"

"I'll try, but it sure seems like it's not happening."

We both pause and think about that. "I'm okay with that," he says finally.

I imagine his arms around me, and the night outside feels less stark and cold. "Me too."

CHAPTER FIFTEEN (DEV)

Friday morning I wake up to a bunch of texts on my phone, one from Damien and one from Coach Lopez that looks like it went to the whole team and several from reporters I've talked to in the past (including Hal) and one from Lee and one from my dad, of all things. The subject of all of them is a tweet that Marshall, a bear on the defensive line, sent, or rather, retweeted. He's one of Colin's friends, one of the guys who walks around with a cross around his neck and a chip on his shoulder, and last night he retweeted a picture of a boat with a caption over it that said "NEW ZEBRA HOUSING."

It's pretty pointed, but what makes it bad is that the account that he retweeted it from belongs to a guy whose other tweets include worse stuff (Lee's text says, and I don't investigate to see what that means because frankly I don't want to waste the energy on it). So clearly Marshall follows this guy, and the media's been buzzing about it because it's Championship Week (almost) and they're anxious for any story.

Coach's text says that we're going to have a team meeting at 9 am, and though he doesn't specifically say what it's about, we don't usually have 9 am team meetings. There's another text from Lux, our defensive coordinator, making sure we saw Coach's text and telling us to get our asses there. So I throw a pillow at Wix to wake him up because it's already past seven am and we've got to have breakfast too.

Most of the guys hustle through breakfast like we do and make it to the locker room by five to nine. Coach Lopez doesn't like tardiness. Even Croz is there on time.

"I'll keep this short," Coach Lopez says. "I want to remind everyone that we're under a microscope because of this game we've got coming up, and anything you do anywhere on social media is going to get seen and blown out of proportion. So keep it bland. We'd prefer you not say anything at all. Got it?"

Everyone murmurs assent. "Good." He checks his clipboard. "Practice today, half-day tomorrow, off Sunday, back to work Monday. Remember Media Day is Tuesday, talk to your agent or our liaison or both, and for God's sake don't do anything stupid. You shouldn't be on social media anyway; you should be thinking about football 24-7."

Behind him, Gerrard nods. I know he doesn't like all the changes Coach Lopez made, but this is one area in which they're in complete agreement. The big moose looks around the room, holding all of our attention. "Good meeting," he said. "Go to your practices."

Lux steps up as the meeting disperses. The maned wolf gestures to me and calls, "Colin," because the fox is walking away. "Can I see you two guys?"

He pulls us into the coach's office and closes the door. "Look, you guys are the captains of the defense. I need you to make sure that this Marshall thing doesn't get too much traction. Colin, you're his friend."

"Kind of." The fox looks away and grimaces.

"I see you hanging out with him, you and Dublovic and Lukos and a couple others."

"He talks to his defensive line more."

"Sure." The maned wolf rubs his ears back. "But you're a co-captain and you hang out with him. So listen, you two figure this shit out. One of you, both of you, keep an eye on things up here. We can't control what people do on their own time, but if things start sparking on the team, we need it to stop right away. If you need to talk to people about it, talk; if you want to listen and let me know who to talk to, fine. I can be the heavy if I need to. But get back with me on Monday and we're going to check in every day to make sure this isn't becoming a problem."

"We got this," I say. "Don't worry about it."

"All right. I also told Doca to talk to Marshall and he'll make some sort of apology or something today, we hope. There might be press sniffing around in the evening but we'll try to keep them away from the practices."

"What should we say if they've already reached out to us?" I hold up my paws. "I haven't responded at all yet."

Colin doesn't say anything, but his ears perk up, attentive for the answer. I'm sure he's gotten some of the same inquiries.

Coach Lux sighs. "Tell them Marshall's going to apologize and that the team is fine."

"Got it," I say.

"Good." The maned wolf gets up. "Take a few minutes to discuss it, and I'll see you out in practice."

The last thing in the world I want is to have to sit down and talk about something reasonably with Colin, but Lux closes the door behind him as he leaves and I don't have a choice. Colin folds his arms and glares at the door.

I don't say anything. He doesn't either at first, and then he heaves an exasperated sigh. "We don't have to talk to anyone. This'll blow over in half a day."

"Agreed," I say. "Just make sure your shitty friend doesn't say anything else out of line."

He snaps his head around. "If you'd make more of an effort to fit in—"

"What, hide what I am? Like you do?"

I've gotten into a couple fights with teammates over the years, and for a moment I think I'm about to add one to the tally. But Colin gets himself under control and sizes me up. "Yes, actually. None of these natural populists have a problem with Coach Lux, or with Carson, or Haluamma, or any of the others."

"They have harassed Carson, and Carlos, by the way, and Haluamma's a rat."

"Rats are foreign, and anyway, he's a Tanezumi rat." This comes with a superior smirk.

I shake my head, tail lashing. "Just because you don't see problems doesn't mean they aren't happening. And what's a 'natural populist'?"

Colin rolls his eyes. "Keep your ears open and hopefully I won't have to talk to you again until Monday."

He gets up and heads for the door. "Hey," I say.

"What?" He doesn't turn around.

"If we do hear something…let's talk before we go to Coach."

I see the instinctive shake of his head, and then he makes an exasperated huff. "Fine." And then he's gone, and good riddance.

I wait until he's out of sight of the office to follow him out and to the practice, where it's nice working with my guys and not having to deal with Colin for once. Looking around, I realize that I never processed that Carson and I are the only non-native species in this group. Why would I? It wasn't a distinction that meant anything until a bunch of people made it. Nobody in this squad or on the team cares about it. And yet, we're not oblivious to what's going on in the world, how those people shouting about distinctions seem to have louder and louder voices. We thought we were safe on our team in our bubble where all that matters is football.

For most of the guys, that's true; or at least, football matters more than what species someone is. Maybe not more than family. Heck, that might even be true for Marshall. Probably is. If you asked him if he'd rather have Josef the boar next to him or Josef's backup, who happens to be a puma, I'm pretty sure he'd pick Josef because Josef's pretty incredible. One of the things I learned about homophobes, and maybe the same is true of Nativists, is that their prejudice doesn't apply as much when they know a guy. It's easy to say, "non-native species go home," but would he really push Josef onto a ship? I don't see it.

"Hey." Croz breaks into my reverie in the few minutes we have before Gerrard starts our practice. "What was that meeting all about?"

He was there, but I've learned that it doesn't matter to bring that up. "Marshall tweeted something dumb." I give him the quick rundown.

"Zebras again?" He rolls his eyes. "You know, these people have some good points, they just don't know how to communicate them."

"Uh…good points?"

"Sure." He grabs a BoltAde and waves the bottle around as he talks in between gulps. "Like, our immigration system is flat busted. I don't mean people like you." He waves the bottle at me. "Your family came over a while ago probably."

"Fifty, sixty years."

"Sure, so, y'know, you guys have established yourselves here. It's not about the zebras, it's about all the people who came in the last five years or so."

This is a weird conversation to be having. "And what are those people doing?"

"Taking jobs! But they don't pay taxes on 'em. And they use our education services, our housing, our health, and so on."

"I don't think that's generally true."

"Sure it is! Look it up." He downs the rest of the BoltAde and tosses it in the trash, and that's when Gerrard calls us over to practice. "Listen," he says, "I don't buy this whole 'stay where you came from' thing. I mean, I'm pretty sure my ancestors are from Deutscherbund. And there's all those people who came here as slaves and the people who fled World War II and all that shit. People should have a chance to make a life here, but they gotta do it legally."

He pats me on the shoulder, and I say, "Right," and we jog off to our drills. But the argument stays in my head the whole morning. The people that a lot of these Nativists are protesting came here legally, but that doesn't matter to them, no matter what Croz says. If there's opportunity, why shouldn't people from poor countries try to make a living here? It's not just that my family came here years ago; it's that I know or have known a bunch of football players over the years who came from poor backgrounds and earned a living (and more) playing a game, and football is kind of a meritocracy. If you can play, you stay on the field (though I think of the gay players who were as good as straight backup players and got cut, and I wonder about that). That, for better or worse, is my vision of how my country works, too. I thought everyone shared that vision, but now I'm not so sure.

Chapter Sixteen (Lee)

Peter's approval of my and Cord's Nativist letter comes in while I'm driving Mike to UG. He alternates between staring out the window at the scenery and checking his phone, probably Twitter. I keep thinking about the whole thing with Marshall retweeting that Nativist guy. It's bad timing for this all to be coming out, but with the swearing in of a federal government that has a lot of Nativist ties, the creeps are coming out of the woodwork, emboldened. If the worst that happens is that someone retweets an offensive picture, then in times like this that's a win. But I also remember fighting for gay rights a decade ago and I feel like this thing is going to get worse before it gets better.

I didn't talk to anyone at the office about it, but Peter added a note that read, "Good timing," when he approved my letter. I'm sure the Marshall thing will blow over quickly. Today there will be breathless takes on whether or not this will affect the play of the Firebirds, and maybe tomorrow there'll be a story about Nativism, but tomorrow's Saturday so maybe not, and by Monday it'll be done. Maybe there'll be a couple awkward questions at Media Day on Tuesday, but likely something else will come up before then.

The University of Goldenwater in Emery has a lovely red brick campus in the middle of one of the most liberal cities in the country. There are old bookstores all over, coffee shops, vegan restaurants, and also Target, Starbucks, and Old Navy. We get lost trying to find Mike's appointment, so he downloads a campus map from their website to his phone and that gets us to a small mob of people in the lobby of a modern building with floor-to-ceiling glass to let in natural light.

The cheerful field mouse in charge of the tour comes up once we've been standing with the group for a minute. Mike gives his name and she turns to me. "Are you his father?"

"No, no," I say, resisting the urge to add that I'm only thirty-one. "I'm his brother."

"That's great," she says, and moves on to the next people in line.

"Step-brother," Mike clarifies to nobody.

My phone buzzes and I bring it out to see the message. "Hey, the Athletic Director just got back to me and she's free now. You mind if I bail on the tour?"

"Yeah, go do your job." He checks his own phone. "I've got the LGBT people after this so want to just meet at like one o'clock?"

"Sure. Here?" He nods, and off I go.

The meeting with Jody goes well. She's a meerkat, so she's receptive to the anti-Nativist stuff. She likes the tone of the letter, suggests a few changes, and tells me she appreciates the local team taking a stand like this. "It'll make a difference," she says. "Maybe not a big one, but every little bit helps."

That's what I'd hoped to hear, so I leave the office with a wag in my tail and an hour and forty-five minutes to kill before I have to meet Mike. I check my texts—nothing from Dev—and then I check my work email, and nothing's really going on there either. I write up a report for Peter on the meeting and tell him I think we'll be good to go with the letter.

Then I put my phone away and spend a happy hour or so wandering around one of the area bookstores, where I find a few interesting books, and by the time I'm done with that I'm getting hungry. I text Mike to ask if he's had lunch and he says no, so I scope out some good lunch places to take him.

We settle on a basic sandwich place that stuffs their deli meat into torpedo rolls. They're great, with a spicy pickle relish and brown mustard, and either lunch or the tour has perked Mike up. When I ask him how everything went, he talks about how pretty the campus is, prettier than Laurel, he thinks. I disagree, but hey, I'm not the one going to school, so my opinion doesn't matter as much. He does say that he's of two minds about the history of activism: he appreciates it but also feels like there's an expectation, especially if you're a minority, that you'll be vocal and agitate for change. "It's a lot of pressure," he says around a mouthful of tuna salad sub.

"What did the LGBT club say?"

"A lot of the same stuff about going to Potomac and all." He shrugs. "I guess if I want the company I'm going to have to get used to it."

"That's the current mindset."

"Yeah, I know." He flicks his tail from side to side. "How'd your meeting go?"

"Good. She liked what we're doing. I think we can go ahead with it."

It isn't until we're finished with lunch and walking back to the car that Mike says, "There was another genderqueer person there."

"At the sandwich shop?" I ask, more for comedic effect than because I actually think that's what he meant.

"In the LGBT club. I talked to them for a bit."

After a half-minute of just walking with no follow-up, I prod him. "And?"

"Oh, it was fine."

"Is this the first other genderqueer person you've met?"

"I've talked to a few online."

"But in real life?"

He nods. "Yeah."

"So?"

He takes a breath. "I dunno. I expected it to match up, like we'd be comparing experiences and it would all be the same. But they said they'd been genderqueer since they were thirteen and their parents were super-supportive, and they just don't classify themselves as either gender. Like they said they agitated for UG's official documents to add an 'Other' choice to any gender question and it went into effect this past fall."

"Mmm." I nod.

"But I don't want to be *neither* gender." His ears go back and his voice gets a little whiny. "I just don't want to be pinned down to one. And I told them that and they said, 'Oh, I used to be that way too, don't worry, you'll evolve.'"

"Ah. I hate that condescending bullshit. You know, back when I was coming out, people told me that I wasn't really gay if I didn't want to sleep with everyone and crap like that. Your journey is your own and just because someone else went through their journey one way doesn't mean you're going to go through yours the same way."

"Yeah." His ears come up and so does his smile. "Yeah. Thanks."

When we're in the car, he says, "There was one thing about it, though. I didn't think I'd like 'they' as a pronoun, but the way they used it, it felt... natural, I dunno."

I navigate us out onto the freeway. My idea is to spend the afternoon in Yerba shopping and sightseeing and then going to a drag club at night, so we've brought some of Mike's outfits to wear. "You want me to start calling you 'they' instead of 'he'?"

He stares out the window. "Maybe. I mean, you don't have to if you don't want to."

"I want to," I say. "Though I won't say it to you, so you won't have to hear it most of the time."

Their ears go back. "Don't tell your dad. Or Mom or Jaren."

"Not until you say it's okay," I promise. To myself I say, *Not until they say it's okay. They're trusting you.* I repeat the pronoun to impress it on my mind.

"I'll tell them sometime. Maybe." They relax back into the seat and stare out the window.

To lighten the mood, I try to think of something silly. "And maybe step-sib instead of step-brother."

Their muzzle twists into a grimace. "That sounds weird."

"Hey, 'my boyfriend' sounded weird to me when I was fifteen." I grin at them. "You get used to it."

They nod and fiddle with their phone, turning it over in their paws. "Okay, I guess."

"And you know, if we don't like it, we can go back to step-bro."

"Ugh." They stick out their tongue. "Step-brother, please. I don't want to be a bro."

"You got it." I laugh, and we go on down the road.

•

Mike was worried about where to change into their skirt, but I assured them we'd find a bathroom somewhere, and there's one in the café we stop into after I finally find parking near Korsat Street. Mike's nervous when I suggest it. "You're sure?" They eye the patrons, a bunch of people sitting around the café with their laptops and phones out, only one couple actually talking to each other.

"Trust me." I grin. "This café has seen way weirder stuff than someone changing clothes in the bathroom. Go grab your stuff from the trunk. I'll stay here so they remember we bought something." Not that that would be an issue here.

So I sit and sip my coffee while they get a skirt and a nice shirt to go with it from the car. Holding the tight bundle of clothes, they wait for the bathroom to be free, then shoot me a nervous glance as they go in. I give my best reassuring smile and try not to get caught up in my phone.

There's a followup to the thing with Dev's teammate, by which I mean that there's an actual interesting news item, as opposed to the dozen or so "what does this mean" stories. The Firebirds and Devils have both released nearly identical statements saying that they support every one of their players and that they don't condone the belief that some people don't "belong" here. It's pretty boilerplate, to be honest, but it's good that they got it out so quickly. I'm tempted to call up Hal and ask him what his thoughts on it are, but he's probably talking to Dev if he's talking to anyone. I look up his Twitter feed and see that he's been posting about an article a day, so he's keeping pretty busy. Nothing today yet, though.

A coyote lady comes over to my table; I double-take and a moment later I realize that it's Mike. "Whoa," I say. "You look great."

They smile, unsurely at first, and then more fully. "Really?" The bundle of shirt and pants that they'd been wearing lands on the chair across from me and they sit down, glancing nervously around the café.

"Absolutely."

"Nobody's staring, are they?"

I suppress a chuckle, because they're earnest and their ears are back and I get a flash of memory of the first time I went out cross-dressing. I wasn't as scared, and maybe that's because it wasn't as tied up in my identity as it is for them. "No, you look fine, and I don't think anyone noticed you coming out of the male restroom."

Their eyes widen and nostrils flare, and they half-check over their shoulder before scowling at me. "They were all-gender restrooms."

"I know, I'm just joking around. You smell right, too."

They don't respond to that, just look around the café again, so I make a mental note not to joke around so much. "Seriously," I say, "enjoy it. How does it feel?"

Their muzzle opens to answer, but they shut it without making a sound. One paw goes to their shirt, smoothing it down, and then they nod. "It's… nice."

"Good."

I check my phone again while they check out the café, and then I ask if they want a drink. "Oh, uh, sure," they say, and examine the menu board. "Mocha, I guess."

"Okay." I fish a twenty out of my pocket. "You want to order it?"

They stare at the bill and then look down at their skirt. It takes long enough that I have to bite back the impulse to go up and order the drink, but finally the coyote gives a decisive nod. "Yeah. I'll go."

They go up to the counter and stand in line, and though they stay pretty still, I'm watching closely enough to see their ears flick down and back up a couple times, to notice how still their tail stays under the skirt. When it's their turn, though, they order their mocha in a clear voice that maybe is a little higher than their usual.

The barista, a huge polar bear, doesn't act as though they're any different from any other customer. As I said, they get a lot of types in here—dyed fur, ear tucks, trans-species—and a female-presenting coyote who maybe smells a little too strongly of a feminine perfume hardly raises any eyebrows here. "Name?" the bear says, picking up the cup.

Here the coyote hesitates, and I perk up my ears. I haven't asked Mike about their name. "Mike" was a name you could pass off as a girl, with some explanation, but I'm curious whether they keep it or select a new one.

The hesitation goes on for a while, and then the coyote leans forward and says something too soft for even my attentive fox ears to eavesdrop on. The barista tilts her head forward, Mike repeats the name, still too softly for me to catch over the music and background conversation. Something like "Maxine" maybe, I think it might be.

They don't come back to the table, just wait over by the other side of the counter. And a few minutes later, the barista says, audibly to my ears, "Maxie," and holds out a cup which Mike—Maxie—takes.

"Maxie, huh?" I say as they sat down and sip.

Their ears flick back. "Just a name I was thinking about."

I nod. "It's nice. I like it. Where'd you come up with it?"

"FBA. We were watching a game and there was a player named 'Maxie Cole,' and Jaren said, 'is that a guy or a girl?' and it turned out to be a girl. But I liked how the name sounded and I started thinking about it when I would think about…" His ears flatten. "Dressing up."

"Cool." I gesture to the café door. "Want to sit for a while or want to walk around?"

"Can I drop the clothes in the car?"

I get up from my chair and pick up the t-shirt and jeans. "Sure. Let's go."

After dropping the clothes off, we walk down Korsat Street past more small cafes and clothing shops, the occasional bookstore. Maxie isn't talking much, so I decide to ask questions. "Tell me how you feel."

They take a few more steps before responding. "I keep looking at people looking at me and wondering what they see. It's a little scary, like someone's going to jump out at me and say, 'what are you doing?' But then…" On the other side of the street there's a sea otter wearing nothing but a Speedo even though the day is misty and cool, his fur shaved into patterns and dyed in rainbow stripes. I wait through Maxie's pause. "People like that really help. But mostly…it feels right. For right now. It's kind of like I'm in 'girl form' or something."

"I like that." I muse briefly on the idea that you could flip your gender around depending on how you feel. It's kinda cool, to be honest.

"But I am a little chilly." The shirt is thin and short-sleeved, and Maxie's got a thin coat of fur from growing up in the desert. "How is it sixty down where you are and like forty up here?"

"Welcome to Yerba." I nod toward a clothing store down the street. "Want to get a jacket?"

"Sure. I—What's this?"

They've stopped in front of a "novelty" store, which has a whole bunch of dildos right in the front window. I grin. "Do you seriously not know?"

They gape. "But that—I mean, like that one there—that's for…"

"Anyone who wants it."

Their eyes flick back to my tail. "Guys too?"

"Uh huh." I grab their wrist. "Come on, you're not allowed in there yet. If you go to college here, you'll spend more than your fair share of time in places like that."

So we go to the clothing store and get a stylish mink named Mia to help Maxie pick out a jacket. She gives them three to try on, and when Maxie goes back into the fitting room, she sidles up next to me and cups her elbow in her paw, resting her other paw against her muzzle. "So…" She draws the word out and bobs her muzzle toward the dressing room. "First time out?"

I crack a smile. "Is it that obvious?"

"Oh, I have an eye. You'd be surprised how many people come here with their first outfit looking to spruce it up or show it off." The mink smiles and taps her nose. "You can tell her that she looks great."

"Them."

She's experienced enough to nod. "Tell them they look great. If I had any advice, I would say maybe brush their fur a little more and brush some powder into it. The scent is good, but there are a few powders you can brush into your fur and then you don't need to spray extra scent all over." She turns and points toward the register. "We have a few powders here if they'd like to browse."

"Sure, let's do that."

Maxie comes out then modeling the lemon-yellow jacket. Mia and I agree that it looks good but that we want to see the others, too. There's a mint-green one in a different cut with mother-of-pearl buttons that I like a lot, and then there's another yellow one, lighter, that Mia likes most. "But," she says, "honestly they all look good on you, so it comes down to whichever one makes you feel the best."

Maxie runs their fingers down the lapels of the jacket, the light yellow one. "I like them all. But if I had to choose one…" They turn back and forth in front of the mirror. "I think I like this one."

"Great." Mia takes the other two jackets and folds them over her arm. "Anything else you want to look at?"

Maxie looks at some of the shirts but nothing catches their eye, so we take the jacket to the counter and look at some fur powders. They get one that they like, and I insist on getting another one that they say they like but didn't want to get. We walk out with Maxie wearing the jacket and holding a little bag with the fur powders.

"I can't wait to try them," they say, swinging the bag. "And thanks for the jacket."

"It looks good. Mia said so too." They seem more confident now, whether it's just the jacket or the fact that they've now gone through a couple public encounters. Korsat is one of the best places in the world to go out in non-traditional gear, so I'm hoping this evening builds up their confidence for some of the less welcoming places, whenever they feel they want to try those.

"Mia said that?"

"Yeah."

They lift their muzzle and smile as we go on down the street.

We grab dinner at one of the places on Korsat, talking more or less normally about family, about the schools, about sports. Nobody brings up Maxie's outfit or makes any comment about them. By the time the dinner's over, they're visibly more relaxed: ears up, tail swishing below the skirt. In fact, they go to the restroom and come back with their tail out over the skirt. I've seen skirts worn both ways and I prefer tail out, but some people like the tail hidden; they say it adds mystery. I think in Maxie's case it's just a measure of confidence, plus a lifetime of wearing pants which force your tail to be out. Then I notice a light scent and realize they've added a bit of fur powder to their tail. It clashes with the perfume, but not in a bad way, and here on Korsat, people wear clashing scents all the time anyway.

The all-ages drag club Cord recommended is a couple blocks away, and now a chilly breeze has kicked up that makes Maxie pull their jacket tighter closed. I'm even a bit chilly despite my winter fur, but I'm not so cold that I can't walk a couple blocks. "One thing to watch out for," I tell Maxie, "is that when you dress up—when you *are* in 'girl form,' guys will touch you."

They nod. "I read about that." Their eyes flick over to me. "Did that happen to you?"

"On a college campus? Fuck yes. It was…" I think back. "It wasn't cool, but at the time I took it like a sign that I was passing, you know? It was kind of like I was putting one over on them." I don't think that's how they feel about it, but maybe passing will be something positive they can focus on. "But here on Korsat, I don't know. Maybe I'll be more likely to be groped than you."

They laugh. "I see what you mean about passing, but it's still not okay."

"No. And hey, if you don't feel safe or you want to leave for any reason, just tell me. I want to make sure you have a good time and if that's not happening, we'll leave."

"Thanks." They shoot me a smile.

It's funny how things can change so quickly, I think, how just a week ago I had a stepbrother named Mike, and now I have a step-sibling who's sometimes Mike and sometimes Maxie and who isn't even quite sure how to navigate those identities. Watching someone come to terms with who they are in real time is fascinating, and being able to help them, even a little bit, is pretty cool. And now that Maxie's dressed up, it's easier to think of them in their new identity, though the fact that they still speak in Mike's voice is a little disorienting.

When we get into the drag club, we encounter another issue that I hadn't even thought of. It's not a canid-specific club, so although there's technically no smoking because of the ban on indoor smoking, there is vaping and there is illegal smoking and the place reeks of pot. Angela, liberal though she is, is pretty fanatically anti-drug and had D.A.R.E. posters up on both Jaren and Mike's bedroom walls until very recently.

So I see Maxie's nostrils flare, and they turn to me with a wide-eyed look. "Yeah," I say. "Pot's legal here now, but honestly it's been semi-legal for a while."

"I smelled it on the streets outside," they say, "but it's really strong here. Can…" They lower their voice. "Can I get high from it?"

I shake my head. "I don't think so, but like I said, if you start to feel bad then we can go."

"Okay." They rub their nose. "It stinks."

"Yeah." I chuckle. "What do you want to drink?"

They get a ginger ale and I get myself the same, because I might have to drive home at any time. Also I don't feel like paying fifteen bucks for a shitty cocktail or ten for a beer. We pad our way across the sticky floor to a corner that isn't so crowded—the tables are all taken—and watch the stage, waiting. We try to talk but the place is like five times louder than the restaurant was.

It doesn't feel like Maxie's having a good time, so at one point I say, "Just wait 'til the first act and then we can go," and they nod.

The emcee comes out to introduce the show, a pure white doe decked out in a red sequined dress, glittering beads sewn into the fur around her ears and in patterns down her tail, tinsel draped from her antlers. Maxie gapes as the deer swings her hips and purrs a welcome to the show. She introduces the first performer, a red fox named Quickly Brown, and slinks off the stage.

Maxie tugs on my sleeve. "I want that dress," they whisper.

That by itself makes me smile, this bold statement from someone who was so shy about skirt shopping yesterday. "We'll see what we can do."

If the emcee was sleek, Quickly Brown is fluffy. Her dress is layer upon layer of frilly pastel taffeta, lemon and siena with crimson trim, a headdress of two-foot tall pure white feathers, and white gloves that cover her natural black. No, I realize; she's dyed the fur on her forearms white and is wearing wrist corsages, white leather straps with yellow flowers on the backs of her paws.

She launches into a pretty good version of "Boy Is A Bottom" that makes me grin and Maxie fidget and tuck their tail down against the skirt. But they don't ask to leave, and in fact we stay through the next three performances before they say they're ready to go.

I am too at that point, so we walk out and away down the street. Even though it's getting on toward eleven, Korsat is still very active, and there are a bunch of clubs with crowds and lines. Maxie eyes them, but I tell them most of the clubs are over-18 only and they sigh.

At the car, they opt to stay in the jacket and skirt, smoothing the skirt out over their lap as they get in. We drive back with music from my phone, both of us quiet until I say, "So the sequin dress but not the fluffy one?"

"No," they say. "It seemed showy."

I can't help a laugh and then clamp my muzzle shut, afraid of offending them, but they laugh along with me after a moment. "I guess everything was pretty showy, huh?"

"That's kind of the point."

"Yeah."

They're smiling. So I ask, "You feel like you might want to be on stage?"

That gets a longer laugh. "I can't sing. I can't dance either."

"You can learn. I couldn't sing or dance when I got to college but I joined the theater group."

They turn to me, interested. "And now?"

I chuckle. "I can…sort of dance."

"What a ringing endorsement." They shake their head.

"I can act, though. I mean, better than I can sing, anyway."

They watch the lights of all the buildings pass by on either side of the freeway. "Can you sing better than Loris Day?"

"Definitely better than that. I mean, I wouldn't drive us out of an otherwise fun drag show."

"Her dress was cool too, though. All green and…" Maxie waves their paws. "Shimmery."

"Better than the sequins?"

They consider, then shake their head. "Nah."

Silence for a moment, and then they say, without looking at me. "Thanks. For taking me out and letting Maxie be out, and…it's just nice to have someone to talk to about this."

"Anytime," I say. "Glad it went well and you didn't get groped or anything."

"I got groped," they say.

"What?"

"By that waitress."

I shake my head. "Still not okay."

"No, but…" They lean back with a smile. "I saw her kissing the bartender, so…"

The bartender had also been female, or at least in drag. "Well, then. Congratulations?"

They nod. "It was a good night."

And a few minutes later a song comes on that I really like, so I sing along, softly. Maxie's ears perk, but they don't say anything until a moment later when they join in the chorus.

CHAPTER SEVENTEEN (DEV)

My Friday and Saturday are thankfully as boring as shit. Practice goes as practice does, I go out with Charm and Carson Friday night for a restrained night out, play FBA '17 with some of the guys from the D line, and wake up Saturday for our half-day. None of the shit with the Nativist guys bubbles up again, so I don't have to talk to Colin, and I know I'm supposed to maybe be thinking of something to do about it, but I also need to keep my focus on football. The biggest game of my career is coming up in just over a week, and while I know I'm as ready as I can be, I've learned over a decade that I can always be a bit more ready. I get treatment for my knee, my ribs, and anywhere else there's a little pain. I don't feel a hundred percent, but I shy away from taking painkillers unless I absolutely need them.

Even though Saturday's only a half-day, I spend the afternoon sitting in the film room with Gerrard and Carson and Price. To my surprise, we're only about ten minutes into it when Croz slams the door open and strides into the room. "Started without me?"

"Have a seat," Gerrard says as though he expected this all along.

To the rest of us, staring at him, Croz says, "Ah, what else am I gonna do on Saturday? Better see what these guys are gonna be up to. Every little edge, right?"

With that, the wolf settles back and we start on a good session of film study that takes us up until dinnertime. Gerrard lists a few specific things he wants us to focus on next week in practice and then says, "All right, good job everyone and thanks for being here. See you Monday."

Walking out, Croz takes me to one side. "He's giving us a day off? For real?"

"He doesn't like it," I say. "He and Coach had it out the first year, but Coach convinced him that taking a break from football can let us come back refreshed and ready, and then Coach ordered him not to schedule anything even voluntary on days off, so Gerrard kinda has to do what he says."

"Guess it took a run to the championship to get a day off." Croz laughs. "Hey, you want to come out tonight? Me and a couple of the guys are going to Templar to this cook-your-own-steak place."

"No thanks. If I want to cook my own steak, I'll fire up the grill," I say, even though I don't own a grill and am not allowed to have one in my apartment.

"Suit y'self," he says. "Look, we're not going to be talking Nativist shit if that bothers you."

"It does, but that's not the issue."

"All right, all right." The wolf raises a paw. "I'll catch ya Monday then."

"Yeah, see you then."

"What are you doing Sunday?" Price asks as Croz takes off in his own direction. "Catching up with the boyfriend?"

"No, he's flying out to—" I'm not supposed to tell anyone about his Cansez opportunity yet. "Somewhere for work."

"Don't ask Dev what his boyfriend's doing," Carson puts in.

"I didn't!" Price punches my shoulder. "I know better. He started telling me."

I punch him back. "My bad, my bad. Sorry. No, Lee's out of town. He's coming back for the game but I don't know exactly when. So I guess I'm going to go see a movie. I'll probably go for a run or something too just to keep everything loose."

"I got streaming if you want to watch movies in the hotel."

Price has good taste in movies from what I remember, so I nod. "Toss in a few beers and you're on."

"I'm supplying the movies. You bring the beer."

"Deal." I turn to Carson. "You in?"

He shrugs but keeps walking with me, which is an enthusiastic yes from him. And it occurs to me that I haven't talked to Carson about Marshall's idiot tweet thing. So we grab a drink in the bar and I ask him about it.

None of the guys on the team harass him, probably (if I had to guess) because he keeps to himself so much. Hell, most of the guys have their families come around at one point or another and I only met Carson's grandmother a few years ago at the last championship game, like six years into being teammates.

But he opens up more about his family than he has in the past. Like my parents, Carson's grandmother has been living in the same town for years, and most of this Nativist shit is about recent immigrants. Us big cats don't come in for a lot of the problems, except when maybe people want to harass me about being gay but don't want to be branded homophobes. Armadillos, chinchillas, sea otters, guys originally from areas of the world that are now poorer countries: those are the ones these shitheads object to. "Originally from" is such a weird term anyway. There's fossil records and historical records to show that, for example, my ancestors came from Siberia, far in the north. I might be tangentially related to some of the old tiger tsars of the 1500s (but probably not). So according to some schools of thought, that's my "homeland." But tigers migrated to what's now Gallia, passing through Deutscherbund and Etrusca and a bunch of other places, and some of them even apparently came over to this country with the Vikings back in the day. I've got an aunt and uncle in Anglia, too. So yeah, my grandfather might've been born in Siberia, but I was born here, and we were far from the first tigers on this continent, so as far as I'm concerned it's all just a load of crap designed to put a logical face on anti-immigrant sentiment.

Carson sees it a little differently, when I get a beer into him and get him to open up. He thinks part of it is searching for an identity, that there's a perception that a hundred years ago the States were just mice and deer, rabbits and foxes, wolves and bears—coincidentally a lot of the species that came over from Europe. You don't see so many of the raccoons and coyotes, the ones who are native to here and nowhere else. Anyway, old Army recruiting posters and commercial ads feature those species you see over and over again, the stereotypically "Statesian" species. People these days feel lost because times are hard for a lot of them, and so they reach back to this supposedly idyllic time and try to hold on to that sense of who they are.

"But it wasn't idyllic," I say. "I mean, my dad told me about times when they had just come to the States and they had to go through garbage to look for food, him and the other kids."

Carson nods. "Someone was throwing away that garbage, though."

"I guess."

He shakes his head. "I'm not saying it's not dumb. Just…there's something there." I nod and don't say much, and he goes on. "I talked to my grandmother about my ancestors, too. Her grandfather brought their family over from Africa to get away from a war. He always talked about how welcoming this country was, and she grew up believing that too. We never did real well here—until me—but we always got by."

"My dad was the same way. Always said we could be whatever we want here." He didn't believe I could be a football player, though to be fair I didn't either, not until Lee showed me.

Carson nods. "I don't think any of the guys on the team really believe in Nativism. It's easy to say shit, but push comes to shove, they'd support the guys they know."

"Push never comes to shove, though," I say. "Not for them."

•

That night, I get back to the hotel room early without much to do. Lee calls me, apologizing again for breaking our two-week break, or maybe now one-week break, but he's so excited about Mike—or Maxie now, I guess, but maybe only when he's dressing up like a girl? Lee doesn't explain it all that well. But whatever, the kid had a good time. I tell Lee I'm proud of him and catch him up on the stuff I've been doing.

"Hey, by the way…you were right about needing to address the Nativism thing. I can't believe I have to police that asshole Marshall."

He laughs. "The universe works in mysterious ways."

"So, uh…can you send me a copy of the letter you guys are doing or is it classified?"

He clicks his tongue. "I don't know if I can send you the letter, but—well, hell, you guys basically sent the same statement out. I'll send you a couple articles I found helpful and I'll write up a quick draft of my thoughts. The letter should go out in a day or two and I'll send it along then."

"Thanks. Okay, doc, I'm gonna go study some film."

"Do what you need to." He blows me a kiss and hangs up.

I get out my tablet and look through a few of the running plays the Devils run that had been worrying me. Their QB is great at play-action, faking the handoff and then throwing a pass, so I look through film to see if I can pick out anything in formations or movement that might tip me off as to what to look for. Gerrard's already been through this, but that doesn't stop me from doing my own research.

He also told me to look at film of some of their trick plays, because those are the ones that often go for big yardage in the playoffs. We've been pretty good about defending them, but the Devils cruised through the play-offs, so they haven't had to pull out any tricks and we have to go back to regular season games to see what they might run. And Gerrard went into their coaching tree to see what else they might have—for example, their offensive coordinator was a head coach in Gateway until he was fired, so I've got Gateway plays from a couple years ago. Their running backs coach used to coach at Taysha State, so I've got TSU plays from when he was there.

I don't even know what time it is when Wix gets back. "Hey hey!" he says, a little too loudly. The door slams behind him.

The current play on my tablet runs its course. I pause the film. "Hey. Good night out?"

"Pretty great," he says, and flops down on his bed. "Oh my god. The ceiling is spinning. Why is the ceiling spinning?"

"Let me guess." I get up and walk to the room fridge to grab one of our water bottles. "Someone bought shots."

"Me," Wix says. "I bought shots. For all the d-backs. One round for uh, thanks." He takes the water bottle. "For every interception in the playoffs."

"They took you to a bar?" I can't believe Colin would go along with someone underage drinking, but he definitely wouldn't let it happen in a public place.

"Nah. I gave Pock some money and he bought the booze and we did shots in the hotel room." He fumbles with the cap, but just as I'm about to help him, he twists it off and lifts it to his muzzle. Some water spills out over his lips and onto his neck, but he doesn't notice or care, just keeps drinking and drains nearly the entire bottle; what's left spills when he sets the bottle on the bed and it falls onto the floor.

"Hang on," I say. "I'll get another one."

"Ugh no, I'm fine, I'm not that drunk." He props himself up on his elbows.

"When the room stops spinning, you're fine." I grab another bottle and bring it over to him. "Remember Deleon?"

"Shit," he says, and takes the bottle, getting the cap off more easily this time. About a third of the bottle down, he tries to set it on the nightstand and I take it so it doesn't fall over. He wipes his mouth. "Thanks."

"I was young and dumb once too," I say.

He grins and pokes my hip. "But now you're not young no more."

"Ha ha." I start to walk away, but he grabs my pants.

"Don't go," he says, holding on. "Thanks for takin' care of me. I really appreciate it."

"No problem. That's what roommates are for."

"Yeah." He looks up and his eyes are wide and earnest. "I told Coach I was gay so they'd give me you as a roommate."

"What?"

He nods. "Yeah. I mean, I am really, but I didn't have to tell 'em. I mean, I wanted to but I could've not, like I didn't tell the other guys. But god damn, I grew up idolizing you. Like the moment I knew I was gay, you were the one who made me believe I could still play football."

"Wait, seriously?" I sit on the bed beside him.

He lets go of my pants and wipes his muzzle again. "Seriously. I came out to my coach in college and he said I shouldn't ever tell anyone if I wanted to play in the UFL and I said 'what about Devlin Miski' and he said if I was as good as you then I could come out. So uh. I decided I was gonna be as good as you and I worked so hard."

I get letters, of course, and Lee reads most of them for me and sends on the best ones. But I rarely come face to face with the guys who say things like this. "You're good enough to play in the UFL," I say. "And I don't think anyone will care if you come out."

"Yeah, but whatever," he waves a paw. "I'm here and you're here and that's cool and I just wanted to say that."

"Thanks." I wait to see if there's more, but his eyes are fluttering shut. "Hey," I say. "Finish the rest of that water before you pass out."

"Uh huh," he mumbles, and drains the bottle.

He seems to be okay, so I go back to my film, but I can only keep watching it for twenty more minutes because I keep thinking about what Wix was saying. I get why he didn't tell me; it would've made our dynamic weird. As it is, it's a little uncomfortable, but at least we have a whole semester of being friends to look back on without having that 'hero' conversation as its foundation. And it's pretty cool to think about this kid striving to make it to the UFL in part because of me.

I wonder if that's how Lee feels about me. It's not the same, of course, and I know he's proud of me. He always makes sure to remind me that even though I worked hard because of him, it was still my work, my effort, my talent that got me where I am. Probably I should say something like that to Wix, but the bobcat is pretty insensible now, so I'll say something in the morning. If he even remembers the conversation. And if he doesn't, I shouldn't remind him. Still, it feels good.

•

The room is dark when I wake up to pressure on my bed and a hissing whisper. "Dev. Dev."

"Mwuh?" Not at my best when I'm disoriented and coming out of sleep.

A paw shakes my shoulder. "Hey."

Wix's breath still smells of whisky. "I know this isn't the best way to do this but fuck it, look, the guys went out to a strip club and I'm fuckin' pent up and I figured maybe you weren't picking up on my signals on account of being old and married and shit but look…"

"I'm not married," I say. "What?"

A couple more wafts of whisky-sour air float past my whiskers. "You want a blow job?"

"Uh." My first instinct is to say no, but Lee specifically told me this would be okay. And fuck, I'm getting hard thinking about it. It's been a week since I fucked my fox and I'm pent up too.

"I'm not drunk anymore. Not really." He moves his paw to my chest. "Look, I just want—you don't have to do anything. I'll go jerk off in the bathroom after. I mean, if you want to, but—I just want a cock in my mouth, I want to get someone off. You know what I mean, right?"

I can't say I don't miss my fox's length in my paw, on my tongue; or that I don't miss his warmth clenching around me. And in the middle of the night, with someone leaning over me offering to give me some release, the decision is harder than I would've thought. But… "You're drunk," I say, to stall.

He shakes his head. "No. I mean, not that much. It's just a blow job." His paw fumbles at the nightstand where my phone sits. "You wanna text your boyfriend and ask permission?"

"No." I'm a little more awake, but still it's the middle of the night and now I'm getting harder because I'm thinking about blow jobs and it's been a week, for fuck's sake.

Wix takes that as assent, and reaches down to grab my half-hard cock through the sheets. "Cool," he says. "Just lay back."

"Hey." He's already getting the covers back, scooting down the bed.

"It's cool." His warm paw closes around my cock.

Dammit. "Hey, Wix. Wixin."

His lips brush it and then his tongue, soft. "Wix, uh." But his mouth opens and enfolds me, and I think again, Lee did say it would be fine, he wouldn't be mad. At this rate it won't take long and that's all it'll be, just a two-minute blow job in the middle of the night and we probably won't even talk about it again.

And then I think, is that what I want? I want release, yes, frankly aching for it at this point. But there's still enough of my non-dick brain active to point out that I can always go finish myself in the bathroom, that this is probably not the best thing for me to do with my roommate. Then I wonder how Wix will feel if I push him away when he's already sucking me off, and by that point it's starting to be clear that if I don't make a decision soon, the time will be over.

So I squirm away from him, push him away by the shoulders. "Hey," I say again. "Thanks, I appreciate the thought, but you know, I don't—I don't think this is the right way to do it."

His eyes shine in the dim room. "Seemed to be pretty right from my perspective."

"No, I know, but…" I waver, again.

He rests a paw on my stomach. "I'm not gonna tell anyone. But if you're not into it…"

And now I wonder about spending another week with Wix after pushing him away, if he'd be resentful or ashamed. He'd at least be annoyed, I'm sure. For god's sake, he's already had his muzzle on my cock; whether I finish or not is almost immaterial at this point. The real question is whether I trust that Lee really will be fine with it, and I have learned over the years to take him at his word.

So I nod, lie back, and say, "Go on," and he does.

It doesn't take very long, and when I'm done, Wix gets up from the bed, pulls the covers back up over me, and trots to the bathroom. In the brief glimpse I get between him turning on the light and closing the door, I see that he's pretty hard himself. I should ask Lee if I can jerk him off in exchange, I think muzzily, but maybe I'll do that in the morning.

Chapter Eighteen (Lee)

When my step-sib wakes up and comes downstairs in a t-shirt and jeans, phone in one paw, I'm already eating my breakfast. "I made bacon," I say, "and if you want an egg I'll make one."

"Sure." He—they (I'm still making that mistake in my head) sit down at the kitchen table, rubbing sleep and maybe a little glitter from their eyes.

I go to the stove and crack an egg. "So is Maxie just when you're dressed—in 'girl form'?"

They nod. "I'm still Mike." They look up from their phone. "Sometimes."

"I think that's really cool. I'm glad you had a good time out."

They're quiet, pensive, playing with their phone but not looking at it. As if realizing only in that moment that they hadn't responded, they snap around to me. "Oh yeah, I did. It was great. It was—really good."

"If you want to go out again tonight, I don't know any specific acts, but we could for sure go walk around Korsat Street. Or even down here, there are a few clubs."

They nod. "Yeah maybe."

"You're flying home tomorrow, and unless you're going to come out to your family—"

"Ha."

"—this might be your last chance for a while."

They don't answer, so I say, "Though you can come visit here whenever you want. If you end up deciding to apply to one of these places, you'll have a good reason, but you don't even need that. I'm happy to have you here for a weekend any time. With some warning."

"Oh sure."

The egg finishes; I slide it onto a plate, add some bacon, and bring it over to him—to them. I don't know why I'm relapsing into thinking the wrong pronouns. Just a reset in the morning, I guess, seeing them in t-shirt and jeans bringing back all the memories.

"I was thinking," Mike says as they eat the bacon and egg, "maybe you could dig out one of your outfits?"

"Oh." I hadn't thought about that. It'd be a nice bonding thing to do for sure. "Maybe, yeah. I'll have to go see what I still have in the closet."

We finish up breakfast, Mike considerably cheerier, and take a trip down to Bautista, to the campus of Bautista State. This is the cheapest of the three schools we're going to see, but the campus is as pretty as either of the others. Mike goes off to have their campus tour and meet with the LGBT club, and I sit in a Starbucks nearby and go through work stuff.

Peter's approved Jody's changes to our letter about the Nativist movement and directs me to send it out to all the athletic directors we work with. So I tell Cord to get that list together and ready to go out Monday morning. Then I go through the rest of the emails piled up from yesterday—Remington's agent again with his client's official statement, notes from a few of the scouts, a letter from Peter about our draft board, one note reminding me about an incident that happened with one of the players we scouted, an injury worse than we'd expected, so I add that to my reply to Peter about the draft board…one thing after another, and then before I know it, Mike's back, tail swishing and ears perked.

I close the laptop and indicate the counter. "You want anything?"

We walk around a bit with our lattes, talking about the visit. I ask how they like the campus and the school and the group. "It's cool," they say. "I like the LGBT group at Golden better, but the school here has this really casual atmosphere that I like. Everyone at the other schools is such a…" They pause. "This sounds bad when I say it out loud, but like, everyone there wants to change the world and be a leader in business or politics or activism or whatever, and I…I just want to learn sports medicine, maybe, and figure out who I am. I don't want to save the world."

"I get that."

"I know that makes me sound like a bad person." They sigh. "Jaren wants to, like, play basketball and make it to the FBA and start a charity for cubs of single parents. He's great, you know, I wish I was like him. But I don't have the energy."

"That's totally cool. I wanted to change the world in college, and I ended up helping run a football team, so I'm not sure how that tracks. Maybe it's better to start with achievable goals and work your way up to bigger things as the opportunities come up." A gust of wind flattens both our ears. "Plus, college is a place where you can figure it out and change your goals and stuff. You could decide you want to write poetry, or maybe study chemical engineering."

Mike snorts, and I nod. "Bad example. Nobody wants to study chemical engineering. But seriously, something might come up. You'll meet new people, take electives…" I wave a paw. "Maybe some cute guy will get you to join a theater group."

"I'm not gay."

"Cute girl, then. The point is, you never know what's going to happen, especially in college. And it's a year and a half away, you've still got to take your tests and apply, you're probably going to check out some schools in Pelagia and maybe Crystal City."

"That's still a little close. Pelagia maybe."

"Sure, whatever."

We go on a little longer and then they ask, "Have you thought about tonight?"

I haven't, not very much, but going back through work for the last couple hours reminds me that I'm not a college student anymore. "You know," I say, "I'd love to. But I have a prominent position with the team now. Going out to gay clubs is one thing—I'm out, I'm proud, everyone's cool with it, or at least they've made their peace. But cross-dressing is something new. Honestly, it's not just what my current job might think of it, it's also my future opportunities. Like the job I'm interviewing for next week."

"Oh. Right." Their ears go back, though the wind has calmed. "I get it."

"Sorry."

"No, it makes sense. I don't have a job or anything and colleges are more accepting, so…" They shrug. "I guess you already made your choices."

They mean it to hurt, a little jibe at how old I am because they're disappointed I won't keep them company. I bite back a lot of snappy remarks and try to remember what it was like being the only gay cub (that I knew of) in my high school. If I'd had a cool older brother—or even an older brother who was maybe half as cool as he thought he was—who was also gay but wouldn't go out to clubs with me for fear of losing his job, what would Lee-the-high-school-junior have said? Something way worse than "I guess you already made your choices."

We pass a theater and impulsively decide to see a movie, and then we grab dinner. Mike's still wavering on dressing up until I point out again that it might be their last chance, and that finally does convince them.

They try a different outfit, and this time they dress at my townhouse and ride that way in the car all the way up. I call them Maxie in my head all the way up and once out loud when I want to get their attention. They turn at that and give me a little smile, acknowledging the name. I feel pretty good about it.

We hang out at a gay bar and because we're obviously together, nobody comes up to us. Maxie asks a little nervously if people will think we're a straight couple, and I laugh and say that nobody thinks that. Then I have to explain that probably the people in the bar buy that Maxie's female, that they don't care about what their underlying biology is, and that it's not what the configuration of our relationship is, it's that we're clearly not cruising.

But I am sort of subtly cruising. Not making eye contact, but checking out who's around. It's been a week and I'm missing Dev a lot, enough that I spend a non-trivial amount of time figuring out how long after we get back I reasonably need to wait before I can jerk off in my bathroom, and whether I'd be better off doing it here in a bathroom. I wouldn't be the first, that's for sure.

So when we head home, because it's a fairly reasonable hour, I give Dev a call. I want to tell him to jerk off, to describe himself jerking off so I can do it too, but I have to at least keep to the spirit of our break. I want to tease him about Wix again because I like the image of the bobcat with Dev's cock in his mouth, but I realize that if I bring it up again, Dev's going to think I *want* him and Wix to fuck. Maybe he'll think I want to watch or something. That might be pretty hot, come to think of it.

I hang up and head to the bathroom to take care of myself, worked up as I am now. Pants down and fully hard, I stop when I hear Mike moving around downstairs. They don't leave their room, but still, I can't bring myself to finish until they've quieted down. Coyote ears are as sensitive as fox ears, almost, and if I can hear them, they can hear me. I've just about figured they went back to sleep when a soft murmur filters through the walls to me. I perk up my ears and regretfully unwrap my fingers from my ready shaft. Quietly, I ease the bathroom door open and pad out into my master bedroom, ears scanning for the source of the sound.

It's Mike, talking in their room. Or maybe just watching a show on their phone. I can't make out the words, so I lean closer to listen and then, as sometimes happens, I take stock of the situation as though I were an impartial outside observer, like Hal writing a headline. 31-Year Old Fox Masturbates While Eavesdropping on 16-Year-Old Younger Stepbrother.

It's always weird when I remember my age like that. I still think of myself as like mid-twenties, but of course I'm not. I fold my ears down and creep back to the bathroom, where I shut the door, take out my phone, and bring up some naked pictures of Dev that I keep for moments like this. I'm as quiet as I can be, and when I'm done and cleaned up and I go back into the bedroom with my pants up, Mike's room is quiet.

•

In the morning, I'm still bleary when I get a call from Dev. "He did it," he says tersely before I even finish my good morning to him.

"Who did what?"

"Wix." He breathes in. "He came back last night drunk, and he talked about how much he admired me and how he's been killing himself to be chill all year, and then we went to sleep and he came over to my bed and sucked me off."

"Oh."

He waits while I register all that. "You said it was okay, right? That's the only reason I let it happen."

"I did say that."

"So it's okay?"

"Yeah, stud, it's fine, I'm sorry, it's like seven in the morning and it's Sunday for Fox's sake."

"Sorry, he's showering now and I didn't know if you'd be busy later."

I roll over onto my back and stare at the ceiling. "I mean, I was half-awake, but I'm still waiting for the other half to catch up. Sorry. Yes, I said it was fine and I meant it. Did you do him?"

"No, he went and jerked off in the bathroom."

"Hey, just like me."

"What?"

I yawn and cover my eyes with a paw. "Glamorous Saturday night. Out at the clubs with my genderqueer stepbrother, come home and jerk off on the toilet."

"Aw, doc."

"Hey, this two-week break was at least partly my idea. We're doing really badly at it, by the way."

"I've noticed." He sighs. "Did Mike have a good time?"

"I think so." It's not worth mentioning his disappointment in me, not right now. "Did Wix?"

He makes a strangled chuckle. "He hasn't said anything yet this morning but I pretended to be asleep when he got in the shower. But I think so. It was really awkward, Lee. Like he was halfway down on me before I tried to make him stop, and then I kept thinking about how maybe he'd get all upset if I rejected him, and you'd said it would be okay."

"Yes, I remember." I can't help a chuckle. "You had guilt sex. That's kind of adorable. And a little messed up."

"He was drunk!"

"Yeah, I know. Was he good?"

"Not as good as you."

"That's what I needed to hear. Good tiger."

"It's true."

"All right, all right. I'm just going to have to reward you when you win the championship."

He exhales, relief and amusement and desire all in a breathy, "Heh heh," and then, "If I win the championship—"

"When."

"If I win the championship, I don't want to fuck your mouth."

"Deal," I say. "And—"

"He's out of the shower," Dev hisses. "Talk to you later."

He hangs up, and I say to the dead phone, "Probably tonight, at this rate."

Chapter Nineteen (Dev)

When Wix comes out of the shower, I'm sitting up in bed so there's no question I'm awake. I'm ready for whatever mood he's got, I tell myself, although where Lee probably would've run through every possibility twice in his head, I'm just repeating, *Lee said it was okay*, over and over.

"Morning," Wix says cheerfully, opening the bathroom door and walking out naked, half-erect, like usual.

"Hi." I keep my eyes on him as he goes to the dresser, humming, and takes out a pair of boxers and a t-shirt. "How you feeling?"

"Minor hangover, nothing a bunch of bacon and eggs won't fix." He pauses. "You okay?"

"Uh huh." I tilt my head. "You remember much of last night?"

He pulls the t-shirt on, leaving his sheath exposed. "What, the blow job?" He cups his sheath. "Did your boyfriend say you can recip?"

"No. I mean, I didn't ask, but no, he didn't say—" I stop. "You remember it, then."

"Yeah." He grins and pulls on his underwear. "Been wanting to do that for a while."

"You said."

Now he stands up from the dresser, sweatpants in one paw. "I did?"

"Yeah. You said you looked up to me, that you'd been crushing on me the whole year."

"Ah, fuck." The pants dangle from his paw, hanging limp as his ears go back and his other paw covers his face. "That musta been when I was drunk. I don't remember coming back to the room at all. Just waking up in bed and thinking I should go suck you off because I might not get another chance."

"We're rooming together another whole week." I'm getting a little hard remembering the blow job, especially now Lee confirmed he's not mad.

"Yeah, but there's practice every day and we'll be getting up early and then as the game gets closer it's gonna be tense." He waves a paw and now pulls his sweatpants on. "Can't believe I did the drunk confessional though. That's so fuckin' lame." He adjusts the snap at the back over his tail.

"It was sweet," I say, partly to tease him.

He rolls his eyes. "Do me a favor and don't tell anyone about it?"

I laugh. "But I can tell people about the blow job?"

"I figure you'll tell the boyfriend, at least." Wix flexes his shoulders and drapes a warmup sweat over his t-shirt, but doesn't put his arms through the sleeves.

"Yeah." I curl my tail back and forth. My hip has a little cramp in it, so I massage it. Might be worth going to the trainer for that later today. "Where you off to?"

"Getting the fuck out of here before some asshat makes me do laundry. Couple of the other rooks are going to spend the day down in Game Burger."

"You're going to play arcade games all day?"

"And pop-a-shot." He mimes shooting a basketball. "I'm gonna show that rhino who's got the sweetest jumper on the team."

"Good luck."

He heads for the door. "What about you?"

"Gonna visit the trainer, get some work done, probably study some film. Maybe grab Ty and go on a hike or something."

Wix shakes his head on his way out the door. "Can't wait 'til I get old," he mutters, and grins at me as he leaves.

•

Down at the trainer, there's a bunch of guys getting treatment. I ask and they say they'll have a spot for me in a minute, so I go next door where a few other guys are working out and I walk on the treadmill, setting it for five minutes. While I'm walking, Colin and Marshall walk in, deep in conversation. They're keeping their voices low, but not many other people are talking, so I can hear what they're saying.

"Fucking snowflakes," the bear's saying.

"I know," Colin says. "It sucks. But it's the team, it's the championship. Just say the fuckin' thing and everyone'll forget about it and we'll win a title and then you can say whatever the fuck you want."

"Thought you'd have my back," Marshall grumbles.

They haven't noticed me yet. "I do," Colin says, all earnest. Maybe a little too earnest. "You just gotta be cool for one more week."

"It was a fucking joke," Marshall growls.

The trainer steps past them into the workout room. "Miski," he calls. "C'mon in."

Fox and bear both swing their heads around to me and shut up. I ignore them and walk in to get the massage on my hip.

"What else hurts?" the trainer asks after about ten minutes of digging into my hip muscles.

"Hard to tell now," I grumble, hip throbbing, though I know it'll feel better in a minute. "But knees."

"Sure." This guy knows me, knows all the injuries that don't go away at this point. "Any other tightness anywhere, anything unusual?"

I point to my left shoulder. "That was twinging yesterday. Seems okay today though."

"Lucky. Still, let's give it some work." And he does, making me regret telling him anything.

When he's done, he drops some ice packs on my shoulder and hips and sets a fifteen-minute timer while he goes to work on some of the other guys.

The immediate physical sensations remind me of my thoughts on retirement. The practices are one thing, because there's adrenaline going—not as much as game time, but to keep doing this for ten years, you've gotta still be able to hype yourself up for practice. But the days off, that's when you feel the accumulation of all the previous years of work. Used to be if I woke up with a twinge in my hip, it'd go away in an hour, and still before that, I didn't wake up with twinges. But you don't think about that, or you try not to, because you can still play through it, and the pain isn't so much that it's driving you to make a change.

Fisher's case is another cautionary tale, but I'm not having memory issues and my concussion tests all come back clear. The shaky departure of the Crystal City quarterback from our semifinal game keeps popping into my head, so when I get done with the ice I grab my phone and try to find out his status, which is harder than usual because they're not playing in a game, so there isn't national interest in his health anymore. Finally I send a text to one of my friends on the Sabretooths to ask if they can verify that he's okay, and then a few minutes later it occurs to me to send Hal a text as well.

I go out to the field for a jog around the track to loosen myself up and I think about the future. This is as good a team as I can remember being on, but if we don't win the title (right now we're three-point favorites, which is about the amount you get from having home-field advantage), then will we do it next year? I went to the championship in 2009, then five years later in 2014, and now three years after that. I probably have one or two top-tier years left, maybe another if I take care of myself, and then I could play another three if we get a star in when Carson retires (I'm sure he'll be gone next year, if not at the end of this one). That's a short window in a league where it's rare to go to the championship two years in a row, where since I've been playing we've gone from sixteen teams to twenty and will probably be at twenty-four in another two years. If what I want is the title, is it worth beating myself up for, taking all that punishment and fucking up the rest of my life even more? If I don't get it, it will all be for nothing but a couple more years of money, and we've got enough in the bank even without Lee's good salary.

My paws pound around and around the track. I remember jogging around this field—no, wait, it was a practice field we don't use anymore. Anyway, back when I'd first come to the Firebirds, Fisher had taken me under his wing. He got me to switch from corner to linebacker, a move the Dragons hadn't thought to try (they talked about moving me to safety when I got off special teams, but they traded me before that happened).

Since then, I haven't suggested a drastic change like that for anyone else, but I've worked with plenty of players on the defense, helped rookies get used to UFL life, and generally feel like I've paid it forward. I don't know whether to count "letting Wix blow me" under that column, but he seemed pretty happy about it, so maybe half-credit.

Where's the balance between the drive to keep playing and the mortgage on my body for the remaining years of my life? Even if we win the title, I can feel that I'll want to win another one, but would that be worth losing ten years with Lee at the back end of things? Or more, as happened to Fisher?

I'm rounding the last turn on my fifth lap and debating finishing up as a fox walks out of the workout room and looks toward me, arms folded. At first I think it's Ty, but the body language isn't right and I realize a moment later that it's Colin.

As I get closer, I slow down, though I don't realize I'm doing it until my fitness tracker beeps at me for going below my usual pace. I tell it the workout's over and walk up to Colin.

"I just wanted to let you know," he says, "that I talked to Marshall and he's deleted that tweet, or undid the retweet or whatever, and he's not going to say anything else until after the championship."

"Thanks." I don't know whether he would've told me if he hadn't seen me overhear him and Marshall, but it's at least a good gesture that he did.

He turns to leave, but I feel motivated to test this fragile détente. "Hey."

His exasperated sigh makes me regret my boldness right away. "What?"

"Do you believe all that shit?"

The fox turns, tail flicking like Lee's does when he's mad. "What shit?"

"I know you think I'm an offense to God or some shit like that, whatever, and you talk about our country's precious heritage all the time, but do you really believe everyone should go back where they quote-unquote came from?" He doesn't answer right away, so I continue. "Does he?"

"I don't know what he believes," Colin says. "We don't talk about it. Why do you care, anyway? You see my cross and immediately know everything about me, so what does it matter? We're not going to be friends."

"I'm just curious. It'd be interesting if we agreed on something, don't you think? Might be good for the defense to know."

He shrugs. "People make good points about immigrants flooding this country. But people who've lived here a couple generations probably earned the right to stay." He flicks an ear at a bug or something. "As long as they haven't been committing crimes."

"Some people at the airport yelled at me to go home," I say.

"What do you want from me? You're pretty good at ignoring advice you don't want to hear, so why do you care what some idiots yelled at you?"

"Yeah, I know." I shake my head. "All right. Thanks for telling me. I guess we're doing that practice thing again Wednesday and Thursday."

He rolls his eyes. "Looking forward to it," he says, dripping sarcasm like he's just walked out of a shower of it.

And yep, that's Colin all right. I do a few leg stretches mostly so I won't have to walk right behind him back into the locker room.

The Nativist thing is still bugging me, though. I appreciate that Colin talked to Marshall about it, but he doesn't seem to know or care what it's about, just that it pisses people off. From the stuff Lee sent me, it feels like something we should all understand, because even though Carson and I don't feel particularly targeted, that doesn't mean that nobody does. It doesn't mean that it's harmless. If I'm being honest, even though it's not aimed at me, it makes me feel excluded, and never mind that it's from a group I don't care to belong to.

But a nebulous feeling of being excluded sounds like "they hurt my feelings," and I can only imagine the reaction of my teammates if I start whining like that. Besides, it's not really my place to preach to the whole team. I'm not sure what to do, so I give myself the rest of the day to think about it.

•

Ty and I go out for a hike for the rest of the day, out in the foothills around Chevali. It's a nice, sunny desert day with cool breezes and hot overhead sun as we walk through scrub brush up to the big brownish-orange rocky bluffs jutting up from the ground. I take a few pictures with my phone to send to Lee at some point, and Ty takes even more pictures to send to his wife and boyfriend. I'm not a huge fan of the outdoors, to be honest, and neither is Ty, but it's a relief to get away from the locker room, and in the winter, it's not too hot and the dusty desert smell is overwhelmed by the blooming flowers and grasses all around.

We talk for a little bit about the Nativist thing, but not a lot because neither of us wants to dwell on it. Mostly we talk about the game, about family, about other sports. It's nice to get away, and when we get back I'm refreshed for the week ahead.

There's one conversation I feel like I need to have, so when Wix gets back to the hotel room I put my tablet aside and say, "Hey, can I talk to you just a second?"

He flops down onto his bed facing me. "Sure, what's up?"

"So, about last night…I get why it happened, and it's cool and all, but that should be a one-time thing."

Wix tilts his head, ears perked. "Was it not good?"

"It was good, yeah."

"So why should it be a one-time thing? I'm not asking for a return."

I look down at my tablet, but of course the answer to that question isn't contained in the film of the Devils running a mesh play. "I don't want to become one of those guys who cheats on his boyfriend all the time."

"You said it was okay with him."

"It is."

"Then it's not cheating." He grins at me.

I close my eyes. "I know technically it's not, but it doesn't feel right to me."

He sits up and leans back against the head of the bed. "I'm just teasin' ya," he says. "You don't want to do it again, I won't force you."

"You probably won't be drunk enough again before the game anyway." I give it a teasing tone.

"Don't have to be drunk," he says, taking out his phone. "Wasn't."

"All right." I don't follow it up because I've made my point. I feel pretty good, in fact. Colin's being slightly less of a prick than usual, Lee's not going to leave me over a blow job, Wix is okay, and yeah, I got a pretty good blow job out of it. Maybe I don't need to worry about Marshall and Colin and the Nativist shit. Maybe the week coming up can just be about football.

Chapter Twenty (Lee)

In the morning, Mike and I run out to the corner coffee shop for breakfast and walk around the little main street of the town where I live (a town that runs seamlessly into all the towns around it, each with its own shopping and restaurant street). We grab lunch at a burger place and then I take them to the airport. They say they had a great time and will definitely come back to visit. "If you're still here."

"I'll probably be here," I say, standing with them at the entrance to the security checkpoint. "There's so much more to do than football here."

Their ears come up. "Good luck with the interviews anyway. I hope you don't move to Cansez."

"Me too. But if I have to, I could take it for a little while."

"I guess I could see that. Wherever I go for college isn't forever."

"Sure." I perk my ears. "You have lots more options for college than I do for work, though."

"I guess. But I have to go where they let me in, right?"

"You can pick where to apply. Your brother only tried U of Chevali and Landon College, so…I'm glad you're aiming higher." I reach out to clasp his paw again. "And that you're figuring out who you are. Now git, you're gonna miss your flight."

He shakes my paw. "Thanks again for letting me visit." He waves and disappears into the security line.

I keep an eye on the flight to make sure it's not delayed or anything, and I call Angela from my car on the way home to let her know Mike's flight is on its way.

"Oh, good," she says. "Sorry things didn't work out so well there."

This catches me off guard. "What?"

"Jaren asked Mike which of the schools he'd want to go to and it sounded like he didn't like any of them. I was going to ask you if you knew what happened."

I'm already reviewing all the visits, but… "I wasn't with him for most of them, but it sounded like they were fine." The only things I can think of that he wasn't satisfied with were the LGBT group meetings, and I can't mention those.

"Teenagers," she says. "You never know what they're thinking. I hoped he might connect with you a little."

"We did connect, I thought. We went out together a couple nights and I thought he had a good time." I catch up to what she said. "Wait, what do you mean 'connect'? We were already friends."

She pauses. "I know I have to wait until he tells me, but he's been quieter since around the wedding. At first Bren and I thought that he was getting used to having a stepfather, but we don't think it's that. So we wondered—we hoped—he was having some sexuality questions."

"You hoped."

"The alternative is depression or drugs, right? He doesn't seem depressed—I mean, he's not having trouble getting out of bed or anything. I used an online quiz and he scored medium as a risk for depression. But he was really excited to go out there and visit, more than he's been about soccer even."

This surprises me; Mike seemed pretty low-key. "Really?"

She gets brighter. "Yes, absolutely. It was a relief, really, because it was going on so long and I wanted him to have something to look forward to. But if he did talk to you about sexuality, you don't have to say anything to me. He'll tell me in his own time."

I weigh the confidence Mike trusted me with against familial duty. "I won't tell you what we talked about, but I will say it's not depression or drugs. I think he doesn't know how to tell you."

She exhales. "It's hard with Mike. Jaren's so easy. He's outgoing, he'll come tell me about things, like when he thought he got that girl pregnant, oh my god. But then it's out in the open and we deal with it. I know Mike has to find his own path, but I really hope I can be part of it."

"You will be. I know he loves you," I say, because that's beyond question. It's the worry about losing the relationship with Angela that stops them from telling her. If they didn't care about her, they wouldn't care about what they told her.

"Thanks, Lee." The smile is evident in her tone. "I know it'll work out all right."

"Sure thing. I told Mike they're free to visit anytime, so," ah shit, I used his preferred pronoun to his mom, fuck, "hope he can make it back out here."

"Who's free to visit?" Angela asks.

My ears get all warm as I fold them down. "Just that I can arrange my schedule whenever," I say. "Sorry, I'm getting off the freeway and dealing with traffic."

"Oh, okay. I hope he wants to go back out there again."

"Me too." Slowly my ears come up.

Angela doesn't have any more embarrassing questions, so as I pull into my garage we hang up. She promises to give my best to my father and I tell her I'll call him either from Cansez or before I head out there.

I have work emails to look at, but I find it hard to focus on them because I really want to know: why didn't Mike want to go to any of the schools out here?

•

Work consumes the rest of my day; if I'm going to take off Monday and Tuesday, I need to get a lot of stuff out of the way first. Mike doesn't call me when they get back to Chevali, nor does my dad call me, nor does Dev.

Who does call me is Cord, to ask if I want to grab a drink at the club by the bay shore, a place the team did a private picnic last year. I've been meaning to talk to him anyway, so I accept. When we get there, there's a stiff breeze off the bay, so we sit inside and look out the patio windows at the shorebirds and the ripples made by the wind.

"Me and Jess talked on Friday," he says after we sit down. "About you and Cansez and everything."

He waits, so I nod. He rustles his wings and goes on. "Anyway, Jess doesn't have as much fur in the fight, but she said I was being a dick, kinda, about that. I thought it through and it makes a lot of sense for you."

"Why were you so mad? I didn't even get an offer, much less decide to take it."

Cord looks away, ears going back. "Ah, you know, we've been doing some good work here with gay rights. That's kinda what I thought you were here for. Outreach to gay athletes, helping spread tolerance in the league. Like that Nativist letter—it's not gay rights specifically, but it felt worthwhile."

"I can still do that in Cansez," I say. "And again, not to press a point, but I don't even have a decision to make yet. You're acting like I already left."

"I know." He rests one paw on the glass, long fingers stretched out. "But you're going out for the interview, and that means there's a chance."

"I really don't want to live in Cansez."

He shakes his head. "Yeah, but if you were definitely not going to take it, you wouldn't even go out for the interview."

I don't say anything, because he has a point there. He acknowledges my silence and goes on. "I know that as an assistant GM, you'd have even more influence, and that's a good thing. But…"

Birds wheel outside during the pause. "But what?" I prompt.

"Who's gonna do that here when you're gone? Is Xu," he pronounces the name carefully, "going to look out for gay athletes? I mean, they feel safe coming here with you and the city and all. If you're in Cansez, will the city be enough for them? Will they feel safe anywhere?"

"You're still here."

He makes a dismissive noise. "I'm practically invisible."

"You don't have to be." I lean forward and he ducks his head. "I like to think we've built a pretty good culture here. It's not just me, it's you too, it's the coaching staff and the other players and even Peter and Michaela. I can't—" I take a breath. "If it all falls apart when I leave, then we haven't built it very well, have we?"

His ears flick back. "If you got the assistant GM job here, would you stay?"

"Oh, probably." I put my paw against the glass as well. It's chilly, sometimes vibrating from the wind outside. I follow the erratic flights of birds trying to battle the gusts. "My house is here, my friends are here. But Xu is a really good candidate. I think they're going to hire him. And…" I try to put my disappointment into words. "I want the best for the team, I really do. But I could've done that and they could've found another position for him. Instead they barely talked to me about the job and everyone's been interviewing him. And I know he's great, he'll really help the team, and so on. I just feel a bit slighted."

"I get that." Cord exhales. "I didn't realize it played out like that."

"This is a business," I say. "They've got no stake in making their employees feel good. They want to win, and after they win they want to keep winning. That's all. So if I'm not a part of the winning plan, will I ever be?"

"Maybe in a few more years you'll have more experience?"

I nod. "Maybe. And that's a good point. Or I could have a few years of assistant GM experience out in Cansez and then I'll start to get looks for GM positions."

"You think?" His eyebrows go up. "I mean, would they…since you're gay?"

"Yeah, maybe not. But maybe. Michaela probably would; she doesn't give a shit what the other owners think. I don't know about this guy in Cansez. I'll have to check it out while I'm there."

"Right."

"But hey. It's still Cansez. I might rather work with Xu here than move there. And even if I go, that doesn't mean you can't stay here and keep working. We're going to stay in touch and I'm not gonna sell the house here."

"You're not? Oh, right." Cord makes a clicking noise with his tongue. "I keep forgetting you're dating a millionaire."

I chuckle. "It's handy for some things. But I can probably buy a place in Cansez with my savings. It's cheap out there."

"All right." He pulls out his phone. "Want to catch a movie? I think there's some good ones down the road."

I've got work to do and packing, but at the same time it'd be nice to catch up with Cord. So I say, "Sure," and we check out the local theater times.

•

Sunday night I'm packing for my trip and still wondering what happened with Mike. I call my dad briefly, but there's only so much I can talk about with him and he doesn't have any more information than Angela did. So I only hesitate a moment before calling Dev.

He chuckles as he picks up. "I didn't call you this time."

"By which I assume things are pretty chill?"

"Yeah. Wix got it out of his system, Colin talked Marshall into undoing his retweet and came to tell me about it, and I feel really good about our chances. The film session today was great and all our practices have been good. Well, the ones I haven't had to do with Colin."

"Is that over?"

He sighs. "Two more next week."

"You can get through it."

"I know I can. What's happening with you?"

I give him the thumbnail about Mike's talk with Jaren, at least, Angela's version of it, and Dev says, "Huh."

"What, 'huh'?"

"Teenagers," Dev said. "Either they don't know what they want, or they spend four months hiding from you and then it all comes out in one night."

"I thought it all went in in one night."

He snorts again. "So just call and ask him."

"What, the very next day? I don't want to seem desperate."

"Okay, so what is it, wait three days?"

"I'll call when I get back from Cansez."

"Sounds good." He breathes in, the sound I associate with him stretching well-worked muscles. I wish he were doing that under me, or atop me. Jerking off last night didn't reduce my tension; it heightened it. "You prepared for that?"

"Yeah, I've been looking at their roster on and off, and the moves they've made the last couple years since Morty's been there. I haven't talked to Morty about his plan for the team. I guess he's going to spring that on me in the interview, so I'll have to think on my feet."

"You'll be fine," Dev says, a deep familiar rumble, and I relax and believe him.

Still, I wake up three times early in the morning before my alarm goes off, nervous in a way I haven't been since we went to the championship. My brain spins around with questions Morty or Devereaux might ask me, other people they might want me to meet who wouldn't like the idea of a non-jock in the position, or a fag, or a fox even. It's the kind of stuff that when I'm fully awake I can dismiss easily—well, pretty easily—or at least I can distract myself. But lying in bed with everything dark, my brain hits another gear.

So I'm not quite as bright of eye and bushy of tail as I might like when I get on the plane, but that's okay because I can sleep on planes, and my first official interview isn't until eleven. I've got a hotel room reserved with early check-in, so I'll be able to freshen up before I head up to the Explorers front office.

Everything goes as planned; I send Dev and my father texts to let them know I arrived safely, another to Morty confirming the interview time, and I shower and change at the hotel, which is a block from the Explorers office.

I'm used to our bright white limestone and blue glass office with the Whalers logo on the front, not huge but visible, and (ahem) a "2013 Champions" banner hanging out front. We have spaces for electric vehicle parking, a little coffee shop on the first floor with a patio out front, and next to us is another office with a couple small startup companies, one that has been working on marketing research for the entire time I've been there, and another that's so new I haven't found out what they do yet, but I like their orange bubbly logo.

The Cansez Explorers make their home in a refurbished old brick warehouse with the logo painted directly on the brick, a grey fox in a pith helmet. The old-timiness of the logo was never something I was a huge fan of (our Whaler at least got a redesign in recent years, but I'm not a huge fan of that either—hey, let's romanticize a destructive archaic practice), but it works really well on the brick. The whole neighborhood reminds me of Hilltown, around where I grew up, only less snowy. Still cold, though, enough that my ears sting by the time I push through the glass doors.

Inside, it's modern and clean, Neutra-Scented up and down. A thin meerkat sitting in the lobby checking her phone jumps up when I come in.

"Mister Farrel? Hi, I'm Tonya. I'm Morty's assistant. I'll take you back to the office now." She gestures to the door and says to the muskrat sitting behind the reception desk, "It's okay, Sherine, he's in the log."

"I know," Sherine says, and flashes me a smile. "Have a great time. Welcome to Cansez."

Tonya leads me down a hallway to an elevator, which we take up to the third floor, all the while talking. How was my flight? How's the hotel? How do I like Cansez so far?

I'm looking around at the carpet that hasn't lost its new smell, at the shiny-clean windows and the view out toward the downtown area, which doesn't really compare to my view of the water of Yerba Bay but isn't too bad. I tell Tonya that everything's great and I haven't really had a chance to get to know Cansez yet, but I'm looking forward to it.

"If you get a chance while you're here," she says, "go down to Smokey's and have the ribs. Best barbecue in the country."

We've arrived at an office that says "Morty DeWitt" on the door, and a familiar rasping voice comes from inside. "Don't listen to her. Smokey's is good but you need to try Devil's Pit."

Tonya rolls her eyes. "You're not from here," she says. "The locals like Smokey's."

"Lee ain't from here, either." I step into the office where the old cougar stands to greet me, chewing what smells like spearmint gum. "An' I know what he likes."

The meerkat touches my shoulder. "Smokey's," she says close up like she's sharing a secret. "Trust me."

"Thanks." I grin and shake her paw, and she closes the door behind her.

I turn to shake Morty's paw, but he's coming in for the hug so I guy-hug him. There's a residue of cigarette scent on his collar, but less than I would've thought. "So, gum?"

He laughs, a rusty "Heh heh" as he sits down. "Had a scare last year, but it turned out to be benign. Still…"

"Yeah. Shit." I take the seat he's waving me to.

"Just another close call." He grins broadly.

"That's, what, eight lives now? Better be careful."

"Ah." He waves a paw. "So you wanna help me get a ring before number nine is up?"

"What've you got going on here?"

"You know the basics." He lays them out for me: good young core, success to build on and attract free agents, good coaching team in place. I ask him about salary cap issues, about their scouting team, about how the owner works with the front office.

"You'll get to ask him that yourself," Morty says with a chuckle. "We're having lunch with him."

My eyebrows go up. "Thanks for the warning."

"You want to change? You look fine."

"No, I just…"

He laughs. "Lee, you'll be fine. I wouldn'ta set this up if I didn't think you could ace it."

I nod. "I appreciate that. Okay, so what about the other stuff? Gay outreach, all that?"

Morty leans back and taps his fingers together over his stomach. "At your discretion," he says.

"Really?" My ears perk up.

He nods. "I mean, look, Devereaux knows you're interested in that. I'll let him talk a little more about it when we have lunch."

"Okay." My tail uncurls, and I grin at him. "So…what do we have to talk about?"

"Why don't you tell me how you been?" he says.

We shoot the shit for a good half hour, talk about my life and then over to the league in general. I'm aware as we talk about the performance of various teams that we're dancing around the privileged knowledge that we each have about our respective teams, and also that Morty is testing me to see what I know and how much I've picked up since I talked to him last.

I think I do pretty well, though of course I have no way of knowing. Around 11:30 he checks his phone and says, "All right, we better get on going."

"We're not having lunch here?"

He chuckles. "Devereaux doesn't come by here too often. He works downtown, so we're going to a place he likes down there. I'm driving."

I make a show of getting out a Neutra-Scent tissue as he stands up and comes around his desk. "I'm ready to get in your car."

"New car," he says. "No smoke."

"Seriously?"

He traces a claw in an X over his chest. "Cross my lungs."

He's not kidding. His car, a new-smelling SUV, carries cougar smell and minty gum smell, but no tobacco or smoke. "You're really quitting this time?"

"I really quit every time," he says, "until I don't anymore."

We make more small talk on the way downtown, arriving at a parking garage right around noon. Morty leads me through afternoon crowds and chilly winds channeled by the downtown buildings to a restaurant called Bayou Buck's. As soon as we come in, the smell of gumbo and jambalaya hits me, a hearty smell that contrasts with the white tablecloths and glass candlesticks on each table. Most of the diners are eating out of bright white china bowls, dabbing their muzzles with stained white napkins, and talking loudly to each other.

Morty leads me through the main dining room to a stairway at the back. We emerge at the top of it into a hallway off of which are two sets of restrooms, and past those, a glass door leading onto an intimate private dining room.

A red wolf in a collared shirt, no tie, and tan slacks gets up from a table that makes the downstairs look like a casual dining place: silver candlesticks, white tablecloth diagonal over a wine-dark base, finely patterned china with gold edging, and, incongruously, a thick stein of cold beer.

"You must be Wiley," the wolf says with a southern drawl familiar from our phone call. His brown eyes meet mine. "Harley Devereaux."

"Pleasure to meet you, sir," I said.

"Ah." He waves aside the honorific. "Save the sirs for the military. Have a seat and tell me what you'd like to drink."

Morty sits on the near side; I sit opposite Devereaux as he sits back down. There's a beer and wine list next to my place setting, but I only glance at it. "I'm good with water," I say.

Devereaux grins at me. "You always drink water, or just when you're on an interview?"

"Just on interviews." I smile back.

"Good." He lifts his beer and turns toward the doorway. "Water for the fox, and a Firefighter Porter for the cougar."

I hadn't noticed the skunk standing there, silent and attentive. He says, "Yes, sir," and disappears.

"I won't pressure anyone to drink, and if you're teetotal that's fine." Devereaux tips the beer bottle to his muzzle. "But I like a fella I can sit down and have a drink with, whatever's in his glass."

"I drink beer with work people." I start to say, "work friends," and then think that maybe Devereaux doesn't want to be friends with his employees, so I change "friends" to "colleagues," but "work colleagues" is redundant, so I end up on "people," which is a dumb word. But Devereaux doesn't notice, or doesn't care, and goes on to talk about the Explorers' structure, to ask me about my plans for the assistant GM job, and to discuss the plusses and minuses of the team as currently structured. I know I don't want to live here, but to make a good impression, I have to be passionate, and I find myself getting excited about the possibilities of this team.

During the conversation, I keep an eye on Morty, who has a good poker face, but not a good poker tail. His tail stays relaxed (so I'm doing okay) through the entire lunch, a delicious jambalaya and soft, moist cornbread. Devereaux also insists I try the side of fried okra he got, and I know what the bitter, slimy vegetable tastes like but I take one anyway, and I have to admit it's the least repulsive okra I'd ever had. The red wolf goes on and on about how authentic the food is here, and only halfway through the meal mentions that he's bought an ownership stake in the restaurant.

The whole thing already reeks of money anyway: the private room in the upstairs with the personal waiter who stands ready just outside the door, clearly not listening to anything except for the sound of his name. Michaela, the Whalers owner, has only had two or three meals with me, and they were all fairly low key. No private restaurants, no private waiters. In fact, all of our meetings with Michaela happen in our conference room, so that's where the meals were.

But money isn't necessarily a bad thing, and the propensity to flash it around, while annoying, isn't either. I want to get a sense of who Devereaux is and why it's so important to him to get me working on his staff. None of that comes through until we leave the restaurant and go on to the second part of the interview.

"Enough of the football stuff," the red wolf says as we walk down the back stairs of the restaurant, him leading with Morty behind me. "Morty trusts your football sense and I've heard enough to know he's right. I know you've got some other interests, so let's go for a drive and I'll show you some of the other things we've got here in Cansez."

The back door opens onto a small garage (heated) in which a Lexus sits. As soon as we step inside, a uniformed meerkat gets out from the driver's seat and steps to the back to open the car door for us. Devereaux goes in first, and then I sit next to him on the long, comfortable seat. Morty walks around to the passenger side and lets himself in the front.

"Football was my hobby," Devereaux says. "I worked so I could get season tickets, and then better season tickets. When I sold my company, I—I didn't approve the sale until I knew there was a football team I could get an ownership stake in."

"Cool," I say. We pull out of the garage and onto the Cansez streets. The silence in the car makes me uneasy, as though Devereaux's trying to trick me and the car isn't actually moving.

He grins, noticing my ear flicks. "This interior's something, isn't it? Rated to screen any noise up to, what is it, Alan?"

"Up to 120 decibels, sir," the meerkat replies.

"I just remember it's the sound of a chainsaw." He points out the window. "A guy could be running a chainsaw right outside that window and all you'd hear in here is a sound no louder than like a paper blowing down the street." He flicks his own ears. "I grew up down the street from a cannery and let me tell you, quiet is the most precious thing in the world."

I nod. "It's great," I say. "Even if Morty can't appreciate it properly."

The cougar snorts from the front seat. "I don't need a hundred thousand dollar car to get quiet, just a coupla fifty-cent earplugs."

"The point is," the red wolf says with a grin, "that look, football is your job and obviously your passion. I love the winning culture you guys have built over there in Yerba. But I know you have other passions too, and I believe all your passions should be looked after."

I've been watching him and not looking out the car windows, but as we turn slowly down a narrow street, my attention returns to the outside silent world. Old brick townhouses line both sides of the street, three stories of regular walls and limestone windowsills and lintels, wooden doors painted green and black and cream leading onto worn stone steps down to a stained, cracked sidewalk. In several windows, rainbow flags or decals shimmer, piquing my interest.

"Down here," the red wolf says as the car rolls to a stop in front of what looks like a closed shop: metal grates down over large storefront windows showing rainbow flags, books, pamphlets, and posters. What's behind the window is familiar even if the grates in front aren't; why would an LGBT Youth Center be closed early on a Monday afternoon? Then a young striped skunk comes out, adjusts his hoodie, and walks down the street away from us.

"Did they just open?" Maybe they open at 1 pm on Mondays and just haven't taken up the grate yet.

Devereaux takes my words the wrong way. "I think they've been around five years or so, maybe ten? I don't know. Anyway, I just wanted to bring you here to show you that we've got some LGBT activity in this town, and whatever you want to do on that front is fine with me. We could even get a little of the club money behind some initiatives, a couple hundred thousand here or there."

It's a generous offer despite the casual words. If this center is any like some of the others I know of, a couple hundred thousand would make up a large part of their annual budget—maybe all of it—and out here that probably wouldn't all go to rent. "Thanks," I say. "That means a lot."

The red wolf is all smiles. "Great," he says. "Hope you understand how much we want you here."

Morty's looking over his shoulder and I catch his eye. His expression is serious, but one eyebrow twitches just a fraction, so I know he's reading my response, even if he doesn't quite get why I'm not more excited about Devereaux's offer. "Sure," I say. "Absolutely. Can I ask something?"

"Of course. That's why I'm here." Devereaux leans forward.

"Why me? I mean, there's got to be a couple dozen good assistant GM candidates out there."

"Two reasons." The question doesn't even faze him; he's got to know it was coming. He holds up one finger. "First, I trust Morty here. He's made a lot of good moves. I asked him for a short list of people he trusted in the league who might be available, and your name was the top of the list."

I catch Morty's eye; he looks away. "And second?"

He holds up a second finger. "When I was building my company, we had a strategy that we would look for the assets other people were overlooking. Sometimes there's a good reason, you know—this parcel of land is next to the water treatment, or that person got fired because they stole from the company, whatever. But sometimes that water treatment plant's been cleaned up. Sometimes that person just took a few USB sticks and who gives a damn?" He fixes me with his gaze. "Sometimes that person is pretty damn smart and good at his job, and twenty owners in the league won't even give him an interview because of who he sleeps with."

I flick my ears back, but I don't say anything, and he goes on. "I built a billion-dollar company in part by evaluating everything and everyone on its merits, and I want to do the same here at the team. Look, you can look up my background. You know I don't have a history of supporting gay rights, trans rights, whatever the current thing is. I won't pretend I do. But I'm sure as hell not against them. It just hasn't been a priority. But if you're gonna bring us a championship, and it's your priority, then it's mine too."

Enough, though he doesn't say it, to find out where at least one gay rights center is in town and drive me past it. It's appealing, I can't deny it.

We make small talk back to the Explorers' office, where the Lexus stops long enough for the red wolf to give me a firm shake of the paw. "Hope you'll consider us," he says. "Morty'll answer any more questions you have. Thanks for flying out here."

And then Morty and I are standing out in the chill breeze on the sidewalk and the car is driving off. "Come on," the cougar says. "Let's get in out of the cold."

We go back to his office, much more comfortable, and this time he closes the door. "Harley can be overwhelming," he says as he sits down at his desk. "You got any questions for me?"

I shake my head. "It's nice to be wanted. Hasn't happened a whole lot. Does that mean there's a firm offer?"

Morty takes out a piece of gum and sticks it in his mouth, grimacing as he chews. "We got a couple other candidates on our list, but none of them have a championship on their resume. Even though you ain't done this job before, we know you know what you're doing. Word gets around."

I think about the players I scouted and talked to who might've ended up on the Explorers. There are two I can think of off the top of my head. "I appreciate that."

He leans back in his chair and links his paws behind his head. "But?"

"But what?"

He shakes his head at me. "Out with it."

I exhale. "It's a really nice gesture to take me by the center. I get what he was trying to do. But what I've been doing with the Whalers, and what I want to keep doing, is more than just giving money to LGBT centers. That's part of it—" A part, if I'm honest, that I've been neglecting. "—but it's more about gaining exposure and visibility for gay people in sports. Football, especially."

"Wouldn't hiring you as the assistant GM do that?"

My tail flicks against the chair. "It would," I admit.

"Uh huh." He studies me for another moment, his tail flicking just like mine. "It's a big change. I can't tell you if it'll work out for you. I can tell you this is a quality organization. Devereaux likes to throw his money around but he's got his nose on the right trail. And assistant GM positions don't fall off trees."

"I know." Morty's assurance has me doubting myself. Would I be a fool to turn down this job? My dad told me that what scared me might be good for me, but also that challenges weren't necessarily the best course. "I'm not turning it down. I mean, if it's even offered, which I know it hasn't been yet."

Morty gives me a good feline grin. "We'll see how our other interviews go. But the sooner you can let us know one way or the other, the sooner we can get moving."

"Before the championship?"

"That'd be best. But I know you'll be a bit distracted that weekend too. Surprised you ain't been checking your phone much this afternoon."

"Turned it off." I take the dead weight out of my pocket to show him. "Didn't want to be 'that guy' in the interview."

"Good fellow."

I flick my ears. "I try. Hey, I don't fly back until tomorrow morning. You want to get a drink tonight?"

He does, so after I try Smoky's barbecue (fantastic) we meet up at a bar and have a few beers. We talk about colleagues we had back at the Dragons, about our families—he's heard that my dad married Angela and he wants to know how awkward that is, so I tell him truthfully that mostly we all ignore it and get along the best we can.

To match familial awkwardness, I ask him about his divorce, and he shrugs and says he doesn't think about it much beyond the check he sends out every month. He's not seeing anyone and doesn't really want to; football is his wife now.

I'm not one of those "everyone should have cubs" people, and probably someone like Gerrard shouldn't have had cubs, but Morty feels to me like he's missing something in his life to take care of. A football team is challenging and the rewards are potentially great (he asks me what it felt like to get that championship; "better than most sex," I say), but a football team won't take care of you when you retire, won't visit you to play cards or talk about the current football players. Morty and his wife never had cubs, which again was probably a good decision, but I think he needs someone, and I wonder if his pursuit of me for the GM job is a little bit due to this emptiness in his life.

I'm probably flattering myself. Morty's fine and doesn't need a surrogate son. But I remind myself, even if I don't take the job, to keep in better touch with him. Wouldn't kill me and Dev to visit once in a while, especially since we've only got one grandparent left between us. And that leads me to wonder how long Morty's got in the league. He's probably in his early sixties now, and has all that smoking in his past.

With those morbid thoughts swirling around in my head, I say good-night around eleven. Morty presses gently, once, to know which way I'm leaning on the job, and I respond truthfully that I can't tell him. I also tell him that that's closer to taking it than I was when I landed.

Back in the hotel room, I do a quick search for LGBT centers in the Cansez city limits to see whether Devereaux deliberately took me to the most run-down one. But that's the only one that comes up. The gay neighborhood here is two city blocks, and not very prosperous ones. There was another center, an article says, but it closed back in 2014. There are two others out in more prosperous suburbs, but they look a way from the city proper.

One LGBT center. Yerba has more than I can count. I close my laptop and stare out the window at the puffs of steam coming from the buildings, like the city's breath in the moonlight.

Chapter Twenty-One (Dev)

For a couple days, things are as quiet as I'd imagined they might be this entire two weeks. Nobody brings up Nativist crap, I don't even see Colin, and Wix is his usual chill, happy self. I go out with Charm a couple nights, one of which Ty joins us for, and I can get ready for Media Day, the Tuesday before the championship.

Lee calls me Monday night to tell me about his interview in Cansez. By this point I guess we've both given up pretending we're taking a break and we talk for an hour about the job and the pros and cons. As best I can tell, he's worried about the owner's commitment to improving life for gay players (we're not allowed to talk about the football side, so maybe there are issues there too, but Cansez went to the semifinals this year, so probably not). He thinks they only want him because he's part of a winning organization, which isn't bad: he did play a part in that championship, I remind him.

"Yeah," he says, "and it's not that. I'm sure I could do the job. I just feel like it's not going to be the same."

"Of course not, doc," I say. "It's in the Midwest."

"Thanks, stud. I remember my high school geography. Plus I'm still here and it's twenty degrees outside and shit."

"You've got thick fur. You can take it."

He snorts. "Do I have a better chance to win another championship there or in Yerba? Or is it about the same? Would it be worth giving up a chance to help a few more gay players just to get myself a ring?"

"Hey, when I get my first ring, I'll let you know."

He laughs, soft and affectionate. "Sorry."

"Don't be. So maybe you're thinking about this job more seriously now?"

He makes a creaky "eh" noise. "Maybe. I'll let you get back to working toward that one. You'll get it this year."

"Doing the best we can."

"Hey," he says, "did you get a chance to read those articles I sent?"

This is the one thing that's been on my mind. "Yeah. I…I've been trying to figure out what to do about it."

"Seems like it's settled down. You could just let it go."

"I could, sure. But…it feels important. The 'you' voice tells me I should make sure Marshall, and whoever else, doesn't think this is just some PC bullshit."

He's quiet for a few seconds. "Yeah. Maybe go to Coach and see what he thinks? If he thinks it's worth talking to the team about, maybe he'll do it."

"Fuck," I say.

"Sorry. I don't know Lopez as well as you do. I just thought—"

"No, that's exactly the right thing to do and I'm pissed I didn't think of it."

He laughs. "You're welcome."

"Love you."

"Love you too."

Tuesday, my media time is slated near the end of the session, so I go to watch Wix field questions. I asked him whether he was worried about his sexuality coming up in the session, and he shrugged. "I'll handle it if it does," he told me.

It does come up about halfway through. Some scruffy wolf says, "You're roommates with Devlin Miski. Have there been any problems?"

"Nah." The bobcat tries to move to the next question, but the wolf keeps going with the air of a sleaze-sniffing professional.

"From a sexual standpoint, I mean."

A few mutters around him, but nobody tells him to shut up. Ears perk to Wix for his answer. "Nah," he says. "Dev's cool."

"And you're not attracted to him?"

"Ya know," Wix says, "I can see where you'd wonder that. He's a good-looking tiger, right?"

The crowd of reporters laughs a little. Wix goes on. "But nah, he's not my type."

This time, a cougar talks over the wolf's attempt to follow up and asks Wix a question about the Port City receivers, and the rest of the session focuses on football (with a couple standard exceptions like 'talk about your family and their expectations for you').

My own thirty-minute session isn't too bad either. The football questions are easy to take, and the only surprise comes when someone asks me about Lee's visit to Cansez. I'm taken aback that they've already heard about it, but I compose myself quickly. "Lee and I are taking a two-week break while I prepare for the championship." The bland lie comes easily now. "I haven't talked to him, but I'm looking forward to hearing about this when the game's over."

"Have you discussed what you'll do if you win?"

I've had variations on this question a dozen times already since the Crystal City game. "I guess we'll discuss that if we win." I put on my best smile. "I'm more concerned about bringing the city of Chevali its first championship. The team and city have been so good to me over the years that I really want this for them."

The questions shift to whether I feel my legacy will be affected by the outcome of the game, and I talk a bit about my legacy being partly paving the way for other gay players to come out. They like that—they've had football questions all day, and any other angle is welcome relief.

Toward the end there is one question about Marshall's Nativist tweet and my thoughts on it, because I dunno, I'm of immigrant ancestry? I haven't noticed whether Carson or anyone else got this same question. Maybe it's because I'm relatively outspoken compared to the rest of the team? Whatever the reason, I say it was a stupid mistake and that's all there is to it, and the session's over.

A bunch of us on the defense get together in the film room a little after that, but instead of watching film, we all take out our phones and read through the coverage online to see if any of us said anything stupid, or if any of the Devils said anything we could use as motivation. One of them called Chevali a city "full of sand rats," which is a pretty shitty thing to say, but it's also so ridiculous that even those of us who've lived in Chevali for years don't really get that upset about it. One of the rookie linemen says that "sand rat" is a slur for chinchillas, which isn't something I'd ever heard, and another says it's a slur for people living in the Middle East, which also doesn't make a lot of sense. In the end we decide it's probably not worth getting worked up about, and we'd rather focus on the guy who said that our defense was "cream cheese," meaning soft.

That last question, and the "sand rat" comment, push me over the edge with the Nativist shit. So I ask Coach if there's a time we can talk, and he fits me in between coordinator meetings. "What's on your mind, Miski?" he asks, leaning his impressive bulk back in his chair.

I printed out some of the material Lee sent me along with his letter, which he sent after it went public, and now I pull those pages out of my pocket. "This thing with Marshall," I say, sliding the papers across the desk. "I know it's blown over and we need to be focusing on football this week, but…Carson and I are getting harassed online, and his family hears it some too. I'm sure there are other guys on the team, like Rain and Carlos maybe, who get it and just don't talk about it."

He picks up the pages, skims them, puts them down again. I take a breath and go on. "My boyfriend had an incident with his team, and that's the Whalers' scouts' statement to the colleges they work with. I don't know if it'll make it to the news, but he said it's fine to share it, that it's out there now. The other things are research he did. I don't know how much you know about it or if you, uh, get that at all."

The moose smiles and tilts his head from side to side so his massive antlers bob up and down. "My species at least comes from this continent. I'm Kanatian. Don't know if you knew that."

"I didn't. Didn't seem to matter."

"Nope. So you want me to talk to Marshall about it?"

I shake my head. "I don't know. I feel like it's a chance to educate people. Not just him, but everyone. But I don't want to distract us from the game. So I figured…" I gesture toward him. "I'd give you all the information. Whatever you decide to do, I'll go along with."

He glances down at the papers again. "This something that bothers you?"

"I can put it aside for football."

"That ain't what I asked."

I take a breath. "A little. More—more in the abstract, I guess. I don't feel like anyone on the team is out to get me because my grandfather came over from Siberia. But also, you know, being the first gay player means I think about shit like this."

"Course." He puts one large hand on the papers. "Thanks for this. I'll take a look and I'll decide if I want to do anything about it. And thanks for coming to me first."

"You're welcome, sir." I exhale and stand, feeling lighter. "And honestly, whatever you decide is cool."

"I know." He grins at me. "I'm the coach."

•

Lee also feels good about how that meeting went when I tell him about it that night, but he moves quickly to praising my press savvy at Media Day. "You know how to play the media," he tells me as I sit out on the balcony of the hotel while Wix lies in bed playing a game on his phone. "Deflect without sounding like you're deflecting, move to something they'll be interested in."

"Thanks," I say, breathing in the exhaust and damp concrete smell of Chevali after a light winter rain. "Only took, what, ten years?"

He chuckles. "They keep changing too. But I think they're getting more like cubs. Anyway, the good reporters don't join that Media Day mosh pit."

"Do people still mosh?"

"Old people like us do when their childhood bands go on tour. Want me to see when Fishbone's coming around again?"

"They're older than we are. You back home now?"

"Yeah, back in the townhouse, lying in bed." He pauses there and doesn't need to tell me he's naked. "Flight back was fine, no cubs near me or anything, no comments about the 'stink.' I watched two episodes of 'Downtown.' It's pretty good. I'll watch it again with you next week."

"What's it about?"

He tells me about this comedic drama, or maybe dramatic comedy, about a Geoffroy's cat who works in a bookstore, a white wolf who works in a coffee shop, and a red fox who drives a rideshare, all three of them trying to get their band more exposure. It sounds fun, different from life, a good escape, exactly what I'm going to want in a week.

One of the things I'm going to want, anyway. I glance over at Wix, still occupied with his game. "Looking forward to watching it with you," I tell Lee. "So what are you going to do about the job?"

"If I tell you, promise not to tell the reporters?"

"Only if they don't ask me directly. You know I cannot tell a lie."

"Of course not. Perish the thought." He draws in a breath and lets it out slowly. "I don't know. Would I be an idiot to turn it down?"

"No."

"You haven't seen the office I'd get."

I laugh. "Doc, you know what's right, even if you don't know quite why. I've never doubted your instincts. If you don't feel it, don't do it. Another job will come along when it's right."

"How could this be more right?"

"It could be somewhere where the weather doesn't suck."

He ignores the jibe. "Morty's working there, the owner likes me, he's on board with the gay activism…even though…" He trails off. "And I've already started something here. Why not let someone else pick this up and go start something in Cansez?"

"Who's going to pick it up?"

He's silent. I wait, but he's silent for so long that I say, "Sorry."

"Dammit, tiger. Why you gotta ask the hard questions?"

"I didn't mean to." But I smile, pleased that I was able to help.

"I wonder if I could work with Morty to help them provide resources for gay players. Is that wishful thinking?"

"Worth asking about, isn't it? But look, when we're practicing here we're taught about focusing on our objective. That might change, but it's critical that we know what it is and not let ourselves be distracted. My objective might be the quarterback, or the slot receiver, or the running back. Whatever it is, I have to give it my full attention."

"Right, but you also have to be aware of the situation as a whole so you know when to shift your focus, right?"

"Sure. My point is, though, is your focus on helping gay players or on getting your second ring? Is it on building your career or on building something else?"

He thinks about that. "Can't I have multiple goals? I want to do all that."

"Maybe you don't have to do it all at once."

"Maybe," he says. "Maybe. Okay, thanks, tiger."

"When do you need to tell them?"

"Probably this week sometime. We'll see."

"Well…you know where I'll be. You coming down for the game?"

"Oh yeah, for sure. Father and Angela are taking the boys and I'll probably tag along." He pauses like he's going to say something else and then just says, "So I'll see you that night."

"Can't wait." I lean on the balcony railing and look into my room. I imagine that instead of a bobcat, there's a fox on the bed, rolling onto his side to show me his creamy white stomach and a pink erection, crooking a chocolate-brown finger to call me inside.

"I mean, I have to prove I'm better than Wix," he says.

Reality snaps back to me. "Argh. Is the only reason you said that was okay so you could tease me about it?"

"You got a blow job," he says, a little smugly. "You don't get to complain."

"If I didn't enjoy it all the way, can I complain a little bit?"

He laughs. "Good night, stud. Love you."

"Love you too."

•

When I report for Wednesday practice, any residual contentment from the conversation with Lee evaporates as soon as Gerrard says, "You're over there today."

He points to the defensive backs' area of the field. "Ah, shit," I say. "Fuck. We're cool. Can you tell Coach we're cool? We don't need to do this again?"

"Tell him yourself." The coyote gestures to the other side of the field, where Coach Lopez is talking to his coordinators. "But do it in the next thirty seconds or you'll be late and probably Javy will make you run laps."

"Goddammit." I jog over to the defensive backs, where the fox barely looks up from his clipboard.

"Miski, you're with Smith," he says. "All right, let's start with double cut drills."

Colin's flattened ears and refusal to meet my eyes when I stand next to him match my mood exactly. I'm glad I don't have to come up with anything to say to him; hopefully my performance will do my talking. Getting out of today with silence would be a win.

It's not in the cards, though. I am better at these drills than I was last week, but still not as good as someone who's been doing them all season. Every little mistake I make, I feel Colin's smug smile behind me.

Halfway through the morning, he finally makes a remark. "For someone who thinks he's so much better than the rest of us, you're not showing it."

This isn't my specialty, and most of these drills aren't for things I'll be called on to do in a game situation, and he knows that as well as I do. So I swallow the temptation to explain that and just say, "I thought we were past this."

"Past what? Having to do our best on the field?"

"This." I gesture between us. "You and me. The point of this is for us to get along."

"Really?" He arches an eyebrow. "I thought this was a punishment for fighting."

"Maybe it's that too." I can't resist adding, "Don't forget where you're practicing tomorrow."

"Maybe you'll be surprised," he says, and at that moment coach whistles us back to the drill, so I let it go.

It bugs me, though. We'd had a reasonable talk about the Nativist stuff the other day and now he's riding me again. When we get a break, I grab a bottle of BoltAde and go sit by myself on the edge of the field.

A shadow falls over me a second before Wix plops down beside me. "Hey," he says.

"Hey."

"Colin rides everyone like that," he says.

"Sure."

"Seriously." He takes a gulp from his bottle. "He's a jerk but that's how he motivates us. Coach Javy had to talk to him about it once when he actually yelled, but now we hardly notice it anymore."

I turn to the bobcat. "He and I have a history—"

"Yeah, I know. And last week, that was worse. I'm just tellin' ya, this week he's not saying more to you than he'd say to one of us." He takes another swig. "If one of us fucked up half his routes, I mean."

"All right." I pat him on the shoulder. "Thanks."

He smiles brightly. "No worries. Now get out there and do better."

"Thanks, rook." I emphasize that last word to remind him that I've been in this league ten years, but he's a fuckin' kid, what does he care? So I push myself to my feet as he springs up and back to his drill partner, and I walk back to Colin.

The rest of the day, I pour everything I have into the drills, and I keep Colin mostly quiet. He chirps a couple times when I make mistakes, but I ignore the remarks and they don't get worse. Meanwhile I'm getting the hang of some of the moves—the afternoon has more cut blocks and tackling drills, which I can do because we also have those in the linebacker drills.

"How was that?" I ask after one set I'm pretty sure I did perfectly, because he hasn't said anything and it bugs me. I want him to acknowledge it.

"Your angle's too high," Colin responds. "It's fine, it's a legal tackle, but it's borderline, and if you do it in front of the ref and you miscalculate, you'll get a flag."

"I know." I can't fuckin' win. "But I wasn't too high."

"Go lower and there won't be any mistake."

"If you tackled more, maybe you'd be able to lecture me on technique."

He gets up in my face then. "You want to compare numbers? Fifty tackles last year. How many did you have, with your many more opportunities?"

"How about this year?" I fire back. We both know our own numbers and I know last year he had a great year, first team all-Defense, while my numbers were down because of the new schemes and a nagging ankle injury. This year my numbers are up and his are down and that's the way things go.

"Hey hey!" Wix gets in between us. "Settle down."

"Mind your business, rook," Colin snaps.

The bobcat doesn't move. "This is my business."

We're both taken aback, and neither of us says anything. Wix goes on. "I've played a full season and more. Maybe I'm still technically a rook, but I'm done with that. I know we've got a great team here and you're both fucking brilliant players and so goddamn stubborn that you can't shut up and even practice together."

"We got along for a while before you came along." Colin's ears are back and his voice is tight.

"Yeah, well, I'm here now and you're not getting along, so just fuckin', I dunno, hit each other or fuck or do whatever you gotta do to keep things quiet."

Colin's eyes bulge. "What did you say?"

I try to push Wix away, but he ignores me. "You both have so much in common. You're two of the best defenders in the league, you're stubborn as shit, you love your partners, probably, and you're both gay."

I thought the fox's ears were already flat, but now they're pasted to his skull. My eyes flick around, but the rest of the defense is keeping their distance, except for Pock, the weasel, who's coming over to either bail Wix out or break this up or toss in his two cents—you never know with him. He stops about three feet away from us at that comment. I'm not sure Wix saw or heard him, but I'm also not sure the bobcat would've cared if he did.

Colin's fury turns to me. "Have you been telling lies about me?"

Fuck it. "Dude." I keep my voice low. "You've been meeting boys for ten years. You think there's anyone on the team who doesn't know?"

"But yeah," Wix says, "he told me, and why the hell shouldn't he? You know what? I'm gay too. What the fuck is the big deal? It's twenty fucking seventeen already. Grow up."

Now Colin sees Pock, but before he can even open his muzzle the weasel raises his paws. "Hey, I knew," he says, "but I didn't say anything about it, it's your business, dude, and whatever, y'know, I mean, a bunch of us chase tail on the road and if yours is boy tail then whatever, to each his own."

The fox looks past him for a moment at the rest of the defense, and I can see him processing that in his head and wondering, *how many other people know?* But he doesn't say anything, just flicks his eyes back to Wix, ears still flat against his head. "That's none of your business, or anyone's business." He turns on his heel and stalks back toward the practice.

Tension flees me all in a rush, and I put a paw to my chest. "Lion Christ," I say to Wix. "You trying to lose us the championship?"

"We're not gonna lose the championship." He looks pretty smug and confident.

Pock comes up and puts a paw on his shoulder. "Damn, kid. I told you not to bring that shit up with Colin."

"You told me not to tease him about his wife."

"Yeah, like, about his wife and fucking around on the road and shit. It was implied."

Wix rolls his eyes to me. "Next time don't imply, just tell me straight up."

"Would that have made a difference?" I ask.

"Nah. It's better out in the open."

The weasel shrugs. "Last guy to say something to Colin about that got traded."

I connect dots. "Maxill? That's why he got traded? Fuck, we could've used him."

"Well, I'm not gonna get traded before Sunday." Wix slaps my shoulder. "Enjoy the rest of your practice."

He jogs back after Colin, leaving Pock and I to shake our heads at each other. "They grow up so fast," I say, and he laughs, and we walk back together.

For the rest of the practice, Colin is silent and precise in his movements. He doesn't ride me anymore, and I find myself getting into the flow of the practice more easily without having to worry about him saying something. The problem now is that I keep thinking about what the fallout from Wix's outburst is going to be. Is he going to be traded somewhere? Or just cut? And what about me? This fragile peace Colin and I have had for the last eight years was already crumbling, but now it's maybe gone.

Maybe I'm confusing it with the feeling I get at the end of a strenuous practice, but what I'm feeling as I leave the defensive backs and head for the locker room is mostly relief. Colin's going to have a lot of processing to do, but it's long overdue. Hopefully one aspect of the processing is finding out that even if everyone on the team knows your secret shame, they don't give a fuck.

What if Colin decides he needs to go to a new team, one where everyone doesn't know him? Shit. I'm sure Wix didn't think about that before his little speech.

Wix stays out that evening playing video games with some of the other corners. While he's gone, I call Lee to tell him about the development. He whistles. "Wix is gonna get himself a new team next year."

"Maybe not. If we win…"

"True. But then Colin has the whole off-season to think about it."

"Ugh." Colin, given time to think, can be dangerous. Then again, I never really bother with him much in the off-season. "Maybe I can talk to him about it tomorrow."

"Don't get yourself sent to another team."

"Hah. I'd retire first."

He's quiet at that, and I am too, remembering a quarterback being helped off the field. "Anyway," I say, "hope the game keeps people from shaking things up too much. We're all pretty focused."

"Good."

"How about you?"

"Back at work, but I'm heading down to Chevali Friday afternoon. I'll see Father and Angela, maybe talk to Mike a bit."

"How's work?"

"I'm interviewing another candidate, some stiff. Peter and Michaela are going to talk to me about the position, but they're going to hire Xu."

"They might still hire you."

He laughs. "Thanks, but I can read other foxes well enough to know. The question is whether I want to stay here as director of scouting or pull up roots and go to Cansez to be Morty's assistant GM."

"Any more thoughts on that?"

"Not yet, not really. I love all the people here and it's a great organization, but that's potentially a fantastic opportunity."

"That's the same thing you said a week ago."

"I told you I hadn't made progress. What do you want?"

I'm not on my guard with Lee. "A blow job."

He laughs again. "Just ask your roommate."

"One of yours. From someone who knows me."

"Well, okay. That narrows it down. I guess I'll put that on the list for Sunday night."

"Sounds good." I smile, my tail flicking against the bed. "See you then."

Chapter Twenty-Two (Lee)

The surest sign that my definite suspicions are reality comes Thursday morning, when the interview I was supposed to have with another assistant GM candidate is canceled for unspecified reasons. The reason, of course, is that they've settled on Xu as their assistant GM.

Okay, the actual sure sign comes Thursday afternoon, when Peter pulls me into his office for a meeting and I find Michaela Martinet there.

The Whalers' owner doesn't visit our offices often, but shows up more than Devereaux does at the Explorers', if Morty is to be believed. Also unlike Devereaux, I've never seen her dressed down, and today is no exception: the tanuki has on a lavender-grey business suit that gleams in the sun through Peter's large window. She's in one of the chairs in front of Peter's desk; my boss waves me to the other.

Before I can sit, Ms. Martinet stands and shakes my paw. "Thanks for coming in, Lee," she says.

"My pleasure. Thank you for, uh, taking the time to talk to me."

"Of course." She sits, and I sit too. Without waiting for Peter to talk, she goes on. "I've got to get to another meeting in forty-five minutes, so I'll cut to the point. You've done an excellent job for the Whalers and we'd love to keep you here. Unfortunately, we can't offer you the assistant general manager position. The consensus is that Dalbent Xu will help this franchise grow and succeed into the future."

"It's not a question of competence," Peter says.

"No," Ms. Martinet agrees. "It's a question of what we can add to the management structure here. We have the opportunity to expand in a way we haven't been able to previously, which could help in many different areas."

"But we also value continuity," Peter said. "So I've asked Ms. Martinet to extend you a future offer."

This is the first unexpected statement. My ears perk up. "A future offer?"

She nods. "We don't expect Xu to be here long-term. I'd say we'll get three years out of him—it might be four or it might be only two—before his ambitions take him elsewhere. He doesn't want to run a team; he wants to go into the business of expanding the league overseas, or maybe an intermediary role between the league and foreign governments. Anyway, assuming you and Peter are still here when Xu moves on, you'll replace him as assistant general manager."

"Oh." I'm not sure what to say to that. It's unusual, and it's nice to be thought highly of.

"To that end," Ms. Martinet says, "we're going to bump your salary by four and a half percent to bring it closer in line with what an assistant general manager would make, and Peter will keep including you on meetings and giving you responsibilities like communicating with agents."

"You did good on the Remington thing," Peter chimes in.

Ms. Martinet gets up, and I get up hurriedly. "I hope that convinces you that we value your service here."

"Oh yes." I take her paw. "It does, it absolutely does."

"Good." She smiles and picks up the briefcase sitting beside her chair. "I've got to run. I'll hope to see you at the team picnic in March."

After she leaves, Peter asks me to sit down again and we talk about what this means, acting as though I've accepted their deal and am going to stay on. Only after twenty minutes does Peter ask, "Is this enough to keep you here?"

I've always tried to be as honest as I can with Peter. "I don't know," I say. "I didn't expect to like Cansez at all, but everyone was friendly there. The owner seems pretty cool."

His ears stay splayed to the side. "All right, that's fair. I just didn't want you to leave without us doing everything we could."

I nod. "I'm sorry for being shitty on the phone the other day. It's kind of a stressful time overall."

"Hey, if my wife was playing for a championship in a week, I'd be stressed too." He grins. "They've had a little bit of shit going on down there, huh?"

"Heh. You might say that."

He tilts his head. "You talk to Dev at all about the research you were doing?"

"Yeah, I sent him some articles and pointed him to our letter when it went out."

"Cool." Peter taps his desk. "The more people on board with this, the better."

He doesn't think the league will make a statement about it, though, and neither do I. Peter doesn't think they will because the league tries hard not to offend any of their potential fans, and Nativists are a sizable enough group to make them worry. I don't think they will because most of the owners are rich, and it's in their interests to have people focused on problems other than how rich people are generally screwing everyone in the country.

I don't make a commitment that day, but Peter's got a lot on his plate and I know he wants a decision by the game if possible. I'd be an idiot to think that he doesn't have a contingency in place in case I leave. He just wants to know if he's going to have to use it.

I schedule a meeting with him Friday morning, since I'm leaving mid-afternoon to head to Chevali. Thursday night I pack and call Father to talk about my trip. He insists again that I stay in their spare bedroom, and I insist again that I've already booked the hotel, it's no trouble, I like having my own space. Then I ask him how Mike's doing and he says, "Fine."

"He hasn't said any more about why he doesn't want to go to school here?"

"No, but he hasn't said much of anything. Teenagers." He chuckles. "He's more talkative than you were at that age."

"Maybe he's got the Abercrombie catalog under his sheets at night too." I keep going before he can respond to that one. I think it's innocuous enough, but I don't want to answer further questions about it. "So we're having dinner Friday night, and then what?"

"Saturday Angela wants to take us all to a play, since Sunday is going to be all football."

"So I should bring a nice outfit?"

"You're the one with the theater degree."

"English degree."

"You didn't get a theater minor?"

"I can check the diploma, but I'm pretty sure it was just English."

"Ah well. Then sure, bring something nice to wear. Or don't. I don't think anyone dresses up for the theater anymore, especially not on a Saturday afternoon."

I grab a couple things out of the closet. "I'll pick something nice, but not too nice. Don't want to show up the rest of my family."

"Ever the dutiful son. How's it going with Cansez?"

I tell him briefly about the interview and how Morty's doing. "I keep thinking about what you said, how the most challenging option isn't necessarily the right choice, or something like that, and maybe that's what's holding me back."

"Change can be scary. But it can also be worthwhile. You know, when I had to make a big change…"

"Hang on." I break in. "Is this going to be about how hard it was for you to marry the lady you fell in love with?"

He gives a little huff. "It wasn't all flowers and hearts. We had to consider you and Mike and Jaren, and Gerrard, for that matter, and Dev's relationship with him. We knew there'd be challenges, but it's all been pretty worthwhile."

"Just 'pretty' worthwhile?"

"Worthwhile." He sighs. "Maybe I'm underestimating the appeal of the play on Saturday. Two hours during which you're not supposed to talk."

"Not supposed to." I smile. "When has that ever stopped me?"

"True. The only one who's ever stopped you from talking is yourself. Like how you're avoiding talking to me about Cansez right now."

I sit on the edge of my bed. "Yeah. If it wasn't in Cansez…"

"But it is."

"And then the Whalers basically offered me a raise and a future assistant GM position whenever Xu leaves."

"That's nice. Did they put it in writing?"

I sigh. "No, I know, a lot can change in three years. But it's a really nice gesture. I don't hear about things like that happening often."

"That's because they don't. Did that help convince you?"

"It complicated things." I flick my tail.

"Really? You were leaning toward Cansez?"

"No—I mean, I don't think I was. What I mean is…" I try to think about how to phrase it. "I didn't think I was leaning toward Cansez, so this should've sealed it. I should've been able to say 'yes' right there in Peter's office. But I didn't, and I'm not sure why."

"From a football angle, which job is better?"

"Cansez, by a little."

"Okay. From a lifestyle angle?"

"Yerba, no contest."

"Uh huh. What other angle is there?"

"Activism."

"Seems like that'd be Yerba, too, wouldn't it? I don't imagine the gay rights scene in Cansez is all that active."

"It's active. But it's a lot more than gay rights now." That takes me a little too close to Mike and Maxie, so I pull back. "I feel like I've been coasting here for a while. Maybe going somewhere else would push me to be more active again."

"Do you need that, on top of the stress of a new job?"

"It all depends," I say, "on whether I'm a football guy or an activist."

"Hmm." Father's whiskers scrape against the phone. "Does it have to be one or the other?"

"Not entirely, but…one's going to get priority, right?"

"I guess so." He chuckles. "We can talk about it this weekend, if that'll help."

"Sure. Thanks." I'm looking forward to it, to getting away from the job stress. And seeing Dev again Sunday night, one way or another.

I haven't thought a lot about the stakes of this game. I mean, it's a championship, maybe Dev's best chance to win one for the rest of his career. He's got two to five good years left and Port City isn't that great a team. Good enough to get to the championship, obviously, but it's a down year all around in the league. On paper, Chevali should win by a touchdown, especially at home, and Dev should have his ring.

And then maybe we'll get our ring, too? The idea of marriage seems so distant to me. We talked about it so long ago, and then again every time he was in a championship, and after a while, life without it became normal.

But marriage is a big step, and if Dev wins, it's on the table. Planning a wedding in the offseason, which we can pay someone to do, but also a wedding means publicity, high profile coverage for me and my new team. Ugh, I'm already hating myself for thinking of it as a marketing opportunity. Best to leave that bridge until we get to it.

Chapter Twenty-Three (Dev)

The next morning, on the way to breakfast, I tell Wix that he should probably stay away from Colin, and he gives me one of those smug kid looks, like I'm his dad telling him not to drive too fast or something. "I've got it under control," he says.

"I'm sure you think you do, because you're a rookie and you think you've got this game mastered after a year."

"It's nice that you care, but look, trust me." He smiles. "I'm glad I could help you out with something for once."

I start to say something, and then what I think of as my Lee voice chimes in telling me to let the kid have his moment, and we're at the cafeteria anyway, so I say, "Thanks," and we eat.

Again, I'm not paired with Colin during today's practice; Gerrard has me working with Price. I watch Colin during the morning drills and he's working really hard at it. He always does, but it seems like today he's head-down focused and he's doing better.

The smart thing would probably be for me to leave him alone, but I feel a little bad about yesterday's spat, to be honest. Wix, though he fucked up, wasn't entirely wrong. We're both gay, me and Colin, and even though he's an asshole, maybe part of that is that being gay and Christian is really hard. We came close to understanding each other over the weekend, and then sparks flared yesterday just to prove that nothing's easy. But maybe if I try to be less of a dick to him, at least he won't be actively shitty to me.

Keeping that in mind, I go over to him on a break and say, "Looking good out there."

He puts down his Bolt and slides me a look, but doesn't say anything. Then he picks it up again, drains it, and tosses the bottle into the nearby recycling bin. After he wipes his mouth, he mutters, "Thanks," and walks off, tail flicking from one side to the other.

Hey. A civil interaction again. How about that?

Buoyed by that minor victory, I kick ass on the cut and weave drills, and when I have a chance to watch Colin, I see that he's taking the advice I gave him last week about setting his feet. That, too, makes me smile. Even dipshits can learn once in a while.

My smile doesn't last past the end of practice. I'm chatting with Price and then the big wolf stops to talk to Gerrard about something. I listen for a bit but I have to pee, so I trot back to the locker rooms.

Colin comes up beside me. "Hey."

It's not like a "hi there," it's a "stop and listen." I slow my walk but don't stop. "What's up?"

"Just so you know," the fox says, "I know something about you, too. So don't go acting all high and mighty around me."

"I wasn't. What do you know?"

"Never mind that." Now he's smirking, but he doesn't luxuriate in the smirk the way he used to. "Just leave me alone and I'll leave you alone."

"Dude, that's all I ever fucking wanted. You're the one who messed with my roommate."

He pauses and reflects on that for a moment. "I still think he'd be better off with me, but I can see you not wanting to room with Dublovic. Being around all that morality would get tiring. For you."

"I'm surprised you're not exhausted," I say, with not as much of an edge as I'd like, to be honest.

"Ah, well, I'm used to it." He shakes his head. "I'm not like you. Don't try to understand what I'm going through."

"I'm not."

He glares. "Everything's so easy for you. Easy jokes, easy life, just do whatever you want." His fingers steal up to the cross on the chain around his neck. "I chose to give my life over to a higher power and that's a choice you can't understand."

"I can understand it." He snorts. "No, really. I mean, what are we doing here?" I tug my Firebirds practice tee. "We signed on to this higher power and we have to follow their rules, right? We can't just do whatever we want or there's consequences. Wouldn't you rather be staying at home this week?"

He makes a guttural noise of disgust. "This is a job. I can't believe you're comparing it to—this just proves—"

"Yeah, I know. But I'm tryin' to understand, okay? I know it's important to you to keep that cross around your neck and still…" I wave a paw. "Do what you do. And I know it's hard."

"You—"

"But also, it's hard doing what I do. And you don't understand that."

He shakes his head. "Just doing whatever you want?"

"Being yourself is hard when there's assholes all around telling you not to be yourself because it makes them uncomfortable." We stop outside the locker room. "Whether it's people who don't want to acknowledge that some guys like other guys, or people who are afraid immigrants are taking all their jobs and culture, or whatever, it doesn't matter what you're doing, it wears you down."

"I'm sure it's so difficult." He huffs and sets his ears back.

"Whatever." I want to end on something of a positive note, as much as I can, so I say, "I learned some stuff in the corner drills. Sometimes it's helpful to look at something you think you know well from another perspective."

"You think you're so clever." He shakes his head and walks into the locker room.

I stand there for a moment and then laugh. I mean, yeah, I thought it was kind of clever, but I guess if you're not ready to hear it, then it's just annoying.

Price comes up to me then. "Did I miss a joke?"

"Nah," I say. "Just Colin being Colin."

We walk in together. "Things back to mutual quiet disgust between you two?"

"Maybe. Probably."

He claps me on the shoulder. "Better than throwing punches. Just keep it that way."

I want to, but also, I remember as I undress, Colin said he knows something about me now. Looking back on my recent past, there's not a lot of things that could mean, and I start to have a nasty suspicion about what it might be and how he might have come to know it.

●

I can't confront Wix right away; I see him at dinner but he's with some of his cornerback buddies, and anyway, Ty and Charm grab me and insist we're going out. Friday and Saturday night we've got an earlier curfew so this is the last night we can go out without worrying too much about getting back.

None of us want to get fall-down drunk anyway, but it's nice to be able to kick back with a few beers and talk Charm out of going to a strip club for a couple hours. "Come on, you don't have to hook up or anything," he complains, but the complaints are rote and more to tease me and Ty—me because he knows I'm not super into strip clubs anyway, and Ty because he is. Charm has sometimes excluded me from strip club trips with Ty because, he says, Ty is "inhibited" when I'm around. I haven't seen evidence of that, but I guess I wouldn't, and I took from his not-very-subtle hinting that he means that Ty won't fuck anyone if I'm along. It's weird being the moral arbiter of my little group of friends, and I wonder what Colin would think if he could hear that.

"This is the problem with kickers." Ty starts another old refrain with me. "They play like six plays a game, so they don't have to worry about being tired."

"That's right." Charm toasts us. "You chumps go out and play the whole damn game. I'm gonna be playing 'til I'm fifty."

I nurse my beer, thinking about that. "I'm not," Ty says cheerfully. "Another year or two, hopefully after we win Sunday, and then I'm out. Gonna have cubs to look after, and I want to spend time with them once they're past the age of screaming in diapers all the time."

"I thought you said only a year or two," I tease.

Charm laughs. "What about you, Gramps?"

The origins of Charm's nickname for me don't matter any more than the fact that nobody else calls me that. The stallion and fox both turn their attention to me. "Been thinking about it," I say. "It's a rough game. How much longer can I play without a bad injury?" I flex my knee, the one that lately has taken to clicking if I sit too long. "Is it already too late?"

"Hey." Charm smacks his beer glass down to the table. "This is a fun night out. No whining about injuries or anything like that."

"We've got a pretty big game in a few days."

"Right, and you're not going to get any better by obsessing about it."

Ty flicks his ears back and gives me another one of those "kickers, geez," looks. "If I just had to run between a pair of goalposts that never moved, I might agree with that. They've got this stuff called film, see."

"Bah." Charm leans back and brushes away Ty's words. "Gramps, you've been around longer than Ty."

"By like a year."

"You still buy into this 'film' thing?"

"I kinda do, yeah." I shouldn't have thought about my knee. I keep testing it with a paw.

"You can only watch so much, though."

"Give it a rest." Ty sets his paws on the table. "Tell us about all the girls from the last two weeks."

Few words can get Charm to change the subject quite that quickly. We're regaled for the next hour by a series of fantastic stories that are anywhere from zero to 75% true, based on previous experience. That doesn't matter, though, because the joy is in the telling.

Between that and the beers, I'm good and chill when I get back to the room and find Wix on his bed, studying film on his tablet. Not a bad idea, and especially after the conversation with Ty and Charm, I want to go over a few things myself. I know that there's a grain of truth to what Charm's saying; a lot of the game is instinctive, and you can't learn that. But you can hone your instincts by watching what the people you're playing tend to do and you can teach yourself to respond more quickly.

I don't want to interrupt Wix's study beyond the quick hellos we exchange. The day's been stressful enough that maybe, I think, I can wait until after the game to talk to him. And maybe I don't ever need to know what Colin thinks he knows about me. As long as we're maintaining our peace, I won't have to have a conversation with him, and that's just the way I want it.

But as I sit on my own bed and start up my tablet, the question eats at me, and even film study does little to dispel it. It's easy for me to drop into analyzing a play as I watch the offensive line, the way the receivers break, the holes that open for the running back. But as soon as the play's over I look at the bobcat on the bed next to mine.

This goes on for a while, until he puts down his tablet to go to the bathroom. When he comes back I clear my throat and get his attention. "Hey, 'sup?" he asks, sitting on the edge of his bed facing me.

"Did you…say something to Colin about me?"

He grins and leans back on his elbows. "I told him I knew you fuck around on the road too." He holds up a paw. "Look, his whole thing is that he thinks he's morally superior, but you're even better than him at that because you're faithful. So I brought you down to his level—in his eyes—and he chilled out. And he said he'd go back to leaving you alone."

I try to process that. "You told him you blew me?"

"Ha, no." Wix grins. "No way would he have let me do him if he knew I did you too."

For a moment I'm sure I heard those words wrong. "You—did him? Like, blew him?"

"Uh huh." He tilts his head. "What? You said you didn't want any more blow jobs, so I figured it'd be fine if I went and found someone else."

"But…" My brain keeps short-circuiting as I try to process Wix going and blowing my worst enemy on the team. "He doesn't care about you."

Wix snorts. "What 'care'? It's a blow job. It's like I have friends I play FBA with, and friends I trade music with, and now there's a guy I blow."

"Wait, this is going to happen again?"

He sighs and sits up. "I didn't want to say anything until after the game, but…yeah. I told him I know you chase off his boys, but that you wouldn't fuck around with me, because you can't tell me to get lost and I won't listen if you tell me to stop. But in return for a few blow jobs now and then, he has to stop being such a shit." He pauses. "I didn't say it like that."

When I don't say anything, he squints at me. "It's gonna be okay. This doesn't have to be a permanent fix, you know, just some duct tape to hold us together until Sunday."

"I don't know." Because I can't formulate my thoughts properly, they just come out. "I mean, it sounds like a really shitty arrangement, but, but you know, you don't really care, and Colin likes to feel superior to people, so it works out for both of you, I guess? And fuck, he's not going to agitate to have you traded now, is he? So I guess he'd just be worried that the other guys on the team will find out about it?"

"Yeah, something like that." Wix waves a paw. "I get it, I mean, I'm not exactly excited to tell people I'm blowing the lead at my position. If it gets out, people will think that's why I'm getting whatever I get and not earning it. So we'll figure out how to keep it quiet."

"Sounds like you've got it all figured out, I guess." I grab my tablet and lean back on the bed, going to the next play in my list. The important thing to take away from this is that I don't need to talk to Colin or worry about him for at least the rest of the week, and that's a load off my mind.

But I keep thinking about Colin and about his whole "I'm not like you." I know he's religious—but he cheats on his wife. He's homophobic—but takes blow jobs from guys. All I really know about his personality, apart from his work ethic (that, we have in common) is this mass of contradictory things, most of which consist of him proclaiming loudly the things he's not.

At least the Nativist people say they're from here. But poking at that makes it fall apart, too. What does that mean, to be "from here"? Your ancestors grew up on this land (though not all of them did, if you go far enough back) and mine grew up on the other side of the world, but we were both born in this country, so what does that distinction mean? It's a stupid way to put up a fence between you and some other people so you can point over the fence and blame them for your problems, the same way Colin somehow blames me for the fact that he's gay and trapped in a religious straight marriage.

I sigh. Three more days. I can't wait until the game, the purity of movement and coordination when I can let my physical instincts take over and trust that ten years and experience and two weeks of hard study have set them properly. I'm starting to feel the nearness of the game now, so I put Colin out of my mind and watch the film of the people I'm going to be trying to tackle in three days.

Chapter Twenty-Four (Lee)

Friday morning I have a short meeting with Peter. I tell him I haven't gotten an official offer yet, but I'm weighing the possibility. He says they've made an offer to Xu and Xu has accepted, and asks me to consider Ms. Martinet's offer, telling me how rare it is. I appreciate the courtesy and promise Peter that I'll have an answer Monday morning when I come back from Chevali. He ends the meeting with an unexpected appeal, telling me that honestly, Xu was exactly what was ownership was looking for and there wasn't any going back once he nailed the interview, and that he hopes I'll be able to see in person how valuable he is.

Being a fox, he of course intends all the layers of meaning that that holds, which I ponder over taking care of my job for the rest of the day (there's not much to do because everyone's excited about the championship, just another email to Remington's agent telling him that his client's statement disavowing Nativists, released that morning to get lost in the swamp of championship news, satisfies the team). I think, if I'm reading it right, that Peter would've preferred me for the position, but that he's hoping I'll learn some of the things that make Xu more valuable at this time.

I like Morty a lot, but if I could pick my boss, it'd be Peter, and not just because he's a fox. That's part of it, sure. The more important part is that we've worked together for years, and while we've had disagreements, we've always resolved them. I've seen him a couple times outside of work, but not often. I'm not sure we're what I would call "friends." Still, he's a great boss, and it'd be hard to leave him.

Cord goes and gets coffee before I take off and also takes the chance to sit down and tell me how great I am to work for. He doesn't ask in as many words about the Cansez offer, but the meaning is plain as the leathery shuffling of his wings. I tell him that he's great to work with as well and that for sure I wouldn't be able to find anyone like him anywhere else. He makes some noises about how he couldn't see himself living anywhere but Yerba, which of course I know; I mean, if I do go to Cansez, I would of course offer him a job there and of course he would turn it down.

And then I'm on my way to the airport for the short flight down to Chevali, reading more material about the Cansez Explorers and their staff, reading articles about Cansez politics and activism, trying to find that one piece of information that will make my decision easier one way or the other.

I don't find it, because it's not there, but when I turn my phone on in Chevali there's an email from Morty. "Official offer coming Mon morning," it says. "Call me before you do anything."

So that's that. It'll be interesting to see what they offer. I'll call Morty, but I'll probably talk to Peter first.

Because that email just came in, it's on my mind when my father picks me up. "How was the flight?" he asks, and I tell him I got an offer.

"Nice." He pauses; we're walking out in public and he's as aware as I am of the crowds all around us. "How much?"

"Don't know yet. The actual letter comes Monday. I just got a heads up."

We make our way down to baggage claim, get my one bag, and then walk out into the dry Chevali air, cool in January but familiar, home in a different kind of way than Yerba or Hilltown. I breathe it in, following Father into the parking garage where he shows off his monstrosity of an SUV.

"This is new." I eye it before getting in.

"The boys have a lot of friends. Well, Jaren does."

"Uh huh." I think about making a comment about my own late high school life and then remember that I never had more friends than I could squeeze into the back seat of our family sedan and I restrict myself to, "Good for him."

We pull out of the airport and I'm just thinking it's odd that Father hasn't said anything more about the offer letter when he says, "Don't accept when it comes in."

"I haven't decided yet."

"I mean…" He taps a claw on the wheel. "Even if you want to take it, take it to your current boss first and see if you can get a better offer out of them."

"What if I really want to take the other job?"

"Then you take that better offer…" His paw sweeps left to right. "Back to Cansez. You can get an extra few thousand. Maybe more. It's pro sports, I don't know how their salaries work, except for what you've told me."

Which is mostly only my salary, because Father manages my retirement accounts. "If I were an all-pro linebacker, it'd be one thing, but front office doesn't usually get the bank broken for them. And my situation is tenuous enough what with my boyfriend and all."

"Have you thought that Cansez might be recruiting you to try to make Dev an offer?"

"Like Chevali did back in his contract year? Maybe. But they haven't even mentioned him, and honestly I'm not sure a few years of a very good linebacker is the puzzle piece they need to get to the championship. Scratch that: I'm sure it's not."

"It'd be nice for you guys to be on the same team, though."

"It would. But it might be one of those things that doesn't happen until later, when he's retired and we can pick him up as a linebacker coach or a consultant on player development or something like that. Anyway, even if they did pick him up, there's no guarantee it'd last."

He smiles sideways. "You guys have talked about that."

"Extensively." The turquoise and salmon décor of the airport shopping mall slides by us, festooned with Firebirds banners. "How's everything with the family?"

"Everything's good. Everyone's looking forward to seeing you."

"Same here." My thoughts drift back to Mike, wondering if I'll get a chance to talk to him about his concerns about the colleges. That seems so far away now that I'm worrying about the job situation and Dev's game. "Looks like the city is enjoying its third championship game in the Miski era."

Father chuckles. "There's a restrained optimism. Third time lucky and all that. At the same time, having lost two in recent memory does something to a fan's psyche."

"They'll win this one."

We merge onto the highway, and he gives me another look. "And then…?"

"We haven't talked about it, but…yeah, I guess. Probably."

"I'm hearing excitement?"

I curl my tail. "It's been so long now that it's secondary to the game. I mean, once the game's over, we'll talk about it."

"Just my two cents, but I don't think a promise you made nearly ten years ago is sufficient reason to get married. I'm sure you two have plenty of other reasons, but you should make sure to find them before you go throwing some of Dev's money at a wedding planner."

"Thanks," I say. "I mean, I know you and Angela only dated for five years before getting married, so maybe you don't understand what it's like to wait."

He snorts. "Fine. You still like fish?"

I wrinkle my nose. "I get a lot of fresh fish in Yerba. What fish do you catch here in the desert?"

"There's catfish farms. Angela has a friend who gets us some good fresh fillets, and she was planning to make them tonight."

"Sure." I turn back to the window. The Chevali skyline inches past, a couple miles distant. "I appreciate the advice about the wedding. It's just something we'll talk about later."

"Yep, okay." Father pauses. "Sorry for shoving my nose in."

"It's fine. Sorry for snarking back."

"I'm used to it."

"Back atcha."

He grins, and the rest of the ride we talk about the upcoming game. There are a few things I know that Father doesn't because of my immersion in the sport, but not as many as he thinks. Dev doesn't talk to me a lot about his team for legal reasons, so mostly I know what everyone else knows. I know a little more about the psychology of a couple of the Firebirds and Devils because I scouted some of them, and others used to play for us, but none of that helps me know who's more likely to win.

Angela, Father, Jaren, and Mike now live in a smallish house near the top of a slight rise that they call a "hill," which makes me snicker every time I see it. Jaren moved into the room over the garage for his senior year of high school, and he and Father ran a new duct out there so he could get the central air from the house. He doesn't have a thermostat, so he has to live with whatever temperature the house wants to be, but he's happy being in his own space. He can even get in through the garage without going into the main house.

Mike was happy enough to stay in the one bedroom upstairs (Angela turned the other into her work-from-home office for her online business making small jewelry from things she buys at estate and garage sales) while Father and Angela have the ground-floor master bedroom. They have a yard, but Father's pretty water-conscious in the desert, so even though he loved the big yard we had back when I was growing up, they've made their yard a nice garden of succulents.

When we get home, the house smells fantastic: frying oil and dough, green beans, and an assortment of southwestern spices of which I can name about half. Angela comes out of the kitchen bringing wafts of spices with her to greet me with a hug, touching her muzzle to mine. "So good to see you again," she smiles, and my tail wags along with hers.

"Nice to see you too," I say. "Thanks for making dinner."

"Oh, it's no trouble. We order out so much, what with the boys being busy and my business doing well. I miss making dinner now and then."

"Yeah, Father told me." We follow her back into the kitchen. "People love the jewelry, huh?"

She smiles. "People always love jewelry."

"But," Father says. "They really love the care she puts into the designs and the way she describes them. Telling a story is half of making the sale."

"Good marketing," I agree.

"But it's not just marketing." Angela stirs the pot of green beans. "The story is what stays with them and they tell it when people admire the jewelry. It's an important part of it. So many people just think they can make a beautiful pendant or brooch and let the item speak for itself."

"Awesome." I smile. "This smells fantastic. Hey, is Mike around?"

"Up in his room, I think," Angela says. She looks at Father, a worried glance. "He stays up there a lot—doesn't come down to play games much anymore. He says he's studying for school, and the browser doesn't show any sites he shouldn't be looking at."

"I'm sure th—he's fine. Can I go up and say hi or does he not like that?"

"Make sure to knock," Father says.

Angela rolls her eyes. "We found that one out the hard way."

"I remember, I think." I gesture to Father. "You told me about it on the phone?"

"Probably." He goes to stand next to Angela. They look good together, fox and coyote, and though they don't exchange more than a light kiss, they do keep their long, bushy tails against each other. "How long until dinner?"

"I was waiting to put the catfish on until you got home, so now…ten minutes?"

He nods at me. "I'll bring him down," I say. It's strange saying "him," and I'm glad that it's strange.

Mike has a poster on their bedroom door of Tally Desposinho, a soccer player currently considered one of the best in the world. I knock right on the attractive zorro's groin. "Mike? It's Lee."

Movement inside, and then they open the door and stand there. "Hey."

"Hey," I said. "How you been?" Behind them lies the clutter of any teenager's room: more posters on the wall, clothes on the floor, laptop on the bed.

"Not bad." They hesitate. "Uh, is dinner ready?"

"In about ten. You want to talk a bit before?"

They think about it, big coyote ears sweeping back, and then they say, "Sure," like it doesn't matter one way or another.

So I step inside and close the door behind me. They take a pile of books off the swivel chair by their small desk and gesture to it, then perch on the edge of the bed while I curl my tail around myself and sit.

"So hey, I had a good time with you last week," I start out. "Hope you had fun too."

They glance at their laptop and then at the door. "Yeah, it was cool. I, uh, don't want to talk about that stuff right now."

"No, I know. I figured, not here. But your mom told me you weren't really thinking about any of the schools we looked at? Did you find another one you liked better?"

"Uh…" They press their paws together. "I mean, not really. I was just thinking maybe I'd stick around closer to home. You know, there's Bianca and Chevali…some good schools there."

"Right, of course, I can see that." But something's bugging me. "You seemed excited about some of the schools we looked at, though. Was I reading that wrong?"

"I thought about it and I dunno, it's far away."

"Didn't you say that even Crystal City would be too close?" He shrugs and doesn't say anything, so I try another tack. "Are there good clubs at Bianca or Chevali? There weren't in my day but it's like fifteen years later now, so I could believe there would be."

"Probably. I mean, yes. I haven't—we haven't gone yet." They play with their tail, affecting nonchalance.

I've talked to college-age kids for a decade now and I can tell when there's something they're not telling me. But I also know that if they don't want to tell me, I won't get it by asking directly. So I press on the point I think is false. "You want to be closer to home to be near your brother?"

"I mean, that'd be cool, but I know he's got his own thing going on. He's all caught up in sports and stuff."

"Your mom?"

They give a half nod. "She's gonna be all alone. Uh, except for your dad."

I grin. "I know they love you guys, but I think they're also looking forward to having you off at school so they can travel around a bit. My father's always wanted to spend more time overseas."

Mike shakes their head. "Anyway, what about you? You went to Cansez for that interview?"

"Oh yeah. It went pretty well."

"So you gonna take it?"

I fold my paws together. "Haven't decided yet. It's a good offer, but I'm also doing a lot of good work in Yerba and I'd hate to leave that behind. But the Cansez job would advance my career better."

Mike lets their tail drop, staring down at it. "Your career is pretty important."

"A lot of things are important." I get a sense of something from their body language and I'm about to ask more about it, but then Father calls that dinner is ready, so we go down, and then I don't have another chance to talk to them for the rest of the night.

Dinner's great, dominated by Jaren talking about his senior year in high school, wanting to tell me about the debate team and how he's going to do debate at the U of Chevali and how there's a cute kangaroo rat and he's been dating her for a couple months. He passes around pictures on his phone of the two of them at debate practice, at the Starbucks near campus, at the protest when the Nativist speaker came to campus.

"Hey," he says to me after that last one. "Speaking of…what are you and Dev doing the middle of February?"

"I don't know. I don't think we have specific plans, but that's the beginning of my super busy time. Why?"

"Oh, one of our debate topics in the spring is the Nativist question, because it's in the news, and it's important here. Our state has the border and all that."

"Right." I look to Father and Angela for cues, but this seems new to them as well.

"So, you know, we're all coyotes and foxes, right, and none of us are targets of that. I have some friends, but Dev grew up a while ago and I want to get the perspective of someone who's been around for a while to talk about how they experienced these feelings twenty years ago as opposed to now. Like, someone who's been there. You think Dev would be okay coming to talk to me?"

"I don't see why not." I try not to smile. "You wouldn't be able to find someone local?"

"Oh, sure," he says. "Our teacher is bringing in a local activist. But it's different when it's someone I know, you know? I feel like I can ask him things I wouldn't necessarily ask someone I'm just meeting."

"Sure. Makes sense." Plus, of course, he'd impress his college friends by bringing a star Chevali athlete to college.

"Thanks." And Angela asks him when he's going to bring this kangaroo rat home, but I don't listen too much to that conversation because Jaren's question has brought something to my mind and I'm chewing it over.

That night, after the coyotes have gone to their respective beds, Father and I sit out on the deck in the chilly evening, bundled up in light jackets against the chilly desert breeze. "I really like the house," I say.

"Thanks. It's…home."

"That's what I like about it." I pause. "You miss Hilltown?"

"You ask me that every month."

"And you always say you can go back whenever you want. You don't say yes or no."

Father smiles. "I'm very happy where I am right now. I'm going to take the family up there on Mike and Jaren's spring break. I figured we'd go to Javive and then skating in the park."

"You never took me skating in the park."

"I did, when you were five. You fell down and hated it and told us you never wanted to go back. So we never took you back."

I can't help but smile as I lean back and look up at the moon. "I feel like you could have tried again at some point."

"Oh, your mother wasn't a fan either. She went for my sake but said the rink there was too small, and since you didn't want to go either, we never really brought it up."

"There it is."

He gives me a look. "Don't blame it on your mother."

"You just did."

"Not entirely on her. I could've pushed harder on some things, but it was easier to just let them go, you know?"

I nod. "I know." I exhale. For all the air is chilly, I still can't see my breath. "Do you think it makes a difference to Mike whether I'm there in the Yerba area or not?"

Father flicks one ear. "I'm sure it makes some difference. Do you think that's the difference between him going to college there or not?"

"I don't know. Maybe?"

"You never seemed that close." Father peers at me. "What happened on his trip?"

And here it is. I really don't want to share Mike's secret, but Father has always been pretty adept at picking up on my lies. I pick my words carefully. "Mike talked to me about some stuff th—he's going through. I can't tell you what, but…I think we bonded."

Father nods and leans back to think. He glances up, and for the first time I wonder if Mike's bedroom faces this way, if he can hear us through his window glass. That's clearly what Father's thinking too, because when he talks again, his voice is low, just the barest trickle of sound. "The divorce was hard on him. Jaren has lots of friends, but Mike withdraws a lot. He saw a therapist for a while and then stopped. We asked him why and he said it wasn't helping him anymore, so we left it at that. But he's always been a little harder to reach, so if you two bonded, then…maybe, yeah." Father exhales and now I see his breath, very faintly. "The counselor told us that one of the ways a divorce can affect a child is making them more prone to take risks. Sex, drugs, that kind of thing."

"I told you, no drugs. And Gerrard didn't leave."

"As good as, especially during football season. We don't talk about it much, because of your relationship with Dev, but when the season's going, he misses about three quarters of his weekends. Angela ends up taking the boys. We don't complain; we love them. But it's hard on them. And I can see Mike not wanting to go somewhere you're going to be leaving."

"But I'll be leaving way before he gets to college. If I even take the job. He won't even be applying until the fall." It feels weird and like a betrayal to use 'he' for Mike now, but it comes back easily as a habit, and I hate that too.

Father smiles. "But if he is worried about big changes…"

I think about going out to the clubs with him, how he didn't want to go out without me, how he asked if I'd dress up as well. How he didn't hit it off with any of the people he talked to at the schools. And part of me thinks, what if I did stay in Yerba? Mike would probably only want to hang out with me for like a few months at best. Once they and Maxie got their feet under themselves, they'd have lots of friends in school.

"Maybe." I'm turning it over in my head. "I thought about going to college in Port City where Aunt Carolyn was, but I didn't want to get away from home that bad."

"Mike doesn't want to get away from home. He'd be happy staying around here."

When I wanted to go to college, though, I was gay and I felt stifled in my home. I wanted a place where I could open up and be me. If I'd known anyone in Yerba, would I have gone there? Maybe. I'd stayed pretty close to home and I hadn't known how to come out to my parents, so I did it brashly, loudly, because I hadn't figured out how to talk to them.

I exhale. Keeping my voice low, I say, "But maybe he'd be happier in Yerba."

Father turns to me. "Don't base your career choice on what your step-brother might or might not want."

"I'm not. But it's a factor, right? And it's not just him. There's other guys counting on me."

"There could be more people in Cansez who don't have anyone."

"Thanks, yes, I know." I sigh and shake my head. "But I don't know those guys. I don't think this has an easy solution."

Father laughs. "Life rarely does."

"Thanks for that profound bit of wisdom."

He snorts. "The good thing for you in this situation is that I don't think there's a bad choice, if that helps."

"A little." And he's right. Either place will offer challenges and opportunities, and either place will advance my career. So…so maybe I've been asking myself the wrong questions.

Chapter Twenty-Five (Dev)

The best thing to do with the information that Wix is blowing Colin and that this is apparently something they both want to make semi-permanent is to forget all about it. The days right before a championship game are stressful enough without worrying about what other things are going on, especially things that I have been told firmly and clearly are not my business.

Friday is the last full day of practice; Saturday is a film study and light practice day to keep us fresh for Sunday. Practice is uneventful and Gerrard says at the end of it, "I suppose this is the best I can hope for," which has us practically giddy heading into the locker room.

Friday night I talk briefly to Lee before he gets on his flight to Chevali, though even the excitement to see him again is tempered by the overwhelming stress of the upcoming game. He still doesn't know what to do about his job and I don't have any more good advice for him, except to express confidence that he'll figure it out. Wix stays out late that night playing video games or maybe blowing Colin, who knows? Not my business. I sit in bed studying film until he comes in and settles down to do the same.

Saturday morning, though, he's slow getting up. I come out of the shower and he's still in bed, lying on his back staring at the ceiling. "Hey," I say. "You feeling okay?"

"You have anything to help you sleep?" he asks.

"I usually go to the trainers if an injury's bothering me," I say. "You didn't sleep well?"

"Tossed and turned a lot." He sits up and smooths down the fur on his bare chest. "I don't think I'm stressed about the game but whatever, I don't want to go into it half-asleep."

"Stress comes out in a lot of ways." I go back into the bathroom to check my bathroom bag. "I've just got painkillers here and you don't want those. I'd go to the trainer."

"I don't want to come off like I have some kind of mental health issue. I just need a good night's sleep."

"So tell them that." Usually Wix jumps in the shower right after I get out, so I don't have to worry about being naked in front of him, but he's still sitting in bed collecting himself, so I grab my t-shirt and shorts and go into the bathroom to change.

"I've seen it already," he calls.

"I know," I say, half-closing the door. "Doesn't mean you have to see it again."

He doesn't move in the fifteen seconds it takes me to pull compression shorts and shirt on over my slightly-damp fur and come back out, but he has thought of a new plan. "Could you go ask for stuff for me?"

"What, so they think I have a problem?" I snort.

"You're older. Older guys have trouble sleeping."

"I'm thirty-two," I say. "Lion Christ."

"I said old*er*, not old. Anyway, you have a good reputation. You've been here for years. I don't wanna be 'the guy who has trouble sleeping.'"

I shake my head. "It's perfectly fine to go and ask for stuff to help you sleep. I know a buncha guys who've done that in the playoffs before. Especially if it's your first championship game, nobody's going to ding you for it."

"Fine." He swings his legs over the edge of the bed and gets up—naked of course, half out of his sheath, but this time he doesn't do anything to make sure I see it, just trots to the bathroom and closes the door behind him.

"Rookies," I mutter, and go down to breakfast.

All through breakfast, though, I think about injuries that kept me from sleeping well over the years, the painkillers I took for them and still carry with me, and I think again about Fisher, about Murell, about other retired players with chronic ailments.

I don't have to decide now, but if this is going to be my last game—if there's even a chance of that—then I've got to make it a game I'm going to be proud of. I'd like to say I always do, but looking back over ten years, there are for sure games where we were ahead and I slacked off to save energy, or games where my knee or hip was bothering me and I worried first about making sure I didn't injure myself further. But I feel pretty good going into this game, as good as I can expect after eighteen football games in four months, and I'm determined that whatever else happens, I'm going to leave this game proud of myself.

Coach Samuelson liked to remind us that we were a team. Coach Lopez says that if each one of us makes sure we're proud of our game performance, that our team will do well. It's hard to argue with his results, at least this year. Carson and Ty and I all think he's a good motivator, but to be honest, we don't talk to Coach Lopez very much. Unless there's a problem.

No problems this Saturday. I see Wix later and he's still working himself up to go ask the trainers for sleeping pills. Stress gets to you in a lot of ways. Back when I was preparing for my first championship game, I was stressed about so many other things that I couldn't pick the game out of them. I still feel like I did okay in that game. I got a sack of an almost un-sackable quarterback, and we played tight defense all the way up to the end of the game. But like Ty, who tried to make an impossible play to win it there at the end, I felt like I could've won it if I'd put extra effort into it. Never mind that I did exactly what the coaches told me to do on the critical play; never mind that nobody's ever questioned the work I did in that game or the other one we lost. From the outside, as long as you're not visibly slacking, everybody assumes you're doing your best. You're the only one who wonders whether you had a little bit more to give. If you're not sprawled flat on your back at the end of the game, you'll always wonder that.

In our film study session, Gerrard goes over the Devils' offense again. Of all of us, he seems the least affected by the pressure, breaking down the different sets and play calls like this is any other game. His steadiness calms us all and helps us focus on the things we need to watch for, the ways we need to react to the Devils' offense, and our assignments once a play's started. We've drilled this stuff over and over all season, and these specifics for the last two weeks, but he delivers them as energetically as if we're hearing them for the first time.

"Light scrimmage in half an hour," Gerrard reminds us as we finish the session. "We're on the backup field."

That means the offense is on the main field with the second-team defense trying to emulate what Port City will be doing; we'll be facing the second-string offense running a bunch of the Devils' plays. It's tough on those guys because they also have to be ready to step in if one of us goes down, so they're learning the better part of two playbooks.

The scrimmage goes well. They score once on us, and we congratulate them, but the rest of the time we keep them pretty well pinned. While we're showering, the defensive coaches huddle up and at the end of the showers they haven't come up with anything new for us to study that night, so that's a good sign.

Everyone seems pretty confident going into our free evening. I check around to see who's doing what, but everyone's busy. Carson's going out with Gerrard, and as much as I like those guys, I don't want to talk football, which is what I'm sure they'll be doing. Ty is "staying in," he tells me with a wink, which means that one or both of his partners is in town for the game and he's going to sneak out to have a nice night with them. Sounds pretty good, and I think about calling up Lee and telling him to meet me at my apartment downtown, but the last thing I want to do is get in trouble for sneaking out. Gerrard isn't Ty's wide receivers coach, who's inclined to look the other way as long as players are responsible.

I call up Charm, but he says he's already booked for the evening. That leaves my roommate, but he's on his way out when I get back to the room. "Hey," he says, "look, I was gonna stay in and have a room service dinner, but then Xalic called and said they got an FBA tournament going on, and they got steaks over there, so I'm gonna jet. But you should eat my dinner—it's steak too, and some veggies and shit, I dunno."

"Um, okay. Thanks." I raise a paw to him and go over to get my tablet and lie down on my bed. I guess I'll spend my evening like an old veteran, reviewing film in my room and maybe playing a game on my phone. Maybe I am old, like Wix says.

I've barely gotten comfortable on the bed when there's a knock at the door and a voice says, "Room service."

"Hmph." I set the tablet aside and am halfway to the door when something about the voice registers with me, or maybe it's the scent I get through the door once I get there. I don't bother with the peephole; I yank the door open and grab Lee, pull him inside into a huge hug.

"Oof," he says, dropping the large duffel bag he's carrying to hug me back as the door swings shut.

"What the fuck are you doing here?" I press my nose to one of his ears, making it flick around. "You could get in trouble. *I* could get in trouble."

"We won't get in trouble." He grins. "I called in a couple favors. Gerrard said it would be okay and gave me Wix's number so I could enlist him to help."

"Wait—Gerrard? Coach Gerrard? Coach 'football is life' Gerrard?"

We've still got our arms around each other, leaning back (and up, in his case) so we can see each other. Lee gives me a very foxy smile. "I argued that I could help you relax and be ready for the game tomorrow, and I had a little bit of help, but that's not important. We can all change a little bit, I think, and better late than never."

"Sure." I don't want to let him go, but now I'm aware of a scent over the smell of fox, coming from the duffel. "Wait, did you really bring dinner?"

"Uh huh." He's no more eager to let go. "That Sonoran place near your apartment? I told them you wanted your usual before the big game. I had to force them to take money for it, too."

"Oh my god." The wave of scent seems to open a giant pit in my stomach, which growls in anticipation. "I know it's probably not the most romantic, but do you think we could have the food before the sex this time?"

"Mmm, I'll allow it." His tail swishes behind him. "If only because the food will get cold but I'm pretty sure the sex won't."

So he breaks out some carne asada burritos, a couple chicken quesadillas, the best tortilla chips in the Southwest, and a bunch of salsa. We sit at the desk and munch happily for a while, me devouring the first burrito so fast that Lee laughs and says, "Take a minute to chew."

"So," I say, licking salsa from my lips, "why are you here? Why not wait until tomorrow night?"

He brushes chip crumbs from his collared shirt. "Couple reasons. I've been thinking about my job and I probably need to talk to Peter about it early Monday morning, and I didn't want to spend a lot of time tomorrow night talking about my job when we should be celebrating your championship."

"So instead we're going to talk about it tonight when I should be thinking about the game?"

He grins and reaches over to rest his paw on mine. "I know you, tiger. You're prepared."

"Hmph. Maybe."

"And if you're not, tell me and I'll go."

I flip my paw to grab his. "Like hell."

He laughs. "All right. But that's really the least important reason. There's another one which I'll get to later. But I was thinking about something else, too, and this is the main one. I don't know if you've been thinking about our agreement at all."

"Not a lot." I regret it as soon as I say it. "I mean, it's been an eventful two weeks."

"It has." He rubs my paw. "I haven't been thinking about it a whole lot either. I did last night, though, and today, and I thought a lot about how hard it was to take a break from each other these two weeks."

"Like I said. Eventful."

"Right." He pauses and his sky-blue eyes open a bit wider, holding mine. I think I know what's coming, and the amazing thing, the wonderful thing, is that I'm not scared at all. "So look. I don't care what happens tomorrow."

"Yes," I blurt out.

His grin widens and he cocks his head to the side. "What?"

"You're going to say we should get married anyway and yes, fox, hell yes, let's do it."

The grin stays there and he doesn't say anything, and I feel a tiny flutter of panic, but not real panic, because I know he's just messing with me. "Unless you weren't going to say that, in which case I don't care because fuck it, we're as good as married and we should go ahead and have the ceremony and the family and all that already."

"No, yeah, that's what I was going to say." He laughs. "Sorry, I don't have a ring and I know that proposing over a quesadilla isn't the most romantic thing in the world. And if you had a big proposal ready in case you won, I'm sorry."

"No." Although that would've been good. Dang, I should've been thinking about that.

"Honestly, I didn't either. I did before the last championship game, and this year I meant to, and then the whole thing happened with the job and all, and Mike…" He shakes his head. "Not important. I'm glad we're on the same page. That was really the most important thing I came here to say."

I don't want to let go of his paw. "I'm glad you did. I wasn't thinking specifically about that but I have been thinking that I was glad I could talk to you through these two weeks. And all the stuff with Wix, I mean, we could've had a big dramatic thing about it, but we didn't. You're the best part of my life and I don't want to give that up ever."

He scoots his chair around so he can lean against my shoulder. "I hope you never will."

I wrap my other arm around him. For a lovely long moment we sit like that, and then he says, "Want to go to bed, or are you still hungry?"

"Uh…" The temptation is strong, but so are other urges. "Like you said, the sex won't get cold."

"If it hasn't after ten years, it won't in another half hour." He tilts his muzzle up to nuzzle mine. "Get all you want now."

"Oh shit, besides, I haven't told you the latest thing with Wix."

So around mouthfuls of my second burrito, I tell him about Wix blowing Colin. Talking to Lee on the phone is nice, but in person I get to see his eyes widen and his paw come to his muzzle to stifle a laugh, which is even better. "Ha ha," he says. "Oh, shit. I don't even know what to think about that."

"Right?"

He shakes his head. "Just think, if you'd thought of that eight years ago you could've had a completely different relationship with him."

I sputter burrito rice at him. "Dammit, fox."

His ears flick and he gets a little of that "made you laugh" smile. "Seriously, I don't want to turn into a 'kids these days' guy, but they're all so much freer with who they are and who they want to be. It's really great. I know back in college we were out on the forefront of change, but Mike has such a broader idea of what's possible for them, even if they're afraid of it. I mean, when I was dressing up in college, it wasn't about my identity or anything. I'm not regretting it—I don't think there's much of me that identifies as female, but even if there was, I wouldn't have known that I could do it back then."

"Wait." I hold up a paw and then swallow the bite of burrito in my mouth. "'Them'?"

"Oh yeah. That's the pronoun Mike wants to use. They started on the visit to Yerba and I'm trying really hard to train myself to use it."

"It's weird. I don't like it."

"It's uncomfortable, but that's what they want. What's annoying is you can't use it in front of Father or Angela yet, because they don't know."

"Wait—they, your dad and Angela, or they, Mike?"

He raises an eyebrow. "Father and Angela don't know about Mike."

"See? It's confusing."

Lee sighs dramatically. "Only if you make it."

"I'll be good around Mike, I promise." I grin myself at having been able to get to him even a little.

"You better be."

"How's he—sorry, how are they doing?"

"They're good. I got to chat with them a little. I really want you to meet Maxie."

He waits, getting me back a little bit. "All right," I growl, finishing off the burrito. "Who's Maxie?"

I get a sweet foxy smile. "Maxie is Mike's female alter ego. They're really fun to be around."

"Oh why, does he—do they—act different?"

Lee considers that. "A little. But it's more…watching them grow into this new identity is rewarding. Or, not a new identity really, but something that's been a part of them for a while and they're only now getting to express."

"Sort of like when we came out."

His paw slides over to mine and squeezes it. "A lot like that."

Chapter Twenty-Six (Lee)

Something Father said nags at me, but I can't quite put my finger on what it is. After we say goodnight, I'm not ready to sleep, so I sit in the guest room (Angela's office) and smell the glue and metal from her jewelry business and look up gay clubs in Chevali. I have the idea that maybe I can show Mike that there aren't as many here, or maybe that we'll go out to one and it'll be shitty and that'll convince them to go to Yerba no matter what I decide about the job.

To my surprise, there are a bunch of gay clubs in the area. Not as many as Yerba, but a respectable number, more than I would've expected in moderately-conservative Chevali. When I read up on them, they're pretty highly rated, too. And one of them is called "Studio 57."

It's a play off the legendarily crazy club from the seventies where celebrities went to drug-fueled orgies (allegedly), with Dev's number 57 in place of the original 54. I look up that club and find that it was founded five years ago and indeed, the owner is a Firebirds season ticket holder.

I wonder if Dev's ever been there. I know I haven't. We should pay them a visit sometime in the off-season.

It's nice, I think, closing the laptop, that even if they do stay here, Mike and Maxie will have places where they can be themselves. And that's the moment when I remember what Father said, and I know what I have to do about the job. So I make a phone call.

Late though it is on a Friday night, Cord picks up. "Sorry to bother you so late," I say. "I can tell from the background noise that you're in the quietest bar in Yerba."

He snorts. "I'm watching a movie in my sweatpants. I guess you're calling to tell me you made a decision. And probably that you're leaving."

"I want to point something out to you, first of all." I lean back on the fold-out couch bed. "You know that for the last few years I've been relying on you for most of the activism stuff we do, right?"

He's silent for long enough that maybe he didn't know that. Or maybe he did and just can't think of a polite way to say it. "Okay," he says. "So, what? I don't need you?"

"You know, I had a whole speech prepared about it, but if you don't need the speech, then yeah, that's my point. You don't need me. What you need is someone high up in the organization who'll listen to you and give your thoughts some weight, and that's been me. But it doesn't have to be. You can talk to Peter directly."

"Mister Emmanuel? I've only met him a couple times."

"I'll introduce you and I'll tell him how important you are to the organization."

"But—"

"Cord. They're hiring Xu because he has connections to a huge market that they don't have an in with yet. Cansez is interested in me at least partly because I have connections to a small market that they don't have an in with. Ms. Martinet isn't going to throw away those connections, especially if I'm taking them to another team."

"So we'll be competing with you for players?" He's cautious, thinking about it.

"Ideally, yeah. Think about that! What if there weren't just two teams that welcomed gay players? What if there were three? Five?"

"Huh." He exhales across the mic.

"And for the record, we'll still be friends and colleagues even if I'm on another team. We might not be able to talk about specific players, but I still want to talk about issues. Maybe we can even get a front office version of Dev's gay player chat group going."

"All right. I mean, if you're going to leave anyway, I want to make the best of it." He's still a little annoyed but coming around. "What tipped it, if I can ask?"

"I was just talking to my father about the job and the kids in Yerba who need help—the gay kids, you know." And the trans kids and the genderqueer and the ones who just want to be able to ask questions. "And he said, 'maybe there are people in Cansez who need help, too.' You know how many LGBT resource centers they have in Cansez? One. One shitty one in a shitty part of town. A couple out in the burbs, but what city kids are going to go out to the burbs for help?"

"Oof," he says. "But I'd expect that."

"And then I was looking up gay clubs in Chevali and there are a bunch. Three good LGBT centers, too. I think—I can't prove this, but I think—that Dev being here made a difference. Slowly, over the years. When he hired a private security firm a few years back for his apartment building, they were cool with his relationship to the point of wondering why it was even an issue."

"You're no All-Pro linebacker," Cord says, but in a friendly jibing way that tells me he understands.

"Nah, but I'll be an assistant GM. My name's gonna come up with the team here and there, and the owner says he supports my activism. So…I'll do what I can. Because the kids in Yerba have you and a bunch of other people to support them. There're gay kids in Cansez, too, and who do they have?"

Cord's quiet again and then he gives a short laugh. "It's funny. I used to say to Jess that you're a good boss, but I wish you were a little more involved in activism. I know football's your job and all, but…anyway, it's funny that now you're more involved and it's taking you away."

"Life's funny that way. But I'm not going away for good. You're gonna stay in my phone and I'll text you, maybe even talk to you more often than we do now. And I believe in you. You got this."

"That's a lot to dump on me," he says.

"When I was hired at the Whalers, I didn't have anyone else, so count yourself lucky."

"I guess you're right." He pauses. "Hey, congratulations on the offer. I never said that."

"Thanks."

"And when you put it like that…I can't argue with you taking it."

"Thanks again." I relax. The decision felt right to me, but I had to talk to another activist to confirm that I wasn't being impulsive. I have a few days to reflect on it before I get the official offer on Monday, but I don't think I'm going to change my mind.

·

I get the idea to go surprise Dev in his room about halfway through the play on Saturday afternoon. It's a good enough play, the story of a jaguar immigrant family, and I think that Dev would enjoy it. Then I think about how he's right here in the city but I'm not going to see him until tomorrow night. And then I think that I don't want to wait because I want to tell him about my decision, and then I think I should wait because the game is really important, and that gets me thinking about the previous two weeks and how we haven't really taken a break and it doesn't seem to matter.

So when the play's over, I review the connections I have to find a way to surprise him. Angela doesn't really talk to Gerrard much, but my step-brothers do. I wanted to talk to Mike anyway, so after the play when we're told there's going to be a forty-five minute wait for a table for dinner, I ask if Mike wants to take a walk around the nearby park.

Father starts to say something, but I catch his eye, and he nods. "Hey," he says, "it's a little chilly out. Why don't we go to the bar and get a drink?"

"Can I get a beer?" Jaren asks, anxious to show how grown-up he is.

Angela smiles and pats him on the shoulder. "Of course. In three years."

The three of them go into the restaurant bar, and Mike and I head outside to walk through the nearby park. There's not much to the park: some trees, some benches, a sculpture in one corner, and an underpass where the main road nearby cuts through it. It is more populated than I'd expected on a winter night, but it's nice to see so many people wearing Firebirds gear. I wish I'd worn my jacket.

"So what's up?" Mike asks after we've been walking a bit.

"I have a couple questions," I say. "The first one is easy."

They nod, a little guarded, but ears still up. "Okay."

"I have an old cell number for your dad. Can you tell me if it's still the right one?"

That surprises them a little. "Oh, sure."

So we take out our phones and compare numbers and I do in fact still have the correct number. "Okay."

"You're going to call him the night before a big game? He won't pick up."

"Maybe not. I have a couple other numbers I can call if that doesn't work, but I wanted to try him first." I explain to Mike that I want to go surprise Dev in his hotel room.

"Huh." They consider that. "I dunno if that's a good idea, but I guess you know him best."

"I've got a good reason," I say. "I think it'll be good enough to convince your dad."

They nod again. "So, uh, what was the other thing?"

We walk along a few steps, cross under the road, and come out the other side. There are fewer people around here, but I still choose my words carefully. "I really enjoyed your visit and meeting Maxie, and I want you to tell me honestly whether if I were for sure going to stay in Yerba, that would affect your decision about the colleges."

That one doesn't surprise them; they were expecting it. "I mean, yeah, kinda. It's always better to have someone you know around. But I dunno, it's not like, I mean…"

They're dancing around a lot. "Did you like the schools there?"

"A couple of them."

"Okay, so why not apply to them anyway? Look, here's my take: it doesn't cost you a lot to apply. See if you get in. I've got to make a decision in two days; you don't have to actually decide for, what, months? A year? If I do go to Cansez, go out again and visit the schools when I'm not there. See what you think. Because I think you're going to have a way better experience in that area than you will around here."

Their ears are out at their sides now, head half down. I go on. "If you go to school here, I think you're going to end up waiting. Maybe you'll—" I look around us. "See Maxie on weekends, if you find a place in Chevali. But I don't think you'll have the community you'd have in Yerba whether I'm there or not. And I don't think you should wait to find out what you want."

Mike doesn't say anything right away, and then they look at me. "Thanks. I don't want to wait, but I'm scared, you know?"

"I know. I came out to my parents like fifteen years ago before it was fashionable. Well, maybe it was always fashionable, but it wasn't always safe. Anyway, it was scary then, too. And I went to a little midwestern university, but at least it was a liberal arts school."

"With a football team." They smile.

"Yeah." I laugh. "They were terrible. Mostly."

"Seems to have worked out okay."

"It did." I consider. "You know what, I think you'll be fine wherever you go. You're a smart yote, and brave too, and you'll find what you need. I guess I don't want you to make me too big a factor in your plans."

They raise an eyebrow. "Jaren also thinks I do everything I do because of him. Is that a big brother thing?"

That makes me laugh. "I don't know. This is the first time I've been a big brother. But maybe it's an impulse to protect you and make sure you're doing the right thing for the right reasons. Jaren and I have both been in situations that you haven't."

"My situation isn't the same," Mike says.

"No. True."

Their tail wags. "But I had a good time hanging out. It sucks that you might be moving."

"What makes you think that?"

"Bren said you'd be a fool not to take the job in Cansez."

I stop, but we're under a tree where there's a trash can that stinks, so I move on again and Mike follows. "He said that, huh?"

"Yeah." They grin. "But he also said that sometimes you are a fool, and that's not a bad thing."

"Hmph." I look around. "Maybe we should head back."

"Let's go around that path." Mike points. "Go somewhere new."

"Sure." I chuckle. "Lead the way."

A little ways along the path, I say, "I think sometimes fathers can be like big brothers. Not always, but they get to know you and sometimes they say the right thing, the thing you need to hear at just the right time."

Mike laughs. "You think you said something I needed to hear?"

I give them a look. "Are you going to apply to the Yerba schools?"

They roll their eyes. "Probably."

"All right then." I give them my best foxy grin.

"I can't tell if that's a big brother thing or a fox thing," they say.

I swish my tail. "Probably a fox thing. I told you, I'm still getting the hang of this big brother thing."

This path takes us up to the main road and a crosswalk, and while we're waiting there, Mike says, "I think you're doing okay at the big brother thing."

I'd been thinking about Dev and that evening again, and so I'm surprised, and I guess it shows. They go on. "I mean, for not having had much practice."

"Right. Of course."

"Don't go getting all puffed about it."

"Sorry." I fluff my tail up. "It's a fox thing. I can't help it."

"Ugh." They mock groan, but grin as they do. "Were you serious about finding places in Chevali? I've looked around and there were a couple, but I never wanted to go on my own."

"Ah. Tell you what," I say. "If I can't manage to see Dev tonight, I'll go out with you."

"Oh, no." They hold up their paws. "Tonight's family night. Mom was very clear about that."

"It's fine." I grin. "Family night doesn't go until 1 am, does it?"

"No, but…" They're thinking about it now. "I'd have to get dressed— leave the house—"

"If you want to do it, we can work it out," I tell them.

The light changes, and we cross. "I hope it works out for you and Dev," they say.

•

Mike goes into the restaurant when we get back, and I call Gerrard. I'm right; he picks up quickly. "Game's tomorrow," he says by way of hello.

"I know," I say. "I think I saw a sign up about it or something."

"What's up?"

"Can you give me Dev's roommate's phone number?"

His tone is clipped and bored. "I don't want you bothering my players the night before a game."

"Okay, here's the thing," I say. "Dev and I have this thing, you know, about if he wins we'll get married, and I think it might be on his mind. I want to tell him that I want to marry him anyway, win or lose. It'll take some pressure off him."

Gerrard thinks about that. "Why not just call and tell him?"

"Come on," I say. "I can't propose over the phone. And if I call and tell him I want to visit, he might hedge, or wonder what's wrong."

"You're just going to talk?"

I cough. "I'm going to propose," I say. "What do you think will happen next? But please," I go on. "This is really important. And I think it would take one more thing off his mind tomorrow to let him play his best game."

He exhales. "Fine," he says. "Fine. But no sleeping over. You're out of there by eleven."

"One a.m."

"Midnight."

"Deal."

"All right. Let me find Wixin's number." He puts me on speaker while he scans through his phone. "You're with Angela and Bren?"

"Yeah."

"How are the boys?"

"They're good. They're both doing really good. They miss you."

"Mmm. Here's the number. I'm going to text it to you."

"Thanks. Hey, not that you need it, but good luck tomorrow."

Gerrard snorts. "We always need luck."

"True." The text comes through. "Thanks again. Sleep well."

He hangs up without saying anything. So very Gerrard.

When I look up at the restaurant, Mike's at the door waving me inside. I start walking toward him and on the way I text Wix. *Hey, this is Dev's bf. Can I get your help to surprise him tonight?*

•

Having already had dinner with the family, I don't eat a whole lot of the Sonoran food in the hotel room with Dev, but the quesadilla is pretty good. It's only like ten-thirty by the time we finish, so we sit on his bed with pillows at our backs and our tails across each other and talk about football.

"So what are you going to do about the Cansez job?" Dev asks.

"I shouldn't tell you."

"Hmph." He noses my ear. "I'll tell you what I think you're thinking."

I lean back into the strength of his arm. "Shoot."

"I think you want to do it for your career. You think it's the right career move. And I think you're a little hurt that you were passed over in Yerba. But I think you feel at home in Yerba and you want to stay there, but you're worried that you're doing it for the wrong reasons. You see a chance to be an activist again in Cansez, but you're worried that you're chasing that for the wrong reasons."

"Pff." I nuzzle him. "I told you all that on the phone. Mostly."

"I know. That's why I'm so sure about it." He grins at me. "But I also think that you're worried that maybe you're too old to make a change."

I get a shiver deep in my stomach, the kind that you get when someone says something out loud that you've barely been able to voice to yourself. Like when you type your password in the wrong field and it shows up on the screen and you're staring at it, so familiar, but in a way you've never seen before, open to everyone. "Why do you think that? I'm not saying you're wrong."

"Because I'm thinking the same thing, but different—am I too old to not make a change? Plus you keep talking about how young Mike is and I get what that means."

I exhale and lean against him. "Okay, so which way am I leaning?"

"I know you, doc." He puts his muzzle right up close to my ear. "If you don't do it, you'll kill yourself wondering what would've happened if you had. Look, Yerba will always be home to you. Keep the house, go back and hang out with Mike when he—when they go to school there. Lion Christ, doc, look how much you got into writing that anti-Nativist letter for the team, fighting discrimination. You've been talking to me about it all week and you did a fantastic job. So go be the activist again, be loud and proud in the Midwest. That's where you're leaning."

I flick my ear against his muzzle. "Even if I weren't, you'd have made a good case for it."

He kisses that ear. "You made your own case. You trust yourself, at the end of everything. Otherwise you wouldn't be here in this bed with me. There have been so many points where it would've made sense for us to break up, not just right at the beginning, but you know, the contract nego-tiation—I mean, also basically every off-season, the fact that we have to be careful what we say to each other, all of that. I feel like at least one of our football friends every year says, 'Is it really worth it?' And we always say it is."

I bury my muzzle under his chin and don't say anything for a few seconds after that. "Mike's going to apply to the Yerba schools," is what I finally manage.

He rumbles against me. "Good. You talked to him—to them?"

"Yeah. Good talk. I feel like they're scared to take that next step, and staying close to home is, you know, kind of a good excuse to not do it. If they move to Yerba, where there's so much opportunity, then if they don't do it it's all on them. Staying around Chevali, well, they can say 'there's nowhere to go out and I don't know anyone.' Which is also a choice, you know."

"Uh huh."

"It's completely different from the choice I'm making."

"I know, fox." He nuzzles my ears again, making me tingle and sigh into his fur.

"Which is also different from the choice you're making about whether to retire."

"Mmm." His arm tightens around me. "I've only been thinking about that on and off. I figure I'll have a lot of time after the game to figure it out. Right now I don't want to, but I really want to play tomorrow, so I'm not thinking about after."

"That's probably smart."

Another pause, and then he nudges me with his nose. "Do you think I should retire?"

"Heh." I inhale his scent, thick in his chest fur. "That's definitely not the kind of question I should answer."

"All right, I'll put it another way. Do you think there's a point where a football player should retire? Age-wise, injury-wise?"

"If you can still play the game, and you still love it, then…" I hesitate. "You know I'm at the wide mouth of the funnel, right? I see all the kids coming in, their eyes bright with wanting to play the game. They're healthy—mostly—and the good ones, when you get them, their joy is exciting to see. I don't work with the veterans, the old guys who've taken one too many to the knee, the back, the head. So I've got a skewed perspective." I think a little more. "There's probably an age where you're more susceptible to a damaging injury, right? But where is that? Thirty-two? Thirty-five? Medicine's better now; forty? I mean…you know the statistics as well or better than I do. So it comes down to a different point for each player. Measure the risks, weigh against the rewards."

He shifts against me. "It sounds so easy when you make it all abstract like that."

I kiss his collarbone. "Sorry."

"Move on when you're ready to move on. Just like you're deciding. Or Mike, for that matter."

My paw rests on his stomach, rubbing gently. "Like Mike?"

"Well, they're deciding if they're ready to move on to the next stage of their life. Hey, I remembered the right pronoun."

"It's not so hard if you practice."

"Yeah." His chest rumbles with pleased noises. "But anyway, yeah. It's… have we done enough where we are? Is it time to change?"

I rub his stomach and take the measure of mine. "I think it's about time to change out of these clothes, at least."

"Oh yeah." He nips my ear. "Was that the last thing you came here for?"

I scoot back from him, getting up to my knees on the bed as I start to unbutton my shirt. "I was thinking, you know. We've had a little ritual over the years, and we haven't done it every game you've won, but I think most of the times we've done it, you have won." I get halfway down and watch his eyes widen as the Port City Devils name comes into view on the t-shirt below my collared shirt. "We didn't do it for the last two championship games. So I thought…" I pull the collared shirt apart and slide out of the sleeves, then run my paw down the Devils logo on my chest. "I thought maybe we should give it a shot."

"I'll give it a shot, all right." He pulls his shirt off in a quick, fluid motion.

I jump off the bed, as much to pull my pants off as to start the chase around the hotel room. "You think you can still catch me, old stud?" I unbuckle the pants and shake them off as he stalks around the bed. I clamber over the other bed and pull my underwear off behind it. Dev grins, pushing his pants and underwear down as he stares across the bed. "What is it Charm calls you?" I tease. "Gramps?"

"Uh-huh." His voice has a low purr-growl in it, his smile wide. "How many workouts did you do this week, fox who is the same age as me?"

"I'm ten months younger—eek!" He jumps onto the bed and as I run, he jumps off to land in front of me. I have no time to react; his arms are around me and I'm falling to the floor, but he's below me and I land not on carpet but on warm tiger muscle, arms keeping me immobile against him.

"Now," he says, "I've got you, you Devil."

I wriggle, but in a moment we've rolled over and I'm flat on my back. We're both hard, my erection pressed into his stomach as he growls and nibbles my neck fur, his poking at my thighs as I squirm around. I clutch his sides, feeling the muscles ripple under his short fur, which sends the fleeting thought across my mind that I should be stricter about my gym regimen. Then his warmth and breath distract me back to the immediate present.

There are no thoughts about work here anymore. He leaves my t-shirt on—that's the whole point—but the rest of our clothes are gone pretty

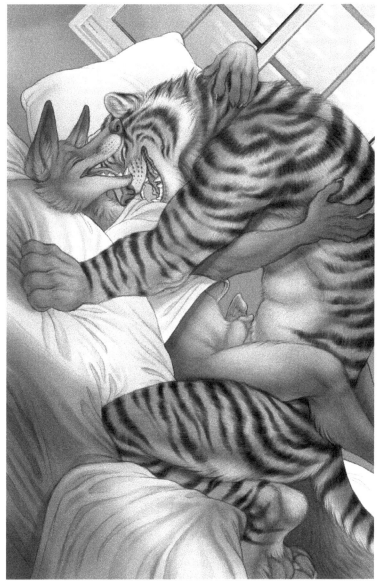

soon. We kiss, we grope each other, roll onto our sides after a little bit mostly because that way he can get his paw between us to grip my shaft.

However routine our lovemaking was before this two-week break, now it feels fresh and new. I can't explain that and don't want to try too hard to. I'm enjoying the scent of him and the love radiating from every touch, as well as his enthusiasm and energy to explore my body. I'm going to be with him for the rest of my life, I think, and that thought fills me with enough joy that I have to stop for a second and bury my face against him.

Eventually we want to move on from paws; he takes my shaft in his muzzle and gives it some attention, and then I reciprocate, and then, panting, he asks me, "Where's the lube?"

I grin up his stomach and broad chest at him. "What?" I ask, "doesn't Wix have some?"

He's surprised, then he jumps for me again, flipping me over onto my stomach. "If I wanted Wix's lube," he growls into my ear, "I would've grabbed it a couple nights ago."

"Okay, okay!" I squirm theatrically. "It's in the bag!"

"Hmph." He gets up, but plants a paw between my shoulderblades. "Stay there."

The rest of it is all very familiar: his slick fingers under my tail, then his hard warmth; his thrusts growing in urgency until he flips me over onto my back; his paw around me, stroking me to match his pleasure. After all these years, we can time our climaxes well, and this time we get pretty close. He slams into my rear only about ten seconds before I gasp and arch and splatter the Devils logo.

And then we lie together, my legs around his hips, his weight on me but not entirely, and we nuzzle and kiss each other and murmur, "love you," back and forth.

"When do you have to leave?" he asks after a little while of this. He's slid out of me by this time, but we haven't put any clothes back on.

"Mm, Gerrard said midnight, and that's what I told Wix."

"So, uh." He twists to look at one of the clocks by the bed. "Like forty-five minutes."

"Yeah."

He licks my nose. "I bet I can be ready to go again in twenty."

I stare up into his golden eyes. "You want to?"

His smile is huge. "Yeah."

So seventeen minutes later, he's inside me again, thrusting, and to my surprise I'm responding as well, and within a few seconds of each other, he throws his head back and moans deep in his throat and I tighten around him and add to the mess on my shirt.

"Mmmf." We might both have said that at the same time. Again we lie there together, still on the floor, until I say, "I better shower so I can get out of here."

"You won't have time to dry off."

"I can do that at Father and Angela's place." I kiss his nose, and reluctantly we disengage. "I don't mind heading home a little damp. It'll be a nice reminder."

He laughs. "I'll join you. Don't want to be naked when Wix gets back."

"Why not?" I say, and before I can say anything else he grabs my muzzle.

"That's enough, fox. Fuck, I wouldn't have let it happen if I knew I was going to be teased about it all the damn time."

He lets go as we get into the shower, and I stay quiet for a moment, and then I say, "Yes, you would, and you did."

"Foxes," he grumbles, and then stops. "No, not 'foxes.' You. *My* fox."

"My tiger."

We hug under the shower spray, and then we kiss, and then he forces me away. "Okay, okay, we don't have time for this."

"There's always tomorrow night." But I get the shampoo and quickly clean the messy areas, and Dev helps, and then I help clean him up. We get toweled off and mostly dry, enough to get dressed again (the t-shirt goes in the bag, which I take with me).

It's 12:03 when I pull the door open and turn to take one last look at him. "Sorry for the super-casual proposal," I say. "I'll get you a ring soon."

He gives me a wide smile back. "I'm gonna get my own ring," he says.

Chapter Twenty-Seven (Dev)

Wix gets back about ten minutes after Lee leaves, and he wants details of the night but I tell him I'll tell him later. "What 'later'?" he grumbles. "We play tomorrow and then we all go home."

"'Later' starts now and goes on indefinitely," I tell him.

He grumbles. "You hang out with foxes, it rubs off on you."

"Something rubbed off on me." I'm happy enough that it's actually an effort not to tell him, but I don't want to get into a whole conversation about it. "I promise to tell you more later. It went really well, though."

"Good."

"Thanks for clearing out."

He salutes. "Glad I could help."

"Get some rest," I told him. "Big day tomorrow, you might remember."

"Oh? Nobody's mentioned anything the past two weeks." He flips me off and saunters into the bathroom.

When he opens the door again, I ask, "Did you get something to help you sleep?"

He reaches back into the bathroom and shows me a bottle. "Got it from Colin," he says.

"Oh, is that where you went?"

"Eventually." He licks his lips and yawns. "Told him I needed a good night's sleep and he gave me one of those. He's got like five."

"I wondered how he sleeps at night," I say. "Now I know."

•

Pills or no pills, Wix gets up before me and is in the shower when my alarm goes off. He comes out completely naked, but at least he's not hard and he's not trying to entice me or anything. And with all that behind us, I can admit that he's pretty nice to look at.

I don't tell him that, of course. I just go take my shower.

The mornings of championship games, in my limited experience, are weird affairs. Everyone's trying to act normal because that's what you do. But everyone knows that it's not a normal day, so there's that underlying everything. We go to the stadium early and it's impossible not to see the banners, to know that people all over the city are buzzing with excitement.

You remember the championship games you watched growing up and how exciting that was, and you think about every single fuckup that happened in one of those games, how often the player never lived it down, and you pray to whatever god you pray to that that isn't you.

That was the first two games, anyway. This morning I feel calm. The evening with Lee reminded me that whatever happens today, there are many more ways to measure the success of your life. There are more important things than a championship (not many, but a few). But also, today, the game *is* the most important thing. I'm going to do my best and that's all anyone can ask. I've established a pretty good legacy in the league, so I'd have to fuck up pretty epically for it to make a difference in my career.

I spend the first hour at the stadium talking to the young guys, the ones who haven't been to a championship game before. I remember all the things coaches have told me over the years and I add in a few of my own. I tell them they're gonna do great, that the coaches have them covered, that we've been out on this field before and everything's going to be fine. But also different, because there's going to be twice as many cameras, the crowd's going to be so intense, and you're going to feel the impact of every single little thing. "Remember it," I tell them. "Own it. Don't let it own you. These memories, win or lose, they're gonna be yours forever."

Croz has been going the opposite direction from Wix. Where my roommate started confident and got less sure as we got closer, Croz is overcompensating for his uncertainty by being even more blustery. "I bet I get three sacks," he says. "Maybe four or five."

Most of the guys chuckle and leave him alone, but I take him aside. "Hey," I say. "You gonna be okay?"

He puffs out his chest. "I'm great."

"Okay. Because you don't have to get a bunch of sacks. Make tackles, hit your assignments. Don't go after interceptions or sacks because you'll overreach and miss a tackle."

"If I hit my assignments, I'll get my sacks. Or an assist, like a couple weeks ago. Eh?" He elbows me. "Johnson's slow. One of us'll get him."

"If it comes, it comes," I say. "Just remember what I'm saying here, okay?"

He draws himself up all indignant, so I hold up a paw. "Hey, look, *I* believe you're gonna get four sacks. I just don't want you to be stuck at three in the fourth quarter and miss a tackle because you're trying to get to the quarterback."

The wolf grins at me and then slaps my paw. "Sure thing, cap. We're gonna get this."

It feels like we've been at the stadium forever. The clock creeps forward and finally Coach Lopez comes in to give us his pre-game speech to fire us up. Usually he's spare with his words, but he hesitates and I wonder if the pressure of the game is getting to him. This would be his first championship, after all. Then he starts, and I realize it's something else.

"All of you in this room came from different places," he says. "Maybe different streets in the same town, different towns in the same state, different states, different countries. Poor families, not-so-poor families, same species families, mixed species families. Maybe some of you are proud of that, and some of you feel like it's part of who you are. You all might not know that I'm Kanatian myself, born and raised. I don't talk about it much because it doesn't matter as much to me. Football matters to me. So that's what I call myself: three-time All-Pro, college champion, head coach of the Chevali Firebirds.

"I don't care what you call yourself. I don't care what part of your family, your species, your hometown, your country you're proud of. Whatever it is, that's fine. But none of it makes you better than anyone else. There's only one thing that does."

We all know what that is, but he pauses. "It's calling yourself a Chevali Firebird. It's winning that game out there. And when we do that, you all get that forever. Nobody can take it away."

The room is quiet. I sneak a glance toward Marshall. He's listening, no expression on his muzzle.

Coach looks around at us and says, "You guys are the best team in the UFL. Let's go out and prove it."

There's more and more of the pre-game ceremony, and even though the TVs in the locker room are on, not many of us are watching. We're talking, listening to music, doing our pre-game rituals. I think about the guys on all the teams that came before this one, about my friends who are retired or on other teams. Gerrard sits near me, and I feel like I'd like to say something to him, but I know we both know everything we'd say to each other.

Or I think I do. "Last night go okay?" he asks.

"Yeah. Great." I glance at him. He's fiddling with his playbook. "Thanks. For helping out."

He nods. "Congratulations."

"Uh. On, um?"

Now he looks at me, eyebrows slightly raised. "Lee said he was going to propose."

"Oh yeah. He did. I mean, I sort of did first, but—yeah, it happened, we said yes."

"So." He nods and extends a paw. "Congratulations."

I shake, wondering what happened to Gerrard the football robot. He holds my paw and meets my eyes. "Now forget about that and let's play some football."

There it is. I can't help the huge smile. "Thanks, Coach," I say.

We come out onto the field, stand for the national anthem, and then I get to go out for the coin flip, with the oversized special commemorative championship game coin. As at the semifinal, Rain calls heads, and this time the coin lands heads. The dingo pumps his fist, looks at me and Colin, and says, "We'll defer."

So we'll get the ball first in the second half, and Colin and I have to get ready to go out for the first series. A few more preliminaries, and the game gets under way.

One of the things I love and hate about football is that you always think it's going to go a certain way and sometimes it surprises you. We hold them on the first series, not quite three and out, but only one first down and then they punt. And on our first series, Rain, who has three interceptions all year, inexplicably throws the ball right to a Devils cornerback, who jogs into the end zone for a score.

A few years ago, our quarterback tossed an interception and almost got into a fight with one of our wideouts on the sidelines over who had made the mistake—the wideout ran a curl but Aston threw to a hitch route. Both of them swore that they'd gotten the right play and even the coaches couldn't figure it out. Today, though, Rain and Ty come back and Rain says, "My bad, I had the wrong play in my head," and Ty says, "It's cool, we'll get it back," and that's the end of it. The coaches don't even have to step in like they were ready to.

That's a good sign, and when the offense goes right back out, they play with the same composure they had to start, which is an even better sign. On our side of the ball we tell each other to tighten up, keep them contained. For the rest of the half we hold them to a field goal, while Rain leads us on a couple pretty drives, one of which gets us a running touchdown and the other of which leads to Charm just missing a long field goal.

So we're down 10-7 at the half, and some of us are worried but I feel okay about it. Dublovic, the cougar who plays safety, keeps going on about the one long pass that set up the Devils' field goal, which went to their speedy cheetah wideout. Even when we get to the locker room, while Carson and I and Croz are breaking down our first-half plays and Dublovic is supposed to be doing the same with the other corners and safeties, he keeps pacing, tail lashing behind him.

I'm pretty good at focusing—we all are—but he's distracting. Colin tells him to sit down, and he does, but only for a second before he's up again. The second time Colin tells him to sit, the cougar says, "Sorry, man, I just—this fuckin' outsider, you know?"

He's talking about the cheetah still, we all know it. In the middle of saying something, I freeze and look at Carson and he looks back at me. Quick as a play on the field, I wait for him to tell me not to go make a big deal out of this. He knows what I'm asking, and he doesn't say no.

Before Croz can parse the interruption and say, "What?" I'm on my feet and moving toward Dublovic.

"Hey." I grab him by the shoulder.

He twists away from me. "What?"

I don't have a speech planned or anything, but words spill out of me. "Didn't you fuckin' hear Coach?"

Anger turns to blank incomprehension. "What?"

"When you say shit like that, you're talking about me."

"Fuck you, I didn't say shit about you. I know better." He sneers. "I'm politically correct."

"Not that. 'Outsider.'" The whole locker room is quiet now. The weird thing is, I don't feel shaky or nervous about this at all. The protestors, Marshall, the people I read about in Lee's research: Dublovic is standing in for all of them and I'm saying things I've wanted to say for a couple weeks, maybe longer.

He shakes his head. "That wasn't about you. That was about that fuckin' cheetah."

"It's about me." I point over to Carson. "It's about him, and it's about," I gesture to the side of the locker room where the offense sits, including by the way our own fucking cheetah wide receiver, "Carlos, and Rain, and Ty, and it's about Lux and Coach, too." He starts to protest and I keep going. "You meant it about Luongo, but you can't keep it in a bottle like that. People say that shit to me and to all of us, and when you say it, that's what we hear."

He looks around for support, but all the guys I mentioned are staring at him, except for the coaches who are in another room. Carson, Ty, Carlos, Rain and even Croz and Price and a bunch of others are staring and nobody's coming to his defense. Marshall's turned away and is fiddling with something at his locker, his back very pointedly to the whole conversation. "I'm just blowing off steam," he says, uncertain now.

"Yeah," I say, "well, use some other words. Or maybe just work on your routes so you're not out of position next time he's your assignment. Then you won't have to blame someone else for your fuck-up."

"Fuck you," he says, "I was—I was covering the fox."

"I saw the replay." I head back to the linebackers. "Anyway, I said my piece, that's all."

"I wasn't—" he calls after me, and then appeals to Colin. "Smith, tell him."

Colin clears his throat. "Sit down," he tells the cougar. "Come on."

Croz is staring at me as I rejoin the linebackers and the murmur of conversation resumes in the locker room. "Fuckin' hell," he says. "In the middle of a goddamn championship, you lecture a guy on his language?"

Carson answers before I can. "He won't forget it, that's for sure."

"I guess not." Croz makes a fist and holds it out. "Mad respect, dude."

I tap. "Thanks. Let's keep going."

Coach comes in a minute later flanked by the coordinators. "Hey," he says as our chatter dies down. "We heard something going on in here. What happened?"

Nobody says anything. I wait for Dublovic to say something, but the cougar's got his head down. Colin looks steadily at me across the locker room, and after a moment he says, "Nothing. We're cool."

The big moose studies the room, but nobody contradicts Colin. "Good," he says. "We've got some ideas for the second half. There's a lot of game left and we're playing well. No reason to be upset at anyone."

Gerrard comes over to the linebackers and breaks down the changes: Here are some things they're doing on offense; here is where they're doubling Dev; here is where they're doubling Croz. When they do that, here's what we do. Here's how they're picking us off the slot receiver; here's how to beat that. We study intently, and even Croz stays quiet.

Nobody mentions my confrontation with Dublovic, except that Ty slaps me on the back as we're heading out, and in the tunnel going out to the field, Carlos finds me and says, "Hey. Thanks."

He and I don't talk much, so this is a bit of a surprise. "No problem."

"I thought about saying something, for like a split-second, you know, but…you did it better."

"Heh. I don't know about that, but—thanks."

"You were great." Rain comes up behind the cheetah, grinning. "Now let's go. We got a game to win."

On our first possession of the second half, Rain, as good as his word, connects with Ty on a gorgeous forty-yard touchdown pass. Fired up, the defense goes out and Dublovic sticks to his assignment and we stop them from moving down the field. I'm not gonna say that yelling at Dublovic fired up the team, but something did. Maybe the coaching adjustments helped, too, and the Devils must not have had as good a halftime.

The next time the defense goes out, Croz drops the quarterback; on their desperation third-down throw, Colin knocks the pass away from the receiver. We eat up some clock on offense and then go out and stop them again, all of us linebackers playing so hard and well that when we come back to the sidelines, Gerrard just says, "Good." Rain goes out and tosses another touchdown, and that's basically that.

With two minutes left in the fourth quarter and the score 31-10, Coach Lopez pulls the defensive starters so the backups get a chance to go in there and play (including Wix), and they promptly give up a seventy-yard touchdown (not Wix; his coverage was solid). But that's it. Our offense goes back out and gets a first down, and Rain kneels three more times to run out the clock. It hits all zeroes and the stadium erupts, the loudest noise I've ever heard in person. The scoreboards flash red and gold and "FIREBIRDS" all over them, and Carson gives me a big ol' hug, and I battle through a crowd to find Gerrard, stoically accepting hugs from everyone.

When he sees me, his muzzle allows the smallest hint of a smile. I extend my paw to him and he grasps it, then pulls me in. I wrap an arm around his back. "It took ten years," I say, "but I got you that ring."

"Tell Lee he's off the hook," he says.

I'm not sure what that means, but I say, "Sure," and then, "You're the best linebacker I've ever known, and you're a fantastic coach."

"You're a hell of a player," he says, and then pushes me away. "Go celebrate. You earned it."

"We earned it." I grin at him, and I don't leave, even as Croz crashes into Gerrard, hugs him, then me, and bounces away. "How's it feel?"

He looks up at the scoreboard, and the smile on his muzzle grows. "It's great," he says. "I wish—no. It's great. I'm proud to be a part of it."

I grab his paw again, squeeze, and then get whirled away into a celebration, with Ty, with Carson, with Charm, with Rain. We go back to the locker room to change before the ceremony, just a quick change—lose the helmets, change out of the jerseys if we want. There's a big box of "WORLD CHAMPION" t-shirts at the entrance to the locker room and the equipment guys are tossing one to anyone who wants one. I want to keep my jersey on, but I take a shirt and stash it in my locker.

Everything is chaos, guys shouting joyfully, still hugging, slapping paws. Amid it all, I come nose to nose with Colin. We both stop and look at each other, but in the joy of this celebration, not even a grudge as old as ours has any power. I smile, and he smiles. We share that moment and then we move on to the other guys who are our actual friends.

After a haze of champagne and hugging and shouting plus an impromptu singing of the Firebirds fight song that's been going around on the radio the last few weeks (it's terrible because none of us really know it), we're all herded back out to the field. I run into Wix for the first time on the way out there and wrap him in a big hug, dragging him along with me and Ty.

"How's it feel?" I ask him.

"I mostly returned punts," he says, "but yeah it feels pretty great."

Ty scruffles the bobcat's ears. "Feels a hell of a lot better to win on special teams than lose on 'em."

"How would you know?" I poke the fox. "You were starting that first year."

He flashes me a grin. "Played special teams too. Thanks for pretending you don't remember."

I laugh, and we come out of the tunnel to the field. They've erected a large platform and the whole team crowds up onto it. The crowd erupts in cheers as we come out, a long, sustained scream that goes on forever, long after the last player is up on the platform and the owner and coach are up at the mic with the corporate suits and the trophy.

Lee's up there in the crowd with my parents and his father and Angela and the boys. I find their section and, lost in the mass of players on the stage, raise an arm and point to them. The head of the UFL quiets the crowd as best he can, and they go on and start the ceremony. I listen with half an ear, and the rest of me is thinking about Lee and how I can't wait to share this with him.

Chapter Twenty-Eight (Lee)

We're already all buzzing for most of the fourth quarter. You can argue about the point where the outcome of a football game stops being in doubt, but for me it was a drive early in the fourth quarter where the Devils had gotten two first downs and faced third and two at midfield and Dev read the short pass across the middle. He got to the receiver, interfered with the catch, and forced the punt. After that the Devils never really mounted a serious threat.

Mike and I sit together with my father and Angela, courtesy of the Firebirds' front office, while Jaren splits his time between us and a couple buddies who got tickets up in the second tier. Two rows down, Dev's parents sit; I say hi to them at the beginning of the game and then not again until the game is done, at which point everyone in the section stands up and starts cheering each other, hugging, tails wagging all over.

I make my way down to where even the restrained Mikhail is standing and Duscha, beside him, still clapping her paws. She sees me first and reaches out to pull me into a hug. "Lee! It's so wonderful! When will they come back out?"

"Soon." I point down to where they're building a stage on the field. "They get that thing up pretty fast."

Mikhail turns to me and extends a paw. "Finally," he says. I bristle a little, thinking he means something like "it took Dev long enough," but he continues with a smile, "they surround Devlin with a team worthy of him."

"Oh, I think the one a few years ago was pretty good. Just the team they played in the championship was a little better." I try a smug smile but can't help adding, "and luckier that day, too. Three fumbles, none lost?"

"Yes, yes." Mikhail waves away my comments and fixes me with a keen eye. "This means you will be planning a wedding, I suppose."

"Yeah," I say.

Before I can say more, Duscha hugs me again, tighter this time. "I cannot wait!" she cries, and steps back, keeping her paws on my shoulders. "You are already part of the family."

I laugh and look away, abashed and very happy. "We'll hire someone to take care of the details, and we'll let you know as soon as—"

"Oh, pff." Duscha shakes her head. "I planned Gregory's wedding, I can plan yours."

"You don't have to," I say, "but we can talk about it later."

Mikhail nods. "Gregory will not like it."

I can't help responding sharply. "He doesn't have to come. But…we do want anyone who would like to be there. And it would be nice if he'd agree to come and be family for a day. Maybe you can help talk to him?"

Mikhail nods. "I will see what can be done."

"Okay." I glance back up; Mike is looking down at me. "Hey, I should get back up to my dad. You guys want to come say hi?"

They make their way up but only have the chance to exchange a few words before the ceremony starts and everyone hurries back to their seats.

It would be really funny if Wix decided to come out during the post-game ceremony, but he doesn't. He doesn't even get to the mic; they talk to Rain, who gets the MVP for, well, being the quarterback of a winning team that didn't really have a standout player. One running touchdown, the passing scores all to different wideouts. Croz got his sack and Colin had an interception, but everyone contributed across the board, so the most important player on the team gets the MVP. Ty gets a brief moment at the mic, the returning hero now with his second ring, and Dev and Colin as the longest-tenured Firebirds on defense (and co-captains) both get a chance to speak. Both of them talk about how great the team is and how great their coaches are, and how Port City was such a difficult matchup, much more talented than the score indicates, all the stuff they have to say.

It isn't until the post-game press, which I'll watch later, that someone asks Dev about getting married, and he has this great smile as he says, "Yep. Next question."

He texts me after the presentation, as the families are socializing and waiting for the exits to clear. *Want to come to the party? Guys ok w it.*

I think about it, but honestly it's not my celebration. *I'll celebrate w you privately later*, I text back. Around me, I see some of the players' wives picking up their phones, no doubt getting similar texts. The party is going to be a big one, lots of people there, going on all night, and for a moment I'm tempted to take back my answer. But no, it's enough to be invited.

Even though the rest of the stadium is slowly emptying, none of us here want to leave. My father and Angela, Jaren and Mike, we're talking to people around us we've only spoken to a few times in the last year or so. I spend a good ten minutes talking to Ty's wife Tami, who's developing a cool-sounding new mobile game, and then we're joined by their boyfriend Arch, who's carrying an eighteen-month-old fox cub. The cub, cradling a bag of popcorn, crunches it while looking around at all of us.

"She was so excited to get her popcorn and then just ran out of energy," Arch explains.

Tami smiles and reaches over to ruffle the cub's ears. "Got your popcorn, though, huh?" she says.

"Mmm." She beams, muzzle full, studying me, the stranger.

"Kella, you know your daddy just won a very important game?"

She blinks back up at Arch. "Your other daddy," the wolf says quietly. "Fox daddy."

Kella looks around, I guess for Ty. Her eyes light on me and then slide past. "He was down there." Tami points to the field. "Remember?"

The cub looks down at the field and then nods and takes another mouthful of popcorn. Arch grins at me and then at Tami. "She's starting to talk but I guess she's shy right now."

"She's getting so big," I say.

"Uh huh." Arch shifts the cub slightly. "She's getting too heavy for Mom. I have to work out just so I can carry her around."

"Glad you guys are doing well," I say. "At least you've got each other most of the season."

Tami raises her eyebrows. "Lonely this year?"

I shake my head. "I've got football too. I don't know what I'd do with another boyfriend."

"Oh yeah." Arch brightens. "So you guys are gonna get married now, I guess?"

Everyone asks that question, from Jenny, a bear I know from many Firebirds events though I can't quite remember whom she's married to, to Ayla, a cheetah I've never met before. Jenny gushes about the playoff share, Ayla beams with pride in her husband, and everyone wants to talk about the game, about the plays their husband made. I do the same, until an usher asks us politely to leave and we notice that the stadium is almost empty. We snap a few last pictures of the huge screen still showing the animated "CHAMPIONS" across it and then head out of the stadium.

Jaren and Mike both get texts from Gerrard; Angela doesn't and didn't expect one. Dev texts his parents and also my father, and I have texts from Peter and Morty and Cord and a bunch of other work people that are almost all, "Congrats! When's the wedding?" and variations on those lines. I don't talk much on the way back to the house, soaking in the feeling.

It's not just that Dev has his championship, earned many times over if you're counting. It's that everyone is so excited about our wedding and happy for us. Friends, family, we're just another couple getting married. Nobody has to know that we decided it the night before, that the game wasn't what made the difference, and maybe never should have been. But it gave us an excuse to wait until we were ready, and we both know we're ready now.

We order three large pizzas from the boys' favorite pizza place and sit around talking about our favorite plays from the game with SportsCenter in the background. Already the sports anchors are asking, "What's next for the Firebirds?" and "Who can they keep for next year?" Dev's under contract, so they don't spend a lot of time on him. I'm the only one who knows he's thinking of retiring.

He texts me around nine to tell me the party's still going, and I tell him to text when he's on his way back to his apartment and I'll meet him there. Father and Angela look like they're settling in for the night, so when Jaren asks if he can go out with his buddies (he sort of asks, like, "hey, you mind, I'm gonna run out and see Karen and Pilo"), I ask Mike if they want to take a walk.

They grab a light jacket and come with me out of the house and down the street. "What's up?"

I have an excuse ready. "I figured we could hit the store up here and get some celebratory ice cream or something."

"We already have ice cream in the house," they say.

"What flavors?"

"Um, chocolate and chocolate peanut butter."

I nod. "So we'll get something else."

Finally, they smile. "All right."

We leave the house and walk down the street. "Pretty good day," they say after a bit of silence.

"Uh huh. One of the best."

They nod. "So what did you want to talk about?"

I scrape my feet along the sidewalk. It's smooth and cool, nice and solid under my paws. "I'm not sure exactly. I'm processing a lot of things, and I think a lot of it has to do with how we define ourselves. So I thought you might be interested. Also I'm not sure who else I can talk to about this right now."

They don't say anything, but give a short nod, and we keep walking along. "One of our players was messing around with some Nativist people. I know Dev had to deal with them too. And I'm thinking about that and about what that even means. It's a bunch of people who define themselves by what, where their ancestors were born? What does that say about you? Nothing much, really. I feel like it's something people cling to when they can't define themselves any other way."

"Don't politicians also use it to inflame emotions and pass bad laws?"

I grin. "Yes, that too. You really should be going to school in Yerba, you know."

They toss their head. "I already said I'd apply."

"The thing is, we're all looking for ways to define ourselves, and when those ways stop fitting or we get dissatisfied, that's when we look for new things. I was thinking about this because I'm trying to figure out why I was waffling on the Cansez job. I think partly my job title is how I look at myself. That's not too bad, you know? It says something about what you're good at. Hopefully it's something you can be proud of. It's a hell of a lot more relevant than 'where were my grandparents born,' anyway."

They step around a puddle on the sidewalk. "I'll keep that in mind when I interview at Jack in the Box."

I chuckle. "Our definitions are different at different stages of life. And there are lots of other reasons to make changes in your life. But you see how this relates to you, I hope."

"A little." They guide me to the left, and a few blocks down the supermarket comes into view, shining in the evening.

"Anyway, I also define myself by championships. I've got one as a head of scouting, but wouldn't it look great to have one as an assistant GM, too?"

"I guess?"

"It would. Trust me. So that's a reason to go. But I also define myself by my activism, by the opportunities I create for LGBT players—not so much the L or the T, I guess, but a rising tide lifts all boats."

Mike squints. "Is that a Yerba saying?"

"Hilltown maybe. We had a lake. Anyway, I don't know that I'd been thinking about that as much the last few years. I felt like maybe I'd done a lot and other people could carry on the momentum. But a couple of Dev's friends who are gay and bi aren't coming out, and here we come back around to the fucking Nativists again."

"Are they anti-gay?"

I wiggle a paw. "They lean that way. Something about continuing heritage and bloodlines. They're not crazy about adoptions, either. But while I'm coasting along on things I put in place five years ago, they're getting more pervasive. I really enjoyed doing the research on them and making a stand for our team. So it's worth going into the heartland and trying to plant a flag there."

The young coyote thinks. "It sounds like it's more about just figuring out where your priorities are."

"Right, definitely a lot of that. But your priorities define who you are, too. Every time you make a choice."

"So if I go to school here…"

"You'll be a Chevali guy. Family priority over—over maybe other things."

They nod. "And if I go to Yerba, I'm putting myself first."

"Self-discovery over family. You're not leaving family behind or anything, but you probably won't be home every weekend like Jaren will be."

"Not *every* weekend," they say, but their eyes roll a little. "And going to Cansez, that's about your career? Or activism?"

I sigh. "I don't think it's that easy. I think there's a chance to be a different kind of activist there, the kind I used to be once upon a time. I got soft in Yerba because it was easy there, and I find myself thinking, 'why don't these other guys come out, these other players?' So maybe I need to go somewhere where it isn't so easy and make it easier there."

They don't say anything for a few steps, until we get to the first stray shopping cart outside the supermarket parking lot. Then they say, "You've always seemed most passionate about the football, the last…I dunno, since your dad started dating my mom. What's the football like in Cansez?"

"Pretty damn good, to be honest. I mean, if I had to pick one of Cansez or Yerba to win a title in the next three years…"

"Isn't that what you're doing?"

"Ha. I guess I am."

We go into the supermarket and get a little tub of vanilla ice cream, and then we pick a cherry cobbler flavor that looks disgusting and therefore, we agree, probably tastes amazing.

"So you're going to Cansez?" Mike asks as we leave the supermarket.

"I think so," I say. "It feels right. And I don't think I'm choosing it because I'm scared not to. I think maybe it is time for a change."

Their ears splay, not going all the way back but definitely down. "I wish you could put it off a couple years."

"Me too." I put an arm around their shoulder and they don't flinch; they lean into it. "But look, I'm keeping the townhouse. It's probably too far for you to commute to any of the schools there, but you can hang out on weekends. And I'll be back every now and then and we can go out to clubs."

"All right. That sounds okay."

"And hey, one more thing for you, too."

They perk their ears and turn, unintentionally sliding out from under my arm. I don't insist on keeping the embrace. "I think you should tell your mom about Maxie. And my dad, but your mom for sure."

They lay their ears back. "I don't know how to tell them."

"Same way you told me."

"What, over the phone?"

I elbow them. "Straightforward. 'Hey, mom, can I talk to you? I've been thinking a lot about things and—'"

"Stop."

"But just like that."

They sigh. "Can you tell them?"

I shake my head. "I mean, I could, but I think it would be a lot better coming from you."

They exhale a long breath of air. "Yeah, I know. All right. I mean, I'll try. Before I go away to school."

"Good enough. If you need help or a pep talk before, give me a call."

"Will do."

We walk a little farther, and then I say, "One other way to define ourselves, you know…we're siblings."

They say a short, "Yeah," but I see the corners of their mouth curve up, just a bit.

CHAPTER TWENTY-NINE (DEV)

The party goes on and on for hours after, from the champagne-soaked locker room to the ballroom at the hotel. (Wix is already pretty trashed, so I escort-slash-carry him to the hotel where he can party more; he and the other underage guys aren't supposed to drink but nobody's enforcing that tonight.) Some guys are limping or holding their arms but nobody complains about injuries, because this is the thing that makes it all feel worthwhile. A few of the guys' wives show up, and then more, until it's a real family party. The owner's kids show up, but not too many other kids; there's booze and even though it's only like nine o'clock by the time we get to the hotel, this thing is clearly going to run to all hours of the night.

I spot Charm across the room with an arm around two different ladies. I hugged him in the locker room but we haven't really talked, so I go over to him.

"Hey," Charm says as he sees me approach. "Ladies, you know Dev? He's the anchor of our defense. By which I mean that he's big and heavy and a huge drag."

He winks at me and I meet his fistbump. "I don't know what this big guy's been telling you," I say, "but you know how he only plays like three or four times a game? It's how he can still be in the league at forty."

They both giggle at our banter, look at each other, and then the bobcat asks if I want company for the evening. "No thanks," I say. "I've got a boyfriend. And I wouldn't want to deprive Charm here of half the paws it takes to get him going these days."

"Hey, hey, nobody wins an old-off," he says. "Look at all these kids around. They're gonna think this is always how things are."

"Honestly, I'd rather have gotten the ring that first year we played here and then never gotten back. I know it eats at you," and here I pause and think about Fisher, still struggling along, and how he would've loved this, "but still. You'd have the rings."

"You've got one now."

"You too."

We grin at each other for a bit and then his eyes widen and he says, "Holy shit, we won the fuckin' championship!"

I laugh, the ladies each kiss one side of his muzzle, and I say, "I'll leave you to it."

"We'll catch up tomorrow," he calls as I leave. "I wanna see your fox."

I do too, I think, but he's already refused to come to the party. I don't want to leave just yet; this giddy celebration still carries me along like a river, excitement pulsing through me. I look for more teammates to corner to make sure we share memories of this moment. I spend a lot of time talking to Carson about the season, to Croz about the game, to Ty about our families (him I tell about my engagement and promise to invite him and Tami and Arch to the wedding; neither of them has come to the party because Tami could come but not Arch and none of them wanted that), and I get buzzed from the champagne and then find myself leaning against a wall next to Gerrard.

He's drinking from a champagne flute, but what he's got in there doesn't look fizzy. I lean over and sniff. It's water. "Too much champagne?" I ask.

"Haven't had any."

"Even in the locker room?" Now that I think of it, I remember seeing Gerrard stand apart from the champagne pouring over heads. "Come on, you've been working for this your whole career."

"I know. It's great, having that win finally."

It doesn't sound great when he says it. It sounds like he's saying it's great to have clean towels in the locker room. So I press a little. "Can't you let go and enjoy the win for a little? Just one night?"

He exhales. "We made mistakes. We got lucky."

"Uh huh. That's what a championship is about. Remember those times we were unlucky? The dice rolled our way this time. But also, we were a better team. What mistakes did we make?"

He comes back immediately. "The defense on that third and seven play in the third quarter, second possession, that was the wrong call. We were lucky they missed the throw. The guy would've been clear for a score. Changes the whole game."

"Okay." I take another drink. "But it didn't happen. If it did, we'd have dealt with it. Mistakes happen on the field, on the sidelines, whatever."

"Next year we'll do better."

I grab his shoulder. "Let's worry about next year tomorrow, or the day after. Have a glass of champagne, for fuck's sake. You just won a championship."

His eyes widen. He curls his tail, thinking. "Everything's fresh in my mind now. I'm not going to be as sharp tomorrow."

"Good." I push my glass of champagne, half full, into his paw, and take his water. "Get a little tipsy, Coach. Talk to your players. We love you, you know. We know you're a big part of the reason we won this. So act like it."

He grimaces and sips the champagne, then takes a longer drink. He stares at the glass. "I'm glad the boys got to see it."

"How about you? You got to see it too. You were part of it, you made it happen."

He nods. "Coach said that too." He finishes the champagne in a gulp.

"All right, so how about you go around to the linebackers and tell them what a good job they did. Enjoy the evening?"

He gives me a look which usually precedes him telling me that he's been in the league longer than I have and he knows what he's doing and don't question his methods, so I cut that short because I'm not in uniform right now. "Yeah, yeah, I know, but come on. Give it a try. It'd mean a lot to them."

"I already told them they did a good job and I'm proud of them."

"Do it again and try to relax." I grab a full champagne flute and offer it to him. "You don't have to drink champagne, but at least look like you're having fun. Okay?"

He sniffs the champagne like he's never smelled it before, like he didn't just down half a glass, and then takes it from me and drinks. "All right. But only for half an hour."

That job done, I keep circulating. I talk to Coach Lopez, who tells me how much he appreciates my leadership on defense this year, and I thank him for his pre-game speech, telling him it was perfect. I talk to our offensive coordinator about his gay nephew and I talk to our assistant GM, who very pointedly says how excited he is to have me around to defend our championship next year. I say that'll be great, although I already know there are going to be changes: Croz is due for an extension and Carson is probably going to retire. I spend some time talking to Price, who like me is filled with a combination of giddy joy and relief at having at least one ring to show for our decade-long career. Retirement being on my mind, I ask whether he's planning to hang up the uni next year, and he laughs. "You kidding?" he says. "I'm gonna play 'til this hip finally gives way for good."

There's something to that, I think. My body at 32 is not what it was at 22, or even at 28, and some mornings after games this season I woke with the feeling that I was a puppet whose strings were fraying at every joint. But every game I still felt good, whole enough to play, and thankfully I avoided major injuries this season. Why not come back for another year?

When Ty and I get a little bit of time, on towards ten-thirty, I guess, as the cubs are shuffled away, the younger players get rowdier and the older players move toward the edges of the room to talk, I mention Price's comment about retirement. "Honestly not sure what I should do," I say. "Right now I want to play another three years. I think we can win again. But if I think about it…I don't want my career to end with me carted off the field, on IR and useless."

"Still thinking about Murell?" Ty asks.

"Kind of. He's out of concussion danger. He's going to be okay. He's coming back next year."

The tall fox grins at me, looks down at his drink, and splays his ears out. "Ok, I'ma tell you something," he says, "but you can't tell. Anyone here, I mean. Or Lee, I guess. That'd be…interference or whatever." He's amusingly drunk right now.

"Okay?"

He leans his muzzle toward me and in his first attempt to speak in a whisper, I can't understand what he's saying with all the noise around. "Say again?"

"I'm going to retire," he says, louder, and then covers his muzzle. "Oops."

"What?" I lean back to look him in the eye. "Seriously?"

He nods. "Yeah. Talked to the fam about it and it's time. We got money for…" He shoots his paw out into the air, fully extending his arm. "Tami's working, Arch is working, figure they can support us for a while and we've got a crazy day fund."

"Crazy day?"

He shakes his head. "Stormy day?"

"Rainy day?"

"Yes." He pokes my chest. "That. So it's good."

"You don't want your cub to see you play?"

Ty laughs. "I'ma get the full video of this game like I got the last one. She can see me play."

I nod. "Okay."

He leans in again. "It's my ankle," he says.

This is news to me. "What about it?"

"You remember a couple years ago I broke it?"

That was before he rejoined the Firebirds, the year after his championship with Gateway. "That was like…two years ago."

He nods. "Never healed right. I can run on it but it's…" He lifts his left foot and shakes it around. "Janky. I played through it, I been lucky, but last summer I went to a doc. Not a UFL doc." He puts a finger to his lips. "Shh."

Going for medical advice outside the UFL isn't a violation of our contract or anything but it wouldn't make the team happy, especially if he didn't share it with our team docs. "What'd he say?"

"Said the uh, the caritage…cartilage…around the joint was degrading because the break wasn't properly aligned…something like that. Fuckin' Tornadoes doctors set it and tried to accelerate the healing." His ears splay out. "And maybe I tried to come back like a few weeks too soon. But it was the playoffs."

"It doesn't hurt, though?"

"A little," he admits. "I play through it. But like…I could fuck it up pretty bad. Lucky this year. But got you a championship, right?"

"Me?" I laugh. "We all got one."

"Sure, sure." He grins at me. "I always liked Chevali, though. They drafted me. And that first game…" He holds his paws out like he's catching a football. "I felt like I let you down. You, Gerrard…" He waves his paws around the room. "The whole city. They brought me in to win and…"

"Hey." I clear my throat. "There were a lot of reasons we lost that game. You're not even top ten on the list."

"It's cool." He flicks his tail. "I put it behind me. Took a while, but winning that championship with Gateway sure helped. And the fam helped too. They're great, really. But that don't mean I still didn't think I could make it right for you. Alla you."

"You did." I reach out and hug him. "You did great."

He hugs back and laughs. "We fuckin' did it, didn't we? They didn't know what hit 'em."

"They know," I say. "It was us."

"So how's it feel?"

I say, "Great," even though I know that doesn't begin to cover it. But Ty understands, he gets it.

"You're not drunk enough," he tells me.

I shake my head. "I gotta drive home in a bit."

"Leaving the party?" He looks around. "Why isn't Lee here?"

"He felt awkward, I guess? Tami's not here either."

"Nah, they're back at the hotel with the cub. I'll probably head back in a couple hours, but I," he presses a paw to his chest, "am gonna take a Ryde."

"Give them my best." I hug him again. "And thanks for coming back. We couldn't have done this without you."

"Sure you could." He slaps my back. "Just woulda been a lot closer. Especially if you still had Varek. That fuckin' stiff."

I laugh. "He was okay."

"Fuck he was. He has speed and nothing else." Ty waves a paw. "Any corner that can keep up with him can defend him."

"All right, we don't need to shit-talk guys who aren't even on the team anymore."

Ty considers that. "Usually you'd be right but for that asshole I'll make an inception."

"Exception."

"Right, that." He slaps my back again. "Give my best to Lee. Let's do something next week or next month."

"Well," I say, "I'm gonna see you at my wedding, right?"

"Oh shit, yeah you will."

"All three of you."

He nods and smiles brightly. "Done deal."

I take a last walk around the room, saying good-byes to everyone, and then I text Lee and tell him I'm heading home. Even as I leave the ballroom, walking out into the hotel corridors and down the stairs to the parking garage, I can't help smiling at every person I pass. *I just won a championship*, I think. *Do you know that?*

Over the years, a lot of guys have told me what it's like to win a championship, and all of them were right and yet none of them completely right. Every other year, either we've watched six other teams go to the playoffs, or we got into the playoffs and ended the season with a loss. This year, we won the last game of football that will be played. There's no more until August. We're the last team standing, the top of the heap, the best of the best. Every tackle I made, every pass I knocked down, every time I read a play in advance, that was part of this win. I'm the starting middle linebacker on the best team in football.

The streets, here near the stadium, are far from empty or quiet. Crowds of people scream and laugh and raise bottles, sing the Firebirds fight song, climb street signs and store awnings, and spill out into the street. There are cops around, kept busy trying to corral the rowdier ones; I spot a fox stumbling out between parked cars and hit my brake just as a cougar cop grabs him by the wrist and yanks him back, while a uniformed tigress and chinchilla do their best to keep the celebration out of the main street.

I'm partly the cause of all this joy, I think, and smile as I roll past, giving the tigress a thank-you wave as I go. The celebration dies out within a few blocks, but picks up again once I get downtown. Around my apartment building, a small cluster of people—a couple wolves, a couple kangaroo rats, a coati, a fennec are the ones I notice at first glance—sing and cheer around a bunch of signs, some with my face and the faces of the other players who live in the building. Another says "THANK YOU MISKI #57." They take notice when the garage door opens, and a few of them try to run in alongside my truck, but Georg, the large bear from the private security service, keeps them back.

"We love you!" they scream as the garage door closes behind me. I lean out the open window to wave back at them, and they scream louder, jumping up and down. All the way to my parking spot I feel great, all the way to the elevator and up to my apartment.

As people moved out of the building, often because they didn't like the attention I brought to it or the security I needed to hire, I recommended the empty apartments to new teammates moving to town. I like the location and so far, most of the fans have been cool about it. Couple stalkers managed to get into the building, but that's gonna happen anywhere. Rain, Ty, even Charm, anyone with a high profile, people find out where you live and try to hang out there. But I've lived in the neighborhood long enough that most of the residents and businesses around here know me and keep an eye out for people acting inappropriately.

Of course, they all know my fox, too. I catch a little of his scent on the door, and as I open it I say, "Honey, I'm home."

"I know." He gets up from the couch, shirtless but still wearing pants. The TV is showing SportsCenter, probably in hour four or five of coverage of the game.

I wrap him in a tight, warm hug, and his tail wags something fierce. "You were fantastic," he says.

"Gerrard thinks we made some mistakes."

"Gerrard needs to loosen the fuck up and enjoy himself."

I grin. "That's what I told him."

"Nah." He pulls his muzzle back, staying in the hug, and kisses me. "You were great. All of you were great but particularly you. That play in the third where you read the run and stuffed it?"

"That was pretty good, I guess."

"That was critical. If you miss that, they get a first and who knows what happens after that?"

I laugh. "It feels so good, fox. I can't even tell you. Well, you know."

"I kinda know." He kisses me again, and this time I kiss back. "I wasn't on the field for mine. It was more like I set up a bunch of pieces on a board and they all did their job well."

I nod. "Yeah, it's just…everything was going right. Really, our coaches were the stars. The halftime adjustments? They put us in position to win."

He giggles. "I heard your postgame media-talk. You don't have to repeat it."

I tickle his sides, making him giggle more and squirm. "No, but I mean it. Everything came together and I was a small part of it."

"An important part."

"All right, maybe one of the more important parts. Hey." I nose his ear. "You're not naked."

"It's a little chilly," he says, "and besides, I thought you might want to watch TV for a bit."

Just then, as if on cue, the coyote sports anchor says, "Let's talk about the role of the Firebirds' defense in this championship. Where do they rank all-time?"

So we cuddle up on the couch and watch the sports anchors debate how good my defense is. A couple of them mention me by name, and one says, "a downgrade from Marvell, but not that much," and the other says he thinks it's a push, which makes me happy, because I'm pretty sure I'm not better than Gerrard. But they also call out Colin as one of the best corners in the league and Croz as a guy with huge potential, so it's not just about me.

We watch contentedly for an hour until the coverage starts to repeat. Lee asks me about my teammates and I tell him most of what happened, except for Ty's news. "Everyone wants to know about our wedding," I say. "I guess we better start planning it."

"Sure," he says. "Where do you want to have it?"

I groan and lean my head back. "I don't want to make decisions."

"We should hire someone local, so we need to make that decision first. Your mom offered."

"Tomorrow," I say.

"Fair enough." He snuggles in against my side. "You thinking about next season yet?"

"A little," I admit. "It'd be tempting to go out on top."

"Isn't that how you usually go?" Lee grins at me, a mock-innocent fox grin.

I tickle him again. "But I feel like I have more I can do. Not just on the field, but for guys like Wix. Like Ty. Even…hell, even Colin. I mean, imagine if being gay wasn't this horrible thing to him? Imagine if it was just normal. He wouldn't have this family life he had to maintain while he gets his dick sucked on the DL. He could just have a husband. They could even be super-religious."

"I'm not sure that playing one more season will change the world," my fox says.

"No, but…it'll do a little bit. Maybe one more player comes out. Wix might; he's pretty chill about it."

Lee snorts. "Seriously," I say. "I told you what he did with Colin."

"That just means he's thirsty."

"Okay, but…I think with another year, with me sticking around… maybe he'd come out."

My fox nods and rubs a paw along my chest. "I've been thinking along the same lines," he says.

"About your job offer?"

He nods. "I didn't think I'd leave Yerba. I kept thinking, maybe if I get something going, in another year…"

That's always the way we think. Another year will change something, another year will get us where we want to be, or at least closer. Sometimes, like this year, it actually happens, and that gives us the hope to keep going. Sometimes it doesn't work out and we have to think back to times when it did. Maybe that's the most valuable thing of all about this championship: the reminder not just that I did it, but that something like this is even possible.

When is the right time to make a change in your life? We don't live in a fantasy movie where we can see what happens on both paths. All we can do is weigh the options, make a choice, and then commit to it as best we can.

"Another year." I kiss Lee's ears. "In another year, we'll be married."

"Yeah." He rests his head against my shoulder. "You know, I'm really excited about that. I can't wait. Like seriously."

"You get to start a new job while also trying to plan a wedding."

"Hah." He exhales. "Not to mention getting back into the activism again."

"The wedding will help with that."

He peers up. "You want our wedding to be a statement?"

"I don't want that, but I don't see how we can avoid it, so…" I shrug. "Might as well lean into it."

He smiles. "We'll see. I'm sure we can strike a balance."

"Mmm." I ruffle his ears. "Assistant GM Farrel. Sounds nice." His tail thumps against the couch, agreeing. "Assistant GM. Big brother. Activist."

Lee's nose brushes my neck. "Linebacker. Firebird. Champion."

At the same time, we both say, "Husband," and then laugh and hug each other. His muzzle finds mine and we both close our eyes, slipping into a warm, passionate kiss. I bring one paw up to hold the back of his head and we stay like that for a good while before breaking apart, his blue eyes sparkling into mine.

There's a commercial on. Lee grins at me and says, "TV is boring now."

"Agreed." So I get up and lead him to the bedroom, and wherever else our lives take us, in that moment, we are both exactly where we need to be.

Acknowledgments

A number of people contributed to this book. Feedback from J "Jadedfox" Strom and my writing group the Unreliable Narrators (Ryan Campbell, David Cowan, and Watts Martin) helped shape the story. AmonOmega and Rukis did a wonderful job bringing the characters to life. Many thanks to Brer for expert layout and design skills, and to FurPlanet for editorial and production help.

Many thanks, of course, to the family I couldn't do this without: Jack, Kit, and Kobalt. They keep me motivated and provide lots of encouragement in all my endeavors.

About the Author

Kyell Gold took up furry erotica writing after high school, making the team at his small liberal arts college as a walk-on. He was drafted late by Sofawolf and blossomed in the professional league, earning four Ursa Major awards in his first three years as a pro for his novels and short stories. He has since won eight more Ursa Major awards, including one for "In Between," the first Dev and Lee story, one for *Out of Position*, which also won two Rainbow Awards for gay fiction, and one for *Isolation Play*, the second Dev and Lee book.

His various online presences are linked from *www.kyellgold.com*, and you can follow him on Twitter at @KyellGold. In the off-season, he lives in California with his husband.

About the Artists

Rukis is a freelance illustrator and writer who grew up in the Appalachian region, working with animals and on farms from a young age. After earning a Bachelors in Traditional Animation, she started a career in freelance art, writing and illustrating a small collection of comics and novels in the Anthropomorphic fandom.

You can see more of her work at *www.furaffinity.net/user/rukis.*

AmonOmega is a Canadian illustrator with a degree in animation and illustration. Having been in the fandom since 1997, his love of drawing fuzzy animals and visual storytelling has kept him warm during the long winters as well as giving him the opportunity to be published in Heat more than a few times, as well as provide the artwork for In the Doghouse of Justice. His biggest inspiration and motivation is his boyfriend, Sleepy Raccoon (who also keeps him warm in the North).

See more of Amon's art at *amonomega.weebly.com*

About FurPlanet Productions

FurPlanet is a small press publisher serving the niche market that is furry fiction. They publish and sell furry-themed books and comics. You can find them in the dealers room at many furry conventions, and you can find their print books for sale online at *furplanet.com* and eBooks at *baddogbooks.com*.

Follow them on social media @FurPlanet on Twitter and FaceBook.

Lightning Source UK Ltd.
Milton Keynes UK
UKHW021830161219
355505UK00010B/382/P